The Nanny

Books by
Melissa Nathan

THE NANNY
PRIDE, PREJUDICE AND JASMIN FIELD

# The Nanny

MELISSA NATHAN

AVON TRADE

An Imprint of HarperCollins*Publishers*

FIRST EDITION

Designed by Elizabeth M. Glover

Library of Congress Cataloging-in-Publication Data

Nathan, Melissa.
  The nanny / by Melissa Nathan.
    p. cm.
ISBN 0-06-056011-8 (alk. paper)
1. Nannies—Fiction. 2. London (England)—Fiction. I. Title.

PR6064.A67N36 2003
823'.92—dc21

2003044319

04 05 06 07 WB/RRD 10 9 8 7 6 5 4 3 2

*To Joshua, Eliana,
and, of course,
Avital, my Tallulah*

In memory of Allan Saffron

✐ Prologue

In Highgate, north London, Vanessa Fitzgerald, accounts manager at Gibson, Adams and Bead Advertising Agency and mother of three, stared at her new nanny, eyes wide with disbelief.

"Leaving?" she repeated. "You mean . . . a holiday?"

"No," said Francesca slowly and firmly. "I meeen *leeving*."

"I think she means *leeeeving*, dear," said Vanessa's husband, Dick.

"I wunt to . . . erm,'ow yoo saiy? Trrabel," explained Francesca. There was a long pause. "Ze *glawb*," she clarified.

Vanessa scrunched up her face in concentration. "You want to . . . ?" She trailed off.

"Trrabel ze *glawb*," repeated Dick, finishing his whiskey. "It's very simple, darling."

"Dick, you are not helping," said Vanessa. "This isn't funny."

"It sounds funny."

"But it's not."

"Righty-ho."

Vanessa returned her attention to Francesca.

"You want to travel the globe? The world?" she tried.

"Yais!" cried Francesca excitedly.

There was a pause.

"And you can't take the children with you?" asked Vanessa.

Francesca frowned at her boss.

"Now who's not being funny," said Dick, putting his tumbler in the sink.

"*Well who's going to look after them then?*" shouted Vanessa suddenly. "*And don't leave that in the sink—put it in the sodding dishwasher!*"

Dick turned slowly to his wife.

"I can't imagine why our nannies keep leaving," he said calmly, placing the tumbler in the dishwasher with elaborate care. "Maybe they don't like being shouted and sworn at as much as I do."

Vanessa shot Dick a look that hit him where it hurt. Straight between the eyes. His was a small brain, but she still knew how to hit it in a single go.

"Or maybe," she told him, "they're just sick of putting your tumblers in the dishwasher for you."

Francesca coughed lightly. Dick and Vanessa ignored her. She'd just handed in her notice, they didn't have to be nice to her anymore.

"It will be *me* who has to find a temporary nanny," Vanessa told her husband, "at the same time as interviewing for full-time nannies at the same time as keeping down my own job—sorry, *career*—because you're too busy poncing around in that bloody excuse for a shop."

"I happen to *work* in that shop six days a week—"

"You drink latte and scratch your balls six days a week, and you know it."

Dick smiled at his wife and changed the subject. Vanessa turned away from him and concentrated on the matter at hand—to keep breathing.

God, she'd thought today had been bad enough. First the tube strike, then that bastard new client rejecting their latest offering because it "just didn't *sing* to him," and then her PA announcing that the tight abdominal bulge she'd passed off thus far as a bad case of lactose intolerance, was in fact a baby, due in four months' time.

The only thing that had kept Vanessa going all day had been the thought of coming home to some peace and quiet, the children all tucked up neatly in bed, some takeout—unless the nanny had happened to leave something from lunch—some vino and a video of last night's *EastEnders*. Instead, she'd come home to a nanny who wanted to trrabel ze sodding glawb.

She took a gulp of Pinot Grigio. To help with the breathing.

"Okay, Francesca, thanks for letting us know," she heard Dick say, as if Francesca had just mentioned that one of the children had lost a sock. Francesca left the kitchen. Dick spoke first, quietly, putting his arm round his wife's shoulder.

"Come on," he said. "You didn't even like her."

Vanessa whined, but Dick squeezed her tighter.

"You know it's true," he whispered, kissing the top of her head. "She *lost* Tallulah the other day."

Vanessa leaned her head on his shoulder, exhausted.

"She found her again," she mumbled into his sweater.

Dick snorted and put his arms round her, his hands resting gently on the curve of her back. "She can't even speak the language properly."

"Neither can the children," pointed out his wife, "but I don't want them to leave. Not for ages."

"Good," said Dick. "Neither do I. Let's have sex."

Vanessa tensed.

"I've got a better idea," she said. "Let's find a new nanny, then have sex."

Dick sighed. He knew better than anyone that Vanessa was perfectly capable of keeping to her word if there was a principle involved.

"How long will it take?" he asked.

Vanessa shrugged. "Depends on how much we're willing to pay."

"Well that's easy then," said Dick. "Let's pay gold dust."

They smiled at each other. It was a deal. After all these years, Dick Fitzgerald knew exactly how to seduce his second wife.

Chapter 1

Jo Green's eyes glazed over as she stared at the half-eaten cake on the table, twenty-three candles now splayed messily around it. *How symbolic*, she thought. One minute ablaze with light, warmly celebrating life's journey; the next, a crumbling testament to the disappointment and guilt that life's little highs invariably bring. Then she decided she really must stop listening to Travis.

She yawned. With the kitchen lights off, a soporific mood had descended upon them all like a sudden fog.

Her father, top trouser button undone, rubbed his hand over his stomach in smooth, rhythmic circles, conducting his body's quiet celebratory wind sonata, in several movements.

Jo and her mother exchanged glances.

"In some countries that's a great compliment," said Jo.

Hilda snorted. "Oh he's multilingual, your father."

Bill belched softly again and proceeded to rub his stomach the other way.

"I don't like to stop him," Hilda muttered. "He has so few hobbies." She shifted herself from the table. "Right. Who wants another cuppa?"

"Don't mind if I do," answered Bill.

"I'll make it," said Jo.

"On your birthday?" Hilda's eyes crinkled up in a smile that created so many lines in her flesh it left almost no room for her face. "Don't talk daft."

Bill slowly and carefully smoothed the edge of the tablecloth with his hand, manfully ignoring the female battle of wills being fought around him.

"Nobody makes coffee cake like your mother," he told Jo, pointing his finger at her.

"You can't have another piece." Hilda switched on the overhead light.

"Oh come on." He blinked. "It's the girl's birthday."

Hilda leaned back against the sideboard, hugging her grey cardigan round her while the kettle boiled.

"Go on then." She sighed.

Bill winked at Jo. "Another slice for the birthday girl?" he asked, wiping the knife clean on the edge of the cake plate.

"A sliver," said Jo. "Thanks."

"And for the chef?"

Hilda swirled hot water round the special-occasion teapot.

"Oh, go on, we might as well finish it off."

Jo watched her parents and when she remembered they could see her, smiled. And then her thought patterns executed a downward swoop of epic proportions. They started high up with *Aren't I lucky?* before nose-diving without warning into *Is this it?* Then, with seconds to spare before exploding into a fireball of self-pity, up they arched, regaining their grip on the world with, *Ooh. Must return video.*

Jo's emotions had been trampolining all day. Her first waking thought as a twenty-three-year-old had been that she had joined the ever-growing group of birthday haters. Until last night, she'd always considered herself one of those lucky types who loved birthdays. She now realized that this was because, up until now, she had been young. Twenty-three, for some reason, signaled the end of an era for her more conspicuously than a Hollywood sound track.

As her emotions continued to yo-yo, with rather more emphasis on the downward than upward "yo," the Green family started their second round of tea and cake in a cosy, yet somewhat reverential, silence.

All too soon normal service was resumed.

"Seeing Shaun and the others tonight?" began her mother.

"Mm."

"Nice lad, that Shaun."

"Mm."

Hilda's concentration was temporarily waylaid by an untidy slice of coffee cake, but before long she was back on track.

"Sheila's a good girl, too."

"Mm."

"Just needs to lose a little weight," added her father, bang on cue.

More cake, more tea.

"Wonder when James'll do the honorable thing and make an honest woman of her," mused Hilda.

"When she's lost a little weight I shouldn't wonder," concluded Bill.

Her parents drained the last of the tea, the predictability of their conversation satisfying them that the earth still spun on its axis, while Jo had
a disturbing snap vision of birthday cake hurled against the floral wall-
paper.

"Thanks for the cake, Mum," she said quickly, and got up. "I'll be off.
See you later."

"Bye, love," chorused her parents, her mother heaving herself up to
clear away the birthday things.

As she shut the front door behind her, Jo took a long, deep breath and
set off for the pub. She tried not to hear in her head the conversation she
knew her parents would be having now about Shaun's intentions toward
her. She tried to concentrate on her walk.

Jo loved walking. It reminded her she was connected to the earth, a
living, breathing masterpiece of functional perfection, an act of God that
proved miracles really did exist, a monument to—

"Who's got a face like a slapped arse then?" came a sudden voice.

Jo turned to face John Saunders, who was loitering on the corner of
the deserted village High Street. Being told your face resembled a slapped
arse would be an insult from anyone, but coming from John Saunders,
whose face appeared to be on inside out, was enough to put anyone on a
downer.

Jo managed a smile for her old classmate.

"All the better to bullshit you with," she said. "Ooh, that Man-at-
JCPenney's look really works for you."

John's eyebrows flickered, his mouth twitched, and a general air of
confusion surrounded him like a palpable aura, which Jo knew meant his
brain was cranking into gear. She decided to leave before steam started
escaping from his ears.

As she walked away from the High Street toward the bridge, her emotional yo-yo flicked neatly upward. The bridge always reminded her of
her first kiss with Shaun. Then she realized that was six years ago—only
one year away from the seven-year itch—and she could almost hear a
whirring sound of the downward "yo."

At the end of the bridge, she turned abruptly to the right without
looking back and crunched her way over the gravel path past the church
graveyard, enjoying the noise underfoot.

She stopped and looked at the graveyard. She was transported back to
her first cigarette (with Sheila on her fifteenth birthday behind *Rachel
Butcherson 1820–1835*). She felt a fleeting moment of remembered exhil-

aration, (upward "yo") before realizing that something as prosaic as cigarettes would never—*could* never—be that exciting again. And downward "yo." There were certain things in life, she reflected—jobs, friends, lovers—one naturally grew out of. They started off as a thrilling challenge, then, before you knew it, seamlessly transmuted into a comfortable fit, then somehow, invisibly shrank. But the excitement of *life*? Was it possible to grow out of that, too? She came to a slow halt. *Oh well done*, she told herself, trying to flick her yo-yo up again. *You've talked yourself into a depression. You must be very proud.*

Then she turned the corner and, despite everything, stopped to take in the view. Every season, every day, every hour, a different perspective of beauty.

On the horizon, trees stretched their bony branches upward and outward to a sky of deep pinks and blues, as if trying to clasp the clouds of gently whisked egg whites.

Empty fields yawned toward her, and an idyllic vision of a country pub cosied itself between two hills like a contented cat. *Ah yes*, she thought. *In the end, life is good.*

There was something to be said for village life, she decided as she approached the pub.

"Oy!" shouted John from behind her. "Slapped arse!"

She stiffened. Yes, there was definitely something to be said for village life. You couldn't escape the village idiots.

Jo was the first one from the gang in the pub that night. She sat in their usual corner looking out at the view. From her side of the pub she couldn't see the sun's swan song blush, so the sky was now a heavy lid of charcoal grey. From here you'd think there had been no sun in the sky all day. She wondered idly about moving seats, fully aware that the effect would be totally spoiled by the gang's complaints and derision.

Was that what was wrong with her life, she wondered idly. Was all the light being blocked by others? Was she simply living in the wrong place, the place without any light? She stopped herself when her thought patterns started to remind her of her mother, an increasing and alarming phenomenon. A wonderful woman her mother, but not the kind of person you'd want to get stuck in a lift with.

She needed distractions. She focused hard on the more somber beauty the view offered. She didn't need to catch the reflection in the window to know what was going on behind her. Old Budsie would be sitting by the bar, smiling at everyone, slowly drinking his life away. The latest load of lads would have arrived for the evening, laughing loudly at their own jokes while scanning the pub for anyone with a decent amount of estrogen and peroxide.

Jo knew every last one of the lads since they were all in school five years below her. She knew that Tom Bath, with his shaved head and eyebrow stud, had played Joseph in the 1990 nativity play and wet himself on stage. He'd said it was the donkey, but everyone knew. Chris Saunders, with his leather jacket and gelled hair, had vomited all over the climbing frame when Annabel Harris had tried to kiss him in Year 4. And then there was Matt Harvey, whose dad was a policeman. Matt had been smoking dope at school since he was thirteen in a desperate attempt to undo the damage his dad's job had done to his corridor rep. Unfortunately, no amount of dope could change the fact that he had ears like a rabbit.

The door opened, and Jo turned toward it. She watched Shaun come in, cheekbones first. *You've got to respect that in a man,* she thought. Whatever might be happening to the rest of him (a slight solidity around the girth, a hint of receding around the hairline, and more and more laughter lines around those baby blues) his cheekbones were here to stay.

"Alright, babe," he greeted her softly. "Happy birthday." He kissed her on the mouth, his hand stroking her upper arm. "My treat," he said, and was off to buy drinks.

Jo watched him wander toward the bar, where he produced a wad of tenners from his jeans back pocket and greeted the barman with a familiar nod. She started to wonder what would happen if she suddenly changed the habit of a lifetime. If she stood up in the pub now, and cried, "*No!* I don't want a Southern Comfort and lemonade! I want a . . . a Bloody Mary!"

She could imagine the stunned silence. The confusion in Shaun's eyes. And the ripple effect—others would feel forced to reconsider their own drinks. It was too much to think about. She could see the piece in the *Niblet Herald* now—

Local Girl Changes Drinks Order
Her Parents Are Too Shocked to Talk

"Niblet-upon-Avon just isn't the kind of place where this sort of thing happens," said the landlord yesterday . . .

On the other hand, she thought, Shaun might be treating her to some surprise champagne. As he turned and approached, she offered him a big smile. He plonked down one Southern Comfort and lemonade and one pint of Guinness on the table with a grand flourish. The flourish, she realized (downward "yo"), was her birthday treat. As he returned to the bar to collect the pints for James and Sheila, Jo briefly considered pouring them all over his head.

Before Jo and Shaun had finished their first swig, James and Sheila, the other half of the gang, appeared by the table. They took off their coats and settled down for the evening.

Sheila had been Jo's girlfriend and life-event gauge for the best part of ten years, and by miraculous coincidence, James, her longtime boyfriend had been best mates with Shaun at school. Miraculous coincidences were considerably less so in such a small village. The foursome had become an institution almost before their individual relationships had.

"You'll never guess," breathed Sheila, all flushed cheeks and bright eyes.

"What?" asked Shaun without turning round, eyes fixed firmly on his pint.

Sheila moved to her seat next to Jo, grinning at each of them in turn, leaving a dramatic pause before answering. Meanwhile, James hitched up his chinos and sat down next to Shaun, opposite Sheila.

"Ah, the ubiquitous Mr. Casey," he greeted Shaun, as if Sheila hadn't spoken.

"Ah, the ubiquitous word 'ubiquitous,'" answered Shaun, pushing James's pint toward his friend.

"Ah, the ubiquitous word 'word,'" responded James, taking his pint.

Jo watched them raise their pints, elbows jutting outward to claim man space. She didn't think she'd ever heard Shaun and James actually have a conversation. They just had endless game-set-and-matches using their tongues and brains instead of rackets and ball. She wondered what would happen if they ever had anything to actually communicate to each other. They'd probably spontaneously combust.

The men eventually put their pint glasses down and wiped their mouths.

"Ah," started James again, "the ubiquitous pint—"

"Shut up, James," cut in Sheila, "or I'll knife you."

James shut up.

"Hey, Sheila," said Shaun. "Just say what's on your mind."

"Hah!" exclaimed Sheila. "You'd never recover, old man."

James mumbled something incoherent into his pint, and Jo thought she caught the word "harpy," but couldn't be sure.

Sheila turned to Jo and gave her a present.

"It's crap, and you've probably got one."

"Wow!" exclaimed Jo. "You shouldn't have! Shall I open it now or—?"

"So!" exclaimed Sheila. "I swear! You'll *never* guess!"

Jo put her present on the floor by her bag.

"What?" she asked.

"Maxine Black and . . ." dramatic pause . . . "*Mr. Weatherspoon.*"

Sheila got the reaction she wanted, even from Shaun. Even the lads in the corner gasped. Budsie stopped drinking for a moment. They all knew Mr. Weatherspoon. Everyone in the village knew Mr. Weatherspoon, religious studies teacher, with a nice line in Aran jumpers and the hairiest forearms this side of the Midlands. Jo was horrified.

"I've only just found out," rushed Sheila. "Maxine was just telling Sandra Jones in the shop—by the baked beans—and I overheard."

Jo was even more horrified.

"Well done, Sheila!" congratulated Shaun.

"But Mr. Weatherspoon's three-hundred years old!" exclaimed Jo.

"Are we talking a quick snog or the full monty?" asked Shaun.

"The '*full monty?*'" repeated Sheila. "Is that what you builders call sexual intercourse now?"

Shaun took a deep breath. "I am *not* a builder, I *own* a construc—"

"Shouldn't we tell the police or something?" asked Jo. "Surely it's illegal."

"Bloody should be," said James. "Maxine Black's a heifer."

Shaun laughed and nodded at his friend over his pint, granting him a point in their doubles match against the ladies.

"He's so *old*," repeated Jo. "Won't it kill him?"

"I've done the math," said Sheila. "Weatherspoon's not that old. When we started in juniors, he was only twenty-one."

They all stopped as this sank in.

"Oh, my God," whispered Jo eventually. "He was younger than we are now."

"That's right," said Sheila. "Barely grown up himself."

"And now," continued Jo, catapulting off her emotional trampoline and landing flat on her arse, "he's so old he needs sex with children to remind him he's alive."

"She's seventeen," corrected Sheila. "And been having sex—or *full monty*—as it's known in the elite world of construction—since she was twelve."

"I think I'm going to be sick," said Jo.

"Me too," mumbled James. "She was like two heifers then."

"Why are you going to be sick?" Shaun asked Jo.

"Because we're older than Mr. Weatherspoon was when he taught us!" cried Jo. "And we thought he was nearly dead then. That makes us officially old."

"Too right, babe." Shaun winked. "You'll be having nippers of your own soon."

Sheila gasped dramatically. "Oh, Jo!" she cried. "I think Shaun just proposed. How *sweet*!"

"Who wants another round?" asked James.

"For the love of God!" shouted Jo. "I am having a nervous breakdown here. I am twenty-three! I have peaked! All I've got to look forward to is illness and comfortable shoes."

There was a pause.

"Don't worry, old girl" said James. "You've still got the legs of a filly."

"Right," said Jo, standing up. "I'm going home."

Twenty minutes later, Shaun, Sheila, and James were satisfied that they'd persuaded Jo to stay by using sensitive, cogent arguments. The fact that her only alternative was a long evening with her parents never occurred to them.

It was nearly eleven when she finally extricated herself from them by promising that she really did want to be alone. She left Sheila flirting with the lads in the corner and Shaun thrashing James at pool, and wandered slowly back to her parents' house, trying to savor the silence, the night sky, and the crisp smell of promise she usually loved about spring nights.

As a child, Jo had always been near the top of her class. Encouraged by enthusiastic teachers, she had dreamed of studying one day surrounded by spires and history, in the company of fellow enthusiasts and inspiring geniuses. She had no idea what subject she wanted to study, just that she wanted a university education.

Then at the age of thirteen, while watching a documentary with her parents one school evening, she discovered that there was a subject called anthropology. A whole subject about studying people and how they functioned within a society! She had instantly announced that that was what she'd study when she was a grown-up. Her mother had glanced up from her sewing, and her father had nodded before switching over to *Wogan*.

Jo didn't mind her parents' indifference to her ambitions. Like any teenager, she firmly believed that her parents' opinions had little relevance to her grand plans. But then, gradually—so gradually she didn't feel it inching its way into her mind-set—she came to see how ridiculous a dream it was. In both her inner circle of friends and her outer circle of vague acquaintances, she only knew people who had studied vocational subjects. Even Billy Smith, two years ahead of her and a towering genius who'd gone to Oxford, had studied medicine, a subject with an obvious reward. And anyway, everyone knew he had no friends and his parents were Jehovah's Witnesses. And seven years' study! Seven years of salary—three hundred sixty-four weeks of paychecks—squandered! While paying for the privilege! It was a mug's game. Anyway, they'd always thought they were above everyone, the Smiths.

And so Jo got used to the idea that spending three whole years studying merely for the sake of studying was a self-indulgence. She was a pragmatist and proud of it.

And pragmatism pointed her in the useful direction of choosing to train as a nanny. She loved children, they seemed to like her, why not use that to earn a decent wage? And so it was that Jo disappointed her teachers, satisfied her parents, and kept her dream safely locked away as a dream by applying to the local college. There she earned herself letters that did not go after her name, but went straight on her CV and got her a good wage within a matter of weeks. After paying her parents a decent rent and helping them with the weekly food budget, the rest was hers. And for the first four years out of college, she thoroughly enjoyed herself.

It was only recently that certain fundamental questions about nanny-ing were beginning to concern her. Such as, why there was already no prospect of *more* money. And why she worked long hours, had no career prospects, and was stuck banging her head on a salary glass ceiling so low she could limbo it.

And why her employers—who had less common sense than she and no emotional intelligence to speak of—worked fewer hours than she yet were able to pay her a fraction of their own salaries?

Every morning, she would stand at the bus stop in the freezing cold dark, then squeeze onto the heaving bus into town. She'd walk to her boss's house, who would still be having her breakfast when she arrived. While Jo started clearing away the breakfast things and taking charge of the children, the mother in question would then invariably climb into a people wagon and drive off to a brightly lit, cleaned, and tidied office, leaving Jo's workspace looking like a war zone. Then, at any time between six and eight in the evening, said mother would return home, tell Jo how exhausting her day had been, then conduct a catch-up meeting with her of everything little Joey or Jack had said, done, and crapped. Only then was Jo allowed the privilege of walking to the bus stop, waiting in the frozen cold dark for her bus, and walking back home.

Now, how could that be right? How could such obedient realism, taken on at the tender age of sixteen, be so little rewarded? She felt like she'd missed the right turning and ended up in a dead-end street before she'd even taken her driving test. Worse, the job offers were coming from younger and younger mothers, and the thought of being paid a pittance by women only a couple of years older than her made her feel less than whole. On top of all that, she was growing concerned that if she and Shaun didn't make an announcement soon, her parents would propose to him themselves. She'd never told them that he'd stopped asking two years ago after she'd refused him for the third time with no more reason than the time not feeling right.

It amazed Jo that if a couple had been together for a while without making an announcement, people always assumed it was because the girl was still waiting for the boy to ask. Even in the twenty-first century, even when people should know better, even when the girl was their own daughter—there sat that ugly, insulting, outdated assumption, chip chip chipping away at her reputation, attractiveness, and intelligence.

The truth was that each time Shaun had sat opposite her in a crowded restaurant, gone pale and proposed, she'd had to hide her dismay. How could he have been with her this long and not realized that with a life decision this important, she'd put rationality over some outdated, controlling notion of romance? Did he really think it was a decision she'd want him to have kept secret from her? Did he really think she'd want to start their married life feeling like his role was to make the decisions, hers to agree or disagree with them? Or that she'd be able to make up her mind in a crowded restaurant when she couldn't even decide what to have for an appetizer? And anyway, it had the nasty taste of sacking someone in a public place to avoid a fuss. Sometimes she wondered if they would now have been married for years if Shaun had actually dared to discuss the subject with her instead of presenting it to her like a multichoice fait accompli.

She reached the top of the hill, pausing a moment to glance at the velvety black shades of hills in the distance, her usual comfort. With a deadening weight in her belly she realized that for the first time in her life the hills seemed to be blocking her view instead of being it.

"Right," said Vanessa, smiling brightly at the pretty young thing in her kitchen while Dick glanced at the girl's CV. "We've just got a few questions."

"Fire away. The girl said, smiling."

Vanessa took the CV out of Dick's hand. "How would you recognize meningitis?"

The girl shuffled in her seat.

"I'd look for a rash."

Vanessa and Dick nodded, staring at the girl.

"Ask the child how they felt . . ." continued the girl, "and if they felt bad, phone the doctor. Or—" she gave them a big smile, "I'd phone my boyfriend. He's a doctor. At King's. We'd be looking for a place together, but he has to live in for now."

Vanessa put down the CV, and Dick took over quickly.

"Do you smoke?" he asked.

"Only outside," she said keenly, her big green eyes fixed on him.

"Only outside? What? You mean you . . ."

"Well, I check that the child is busy, watching telly or something, and nip outside. I don't think it's good for them to see me smoke."

"Well, thank you—" started Vanessa.

"So," said Dick quickly. "What do you like cooking for a child?"

"The same things I like, really. I feel children should start eating adult food as soon as possible. I don't always think it's healthy for them to eat children's food. It makes them spoiled."

Aha. They both leaned forward.

"And what sort of food do you like?" asked Vanessa.

"Fish fingers. Burgers. I love chips. And of course Tommy K."

"Thank you so much for coming," said Vanessa. "I don't think there are further—"

"Do you have any questions?" Dick asked the girl.

"Ooh yes, actually," she said. "What brand of mobile phone would I have?"

Ten minutes later, they sat waiting for the next nanny to turn up.

"That's two full weeks and ten girls we've seen," said Dick. "This is ridiculous."

"It's two full weeks and ten girls *I've* seen," said Vanessa. "You've seen three. And I'm not doing another Saturday on my own, I'm telling you now."

"Fine," said Dick. "But we're getting nowhere."

"Well what do you suggest?" asked Vanessa.

"I just think maybe we're being a bit harsh."

"Harsh? This is the person who'll be bringing up our children! Of course we're harsh!"

"Well, I just think perhaps you're—*we're* not being realistic."

"Of course I'm not being realistic!" cried Vanessa. "I'm emotional, subjective, demanding, and full of *hope*." She slumped. "Why do you think it's so depressing?"

"Maybe the pick of the crop is just out of our financial range."

"Noo," moaned Vanessa. "It can't be. We work so hard. We deserve the best."

"But they're only human, Ness."

"I know." Vanessa sighed. "The person who patents a robot nanny will die rich."

"Is that what we're looking for?" asked Dick. "A robot?"

"No, I'll tell you what we're looking for." Vanessa sat up straight. "We're looking for a nice youngish girl from a nice, stable family background who has absolutely no social life, a boyfriend who lives a long way away, no hobbies, and definitely no phobias. She mustn't smoke, she mustn't watch daytime TV. She must be able to drive and be obsessed with our children—they must be her *life*—until we come home and then she must back off and sit in her room all evening, watching her walls. She must be health-conscious for them, but not for herself. She must be soft-spoken but firm, NNEB trained, bright and full of common sense, she must be selfless, tidy, warm, good at art, imaginative, and clean, with a high boredom threshold. And she must look worse than me in a bikini."

There was a pause.

"Well," ventured Dick. "I think maybe you're being a tad unreasonable."

"Of course I'm being unreasonable!" Vanessa cried. "I'm a *mother*! Honestly, Dick, sometimes I wonder if you've been listening at all."

"Ah, dear," breathed Dick. "No wonder this process takes so long. Any other requirements I need to know about? Is there an ideal shoe size?"

"And I must like her," remembered Vanessa. "Not as a friend, I don't want a friend, I want an employee. But she'll be living in my house—"

"*Our* house—"

"And she'll be someone I have to want to talk to every evening while you're watching television."

There was a long pause, during which Dick poured them each a stiff drink. "Why are they all so young?" he wondered aloud. "In the olden days they were buxom ladies with starched pinnies and faces who ruled the roost while the parents had a life."

"Yes, dear, and they were secretly in love with the butler."

The doorbell rang.

"I'll get that, darling," said Dick. "Just see if there's a miracle waiting for us."

He opened the front door. Standing in front of him was a woman in her midfifties wearing a type of checked two-piece suit that he didn't know still existed. She had a bosom like a barrier and a face like a frog. He was actually frightened.

"Come in," he said warily. She followed him down the hall and by the time he got into the kitchen he was almost running. Introductions were made, and the interview began.

"What do you like cooking for a child?" asked Vanessa.

"They must eat fresh fruit and vegetables twice a day," said the woman firmly. "I would check my weekly diary with you and then get them used to a routine. It gives children stability and teaches them that they are not the ones in control, you are, via me."

"Thank you," said Dick, beginning to stand. "I don't think there are any—"

"Do you have family of your own?" asked Vanessa. Dick sat down.

"Both my daughters live abroad," said the woman. "I was widowed in '79. I'd be delighted to baby-sit any night. And at weekends."

"I think that's everything; isn't it, darling?" Dick turned to Vanessa, who ignored him.

"What are your hobbies?" she asked.

"Knitting and cooking."

"Do you smoke?"

"No. Disgusting habit."

"Would you like to see our children?" asked Vanessa, ignoring the tiny rocking movement coming from Dick.

"No," said the lady. "I like children whoever they are."

Vanessa didn't answer immediately.

"Oh," she said. "I see."

"Right!" said Dick, almost jumping up. "Thank you so much for coming, awfully good of you, I love that suit . . ." He saw off their last interview that week as Vanessa stared miserably into space.

Monday in Niblet-upon-Avon was a fresh, bright day, so the park was fairly full—full enough for Jo and her nanny friend Edwina to be forced to share their bench with an old woman who sported an old man's coat and a young man's moustache.

They sat down while keeping their eyes firmly on their charges, who were, naturally enough, charging around. Three-year-old Davey was Jo's latest little boy. His sister was already in big school, and it wouldn't be long before he'd be going to nursery for three hours every morning. He couldn't wait, which Jo and Davey's mother tried not to take personally. Jo had been Davey's nanny since he was six months old, and she adored him. Once he was in nursery, what job satisfaction she did get would be significantly reduced.

She turned and watched Edwina, who was scouring *The Lady* for a new job. Edwina's charge, Nancy, was a needy little sweetheart thanks to the fact that her parents were quite the opposite. Edwina had finally reached her tolerance level with the mother and, like so many of Nancy's nannies before her, spent most of her time with the little girl desperately searching for other jobs.

Jo turned to find the children. After a few moments, she found them sitting together by the tree in the far corner.

"Hmm," she said to Edwina. "Should Nancy be doing that?"

"Probably not," muttered Edwina, without looking up.

Eventually, Edwina glanced over to her charge. Nancy was taking off her knickers and showing Davey where Barbie had personally autographed them in pink.

"Oh not again." Edwina put down her magazine, got up off the bench, and wandered reluctantly toward Nancy.

Jo watched the two children place the Barbie knickers over both of their heads, blissfully unaware that their quality assurance test was soon to be seriously curtailed. Then a shadow fell across them and four innocent eyes looked up at Edwina through lace-frilled leg holes.

Jo looked at her watch. Another half an hour of playing before pickup time. A welcoming warm breeze suddenly tickled the air, and she closed her eyes for a moment and leaned back on the bench. She was calmed by the sound of children giggling and dogs barking. *Live for the moment*, she told herself. *Just live for the moment.*

She must have fallen asleep, because the tender ripple of glossy pages turning in the breeze feathered into her consciousness, rousing her from a daydream of Hugh Jackman wearing a pinny at her mother's kitchen sink. She opened her eyes and looked down at the magazine Edwina had left on the bench beside her. She had never had any interest in *The Lady* before—all of her jobs had somehow found her—but something made her pick it up. She thought of Alice in Wonderland picking up the bottle marked DRINK ME.

She skim-read pages of ads for nannies and became aware of herself as a much-needed commodity. She started to turn the pages, feeling as if she'd just discovered a new layer of chocolates after thinking there had only been orange marzipan left. Finally, her eyes lighted upon one in particular. It had a very nice black frame.

Kind and loving nanny wanted for busy professional household in Highgate Village, London. Clean driving license, nonsmoker essential. Sole charge of eight-year-old, six-year-old, and four-year-old. Sole use of Renault Clio, suite of rooms with television and DVD.

She thought at first that the weekly salary was the PO box number. She read it again, slower. Then she read it once more.

Highgate Village. It was a pretty, quaint-sounding name, yet it was in London. She hadn't been to London since her midteens when a crowd of friends had gone clubbing there. She remembered the exhilaration at how alive with possibilities it had felt, even in the middle of the night. She looked back at the ad.

Three children—she'd never looked after three children before, but she knew as sure as she knew her own name that she desperately needed a challenge. And the car . . . And the suite of rooms.

After reading it a couple of times, she could feel her heart beating. New and dazzling thoughts began to starburst into her mind. With that much money, she could actually put some aside—maybe even save for the first time in her life. Come back home and put a deposit on a little flat. Or use it to pay for a college course . . . she was still young. She could start again; her parents would understand—

She suddenly pulled in the reins—she could never leave Mum and Dad. It wouldn't be fair—they needed her now more than ever.

"You can keep it," came Edwina's voice. "There's sod all in there for me."

Jo looked up at her.

"Oh no—"

"Here," said Edwina. "Take it." And she lifted it from Jo's hands, folded it roughly, and squeezed it into Jo's bag between Davey's beloved Thunderbirds companions Scot and Virgil.

That night, Hilda and Bill weren't talking. Bill had had his tea at the pub—steak and chips—instead of waiting till he got home for steamed greens and cod. They were furious with each other, and the television became that night's weapon of choice.

"You're not watching this crap, are you?" said Hilda, every time Bill zapped the channels over to the program he wanted to watch.

Jo didn't particularly want to look at the screen, but neither did she want to catch her mother's eye. For want of anywhere else to look, she looked at the door into the hall.

"What's up?" asked her mother.

"I'm going to make a call," she heard herself say.

"Alright, love. No need to ask permission."

And with that, Jo went into the hall and phoned the Fitzgeralds in Highgate, London.

Chapter 2

There was so much to take in, Jo didn't know where to look first. The Highgate house had seemed small from the outside, smaller even than her parents'. It was a nondescript end-of-terrace Victorian house with no front garden. It had only one window facing the ugly north London road that looked nothing like a village, with or without a high gate. And the road was so jammed with enormous four-by-fours Jo wondered if they were occasionally used as extra rooms.

She rang the doorbell and waited. Eventually a hassled Francesca, soon-to-be-ex nanny, opened the front door, and Jo stared at the Tardis in front of her.

The entrance hall was practically a room in itself, with bright Victorian floor tiles and ceiling cornicing framing a filigree radiator cover. A chaise longue stretched across the opposite wall, with a mock Victorian-style telephone on the minute table next to it. The walls were painted a sumptuous red. Wordlessly, Francesca motioned Jo to wait in the living room and shut the door behind her. There Jo stood, executing a slow-motion 360-degree turn, trying to take in as much as possible in as little time as possible. The lounge and dining room had been made one room, so what looked from the outside like a tiny front room was in fact a very comfortable sitting room and adjoining dining room with extremely high ceilings.

The living room was furnished with large, deep, white sofas on the varnished real oak floor. The walls were a different shade of deep, rich red, and a stunning Victorian fireplace stood in the center of the wall, framed by minutely detailed, shining Victorian tiles. Above it was a painting in vivid primary colors that Jo imagined must have been done by one of the children.

In the dining room stood a splendid, vast wooden table with matching vast wooden chairs. On the walls, wrought-iron sconces held fat, mis-shapen candles, as did the central chandelier-style fitting. The only electric light was in the far corner, over the polished upright piano, on top of which sat two descant recorders. Next to them languished a slow-blinking cream cat, staring at her. Jo started at its first blink, feeling she'd been caught red-handed, spying. She smiled shamefacedly at it before tutting at herself and looking away.

Every window was a sympathetically updated sash, and the curtains were a sumptuous, even darker, richer red than the walls, tied back by dramatic wrought-iron fittings.

Jo heard the sound of a man and a young woman saying their goodbyes in the hall, the woman very obliging, the man monosyllabic. Then the front door shut and after a moment of silence she heard the man say loudly, "Sweet mother of Jesus."

Jo sat down quickly as the living room door opened and the man appeared. She stood up again.

"Jo Green?"

"Yes." Jo walked toward him, and the man nodded briefly, before saying, "Follow me."

Jo had already put her hand out to be shaken, and the man seemed somewhat taken aback.

"Oh," he said, coming forward into the room and shaking her hand. "Dick Fitzgerald."

"Pleased to meet you, Mr. Fitzgerald," said Jo.

"Oh, Dick, please. Pleased to meet you too. Um, do follow me."

Dick led Jo down a narrow corridor to the back of the house, where he opened the door for her and followed her into the kitchen.

"My wife will be along in a minute," he told Jo's back.

Jo hardly heard. She was standing in the biggest, brightest kitchen she'd ever seen—the size of her parents' entire downstairs floor. Ceiling spotlights shone in the distance onto a glass table in a separate dining area from which enormous, elaborate French doors led onto a perfectly proportioned, perfectly manicured, long, narrow garden. Upon the table languished another cream cat, staring at her like a frosty queen, and Jo wondered uneasily whether this was a twin of the cat on the piano or the piano cat's idea of a joke. Unnerved, she edged farther into the room. The kitchen was painted a color she didn't even know the name of. Was it purple? Lavender? Blue? Lilac?

She kept on walking, and round the corner in an extended conservatory to the side was a matching (purple? lavender? blue? lilac?) two-seater sofa. Opposite it was the biggest television she had ever seen in her life. She tried not to gasp. The television was so large it was practically another presence in the room. Her dad would be in paradise in this kitchen. All he'd need was a toilet attached and he'd never want for anything. Sod it, he'd make do with a potty. She noticed that the two-seater opposite the television had a throw folded over one arm—the room's one concession for life with children. This must be the nanny's habitat. She found herself grinning. She could be very happy here.

Dick offered her a seat and she sat down at the glass table. She tried not to look at her legs and feet through the glass, but it was a most odd sensation. She followed Dick with her eyes as he tidied some mugs away into the dishwasher. This kitchen had curved doors and curved doors handles. It also had every possible modern convenience, including coffeemaker, pasta maker, and bread maker. It was like being in a state-of-the-art witch's grotto. Every convenience, including the space-age kettle and vast toaster, were made of shining chrome. Not a flower in sight. Her mother would suffer withdrawal symptoms here. And as she looked at the objects all lined up on the wide window ledge of glazed Mediterranean tiles, Jo felt tempted to agree with her mother. She felt like she was in the middle of a chrome battlefield.

Meanwhile, necessities like the fridge were disguised behind matching (purple? lavender? blue? lilac?) doors. Only the fridge was conspicuous thanks to its icemaker, and near it, the large, kidney-shaped sink was completely empty and clean, thanks to the expertly disguised dishwasher. Jo tried to remember if she'd ever seen her mother's sink empty. Instead of two taps, the sink had one burnished brass tap that looked like an old-fashioned pump. Surrounding the sink, and stretching out luxuriously over all the cupboards, a shining, curvy pine work top glistened luxuriously.

Jo took it all in then glanced back at Dick, nodding pleasantly. She might never see this place again—she had to take in as much as possible. Dick moved to another door behind him, and what Jo had assumed was a cupboard was in fact a good-sized utility room, with another, larger though less beautiful, sink. There the dryer, washing machine, ironing board, and iron were kept. The room was as big as her mother's kitchen. Jo was beginning to wish she'd brought a camera.

Dick let her stare. God, he loved this bit. It was well worth taking a Saturday off work to enjoy all this young, provincial adoration. And he loved it when they tried to pretend they weren't bowled over by the house, as if he couldn't read it all over their faces. This was where they usually became deferential and tongue-tied.

"Your home is absolutely beautiful," said Jo warmly. "I feel like I've stepped into a glossy magazine."

Dick laughed with some surprise.

"Oh! Well! Thank you," he said. "You're very kind. My wife should really take all the credit—"

A woman appeared at the kitchen door. "Are you talking about your ability to dress yourself again, darling?" she interrupted Dick as she approached Jo. "Vanessa Fitzgerald."

"Jo Green."

"Thank you so much for coming down to see us."

"Not at all. Once you're on the train it isn't—"

"Where are you from again?" Vanessa wandered toward the kitchen table and thrones.

"Niblet-upon-Avon, a tiny little village just near Stratford."

They shook hands firmly.

"How lovely."

"Oh, have you been to Warwickshire?"

"No. But I hear it's on a par with Tuscany."

"Um. Well, it's very beautiful."

"Right," said Vanessa, shooing the cat away. "Let's start." The cat resettled itself farther down the table, ready for the show.

The two women sat down. Vanessa gave Jo a tight grin.

"I'll just file the previous applicants." She scrunched up five CVs and threw them in the bin. "We're hiring a nanny," she smiled, "not doing 'Care in the Community.' "

"God, darling," said Dick from the kitchen. "I love it when you're inhuman."

Unable to watch Vanessa read her CV, Jo studied Dick as he busied himself in the kitchen. He was what Jo could only describe as a handsome older man. If he had been twenty years younger she would be feeling significantly rosy-cheeked. But age had certainly softened his edges. He was in his late forties possibly early fifties and was wearing a navy crew-neck sweater with the latest fashion jeans. Somehow they didn't look too youthful on him. She glanced back at Vanessa, who, though tired, was really rather beautiful. Soft brown eyes, vanilla skin, and thick dark hair that made Jo think of ice cream. Probably late thirties. She was wearing a fashionable knee-skimming skirt and a short, close-cut top, which showed off her curves.

Jo began to feel the first signs of hope that she'd felt for a good while. Here were two attractive people who had waited until they'd found the right partner before starting a family, rather than doing it just because everyone else had started around them. Together they had everything— looks, money, large family, and a television the size of a small cinema. *Look and learn*, she thought to herself. *Look and learn*.

"Tea? Coffee?" asked Dick from the kitchen.

"Oh tea would be lovely." Jo smiled.

"Earl Grey, English Breakfast, herbal, or lapsang souchong?"

Jo stared at him. Had the interview started?

"Stop showing off, darling. Make us a pot of tea and shut up."

Jo stared back at Vanessa. Never in a million years had she ever heard a woman tell a man to make the tea and shut up.

While Dick made the tea, humming as he did so, Vanessa caught Jo eyeing the enormous television behind her.

"It may be big," said Vanessa dryly, "but it still shows the same crap as any other television."

"Surround sou-ound," sang Dick, busily placing cups and a teapot on a tray.

"Surround sound, my a-arse," sang Vanessa back, still smiling at Jo. She leaned in toward her, and said conspiratorially, "Men think the bigger and faster anything is, the better it is. Except for their women, of course, whom they want small and slow. It's precious, isn't it?"

Jo stared at her. Had the interview started now?

Dick approached with the tray, stepping carefully, over cat number one, who had come in from the living room and positioned itself, sphinx-like, in the middle of the floor. He placed the tray on the table and sat down next to Vanessa, facing Jo.

Jo had never seen so many different brightly colored cups and saucers. Dick carefully arranged them so that not one of the cups and saucers matched. The turquoise cup sat on the fuchsia saucer, the emerald cup on the aquamarine saucer, and the aquamarine cup on the turquoise saucer. Her mother would be out in hives if she could see them.

Vanessa and Dick both smiled at her politely, indicating that the interview was about to commence. She managed to return the favor, feeling increasingly uncertain.

"I have a previous marriage," Dick started as he poured milk (from the lilac milk jug) "so it's not just the three children who are living here at the moment. There's Toby, who's thirteen, who my ex-wife, Jane—"

"*Whom*," corrected Vanessa.

"—will bring round here every Friday evening, six sharp. Toby stays until Sunday afternoon." He paused before saying, "I think you'll find it was 'who,' darling."

Vanessa smiled sweetly at Jo over her cup of tea (turquoise), as if Dick hadn't spoken.

"Have you ever looked after a child that old?"

"Nearly," said Jo emphatically, trying to ignore the novelty of watching a couple point-score over grammar. "My previous but one family ranged from five to eleven. Actually I've missed the conversation of the older children. It was one of the reasons I answered your advertisement."

Vanessa stared at her. "And, perhaps more importantly," she continued, "have you ever looked after a child of Satan?"

"Darling," reprimanded Dick.

"Well, you've said it yourself," Vanessa reminded her husband. "Jane the Drain is the devil woman."

Jo interrupted before the argument took hold.

"I've always thought that all children—like all adults—have the potential to be nice and nasty," she said. "If you get on with people, you can get on with children."

Dick joined his wife in staring at her.

"Then there's Dick's other son," continued Vanessa after a pause, "who's twenty-five."

Jo raised her eyebrows in surprise. It was the right thing to have done.

"I know." Dick grinned, genuinely trying to look humble but genuinely unable to pull it off. "Child groom. Unfortunately, I married a child bride. We didn't stand a chance."

Vanessa added, "Now you're just a child father-of-five, and she's a bitter bitch from hell."

"Thank you, darling, very helpful." Dick turned back to Jo, not remotely put off by his wife. "Josh is a chip off the old block. Good-looking, eye for the ladies, always got a few on the string at the same time if you know what I mean, been living with his mates in Crouch End—*very* trendy area just near here—for a couple of years, very successful accountant, on his way to becoming a partner in a large city firm."

He paused dramatically, to let it all sink in. Jo raised her eyebrows and nodded, to register immense respect for all this information.

Vanessa turned to her husband and smiled tightly at him. "And what block is that exactly?"

In the silence that followed, the cat on the table suddenly yawned, displaying its incisors to all with complacent pride.

Dick turned slowly to his wife and locked eyes with her. They were sitting a fraction apart. He looked down at her lips. Jo couldn't work out if they'd forgotten she was there or were performing to her.

"Oh come now, sweetheart," Dick murmured. "You remember my block. It hasn't been *that* long, surely?"

Vanessa seemed to consider this before giving him a conciliatory smile and turning back to Jo's CV.

"Anyway," said Dick, turning to Jo suddenly, "Josh pops in from time to time—"

"—when he's visiting us," interrupted Vanessa, "from Planet Josh."

Jo had absolutely no idea how to react, so she did the first thing that came into her head.

"Ooh, how lovely!" she enthused. "He sounds . . . *perfect*. I mean, I can't wait. I mean . . ." she trailed off.

They both eyed her suspiciously.

"What I mean *is*," she said, considerably slower, "that sounds nice."

Their eyes shrank, as if to focus past Jo's face, on her mind.

"For you," said Jo quickly. "And of course for the children."

"Not really," said Vanessa. "He's been known to get them so excited they vomit."

Jo nodded seriously. She felt her control of the interview slipping out of her hands. Something had to be done.

"I have a boyfriend," she told them. "We've been together for six years."

Vanessa's and Dick's eyes widened again.

"So I take it it's serious?" asked Vanessa.

Jo thought. "Yes," she said at last. "But it used to be fun."

Dick laughed loud and strong, until Vanessa said dryly, "I know the feeling," and then he stopped.

"I like your goldfish," said Jo desperately, nodding at the vast rectangular goldfish bowl high up on a wide shelf above the kitchen counter. "Isn't he big!" The shelf must have been built specially because it was exactly the shape of the bowl, allowing nowhere for the cats to climb or perch. In the bowl darted a single large goldfish, eyeing the cats.

"Thank you!" said Vanessa. "He's the children's. He's called Homer."

"Oh I love *The Simpsons!*" said Jo eagerly.

"He wrote *The Odyssey,*" explained Vanessa.

"Do you have a criminal record?" Dick asked Jo gravely.

Vanessa put her head in her hands.

"No," said Jo with a polite grin. She attempted a joke. "Although if I did, I don't suppose I'd tell you. Especially not in the actual interview."

Vanessa turned to Dick.

"See? I told you that was a stupid question. Ask a criminal if they've got a—"

"I'm not a criminal—"

"Of course you aren't," said Vanessa, "but the point is—"

"The point is she's not a criminal," said Dick.

"The point is you're an idiot," answered his wife.

"Don't pick a fight in front of the staff, dear," he replied, with a smile so forced Jo could almost hear his teeth grind. "It might make you look uptight. We don't want them all leaving as quickly as Francesca, do we?"

Vanessa bristled.

"At least I *have* staff, darling," she replied.

Jo was staring at them both. She'd never before seen an argument achieved with smiles, affectionate names, no screaming, and the odd allusion to a sex life. She felt like she'd stepped into an alternate universe. When her parents argued you knew where you were. As did most of the neighborhood. Her parents' messy, explosive rows were usually set off by the fact that they simply couldn't understand one another. Jo had always thought that was their fundamental problem. Yet here was a marriage where the highly developed knowledge of the potential enemy served simply to improve the aim of the deadly, heat-seeking verbal missiles.

Meanwhile, Vanessa was staring hard at her: Jo cast her eyes around the kitchen, politely letting her stare, wondering what on earth she could be thinking. Vanessa was in fact beginning a relationship with her. And as with so many relationships, it began all in the head.

Hmm, Vanessa was thinking. *Pretty, but in an endearing, girlish way that the children will be able to relate to and Dick won't. Bright, but open and honest. And, unlike any of the others, has done A-levels, so not only can she speak English, she can write it, too. Doesn't talk like a docker, smell like a fishwife, or look like a troll. She has a clean driver's license. And perhaps most important, she is almost completely sane. Is she too good to be true?*

Jo sat watching Vanessa and Dick in tense silence. Vanessa and Dick watched *her* in tense silence. Then Vanessa turned to Dick, tensely. Silently, Dick turned to his wife. For a good minute no one breathed out. If there had been plants in the kitchen, they'd have died of lack of carbon dioxide.

At last, Vanessa spoke to Dick.

"Well? Darling?"

Dick smiled.

"You're the boss," he replied. "Darling."

Jo had never heard the word "darling" used as a term of abuse before. There was so much to learn.

Finally, Vanessa turned to Jo.

"Do you have any questions?"

Jo pondered this. Yes, certain key questions did surface. Have you two considered couple counseling? Have you ever used the bread maker? Will I have to use the bread maker? Will I be able to watch the TV? Can I bring my dad to watch the TV? Can I bring the village to watch the TV?

"What are your ideas of discipline?" she asked gently.

Vanessa smiled sweetly. "If he has an affair, I'll cut his dick off." She proceeded to giggle suddenly at her own joke.

"I think she meant with the children, dear," said Dick, crossing his legs.

Vanessa took a deep breath. "I don't like lying," she began, "more than two hours' television a day, intolerance of others, and I can't abide laziness. Chocolate only once a week—to prevent late-onset diabetes—and homework to be done immediately after school, to prevent Sunday evening tantrums."

Dick attempted a smile. "We just want them to be happy."

Vanessa turned on him. "Are you criticizing my parenting skills?"

"God no," he replied. "It's only aesthetics that keep me wearing the trousers, darling."

Vanessa's eyes shrank. "Don't you dare turn this into a gender issue, Dick," she said.

"Our parental hierarchy is based strictly on effort and results. *I'm* the power base because *I've* put in the hours, *I* hold ultimate responsibility—emotional and financial—and *I* didn't go to Klosters while they were gestating, unlike someone I know in this room."

Jo shrank in her seat. She was fairly certain she'd never been to Klosters, but the urge to apologize was almost overwhelming.

"Children are like life," Vanessa muttered under her breath. "You get back what you put in."

"Perhaps I could see the children?" asked Jo in a small voice.

Vanessa and Dick both looked at her in surprise.

"They're upstairs in the attic, playing," said Vanessa, while Dick walked out to the hallway and bellowed their names so loudly that when he returned, his face had turned the same color as the walls. Within moments, Jo became aware of the sound of a herd of buffalo trampling through her brain.

"Hark! Do I hear the sound of angels singing?" said Vanessa, as four children launched themselves into the kitchen. The room seemed to shrink.

"This is Cassandra, or Cassie," said Vanessa, as a tall, thin eight-year-old with a shock of red hair glared at Jo. She wore combat trousers, a tight little T-shirt which announced PSYCHO-BITCH, and glittery hair accessories. She looked like a warrior pixie. "Only my friends call me Cassie," she announced.

Standing slightly behind her, literally in her shadow, was a four-year-old, staring intensely up at Jo. To their right slouched the boys. Toby, at thirteen, was clearly a god; Zak, at six, his happy cult member.

"Yeah," Toby sneered at Cassandra. "That's why no one calls you it."

Zak giggled behind Toby, and Cassandra stuck her tongue out at them both with a movement that used up her entire body.

"Oh, well argued, darling," Vanessa congratulated her daughter. She turned to Jo. "As you can see Cassie's going to be a politician when she grows up," she said. "And Toby's going to be a pig."

"Did you see *Hannibal*?" Toby asked Jo. Zak grinned.

"No I didn't," said Jo.

"He eats a man's brain," said Toby. "My friend's got it on DVD, and he eats a man's brains out and cooks it while he's still alive."

"Ooh!" said Jo. And then in the ensuing pause, she said, "Ooh!" again.

"There's blood trickling down his face," added Cassandra helpfully.

"And he starts gibbering like a baby," added Zak.

"It's *brilliant*," concluded Toby. "I've seen it twice."

Jo turned to the four-year-old.

"And you must be . . . ?"

"This is Tallulah," said Dick softly, as if presenting a prize jewel.

Tallulah edged back slightly, behind Cassandra. "It's okay," she told Jo extremely quietly and slowly. "I'm fine. Thank you."

"Would you like to see my Roving Willy?" asked Zak, stepping forward in front of Toby. "He's a robot."

Before Jo could answer, Vanessa interrupted.

"I'm sure Jo would love a guided tour, darling. But not now."

"Up you go," said their father.

To Jo's astonishment, the buffalo faded away into the distance. In the peace and quiet, Jo turned back to Vanessa and Dick. They smiled proudly at her, waiting for her comment.

"They're . . . they're *darlings,*" she said, enjoying the sound of the word in her mouth.

"They're brats," said Dick with false modesty.

"Which is how we know they're all yours," said Vanessa.

Dick turned to Vanessa. "Oh, well argued, darling." He turned to Jo. "My wife's going to be a politician when she grows up," he said.

"And Dick's going to be a pig."

Jo laughed nervously.

"Do you have any other questions?" asked Vanessa.

Yes, thought Jo. *What's the quickest way out of here?*

"You mentioned use of the Clio?" she said.

"Yes," said Vanessa keenly. "It's yours, sole use, air-conditioning, central locking, and sun roof. Do you want the job?"

Jo blinked for a nanosecond and felt her head nodding.

"Can you start next month?" asked Vanessa.

Another nod.

Dick and Vanessa smiled at their new nanny. Jo's mouth smiled back at her new employers. They smiled wider at her. She smiled even wider in return. Would now be a bad time to back out?

"You'll be pleased to know there's a television like this in your suite," said Dick.

"Come and have a look."

"Really?" beamed Jo, winning the smiling competition. "Perfect!"

The bunk beds in what was once Tallulah and Zak's room were perfect for secret meetings, even though Zak no longer slept there.

Monday morning school hung over them like three little dark clouds. They somehow knew that sharing their feelings would only make it one big one; Monday morning school was one of life's inevitabilities, like new nannies.

"I thought she looked alright," said Cassandra.

"So did Francesca," said Zak. "She hadn't seen *Hannibal*."

"So?" asked Cassandra.

Zak racked his brain for a suitable answer. He wished Toby didn't have to go back on Sundays. Toby would have known what to say to that one. Toby knew everything. Although not as much as Josh. Josh was even better than Toby. Josh looked like a man but acted like a boy. Josh was funny.

"I liked her hair," whispered Tallulah through her thumb, which had come home to her mouth after a hard day's work. "When I grow up I'm going to have black hair."

Already under her duvet, she was half-asleep, her strawberry blond hair fanned out against her *Tweenies* pillow.

"I wonder what *her* brain looks like. Zak said, grinning.

"We could take yours out and guess from there," said Cassandra.

"Oh ha-*ha*," said Zak. "I'm a boy, so my brain's different."

Toby would have laughed at that. Josh would have said "Touché, mate," then winked.

"Yeah. It's smaller," said Cassandra. "With a willy on it."

Tallulah laughed a delicious, half-asleep, baby laugh.

"Oh ha-*ha*," repeated Zak, aware that repetition rendered this witty rejoinder relatively useless.

Cassandra hated Zak on Sunday evenings. By Monday morning he was his old self again, but every Sunday evening he was filled with an uncharacteristic, bullish cockiness after spending twenty-four hours with Toby. *Unfortunately*, she thought, *Zak doesn't have Toby's intelligence, because his brain is still growing, whereas Toby's stopped growing years ago.*

Zak frowned heavily. Sisters were crappy. Why did he have to have two, while some people got to keep their big brothers all week long? He would ask Mummy tomorrow if he could have a baby brother.

He got off Tallulah's bed and readjusted the ankles of his Arsenal pajamas. "I'm going to bed," he said, and left. "Night, Lula."

He took the stairs up to his room two at a time. Toby would have been impressed, though he'd never have said. Josh would have cheered and thrown him round the room till he felt dizzy. The physical effort of such heroic stair-climbing resulted in two small trumpet sounds echoing from his nether regions, and Zak was forced to admit to himself that they rather ruined the skill of his footwork. Perhaps it was better Toby and Josh weren't there after all, he thought, as he opened the door to his own bedroom. Sometimes it was nice to be alone.

It was still exciting to be going up to his new attic bedroom. Toby's bedroom was next door and acted as the playroom as well because although Toby was older, he was only there two nights a week. Zak felt a bit smaller when Toby wasn't in the room next door.

He carefully attached a piece of string to his door handle and to his light saber on top of the door, setting a trap for robbers, slid under his duvet, and waited for Mummy to come up and say good night. It was much better than being in the top bunk and sharing with a girl. The window in his new bedroom was in the ceiling instead of the wall. No other room in the house had that. Being a boy was the best.

Below him in Tallulah's bedroom, Cassandra looked down at her sister, who was sinking into a deep sleep. She sighed. Sometimes she wished she could be four again, when everything was possible and you believed that if you wanted black hair when you were older, you'd get it.

She stomped into her bedroom, kissed her boy band poster, asked God to make her famous, and went to bed.

Unaware that her sister and brother had left her bedroom, Tallulah breathed softly and evenly. She was already Princess Jo with long, sleek, black hair, beautiful, cat-shaped blue eyes, and long, slender legs.

Upstairs, at the top of the house, Zak lay in his bed staring at the stars. They stared right back at him. He wished Mummy would hurry up. He hated Cassandra.

He closed his eyes, then opened them again quickly.

Did his brain really have a willy on it?

Later that night, Vanessa and Dick got to bed.

"What was it this time?" Dick asked Vanessa.

"Light saber, little bastard."

Dick chuckled. "That'll stop the burglars."

"It'll stop Mummy coming to tuck him up every night."

Vanessa lay on her back, positioned her arms beside her, closed her eyes, and started to breathe very deeply from her diaphragm. Thanks to three years of hypnotherapy, she was able to pull her thoughts away from all things stressful and focus on all things pleasant. Her hypnotherapist always used a beautiful summer garden or a calm, sandy beach. Vanessa preferred Harrison Ford in shorts. Worked for her. She focused hard on two strong, long, tanned thighs.

"So," growled Harrison into her ear. "We got a new nanny then."

Like a schoolgirl creating a fantasy scene with stickers, Vanessa visualized Harrison holding her in his arms after saving her from snakes and Nazis.

"Wasn't there a concluding part of that deal?" whispered Harrison, his scar shimmering in the dark.

Lying perfectly still, Vanessa's mind arched toward Dick. At least he'd taken a day off and helped her with some of the interviews. At least he'd made the tea. She nodded as Harrison started stroking her stomach.

Chapter 3

"*Leaving?*" repeated Hilda. "What do you mean? *Leaving?*"

"Well," started Jo. "I-I-I thought, I—"

"I'm going to have to have a word with that boy."

"Dad!"

"That man's wasted the best years of your life."

"Thank you."

"Well, you're no spring chicken—"

"It's got nothing to do with Shaun."

"Rubbish."

"*Bill!*" shouted Hilda.

"Well, I *mean!*"

They all fumed in silence.

"Are you unhappy living with us, love?" asked Hilda.

"No! Of course not."

"Then why?"

Jo looked at her hands.

"Mum."

Hilda nodded.

"I'm twenty-three years old—"

"I know, love, I was there."

"—and I've never lived away from home."

"*You would have if that bastard had proposed!*"

"*Bill!* Let the girl speak."

Bill started pacing the tiny front room with such ferocity that he looked like a caged line dancer.

"Sit down," ordered Hilda. "It's not good for you to get too excited—"

"I'll tell you what's not good for me—"

"*Stop shouting!*"

"*I'm not shouting!*"

"*You are! No wonder she wants to leave home.*"

Bill slumped heavily into his armchair.

"It's all your nagging and fussing," he told Hilda. "It would do' anyone's head in. If I had the choice, I'd be off to flipping Highbridge or Gatesbury or wherever it is—"

"Chance'd be a fine thing," said Hilda.

"Eh, do they need a builder, Jo?"

"Hah!" shot Hilda. "They couldn't afford the food bill—"

"*Oh give it a flaming rest, woman!*"

"*You're shouting again!*"

"*Course I'm frigging shouting!*" Bill's face was turning red. "*You're driving me mad!*"

"*Calm down!*" Hilda was nearly crying. "*It's not good for you!*"

"*Stop telling me what to do, or so help me, I'll—!*"

"Right," said Hilda, standing up suddenly. "I'll put the kettle on."

Jo and her father sat in the living room listening to the sound of Hilda in the kitchen furiously taking out mugs, the milk jug, and the teapot.

Eventually, Jo caught her father's eye.

"I think that went pretty well, don't you?" she asked.

They both snorted, until Bill said, "If Adolf Bloody Hitler invaded, she'd put that frigging kettle on."

"And you'd shout till you were red in the face."

Bill shifted in his armchair.

Hilda brought the tray in, and they watched her pour the milk and tea into the mugs in silence. They took their mugs meekly. After a few sips, Bill sat forward in his chair and rubbed his hands together.

"So," he said. "London, eh? Big-city lights."

"That's right," said Jo. "I'll just see how it goes. Probably come back home every weekend."

Hilda's lips were a thin line as she sipped her tea, and Jo and Bill tried to ignore how much her hands were shaking.

Bill gave Jo a little wink.

"Nothing like your mother's cuppa."

Jo smiled, and they drank their tea in silence.

That night, Jo and Shaun were separated by a pink tablecloth, matching candle, matching candlestick, and matching single rose. They drank their wine, then took another mouthful of heavy French food, then another sip of wine.

Shaun looked like he was in shock. There was no other way of putting it. When Jo had told him that she'd been offered a job in London and had accepted it, his body actually did a little jerk, like a puppet whose puppeteer had just hiccuped.

"I'm not finishing with you!" she gabbled. "I still want to go out with you—if you still want that."

"So what the fuck are you doing?" he asked, seemingly incredulous. "You think long-distance will *improve* things?"

"I just need to get away, think things through."

Shaun kept his voice low. "If you're moving to London because you haven't got the balls to finish with me," he said. "I—"

"I am not finishing with you," said Jo firmly. "Shaun, listen to me. I can't see me ever wanting to be with anyone else. I'm as confused as you are as to why I . . ." She struggled to find the right words. "Can't say yes."

Shaun took a deep breath and looked out of the window. Jo continued.

"I think I'm just not happy generally. About my life, about so many things. My parents, my job, even Sheila—they're all driving me mad and making me feel . . . depressed, unhappy . . . I'm low, Shaun. Very low. I have been for a while. I've only just admitted it to myself. I think my birthday made me confront it properly for the first time."

She sat back in her seat, feeling as if she'd just done a very bad first striptease. What would Shaun think of her now? Would he think she was mentally unstable? Would he want out?

"And what about me?" he asked, still staring out of the window.

She stretched out toward him, but couldn't reach him, so left her hands on the table.

"Shaun, you're the one thing that's keeping me sane. You have to believe that. But I need to get away so I can work out what it is that's confusing me."

"Confusing you?" he sneered. "I thought you said you were depressed?"

Jo struggled to make herself clear.

"I'm confused because I don't know why I keep getting depressed. I mean, I have everything a girl could want. Don't I?"

Shaun gave her a look.

"Do you?"

"You know I do," said Jo, putting conviction in her voice. "Which is why I don't understand how come I'm not feeling . . . lucky."

"Maybe you just expect too much from life."

"Don't say that."

"It's true," said Shaun. "You think too much, that's your problem."

"I can't help it."

"Course you can."

Jo sighed.

"What if you find out that this *is* happiness?" asked Shaun.

There was a pause.

"If this is happiness, Shaun, I'll kill myself now." Hearing the words out loud frightened her.

"Cheers," whispered Shaun, taking a gulp of wine.

"Shaun, I know it's a cliché, but this really isn't about you. It's about me. I'm worried—"

"Oh spare me!" Shaun let out a hollow laugh. "You're going to tell me you'll always love me as a friend next, aren't you?"

"Just . . ."

"What?"

"Give me time, Shaun. Please—"

Shaun crouched suddenly over the table toward her. "I've given you six fucking years," he hissed almost extinguishing the candle. "What do you want me to do, Jo? Fight for you? Is that it? Is this a test? See if I love you enough to visit you in London?"

"No!—"

"Then what, Jo? 'Cos I'm fucked if I can work it out."

If she'd had the energy, Jo was sure she'd have cried. "Just be on my side, Shaun."

"You mean like in a marriage?"

"No, don't—"

"Oh don't panic," he said quickly, holding his hands up in mock arrest. "I'm not proposing to you again. I have got some pride left you know."

They sat in silence.

"See me every weekend," pleaded Jo eventually. "Please, Shaun. I need you."

The waitress came over and asked if they'd like to see the dessert menu.

Shaun lifted his head toward her, his eyes only reaching her skirt.

"No. Can we have the bill please?" As the waitress walked away, he turned back to Jo.

"There are women waiting for me, Jo," he whispered.

She nodded.

"Queuing for me. In the wings. I've had offers—" He stopped himself.

She nodded again. She didn't want to hear any more.

When the waitress came back and put the bill next to him, Jo looked out of the window.

The next day Jo told Sheila. Sheila listened in silence to it all, so it didn't take that long. Afterward there was a pause while Jo racked her brains for anything else she could say.

"So!" Sheila finally said. "How did Shaun the Braun take it?"

"How do you think?" asked Jo.

"Like a man," said Sheila. "Badly."

Jo nodded as she took a sip of her coffee. "Maybe I'm making a mistake," she said.

"If you ask me," said Sheila, "I think it's a great idea."

"Do you?"

"Yeah."

"Why?"

Sheila shook her head. "Oh no you don't," she said. "Don't start all that analysis shit with me. I just do."

"But why?"

Sheila studied her. "You think too much."

"That's what Shaun said."

"Did he? I take it back."

"What else do you think?" asked Jo. In for a penny, in for a pound.

Sheila stubbed her cigarette out in the ashtray before fixing Jo with a hard stare. "You really want to know?"

Jo grimaced. "Maybe not."

"I think you and Shaun are stuck in a rut 'cos neither of you can face finishing it."

Jo leaned forward over her stomach. "So why does he keep proposing?" she asked.

Sheila shrugged. " 'Cos he wants it to propel you into finishing it? You know what blokes are like: never do anything you can get her indoors to do for you."

"I'm not sure—"

"So you're both stuck in an emotional limbo land, and you need to get out so you can get on with your lives. Which explains why you've been feeling so low lately and why he's even more of a boring bastard than he was before he met you. You know it, and I know it," said Sheila, finishing her drink. "You deserve better."

Whatever Jo was feeling at the moment, it wasn't that she deserved better. But the thought stayed with her all week.

She hadn't known what to expect from anyone, but the reaction from her boss was the biggest shock of all.

"Well," said Davey's mum quietly. "I suppose I knew it would have to happen sooner or later. I just hadn't realized it would be quite so soon."

"Sorry."

"Don't be sorry," she said. "I knew you were too good to be true."

"Thank you."

I should have paid you more."

"No."

"I should have treated you better."

"No—"

And then, to Jo's amazement, she started crying. Jo put her arm round her.

"I'm a terrible mother," she sniffed. "I'm a terrible wife and a terrible mother." Jo tried everything to convince her this wasn't true, but she proved inconsolable. It was only when Davey came in to ask for some chocolate that she managed to stop crying and stoically turned her back on him. Jo fetched him some chocolate and he, oblivious to anything but the precious cargo in his hot little paw, trotted happily back to his Indian fort, chocolate already beginning to appear all over him.

Half an hour later, by the time Jo's boss's husband had returned home from the office, Jo had discovered that her boss hated her job and felt traumatized leaving the children every morning but was terrified of leaving work because she'd seen so many friends do it, only to find themselves three years down the line with long, empty days and an out-of-date CV.

"I've been so jealous of you when the children have asked for you instead of me," she sobbed to Jo. "I've *hated* you sometimes, *hated* you."

"Oh dear."

"And now," she said through racking sobs, "I hate you because you're *leaving me.*"

Jo passed her another tissue. When the husband reappeared from upstairs in his jeans and sweater, he took one look at his wife, muttered "Not again," and left them to it.

Davey's mum blew her nose loudly into the tissue and grinned meekly at Jo, eyeliner cross-country running down her cheeks. "I bet your new family aren't as dysfunctional as us," she sniffed pathetically.

Jo smiled at her boss. "I bet they are," she said.

It was only when she had to explain to three-year-old Davey that Jo realized telling everyone else had been a piece of cake.

His little face crumpled in confusion. "Why?" he asked.

"Because I've got a new job."

"With a new little boy?"

"No. A big boy and two girls."

Davey thought for a while. "Will you still be able to pick me up from nursery?"

"No, sweetie."

"Will you still be able to bathe me?"

"No, sweetie, I won't."

"Will you still be able to blow my nose and call it an 'elephant blow'?"

Jo picked him up and put him on her knee so he couldn't see her face. "I'll come and visit you loads," she whispered into his hair. "And I'll send you funny postcards in the mail. Won't that be fun?"

"Will you come and see me at bedtime?" asked Davey.

"And you'll have a nice new nanny who'll love you just as much as I do."

"Will I like her back?"

"Oh yes!" said Jo, trying not to think of her. "Of course!"

"Will you miss me?"

"Of course I'll miss you."

"So why are you leaving me?"

Jo hugged Davey fiercely. "Sometimes we have to leave people we love," she sniffed.

"Why?"

Jo sighed into his hair. "Ah," she whispered. "That's the one question I can't answer."

Jo had arranged to catch a Sunday morning train, and her parents were the only ones able to see her off. Sheila had a Sunday shift at work. Shaun had said he'd wanted to come, but he needed to be on-site that day as his firm was starting work on the biggest contract they'd ever had the next morning, and last-minute details needed to be finalized. Jo chose to accept this. After all, she could hardly expect him to support her career moves, then not support his. But she did insist that she needed to spend the last night in Niblet sleeping in her own bed, at home with her parents, and they both knew that it was her little way of punishing him for not taking half an hour out of his Sunday morning to see her off. Their good-bye was a muted affair late Saturday night, after a tortuously touchy day together.

"I'll phone you as soon as I get there," she'd promised him.

"Cool," he'd said. "Take care, babe."

He kissed her lightly on the mouth, and she left, sniffing all the way home. When she got back, her parents left her alone, convinced that the tears were because he had not fallen for the bait and still hadn't proposed. Bill had half a mind to go and show him a thing or two and would have, if he hadn't known Jo would never forgive him, and if Hilda hadn't furiously barred the bedroom door while wearing her dressing gown and curlers, which had made him feel slightly ridiculous.

So bright and early Sunday morning, the three of them set off to Stratford-upon-Avon station. Jo had not been able to think of a kind way to explain that she really didn't need both of them to wave her off. It was only on the drive there that she realized she was letting them think they were doing her the favor because it might be the last time they'd feel needed by her, which was probably the first time she'd ever felt like the protective adult among them. *Typical*, she thought. *Just when I'm leaving.*

The train arrived twenty minutes early. Bill carried Jo's suitcase onto the stationary train, then turned to her before returning to the platform. He spoke quietly and quickly. "Mind you phone your mother. She'll miss you."

Back on the platform, he gave Jo a brusque hug, coughed, then turned away and started to saunter back toward the main concourse, whistling and jangling the change in the pockets of his grey slacks.

Hilda and Jo watched him as he went.

"Pierce Brosnan, eat your heart out," said Hilda.

Jo laughed.

"He loves you, you know," Hilda told her daughter.

"I know."

"Don't be a stranger. It'd break his heart."

They hugged, then Jo turned away and got on the train. She busied herself, getting out her book and finding her seat. When she sat down, she looked out and could still just see her mother slowly following her father down the platform.

Chapter 4

When Jo's train pulled out of Stratford-upon-Avon station she was a brave, strong adventurer with hope in her soul and a song in her heart. By the time she arrived at the Fitzgeralds' she was a gibbering wreck.

The London Underground had changed since her visit just a month before. When she'd used it for the interview, she'd been a tourist. Its sights, its sounds, tempo, smells, idiosyncrasies, delays, anonymity—everything was quirky and exciting.

This time was different. This time was for real. People moved to a rhythm she couldn't follow. She felt like the new girl at the front of a ballet class in a mirrored room. As the escalator took her deeper and deeper down, a great heaviness expanded inside her chest like she was drowning from the inside, a feeling she assumed must be loneliness. When an advertisement on the walls talked about coping with loneliness she had to turn away.

She tried to ignore her feelings and adopt the air of a seasoned traveler; after all, she'd made the journey to Highgate once already, she knew exactly where she was going. How hard could it be, she asked herself. She answered herself pretty succinctly by arriving in High Barnet.

Half an hour later, she arrived in Highgate, a stressed, traumatized nobody, aware of the ultimate meaningless state of existence and wearing the "Come any nearer and I'll pull the cord," glint in her eye.

Reaching ground level at Highgate, she waited to feel the recognizable smell, taste, and texture of fresh air. When she didn't, she almost wept. London had different air! Of course. She could almost feel pollution plugging up her pores.

As she walked up the hill toward the village, her rucksack assaulting her back at every single point of contact, head like a cartoon hammer and feet proving themselves once and for all to be a major design flaw, she wondered if Vanessa Fitzgerald would mind if she greeted her with "One hot bath, bitch, or three dead babies." Then she realized that she would be unable to form such a complicated sentence.

She needn't have worried. Vanessa wasn't in, as it was the first Sunday in the month,

Dick was in sole charge of the children. Only one generation ago that would have meant a day of discipline. Now it meant someone else who wanted to watch crap TV and eat junk food.

"Good journey?" asked Dick as he took Jo's suitcase from her hand and placed it two feet away from her in the hall. He ignored the multicolored rucksack coming out of her head.

"Oh, you know," she said, forcing a smile. "No."

"Good," he said. "The children are upstairs—"

"DA-AD!" yelled one of them.

Dick smiled helplessly at Jo, tutted happily, and left her to it, bounding up the stairs two at a time.

Feeling like an uninvited guest at the party from hell, Jo stood for a moment getting her bearings. Having got them, she decided she wanted very much to change them. Then at the sound of Dick bounding back down the stairs, she mindlessly picked up her suitcase and lumbered through to the back of the house, through the kitchen, and into her suite of rooms.

There she dropped her suitcase and slowly collapsed onto her back, landing on the rucksack. She wriggled her body out of the straps, where, instead of it floating up to the sky as she imagined it would, it refused to budge. There she stayed, like a beetle dying on its back, for a considerable while.

When she felt her eyes well up, she heaved her body into what could loosely be termed a sitting position. Once up, she forced her body into a vague approximation of a standing position. Once standing, she conquered her inner fear, invoked her fighting spirit, and placed one foot in front of the other. She tripped over her suitcase, swore and stamped over it to her other room.

She stood in the doorway and took it all in. An enormous wardrobe dominated the far corner, a vast television squatted in the middle, and a dressing table perched in the near corner. Opposite them all was a funky futon-cum–double bed.

If I had the energy, she thought, *I'd bring all my stuff in here and unpack it next month.*

Instead, she walked in and opened the vast wardrobe, half-expecting to find herself in Narnia. She stared sadly at the solid back of the empty wardrobe. It was absolutely enormous. She frowned and stared at it some more. *Hmm,* she considered. *I'll need more clothes.*

She walked back through her bedroom, tripping briefly over her luggage, into the en suite shower room. It was also enormous. Unfortunately no bathtub (Jo's parents had never had a shower installed), but the shower took up almost as much room as a tub would, and there was a toilet, sink, and a floor that could have doubled as a small dance area.

If I had the energy, she thought, *I'd bring my stuff in and leave it in the middle of the floor for a month.* Instead, she washed her face and looked at herself in the mirror. "This must have been how Lady Di felt when she arrived at the palace," her reflection seemed to say. Suddenly a small voice sounded behind her.

"It's teatime."

She spun round and looked down to face Tallulah. "Hello!" Jo knelt and grinned at her like a long-lost friend.

Tallulah inspected her gravely. "Hello," she said politely.

"How are you?" asked Jo.

"I'm fine, thank you," answered Tallulah. "How are you?"

"I'm fine, thank you," said Jo.

There was a lull in the conversation.

"It's teatime," announced Tallulah.

"Ooh, lovely," said Jo. "Thank you."

"Daddy says will you be wanting brioche or focaccia?"

Jo thought for a moment, trying to work out if the little girl had just sworn at her. She repeated the sentence in her head a few times. "I'll come and find out, shall I?" she said eventually.

Tallulah frowned. "If you don't know now, you won't know then."

"Oh!" said Jo. "Is that what you think, eh?"

"Yes."

"Well then," said Jo, gently taking Tallulah's hand in hers, "you'll just have to decide for me."

"I can't do that," said Tallulah, leading Jo back through her bedroom.

"Why not?" asked Jo.

"Because I can't."

"Of course you can. I trust you completely."

In the kitchen, Tallulah blinked contemplatively up at Jo. Just before the other children advanced toward the front line, Jo thought she caught the glimmer of a smile on the little girl's face.

"I'm having chocolate spread," announced Toby, leaping onto one of the velvet-cushioned iron thrones, almost squashing the two cream cats, who leaped out of the way and cast him looks that would have shrunk a lesser man.

"It's Nutella," corrected Cassandra, plonking herself opposite him.

"I'm having chocolate spread, too," announced Zak.

"It's *Nutella*!" repeated Cassandra.

"I'm choosing Jo's tea for her," Tallulah told them all.

"It's chocolate spread, smarty-pants," Zak told Cassandra.

"It's Nutella, poo pants," Cassandra told Zak.

"Now, now," Dick told them all.

"And I'm not having chocolate spread on bread," said Zak, "I'm having it on chocolate digestives."

"Hummus, anyone?" asked Dick.

"Bleagh!" spat Toby.

"Yes please!" said Tallulah.

"Hummus tastes like sick," explained Toby.

"I love hummus," Tallulah quietly informed Jo.

"It's made with chickpeas," Cassandra told them.

"Oooo-oo-ooh," mocked Toby. "It's made with *chickpeas*!"

Zak collapsed in hysterics.

"It's made with *chickpeas*!" he repeated.

"Well it *is*!" said Cassandra, frustrated.

"Well it *is*!" repeated Toby.

"Now now," said Dick. He turned to Jo. "There's mixed salad with balsamic vinegar and sun-blushed tomatoes—the children find sun-dried a bit too salty—and focaccia with hummus, tzatziki, or guacamole. Or if you have a sweet tooth there's brioche, butter, and chocolate spread or raw honey—most of it organic. I'll grind some coffee when the kids are sorted. Half-decaffeinated, organic, Brazilian, hope that's okay."

After deciding that Dick was being serious, Jo looked down at Tallulah. "Tallulah's choosing for me," she said. "I'll have whatever she's having."

Without further ado, Tallulah poked her little pink tongue neatly out of the corner of her mouth and started making Jo's tea.

"Chocolate spread! Chocolate spread!" shouted Zak, victorious.

"It's Nutella!" cried Cassandra. "Look at the label!"

"Dad said chocolate spread!" shouted Zak.

"Da-ad!" wailed Cassandra.

"Now, now," said Dick.

Tallulah chose buttered toasted brioche with lots of chocolate spread and hummus. Luckily, homesickness seemed to be temporarily numbing Jo's taste buds.

"I like the cats," she said, hoping the act of talking would distract her body from the act of having a minibreakdown.

Dick smiled.

"They're Molly and Bolly," said Tallulah, solely to her. "Molly's the boy, he's the bigger one, and Bolly's the girl."

"Molly's a strange name for a boy," said Jo.

"It's short for Molière," said Tallulah. "Mummy's favorite playwright. He's French."

"I know. I studied him for French A-level."

The table went quiet.

"Bolly's short for Bollinger," continued Tallulah. 'It's Mummy's favorite champagne. Bolly's always busier than Molly but doesn't eat as much as him. They're Burmese, but they don't have a funny accent."

The conversation was then drawn to a close as the table started arguing about what sort of accent the cats would have if they could speak, Dick playing as active and passionate a role in the argument as his children.

While they were eating, Jo became vaguely aware of the sound of the telephone breaking into the cacophony around her. She waited for someone to answer it, and when no one did, wondered briefly if it was only going on in her head. But no, Dick was starting to notice it, too. He kept frowning at it and tutting. Was this a test? To see if she was able to take responsibility? Was it Vanessa calling? Or could it be her parents checking that she had arrived in London safely? She hadn't had a moment to call them. The longer it was ignored, the more frantic she started to feel. Eventually, unable to contain herself any longer, she said to Dick, "Would you like me to get that?"

"Oh yes, please," he answered eagerly.

As Jo approached the ringing phone, the family as one became silent. Jo realized she didn't know the phone number, yet didn't feel she could answer informally, as if she were mistress of the house, especially if it was Vanessa on the other end. She also realized she had no idea how to answer the tiny chrome instrument. She grew suddenly self-conscious. She picked up the phone and heard herself say, in a stilted voice, "The Fitzgerald residence. May I help?"

"Press the green button!" cried the suddenly hysterical Fitzgeralds.

Jo managed not to throw the phone in the air and pressed the green button. *"Speak!"* they yelled at their new nanny.

Jo turned her back on them.

"The Fitzgerald residence," she said brusquely. "May I help?"

There was a long pause. She could feel the entire family staring at her back. The pause continued. She could hear someone breathing at the other end of the phone.

"The Fitzgerald residence, may I help?" she repeated.

Another pause. She turned away from the family a bit more.

"Or not?" she whispered pointedly.

"Hello," came a warm male voice.

"Can I help?" she repeated.

"Help who?" came the grinning voice. "You're the one who sounds like you've got a poker up your arse."

Jo's body underwent a thermal flush.

"Thank you," she said. "To whom would you like to speak?"

"Dick. Is . . . of whom I would like to speak. To."

Jo tried to hand the phone to Dick as if it was a hot bomb, but Dick was having none of it. He shouted into the mouthpiece, "Who the hell is disturbing my Sunday tea?" Jo took a deep breath, gritted her teeth, and turned her back again.

"Who shall I say is calling?"

There was a pause.

"You shall say Josh is calling."

"And what's it about?" yelled Dick across the kitchen.

This must be a test, she decided. *No wonder their nannies don't last long.*

"Will he know what it's concerning?" Jo said into the phone.

"No," said the voice. "I don't even know what it's about yet," it said. "Let's just live dangerously and see what happens, shall we?"

Jo wondered how on earth she had become a figure of fun for someone who hadn't even met her yet. She felt a stab of longing for home and yearned for the chance to be the one mercilessly ridiculing others and not the other way round. Was she ridiculous to the Fitzgeralds? Were they all laughing at her? She turned to face them. They were all grinning, and Dick was stuffing his face with salad. She felt a sudden need to be back in her neighborhood pub with Shaun, getting her usual without asking. She handed the phone to Dick and, imagining Shaun, Sheila, and James were listening, found a spark of her former self and said, "It's Josh. He doesn't have a strategy for the conversation, but is willing to live dangerously if you are."

The Fitzgeralds burst into happy laughter, and all tried to grab the phone.

"Firstborn!" shouted Dick into the phone. He held the phone out to his children, who all yelled their greetings.

Jo pretended not to hear Dick repeatedly say into the phone, "Did she? Did she?" punctuated by hearty laughter.

She contented herself with the knowledge that whatever Josh was saying about her was clearly puerile, and, anyway, she felt the same about him times infinity, with knobs on.

Josh, via the telephone, was handed round to every child, and she had to hear every single one laugh at something he said, then say, "No, she's really nice," until she wanted to scream.

"He called you Mary Poppins," explained Tallulah eventually. "And did an impersonation of your voice on the phone."

Jo was so impressed that a four-year-old knew what the word "impersonation" meant that she hardly had time to be mortally offended.

Zak and Toby laughed.

"Don't worry," Cassandra whispered. "I love Mary Poppins."

Jo smiled at Cassandra. "Thank you," she said.

"It's alright," shrugged Cassandra. "Josh is just"—she looked at her brothers—"a boy."

As the boys cheered, Jo, Cassandra, and Tallulah all shared a moment of mutual understanding.

Before tea was over, Vanessa arrived home. She wandered into the kitchen, put various shopping bags on the floor, and amid the screamed questions, "Did you get me anything?" "What's in the blue bag?" "Why's your hair a different color?" assessed the situation fairly accurately.

Hands on hips, she stared at her family until they all shut up, then said quietly, "I thought I heard a bomb while I was in Hampstead, but I had no idea it had hit my own kitchen."

The children, including Dick, laughed at this, so it was Jo alone who took in the scene through Vanessa's eyes. The kitchen was a disaster. She felt a pang of pity for Vanessa until Vanessa said to her, "I'm sure Dick'll give you a hand with this lot," when she felt a much bigger pang of pity for herself. Vanessa was still talking, "Then when you've finished, we can go through the week's schedule. Right!" She turned to her family. "I'm having a hot bath. Approach at your peril."

And before Jo had time to cry, "Wait for me!" she was gone.

By the time Jo had cleared away the mess in the kitchen, learned from Dick where everything belonged, and had just enough time to open her suitcase and look at it for a while, Vanessa felt like a new woman.

They met at the kitchen table for Jo's first Sunday evening debriefing. Vanessa was in her fluffy bathrobe, her hair in a towel, and her face cleansed. Jo was in a foul mood, her hair in a mess and her face clenched.

"Right," started Vanessa, taking a big breath. "Zak goes to St. Albert's in Hampstead—I recommend beating the rush hour, otherwise, you'll be in traffic all morning. Cassie goes to St. Hilda's on the way in Highgate, doesn't mind being dropped off halfway up the hill if there's traffic. Tallulah goes to the local Montessori, but we do like her to walk, so we'd rather you drive her back home after dropping the other two off and then walk her up there please. It's wonderful exercise, one big hill! Lulah gets picked up at midday. Once a week she does Tumble Tots and once a week she does ballet, her tutu's on the back of her bedroom door, don't forget it please, she has been known to cry until she turns blue. The other two are out at twenty past three, Zak first, because Cassie's old enough to start walking home with a friend or doesn't mind waiting— always find out which in the morning, she often forgets to tell you. After school Zak does Beavers and karate and has tutors for math and English at home, in the dining room. Cassie does drama and music at school, Brownies, ballet, tap, and jazz outside school in Muswell Hill, she can change there, address on the fridge, A-Z with the cookbooks by the kitchen door.

"The two older children practice piano and recorders once a week each at least, in the dining room. (The local pharmacist has very good earplugs.) Zak needs his recorder for school on Monday, Cassie—treble *and* descant—on Friday.

"Their weekly schedule is on the fridge calendar—off the top of my head I can't remember which day is which. All I do know is that we had a nanny once who took Cassie to karate, Tallulah to Beavers, Zak to ballet, and she was back in the bosom of her family in Norfolk that night. Oh! And of course, whenever she can squeeze it in, my mother, Diane, pops in to see the children—they adore her. All you really need to remember is that Tuesday's the nightmare day when it's so stupid you have to make packed teas for all of them as well as lunches—oh that reminds me, Zak's packed lunches must always have cheesey straws in them, otherwise he literally doesn't eat anything else. All day. He also has every pair of pants ironed. Otherwise, he won't wear them. Tallulah's lunch box is Tweenies—Zak's is Superman—Cassie's is Buffy. Please don't mix them up or they will be bullied." Vanessa frowned suddenly. "Any questions?"

Jo's brain started curling at the edges.

"Ooh," remembered Vanessa, diving into her handbag. "Here's your new mobile phone." She handed Jo a tiny, silver mobile phone. "Needs to be recharged at least every other day—don't we all?—your number is here on this card. Please keep it on at all times and feel free to give the number to friends and family. It is yours now. You may get calls for Francesca but that won't go on for long and you'll always know because they can't speak English and don't expect her to be able to either.

"My work number is here." She handed Jo her card. "Extension 4435 if the girl on reception doesn't put you through immediately or cuts you off. Dick's work number is here." She handed Jo Dick's card. "No extension number, but sometimes he doesn't answer because there's a customer in the shop and he's out celebrating.

"Here is your set of front door keys, our home alarm code is 4577 hash or gate, under the stairs, write that down if you need to but never keep it in the same bag as the door keys, because if you lose it and we're burgled, we won't get anything back on insurance and Dick will hire someone to kill you. Please activate it whenever you go out. We don't turn it on at night just in case one of the children wanders downstairs and sets it off. Here are your car keys, you are third-party insured and a member of the AA. There are speed cameras on every road that doesn't have speed bumps. The children get carsick over sixty miles an hour. Always keep spare paper bags in the glove compartment."

She frowned again. "I recommend you clean out the cats' litter tray at least every other day. Otherwise, it gets unbearable. Just feed them at lunch, cat food in the utility room, I do breakfast and Dick does dinner. It's the one job we've managed to share. Fish food is in the utility room, the children feed Homer once a week, usually Fridays, but they do need help getting him down. I don't want them climbing the work tops. And I don't want cat food in the fish tank, as the last-but-one nanny found out when it lost her her job and killed the fish."

Vanessa leaned in and whispered. "This is actually Homer II." She tapped her nose. *"Entre nous."*

They blinked at each other, Jo feeling the blood draining from her limbs.

Vanessa leaned out again. "I suppose you want to unpack now," she said brightly.

"Not really," said Jo.

"Maybe tomorrow then," said Vanessa, sympathetically.

Jo nodded without moving her head.

Vanessa stood up and walked to the fridge, took out a bottle of wine and, looking back at Jo, pointed at it, her perfect eyebrows arked in a question.

Jo shook her head. "I think I might go to bed actually, if that's alright."

Vanessa's eyes widened.

"Of course!" she exclaimed. "You must be exhausted. Just say good night to the children and you're a free agent."

Jo saying good night to the children was clearly more for Vanessa's good night's sleep than for Jo or the children's. Following Vanessa's directions, Jo popped her head round the corner of Tallulah's room. Tallulah was already in bed thumb in mouth, eyelids drooping as Daddy told her a story. Jo whispered good night to her and got a beguiling smile back. She knocked on Cassandra's door and found Cassandra sitting up on her bed, writing furiously into a furry pink diary. Jo said good night and Cassandra looked momentarily distracted, answered politely, then returned to her writing. Then Jo went upstairs to say good night to Zak.

She never saw the light saber coming and didn't stand a chance. At the sound of it hitting her skull, Zak bounced out of bed squealing with delight. His plan had worked! No burglar would see it coming! He was an Action Hero! He clutched his willy in excitement.

Vanessa was very sympathetic. "Little shit," she confided to Jo, while rubbing arnica in her forehead. "One day I'm going to stick that light saber where the instructions specifically tell you not to."

As way of an apology for her son's behavior, Vanessa insisted Jo join her and Dick for a welcome toast, which had the fortunate side effect of putting off their Monday morning's approach even further.

"Sunday evenings are the pits, aren't they?" murmured Vanessa as she poured her a generous glass of wine.

"Mm," agreed Jo. "They can be."

"Not for everyone, darling," said Dick. "Maybe, unlike us, Jo enjoys her job."

"Don't be ridiculous," said Vanessa. "No one enjoys their job."

"I do," said Dick.

"That's because it's not a job," countered his wife. "It's a hobby."

"A hobby that pays for the children's education, all our holidays, half the bills, and luxuries like a full-time nanny," said Dick quietly.

Vanessa turned to Jo.

"Dick's daddy left him a trust fund in his will," she told her. "So he bought a record shop to play with. For the three people left in the country who haven't taken to those newfangled, one-night-wonders CDs."

"Now, now," said Dick, before turning to Jo. "CDs are a passing phase. Records are imbued with memories."

"Which is why people never got rid of them in the first place and don't need to buy new ones, darling."

"There's a flat above the shop," Dick continued to confide in Jo, "which I did up myself at great personal cost and rent out at spectacular rates." He sighed. "It's not easy being a landlord. Big responsibility. Which is how we never have to worry about a single bill and my wife can enjoy all the latest fashions and an extensive beauty regime."

"With what's left over from the mortgage and children's clothes, school equipment and toys, obviously," finished Vanessa. "It was before he met me, of course," she continued to Jo, as if Dick hadn't spoken. "Otherwise, he'd have got a proper job and invested it in something that would have been of some use to his family, like shares or a villa in Nice or a yacht. But boys will have their toys."

"Not all of their toys, darling."

Vanessa responded to this under the pretext of filling Jo in on vital background information.

"I insisted on a dining room table in the dining room instead of a train set," she explained. "Poor Dick. He'll never get over the disappointment."

"But it's alright," he added to Jo, their new couples' counselor, "because we've now got the ugliest dining room table in the world."

"To match your first wife," said his second into her Pinot Grigio.

"More wine?" Dick asked Jo.

"Yes, please," she replied.

Jo found herself in her new bedroom suite, completely on her own, with the entire evening at her disposal, at precisely midnight. She tripped briefly over her open suitcase and discarded rucksack and lay on her bed too exhausted to cry. After a few moments, she hauled her clothes off her body and got straight under the duvet, where she suddenly became wide-awake. There she lay, blinking in the dark for four hours. By 4 A.M., she hated London, hated the Fitzgeralds, hated children, and hated her life. By 4:01 A.M. she fell into a heavy sleep. And just two-and-a-half short hours later, she was very rudely awakened.

Chapter 5

Jo could probably have coped with the wake-up call of a pneumatic drill thundering through her skull had she not just been dreaming about chancing upon a mute, shell-shocked, virgin Ben Affleck skinny-dipping through her private lagoon. No time is good to wake up to the sound of a pneumatic drill thundering through one's skull, but this really did feel like an all-time low.

She opened her eyes and waited for the familiar sounds of the not-so-distant River Avon to emerge from the clamor inside her head. She kept on waiting. Eventually, she poked her head out from beneath the duvet. She was most disoriented to discover that she was not in her bedroom, but in some IKEA nightmare. And then suddenly, it all came back to her. She was in hell, north London.

She lay in her bed, staring at nothing and hoping for a quick, painless end when, as suddenly as it had started, the pneumatic drill stopped. Bliss. Utter silence. She treated herself to a flashback of a mute, shell-shocked, virgin Ben Affleck discovering her private lagoon's hidden waterfall when she was disturbed by the sound of an avalanche outside her window. She screamed and leaped out of bed.

Nervously, she tweaked the curtain aside and came face-to-face with three burly builders, one wheelbarrow, and a builders' chute down the side of the neighboring house. The builders all spotted her and as one, grinned the male grin, a highly efficient communication shortcut, specific to their gender, that makes their minds transparent. She pushed the curtain back and leaned against the wall.

After her power shower, Jo picked the first outfit from her suitcase that didn't look like it had been through a wringer, dressed quickly, and appeared in the kitchen. It was empty. She put the kettle on and tried to remember where the tea bags were kept, while keeping an ear out for upstairs. When the pneumatic drill started up again, she decided to venture up to the children. Perhaps she could ask them to hide her.

No one was awake. She looked at her watch. It was late. The children had to be in school soon. She knocked gently on Vanessa and Dick's bedroom door, then on Tallulah's and Cassandra's.

Within seconds, there was grand-scale panic in the Fitzgerald household.

"We've overslept!" Vanessa yelled to the world, putting up an impressive contest with the drill. *"Get up now! Jo will be taking you in ten minutes flat."*

Jo decided it would be a good time to work out where the schools were, so ran downstairs to get the A-Z.

"Where are you going?" cried Vanessa.

"Downstai—"

"Dick needs help getting the kids up while I shower!"

Dick did indeed need help. Tickling children in their half sleep until they accidentally punch you in the face has never proved to be the fastest way of waking them up.

Starting to feel panicky herself now, Jo opened their curtains and told them that if they were down in ten minutes, she'd make them a surprise treat for dinner. And the first one down could have the biggest helping. It worked wonders as they had yet to sample her cooking.

Jo hardly noticed that when she left for school with the children neither Dick nor Vanessa had left their home, and Dick was not even dressed. All she did notice was that she hit a traffic jam almost immediately and her car had a much lower clutch than she'd imagined. She spent most of her first school run moving her car seat backward and forward, pretending she knew what she was cooking that night and taking a wrong turn. There simply wasn't time for them to drive home and walk Tallulah to school, so Jo made an executive decision. "If Mummy and Daddy can't wake her up in time, I can't walk her to school," she self-justified. "Maybe it will teach them not to do it again."

As she and Tallulah drove down Highgate Hill, Jo saw with increasing trepidation just how steep it was. She had visions of her crawling up it in future. She told herself that within weeks her legs would be shapely as well as slim, and her heart would be at its peak of good health. Either that or she'd be dead from exhaustion.

When she got home after dropping Tallulah off, she had to clean the kitchen and finish the ironing. She also wanted to phone Shaun. She assumed the kitchen would be an easy job, but discovered that it couldn't possibly have been cleaned properly since the nanny before Francesca. Afterward she was exhausted and made herself a quick cuppa, stretching her back out while the kettle boiled. With a mug of tea to fortify her, she started the ironing. She made another interesting discovery. Everything was in the ironing pile. Jo was just about to take her first swig of tea and call Shaun when she realized that if she had to walk up the hill to Tallulah's school, she would be late if she didn't leave five minutes ago. She picked up the keys and left the house, remembering to set the alarm first.

Her calf muscles were trembling and sweat was clinging to her back by the time she turned into the little side street where Tallulah's Montessori nursery was. She saw the single-file line of parents queueing outside the school. She stood, at the back of it, wondering how Tallulah would feel about carrying her home.

Vanessa had mentioned that for security reasons each child was passed individually to his or her "carer of choice" by the teacher, rather than allowing anyone to wander in off the street and take any child away with them. She had expected to have to explain who she was and give everyone a potted history of her CV, as any new nanny in Niblet would have had to do. But not here.

After a few moments a woman arrived behind her, and Jo thought that at last someone friendly had come to save her.

"Hello," came a voice behind her.

She whipped round and was about to answer when she heard the woman in front of her start up a conversation with her would-be companion. And then to her disbelief, the two women continued a wholehearted conversation around her as if she was invisible. As they spoke about the merits of Hatha yoga compared to Iyengar, Jo tried very hard not to think of her parents.

By the time Tallulah sprang out at Jo, smiling and waving her little hand, Jo wanted to hug her till she cried. Luckily, Tallulah was too interested in what was for dinner to notice anything amiss. The two of them walked down the hill, making conversation about the surprise treat.

"Is it chicken?" asked Tallulah.

"No."

"Chips?"

"No."

Tallulah gasped. "Cheese fondue!" she cried.

Take me home, thought Jo. "What is your all-time favorite food?" she said instead. The question was a sure winner. Every four-year-old's favorite food fitted in nicely with her easy recipe for chocolate Rice Krispies.

Tallulah was quiet for a while. Then she opened her eyes wide, and said in hushed awe, "Homemade hummus on home-baked brioche with garlic-stuffed olives."

Jo knelt beside her. "Well, sweetie," she exclaimed. "It's not that."

Jo planned to phone Shaun during Tallulah's ballet lesson but made the fatal error of deciding to catch a quick glimpse of Tallulah in her full tutu glory before nipping out to make the call. After half an hour of standing mesmerised by eleven fairies in the fairy wood, she realized she'd missed her chance. So she joined the other parents on the small chairs at the end of the room.

Tallulah was being a tree. Stretching up, up, up into the sky in a pink glittery concoction of feminine fancy topped with a pink flowery headband. Next to Tallulah stood, treelike, a tiny, squat four-year-old wearing a thermal vest under her tutu, ballet shoes that she would grow into well within the decade, and the face of a fairy elephant. Her mother sat beside Jo with love in her eyes.

"That's right, Xanthe!" sang the teacher, "join in."

Xanthe was far more interested in pensively picking her nose and watching Tallulah being a tree.

"Ooh, Tallulah," chirruped the teacher, "you're *a lovely* tree. Isn't she a lovely tree, everybody?"

Ten four-year-olds stopped being trees for a while and looked at Tallulah. Tallulah opened her face to the sun and thought tree thoughts.

"*What* a lovely tree," cooed the teacher. "Are you an oak or chestnut?"

"Banana."

"Oooh," said the teacher. *"Lovely."*

Jo only just stopped herself from tapping the woman next to her and telling her that she was Tallulah's nanny. Before she knew it, the class was over and she realized she would have to wait to phone Shaun until after they got back home.

By the time they got back, Jo's schedule was tight. Tallulah had to be changed from a fairy to a four-year-old and eased down from the dizzy heights of tree stardom while tea had to be thought about and prepared, all within the strict deadline of pick-up time for the older two children.

As the afternoon wore on, Jo's need to speak to Shaun grew increasingly uncomfortable, like an unheeded blister. Usually by now they'd have spoken briefly first thing in the morning, had a lunchtime catch-up and then squeezed in a quickie mid-afternoon to make tonight's arrange-

ments. She'd have had macro- and micro-details of his day from the traffic jam on his way into work to today's sandwich fillings and, if there'd
been time, they'd have even managed a row. After being together for so
many years they could fast-track from easy-going chat to heated row
within moments. But today, there had been no time to even start one. Not
talking to Shaun gave Jo the oddest sensation of having gone too far out
at sea and lost sight of the shore. But every time she picked up the phone,
Tallulah bounced in with another query or demand, with the energy and
persistence of a delirious pup.

To her amazement, Jo got tea, Tallulah and herself as ready as they both
needed to be in time to pick up the other two. She'd have to phone
Shaun this evening, she told herself firmly, and until then she'd just have
to cope with being all at sea. Just as she was about to leave the house, the
phone had rung. It was Diane, Vanessa's mother.

Luckily, she explained to Jo, she could squeeze in a little visit before her
bridge game, as long as the children were home on time. She would be
there at four *on the dot*, so Jo promised that would be fine and was now in
a hurry. Tallulah was only too pleased to hurry along beside Jo, because
she had been the best tree and she hardly had room in her little body for
all the happiness. In fact, bits of happiness kept bursting out in the form
of unexplained giggles and skips.

They got to Zak's school in good time. Zak caught their eye in the
playground and nodded briefly with an easy smile. Then he went to shake
his teacher's hand and doff his cap before obediently approaching, handing Jo his football as if she had been waiting for it all along, taking her
hand in his, asking her how she was, then telling her about his day in intimate detail.

Zak and Tallulah spent an enjoyable ten minutes in the car together, as
Jo drove to pick up Cassandra. They found her sitting on her own on a
low wall wearing a glum expression of world-weariness. With barely a
flicker of recognition, she got wordlessly into the back of the car. All
three children were in their own little worlds, and Jo left them to it, concentrating on getting home without traveling via Manchester.

"I was a tree," Tallulah told them all.

When Jo got them all home at one minute to four, she discovered
she'd forgotten the alarm code. Zak remembered it, but fell over on the
way to the understairs cupboard and wailed so loudly he almost deaf-
ened the beeping of the alarm, but not quite. Tallulah went to look at
Zak's knee while Cassandra calmly punched in the four-digit code and

told Zak to stop crying like a baby. Jo wondered if now would be a good time for her to slip away home. She looked at her watch. Thirty seconds until Diane arrived. She wondered if Diane would be anything like her daughter.

Meanwhile, Diane's daughter was rather enjoying her day. Most of it had been run-of-the-mill. That morning, she walked briskly past reception at Gibson Bead Advertising Agency in Soho, holding a steaming black coffee in one hand and a bulging briefcase in the other. She headed for the lift, her strappy shoes clacking on the marble floor. She pressed the lift button and checked her makeup in the glistening reflection of the lift door. Her eyes drifted behind her. There she saw Anthony Harrison from Creatives enter the building, wink at the receptionist, and stride toward the lift, whistling as he approached. She turned her head away from him and pretended to look at something on the far wall, a gesture which her subconscious knew was far more likely to attract his attention than actually engaging him in conversation.

Anthony Harrison was one of the few of the Creative team copywriters with whom Vanessa would have actually liked to work. Creatives were notoriously pampered, spoiled, and impossible, but Anthony Harrison managed to turn those traits into engaging proofs of genius. He was the man who had come up with the hugely successful *Bloody Hell—It's That Time Again* tampon campaign and the gloriously ironic copy of the L'Oréal line, *Equality—Because I'm Worth It* campaign. He seemed to be able to slip effortlessly into women's heads. Probably because he had similar access to their knickers. Vanessa prided herself on being the only woman in the entire office who was impervious to Anthony Harrison's charms. Yes, he was good-looking, creative, intelligent, and charming, she could see all that. But from about the age of three, when Vanessa had first started loving everything about the male sex, she had been attracted only to dark men. As far as she had always been concerned, blond men were as manly as Barbie. It just didn't work for her. All her boyfriends had been dark-haired, and her husband was dark-haired and olive-skinned, with soulful brown eyes. Anthony Harrison had thick hair that flopped over his forehead in an endearingly boyish way, but it was flaxen. His skin was smooth as silk, but it was fair; his eyes were deep and penetrating, but they were blue. Vanessa was safe.

Anthony stood next to Vanessa, and she kept her eyes firmly on the wall, conscious that he was managing to give her the once-over without moving his head. She smiled inwardly. Men were so predictable. Which was, she knew, one of the many reasons she adored them.

The lift chimed and its doors slid silently open. Here she acknowledged Anthony's presence for the first time, at which he gestured for her to go in before him. She smiled delicately, just the right amount to accentuate her apple cheekbones and remain enigmatic. They stood next to each other in silence as the lift ascended. Vanessa got out first. Creatives was on the top floor—or the "penthouse" as it was known—offering superior views and thicker carpets than the rest of the building. As she walked away, she could feel Anthony Harrison's eyes scan her figure once more. In the reception mirror she could see him ignoring the glances from women already at their desks, keeping his eyes focused on her retreating view as long as possible, tilting his head sideways as the doors shut in front of him. She felt her endorphins skip with vengeful satisfaction at the thought that men still found her sexy.

She walked swiftly through the office, her coffee high, her head higher, and her self-esteem somewhere in the clouds. It was the best part of the day. Unfortunately it was nearly over. She swept confidently into her office, shut the door, and walked over to her desk. She put her coffee next to the up-to-date photos of the children, hefted her briefcase onto the desk, and sat down, moving fast to distract herself from the deflation already setting in.

There was a rat-a-tat at her door.

"Come!" ordered Vanessa.

The door swung open dramatically and Max Gibson, agency founder and onetime advertising guru, stood theatrically in its center, with a smile on his face wider than his bow tie. Max's days of inspired campaign ideas were long gone, but his onetime pulse-of-the-nation slogans were now so anachronistic they were postmodern in a totally up-to-the-minute way. He was enjoying his retrospective phase far more than he enjoyed his initial success, when he'd been too ambitious to enjoy anything.

"Vanessa, sweetie," he bellowed through his cigar. "VC wants an agency review! We've been asked to pitch!"

Vanessa blinked in amazement. Archrival, McFarleys', had held the much-coveted Vital Communications account for almost five years. Their latest campaign—a very trendy teddy bear with his own mobile phone and website—had slowly grown stale, but because the sales were still up, everyone in the business assumed McFarleys' would be safe for years to come.

"You're kidding!" Vanessa cried.

Max roared with laughter. "Would I kid about something this big?" he twinkled. If his bow tie could have spun it would. "Those bastards must be shitting themselves." He laughed, then suddenly turned deadly serious. "I want the best creative team we've got. I don't care how up their arses they are, in fact the higher up the better. I want a creative team who are *so* up their own holes, they're fucking *potholing*. I want them to give you *migraines*, I want a team that are so goddam good, they make your life a *nightmare*. I want you *committing suicide* over this, sweetie."

"You want me to head this?" gasped Vanessa.

"Head it? *Head* it?" exclaimed Max. "I want you to *mastermind* it! I want you to fucking *Mussolini* it! And I expect you to pick the best. The crème-de-là-fucking-crème."

"Right," said Vanessa, pen in hand.

"Anyone in mind?"

"You know," said Vanessa. "I've never worked with Anthony Harrison and Tom Blatt before."

"You're shitting me?" exploded Max. "That's criminal. How long have you been here? What? Eight years? Call a lunch meeting at Groucho's pronto."

"Okay," said Vanessa. "You're the boss."

She picked up her coffee, and Max winked at her through the cigar smoke.

Anthony Harrison looked out past the line of awards on the window ledge, out toward Soho, which was starting to buzz with anticipation of the approaching summer. The rumors about the VC pitch had already started.

Tom Blatt was Anthony's partner in crime, a graphic artist, who, in his own modest words could create images that got "blue-rinses to buy piss in a bottle." Tom wasn't a wordsman. He sat in the office he and Anthony shared frowning so hard it was giving him one of his heads.

"If Goofy and Grumpy get it," he told Anthony, "I'm leaving. Leaving. That's it. Moving onto a houseboat to paint flowers on fucking watering cans."

"For Christ's sake," said Anthony. "Why do you immediately assume the worst?"

Tom shrugged. "Helps me deal," he muttered.

"With what? Nothing's happened yet."

"When it does, I'll be ready. Healthy pessimism. Worked for van Gogh."

"How? He cut off his ear and killed himself."

"But look how famous he is now—"

"Tom. You're in advertising. You're not going to cut off your ear, and you're never going to be famous."

Tom slumped down on the leather swivel chair opposite Anthony's desk. "I bet that bitch gives it to Goofy and Grumpy. She wouldn't know talent if it crapped on her face."

"What bitch. Who's heading it?"

"Vanessa Fitzgerald."

"Bugger! I was in the lift with her this morning. Should have given her a bit of the old Tony treatment."

Tom let out a big sigh. "How come the suits wield all the power, and we're the ones with the talent?"

"Dunno, Tom."

Anthony's phone rang. Anthony and Tom stared at each other, and after three rings, Anthony picked it up.

"Anthony Harrison."

"Anthony?" It was a female voice, firm but friendly.

"Yup."

"Vanessa."

"Hi, Vanessa!"

Tom sat up in his chair.

"I won't bush-beat," said Vanessa. "You know we've got the VC pitch?"

"I had heard some rumor."

"You and Tom interested?"

Anthony grinned at Tom.

"Yeah, why not? I'm sure we could squeeze it in.'

"Let's have a meet," Vanessa continued. "Monday's the earliest I can do it. Groucho's, 1 P.M. You, me, Tom, and Max."

"Great. I'll let Tom know." He put the phone down and punched the air.

Downstairs, Vanessa replaced her phone slowly and replayed Anthony's answers in her head, reveling in the controlled excitement she'd heard in his voice. There was something extremely endearing about a man pretending he didn't feel your power over him.

★　★　★

At four o'clock, Vanessa found a window to phone Jo at home.

"Hi! How's it going?"

Jo cradled the phone on her shoulder. She kept an ear out for Diane, due to arrive any second, while the other ear was still ringing from the sound of the house alarm. She knew she'd have to get the Rice Krispies started if she was going to get them finished in time for tea.

"How was school?" asked Vanessa, while finishing her progress report on a cereal ad. Jo tried to think. "Fine. Zak had a spelling test. He got "whether" right with an "h." The teacher was very pleased. He needs a new recorder because the big boys used it as a goalpost and it got broken. Cassandra had a math lesson, and Tallulah sat next to Ella for painting." She assembled all the ingredients together on the worktop and smiled. She knew the Children Commandments. There Shall Be Ingredients for Chocolate Rice Krispies in the House at All Times.

"Mmhmm," said Vanessa, signing the bottom of her notes. "Please put that in the diary, I'll buy him a recorder on the weekend."

Spider-Man hurled himself into the kitchen, unaware that baggy, saggy underpants ruined the overall effect somewhat. "Have you moved my cyberdog?" he asked Jo, his voice rising unsteadily.

"I thought you were getting ready for your nan?" said Jo, looking down at Zak. "She won't want to see you like that, will she?"

Max poked his head round Vanessa's office door. "Did you speak to Anthony?" he bellowed, ignoring the phone in her hand.

Vanessa grinned and nodded at Max, while saying "What's he wearing?"

"How the fuck do I know what he's wearing?" asked Max.

"He's Spider-Man," answered Jo into the phone.

"Oh dear."

"Have you moved my cyberdog?" repeated Spider-Man, hitching up his pants and getting tearful.

"I talked to them earlier this morning," Vanessa told Max, giving him the thumbs-up.

"Did you?" asked Jo. "They didn't tell me."

"No, the Creatives, not the children."

"The what?"

"I can't find my cyberdog!"

"If you can get into your smart trousers and shirt, I'll come and help you look for it," said Jo.

"Has he been holding his willy at all today?" asked Vanessa.

"I hope to Christ you're not talking to a client," snapped Max.

"Must dash," said Vanessa. "I'm frantic. Bye."

Jo clicked off the phone, gave Spider-Man a secret mission to get into his smart clothes that Nan liked (thus putting the baddies off the scent), put the phone in the fridge, took the phone out of the fridge, and continued to make chocolate Rice Krispies.

Twenty minutes later, three children in smartish clothes looked silently in the bowl.

"Does Mummy know you've made this?" asked Cassandra.

"No," said Jo. "Would she like some?"

"She doesn't let us have too much chocolate," said Zak. "It's bad for our teeth and, long-term, for our entire systems."

Jo thought about asking whether Mummy's mummy was of the same mind, when the phone rang.

With her eyes on the children, she went to pick it up.

"Hello," she said into the phone. "*Don't* eat it yet!" she yelled at the children, who were venturing nearer the bowl.

The children stared at her, and she stared back at them, holding a wooden spoon as threateningly as she could. When a voice sounded in her ear, she got a little shock.

"Hello, is Jo there please?"

"Shaun!" Jo almost wept with relief. She'd forgotten she'd given him the house number before leaving.

"Blimey is that you? I didn't recognize you."

"I miss you! *Don't eat it now!*"

She leaped across the room and rescued her mixing bowl.

"This is for dessert *after* homework," she told them. "Or it's a wooden spoon up the bottom."

"Whose bottom?" asked Cassandra.

"You said it was a treat for waking up," said Zak. "Not for doing our homework."

"Can it be Zak's bottom?" asked Cassandra.

"No," said Jo.

"Why?"

"Much as I love listening to dysfunctional children," came Shaun's voice in her ear, "I'm a bit busy at the moment. Shall we speak later?"

"Yes," Jo told the wooden spoon.

Cassandra took the phone from her. "Could Jo call you back please?"

Jo heard her say to Shaun. "She's a bit busy right now. Does she know your number?" Then as Jo wiped chocolate off her ear, she heard the little girl say, "If she doesn't call tonight, she'll call you as soon as she can. Thank you for calling. Bye now."

Cassandra switched off the phone. "He said that's fine," she told Jo, handing her back the phone. "Do you know where the cake tins are?"

Nodding mutely, Jo could hear the sound of a doorbell in the distance.

"Right! Homework time," she announced, hurrying to the front door, practicing her capable smile. When she opened it no one was there, but at the front of the garden an immaculately dressed woman was dead-heading the rosebush. The woman turned suddenly to look at her, and then began to approach. She was unmistakably Vanessa's mother. As they met at the door, Jo showed the woman her smile, and the woman handed her some rose stems and stepped into the house. Her skin was taut and smooth, her makeup flawless, and her clothes expensive. She was exceedingly well preserved and seemed unable to smile properly, a bit like the Mona Lisa, thought Jo. But it was her hair that caught Jo's eye the most. It looked like a new crown of spun gold and copper, and her every movement was as if she was still practicing walking with it on her head.

"I've come straight from the hairdresser's," she said, taking off her coat and handing it to Jo. "So I can't stay long."

"Right," said Jo.

"Hello, darlings!" she called out into the house. "I've been to the hairdresser's, so I can't stay long!"

She turned to Jo, said, "Just one tea please, I'm playing bridge tonight," and sallied forth into the kitchen, where she found the children in various stages of eating raw chocolate Rice Krispies off a wooden spoon.

"Lula!" cried Diane in dismay at Tallulah's sticky brown mouth. "You look like a clown!"

"So do you!" exclaimed Tallulah, impressed. "I want lipstick!"

Diane turned to Jo. "Is that chocolate?" she asked.

"Yes." Jo sighed. "It's a long story."

"I know the story of chocolate," said Diane crisply. "It originates from the cacao bean and was introduced to Europe by the Spanish when they conquered Mexico. That wasn't my point."

Jo blinked at Diane. "I didn't mean that story," she whispered.

"Jo promised us a treat if we got up this morning," Cassie explained.

"Goodness me, whatever next?" Diane asked the room. "Gifts for sleeping?"

"They overslept, so—" started Jo.

"I can't stay long," repeated Diane. "Who wants to watch Grandma do her nails?"

The girls cheered, and Zak blew an expressive raspberry.

"Zachariah!" cried his grandma. "I don't think there's any call for that, is there?"

Jo heartily agreed with Zak, so quietly got on with making the tea.

"Sorry," said Zak, before mumbling, "And it's ZacharIE."

"I should think so."

"They were just about to do their homework actually," said Jo.

"Yes," said Zak. "I've got lots." And off he vanished.

"Girls," said Jo, "After you've finished helping your nan—"

"Grandma," corrected Diane in her best Lady Bracknell voice.

"—you can do your homework," finished Jo lamely. She then found the cake tins and started pouring her raw mixture in, while the girls crowded round Diane doing her nails.

The quicker I do this, thought Jo, *the more time I'll have to call Shaun before the children's tea.* As soon as the Krispies were in the fridge, the phone rang. Jo glanced over at Diane, who waved wet nails in her direction. As Jo went to answer the phone she heard Diane say to the girls. "Let's see how good your new nanny's phone voice is, shall we, girls? It's the perfect test of a lady." Excited, Cassandra and Tallulah watched her keenly.

Right, thought Jo. *You asked for it.*

"Good afternoon," she said into the phone, impersonating Eliza Doolittle's post rain-in-Spain moment. "The Fitzgerald London residence. How may I help?"

In the pause that followed, Jo caught Diane's plucked eyebrows arch toward her golden crown.

"Blimey," came a warm male voice that Jo recognized immediately. "Do you wear a pinny and a hat, too?"

Jo stared blankly at Diane, harpooned by the woman's scrutiny. "To whom do you wish to speak?" Jo was now on automatic-pilot, paralyzed from the fringe down.

"To you." Josh laughed. "You're priceless."

Diane started to smile graciously at Jo, who felt encouraged enough to continue. "Would you like to speak to anyone in the Fitzgerald family?"

"God no, they're all mad."

"The children's grandmother, Diane, is here playing with the girls."

"Why? What have they done wrong?"

Jo controlled her smile. She managed to half turn away from Diane, which felt recklessly rebellious. "They almost ate chocolate," she said primly.

"Oh my gosh!" mimicked Josh. "I'll call the police while you make them sick it up."

"They're with their grandmother now," complied Jo, "so I don't think that will be necessary."

Josh's "Fuck me, are you for real?" spoiled the first warm feeling she'd had since she'd been there. It was one thing to be mocked, but quite another to be mocked by a moron who couldn't tell a joke when he heard one. Disappointment fueled her anger.

"Can I put you on speakerphone?" he was saying now. "The guys in the office don't believe me. Rupert wants a date if you let him use a dummy."

Jo gritted her teeth. "I'll tell the Fitzgeralds you called," she said, and hung up.

Slowly, she turned back to Diane who was sitting very still, her head slightly tilted, her gaze questioning. The girls were long gone, finding Jo's phone conversation almost as boring as watching nail polish dry. Instead, Diane was now flanked by the bookends Molly and Bolly, who joined her in giving Jo a superior, unflinching stare.

"It was Josh," Jo told them.

They all looked singularly unimpressed.

"Was it?" muttered Diane.

"Between you and me," attempted Jo, "I don't think he's a very good influence on the children."

"Of course he isn't," said Diane, standing up. "He's the son of Dick's first wife, Jane, who you will soon find out is a cow. In a none-too-effective disguise. Doubtless you'll meet her when she drops off her boy Toby. He is the devil."

"Right," said Jo, as Diane wafted past her into the hall, followed by the cats. "I'll look forward to it."

"Good-bye darlings!" Diane called up. "Grandma's going!"

"Guys!" shouted Jo. "Say good-bye to Grandma before her bingo!"

"Bridge!" exclaimed Diane, horrified.

"Oh, I'm so sorry. I always confuse those two."

Diane shouted upstairs again. "No need to come down, I'm in a rush!"

"Bye!" shouted three children from various rooms upstairs.

Jo handed Diane her coat, and Diane took a long last look at her as though Jo had just handed her a bouquet of flowers in thanks for opening a fête. Then after Jo had opened the front door for her, Diane instructed Jo to instruct Vanessa to instruct her gardener to dead-head the roses, and, followed by the silent cats as far as the front gate, wafted away.

"Mmm, broccoli," lied Jo, as she took a bite.

"I hate broccoli," said Tallulah, as the other two watched Jo, equally unconvinced.

"Imagine it's covered in chocolate," said Jo. "That's what I always do."

"Why don't you just not eat it?" asked Zak.

"Or cover it in chocolate?" asked Cassandra.

"I just like eating stuff that makes me grow," lied Jo again.

"Why?" asked Cassandra. "You're already tall."

"I'm going to be tall when I grow up," said Tallulah, eating a piece of broccoli.

"I'm just going to wear high heels," said Cassandra.

"I was a tree," said Tallulah.

Jo had just got everything into the dishwasher and was about to bathe Tallulah when Dick arrived home. She almost sank to her knees in gratitude as the three children hurled themselves at him. As she watched him roll on the floor with them, she wondered how this "daddy bear" was the same man from her interview. As the children started using him as a trampoline and he grinned stupidly up at her, she decided first impressions could be very misleading.

She looked at her watch. 7 P.M. She'd worked a twelve-hour day without a single break, and she still hadn't finished the ironing. Did all Londoners work these ridiculous hours or was it just the Fitzgeralds? Dick noticed her look at her watch.

"I know," he said, from underneath a child. "Odd hour to be home."

"Ah," sighed Jo, relieved. "I thought it might be."

"God yes!" he said. "But as it was your first day, I just shut up shop and came home early."

Chapter 6

A fortnight later, back in Niblet, Shaun reached the pub before dusk. He saw Sheila before she saw him, ducked behind the bar, and ordered himself a swift pint.

"Heard from Jo yet?" greeted the landlord.

"Yeah," said Shaun. "She's rushed off her feet."

"Ah, poor girl. Usual? Hello there, Sheila, what can I get for you?"

Shaun turned to Sheila, who was standing right behind him.

"Hello!" he said. "Didn't see you there."

"Pull the other one," said Sheila, "it's got Big Ben on it."

They stood at the bar.

"Spoke to Jo today," he said eventually.

Sheila smiled at him. "How long did you hold out then?"

"How d'you know she didn't phone me?"

"Because in two weeks she's only phoned me twice. And I don't care what they say about true love, there's no way she'd have phoned you more than me."

Shaun took a swift drink.

"I'm right, aren't I?" she asked.

Shaun took his pint and went to sit on his own. Sheila got herself a drink and followed him.

"Don't take it personally, Shaunie," she said, joining him by the fire. "I'm sure she'll be phoning much more important people than both of us now she's living in London." Shaun downed half his pint, took a deep breath, then downed the other half.

"I bet you're really pissed off," he said eventually. "Knowing she can cope without you."

Sheila shrugged. "Oh, I'm fine. It's good for her to get away. Branch out."

Shaun let out a laugh. He wiped his mouth.

"So," said Sheila. "How are you keeping yourself busy of a Saturday night?"

"Don't look at me," he said. "How the hell are you keeping yourself busy of a Saturday day? No all-day-long shopping expeditions to tempt her away from me."

"I never had to tempt her actually."

Suddenly Shaun shouted out at James, who'd just appeared in the pub doorway. James nodded and came over.

"Usual?" Shaun grunted at Sheila.

Sheila nodded. Shaun went to join James at the bar.

Meanwhile, miles away, in a heaving City bar, Jo's phone calls were the subject of another, rather more animated conversation.

Josh had just done his impersonation of Nanny on the phone to his mates. Sally from Accounts had joined them tonight, and it wouldn't have been arrogance on his part to claim that he knew why she was there. The more the gang laughed at his imitation, the closer Sally got, until her stockinged thigh was practically on top of his. The day was getting better and better. First a phone call from his dad for a man-to-man chat, and now Sally from Accounts practically on his lap.

"So where did they get this nanny from then?" asked Jasper.

"Fuck knows," said Josh, growing distracted. "The Tight-Arse Nanny Academy I suppose."

"I've got to talk to this woman," said Rupert. "I'm getting a boner just thinking about her."

"How much is it worth?" asked Josh.

"A tenner."

"Hah!"

"Twenty!"

Josh laughed again.

"Fifty! But if she's not as good as my dreams, you owe me."

"Done!" shouted Josh, and they all cheered. "Next time I talk to her I'll put her on speakerphone and when I tip you the wink, you can have a word."

And with that, Sally slid herself onto Joshua's lap, her skirt momentarily rising so high he caught a glimpse of dappled, bronzed thigh. And for the rest of the evening, the tight-arse nanny was completely forgotten.

* * *

Over the next couple of weeks, the tight-arse nanny's life was reaching a new and somewhat spectacular low. By the end of her third week in the Fitzgerald household, she found herself lying on her bed, staring at her open suitcase, abandoned rucksack and still-packed box, too exhausted to move and trying not to cry.

Technically, Jo had weekends off, unless previously arranged as paid baby-sitting. But she'd spent her first weekend catching up on sleep, the second being cajoled by Vanessa to just pass her this and just pop something into the dishwasher and just nip upstairs and bring down something. On the third weekend, she was reduced to going to the cinema on her own just to make the point that she wasn't technically meant to be working. She was surrounded by rowdy crowds of teenagers who kept staring at her and young couples who didn't; then she fell asleep at the feel-good climax, waking with a start and saying aloud, "Are the cats in?" which felt like the least humiliating two minutes of the whole evening.

She'd have loved to go home for the weekends, but she knew that if she did, she'd never come back, which would mean the end to her dreams and the beginning of a life of being reminded "I told you so" by all her loved ones. As for Shaun coming to visit, his firm was still in the first all-important month of their biggest-ever contract, so she knew he'd practically be living on-site, weekends included. If he hadn't been able to take time off to pop to the station to see her off, he would hardly be able to come and stay. Occasionally, very occasionally—and usually at night—she did find herself wondering if her parents' generation had got it right by insisting that the woman's career was to follow the career of the man who'd chosen her. Okay, in some circumstances it may not have been as pleasant for the woman, but it was certainly less complicated.

She'd contacted her parents nearly every day, and as long as she did so when there was at least one child in the car she didn't feel tempted to cry. Apart from the exhaustion and early nights giving her very little free time to make long personal calls, she simply didn't have enough energy to phone Shaun and was rarely in the right frame of mind to phone Sheila. In the rare moments of quiet, she missed her parents; in all the other moments she ached for the familiarity of Niblet.

On the Friday morning of her fourth week at the Fitzgeralds', Jo waited in the schoolyard, pondering on her learning curve since leaving home.

She had known that the Fitzgerald household was going to be different from her own, but she had thought the differences were only in the details. She now realized that details were what made a house a home. And the Fitzgerald house wasn't a home, it was a station for remote controls. There were so many remote controls in it that they needed a remote control to find them. There was one for each stereo in each room, one to dim the lights in each room, one for the fireplace, even one for the lounge clock—an unnerving light-effect number that you had to, of course, point your remote control at for it to work. A small mound would then rise, phoenixlike, from the coffee table and shine at the blank wall ahead. And lo, there would slowly appear, Cheshire-cat-like, a wall clock. Usually by the time it had appeared to show you the time, you were late. And of course, there was a remote control for every television in the house. If there was a robbery of their remote controls, the house would no longer function. It would just be a shell.

As for Jo's suite of rooms, television, and enormous wardrobe, it was proof, if proof were ever needed, that money does not bring happiness. Her body yearned for the easy comfort of her tiny room, its stirring view of the River Avon, and the reassuring sound of her parents' yelling from downstairs.

As she watched the queue in front of the nursery it occurred to her that she might not be strong enough for this. After only one month, she might have to go home, defeated. "Cheer up," came a voice behind her. "You look like you've just lost a baby and found three."

Jo assumed the voice wasn't talking to her, but took a sly glance behind her anyway.

There stood an expensive-looking, tall, blond, tanned girl about her age, holding a car seat in which dozed a baby the size of a doll.

"You're a new nanny aren't you?" the girl asked, with an amused grin. Jo nodded.

"Thought so," the girl said. "If you were a mum, you'd just be looking bored, not brain-fucked. I'm Pippa, and this," she said, holding the car seat forward, "is Sebastian James."

Jo looked at Sebastian James. He must have been weeks old.

"Say hello to the nice lady, Sebastian James," said Pippa.

Sebastian James's left eyebrow fluttered briefly. It wasn't much, thought Jo, but it was more than she was used to.

"Pleased to meet you Sebastian James," she said, and held out her hand.

Sebastian James's bottom let out a ripple.

"The youth of today," tutted Pippa, swinging the car seat back onto her hip. "No respect."

"Well, they haven't lived through a war."

"His mother's having her piles done." Pippa grinned.

"Ooh, lovely."

"Well, it is for the Harley Street specialist. Twelve hundred smackers for forty minutes."

Jo whistled long and low.

"Mind you," confided Pippa, "he does have to locate them. Probably needed a finder's fee."

Jo discovered that Sebastian James's sister, Georgiana Anne, was in Tallulah's class.

"Their parents are nanny virgins," explained Pippa. "I'm their first, bless them. And I've been with them for three years, so I'm now technically their boss. I have three aerobics classes a week and a facial on them, they're so terrified of losing me. And the guilt! It's amazing. There are people out there murdering children and all this couple do is work every hour God sends to earn enough money to bring up a small family and go private, and you'd think they'd committed genocide. Poor sods. Mind you, very useful. Got my own attic flat in Highgate, with separate front door and a south-facing terrace garden. And I've just come back from a prebaby 'work' holiday with them all in the Bahamas. They wanted to do Antibes, but I said it had to be the Caribbean. Do yours work?"

"Yes."

"Excellent."

Sebastian James belched. Pippa and Jo looked at him.

"Men," tutted Pippa. "Time for a coffee?"

Jo's eyes went round.

"Actually," she said, "I haven't got time for a crap."

"Oh dear, that's not good."

"No," agreed Jo. "It's not good."

"I wondered why you were standing like that."

Jo's laugh was sudden and loud, as if she'd forgotten how to do it. "Oh, that's just how I stay upright after walking up Highgate Hill."

"What have you been doing weekends?"

"Oh you know, odd jobs for my boss, weeping in my room, falling asleep in cinemas, that sort of thing."

"What are you doing this Sunday?"

"Resigning and going home to marry my boyfriend."

Pippa squeezed Jo's arm. "Meet me for coffee this weekend," she urged. "Costa Coffee, Highgate High Street, 11 A.M. Lesson number one, if you don't have set plans at the weekend, they treat you like you're working. But never make it too early in the morning, because then they'll act like it's a weekday."

"Oh," said Jo, eyes even wider.

Pippa beamed at her. "You have much to learn, Grasshopper," she said.

"Thank you," said Jo.

The nursery door opened, and one by one, ten eager little bunnies came out, blinking in the sun. Behind them wandered Tallulah.

Georgiana Anne approached Pippa, kissed her baby brother hard on his forehead, her teeth leaving marks in his crepe-paper skin, handed Pippa a papier-mâché objet d'art that looked like a penis in a wig, hitched up her tights, and announced, "It's for Mummy."

"Wow!" exclaimed Pippa. "Lucky Mummy!"

"I want chicken nuggets for lunch."

Jo knelt to Tallulah's height to hear her better. Tallulah looked her straight in the eye.

"Hello," said Tallulah.

"Hello, did you have a good day?"

"Yes, thank you. Georgiana's my friend."

"That's nice."

Tallulah looked over at Georgiana.

"Sometimes," she allowed.

Halfway home, Tallulah looked up at Jo.

"Can I skip?" she asked.

"Of course you can, poppet. Just wait for me at the curb."

"I like your hair," said Tallulah, before focusing her mind on more important things. She had skipping to do.

Back at home, while Cassie and Zak were busy with their homework, Tallulah needed occupying after a busy day of tumbling like a tot.

"What would you like to do?" asked Jo, hoping the little girl would say "Find you a new job while you call your boyfriend and make him the happiest man in the world."

"I'd like to paint," announced Tallulah.

"Right," said Jo. "What would you like to paint?"

"A Kandinsky."

Jo smiled. She was talking funny again. "A Kan-*what*sky?"

Tallulah giggled. "Kandinsky, silly." With that, the little girl took Jo by the hand and led her into the living room and pointed at the brightly colored picture over the fireplace that had clearly been painted by a four-year-old. "That's a Kandinsky. Not a real one, obviously, a copy," explained Tallulah.

Jo knelt "Do you know," she confided. "I only understand every third word you say."

Tallulah nodded and sighed. "I know how you feel," she said quietly.

Half an hour later, with Kandinsky Technicolors sprayed delicately all over her, Jo answered an insistent ring on the doorbell. She heard the buffalo horde racing down the stairs, and braced herself for the one remaining experience yet to be savored at her new household. She was almost looking forward to it. As yet, she had missed meeting Toby's mother, the notorious Mrs. Fitzgerald the First. Two Fridays ago, Jane Fitzgerald had been in such a rush to get away for a spa break that all Jo saw of her was the back of her Peugeot, and the previous Friday Jo had been busy with Tallulah in the toilet at the precise moment Jane had arrived, so Zak had let Toby in. Jo opened the door. There stood a scowling Toby and a concave-woman in shades that must have weighed more than her body. Toby rushed past Jo without a word, where he was greeted noisily by Zak in the hall.

"Bye bye, darling," Jo heard the woman say behind her. "I'll miss you, too."

Jo turned back to the woman and was about to say hello when the woman took off her shades, revealing two sharp blue eyes and said, "Is the bitch in?"

Jo's jaw dropped.

"Are you the latest nanny?" asked the woman.

Jo nodded and watched as the woman slowly looked her up and down. She shook her head and tutted. "I give you a week," she said with a shark smile. "How are you enjoying it so far?"

Jo shrugged.

"One week," repeated the woman. "The only reason they're still married is because she won't do anything I had to do. I'm in therapy, you know, eleven years after the divorce."

Jo blinked. Jane crossed her arms across her cagelike chest. "So how d'you like Dick-brain?" she asked.

"Um—"

"And Pamela Ewing?"

"Um—"

"I see they hired you for your brains then," she muttered, and started to walk away. At the front of the garden, she turned briefly back, and said, "Good luck with Toby. He's a shit. Like his father."

And with that, she was gone.

Jo watched her go and slowly closed the door behind her. She stood for a while in the hall.

By the time she had followed Zak and Toby into the conservatory, Zak was dealing badly with the poignant truth that after life's peaks come its inevitable dips. He was stamping his feet, saying "It's not *fair*," and sobbing ineffectually while Toby, the playmate he'd longed to have all to himself since Sunday night to right all the world's wrongs, was coolly indifferent to him, and had now wandered over to Tallulah.

"What's your favorite Teletubby, Lulu?" he asked.

Tallulah sighed and without taking her eye off her painting, replied, "My name is Tallulah. Not Lulu."

"So *Tallulah*, do you like Poo-poo or La-de-la best?"

"I'm not a baby," responded Tallulah almost inaudibly.

"Oh, I see. So what do you watch, now that you're such a big girl?"

"The *Tweenies*."

Toby snorted and muttered "lame." Then he turned to Cassandra, who was frowning over her math homework.

"You're in a bad mood. Is it your girl's period, Catastrophe?"

Cassandra spoke in a monotone.

"Your daddy left your mummy for a girl half his age, then fell in love with ours," she said.

Toby shrugged. "Your mummy's a selfish bitch."

Then suddenly all the children jumped at the sound of a piercing scream. They stared at Jo. She finished screaming and stared back at them, such disgust on her face that they all began to feel a little ashamed. "Right," she whispered menacingly. "Any more comments like that, and I'm shooting the lot of you."

"You can't," tutted Toby.

"Except Tallulah," continued Jo, "who was perfectly within her rights."

"You'd be taken to prison," continued Toby, "where they'd probably beat you up."

"I don't care," said Jo. "It would be worth it to leave you lot."

The children looked at the floor.

'Toby, Zak, get upstairs,' she continued. 'I don't want to hear another peep out of you until I say '*peep*.' "

Toby and Zak went upstairs, Toby with a nonchalant air that told the world he had been about to go upstairs anyway. Cassandra and Tallulah stared at Jo as she went back to making their tea.

After a while, Cassandra spoke. "Would you really shoot us all?"

"No."

"Thought not," she muttered, and returned to her homework.

Jo counted to ten very slowly. "Right," she said. "I'm going to make a phone call. Cassandra, please watch that your sister doesn't get paint everywhere. I won't be long."

Jo heard Cassandra grunt as she left the kitchen and slammed shut the bedroom door behind her. She was just about to get her mobile phone out of her bag to phone Shaun—no, Sheila—no, her mum, when the other phone rang. She sat heavily on her bed, swore even more heavily, and picked up the phone on her beside table. It was the first time she'd ever taken a call in this mad place without being scrutinized by someone. She felt wild with the risk of it.

"Hello?"

There was a click and a funny echo sound and for a moment Jo thought it must be Sheila calling her from her office and putting her on speakerphone, like she did when her office buddies wanted to join in the gossip. She felt a moment of intimidation at the prospect of putting on a performance for Sheila's gang. She wasn't up to it. Then the sound of Josh's voice came on the line.

"Good afternoon," he said in a loud voice. "Please may I speak to Mary Poppins?"

Jo felt her jaw lock. "No," she said bluntly. "You can't."

"Oh," said Josh and stopped. "Why?"

"Because she's out on the tiles. Literally. With Dick van Dyke."

There was a pause. Jo heard voices in the background.

"Who is this?" asked Josh.

"This is Jo Green. The soon-to-be-ex nanny. I'm not Mary Poppins, I'm not wearing a pinny or a hat, and I'm not here for your amusement. I'd love to chat, but unlike you I don't have time to make puerile phone calls at my boss's expense. Or worse, to crowd round someone *else's* phone and listen to *his* puerile calls, like the rest of your office." And she slammed the phone down and threw herself back onto her bed.

Josh stared at his phone. Around him, the gang shifted, some scanning the room for hidden cameras, others making their way back to their desks quickly.

"I think you owe me fifty smackers, mate," said Rupert. Sally was gone.

Josh blinked a few times at the phone, then swore with more gusto than imagination.

Chapter 7

On Sunday morning Jo discovered that all advice from her new friend Pippa would prove invaluable. She woke before her alarm, but forced herself to stay silent in bed. She could hear the children in the kitchen, pouring breakfast cereal somewhere near cereal bowls, breaking the toaster, shushing each other and bickering over who had the remote control, while Sunday morning television blared out obliviously. Miraculously enough she must have dozed a bit, because the next thing she heard was Dick trying to compete with the television for his children's attention, failing miserably, making himself a coffee and arranging on the phone to meet up with Josh for lunch. When she next awoke, Vanessa was the one shushing the children with the surprising words. "If you wake Jo, she'll leave, and I'll have to send you into care."

Jo was quite flattered when this worked. At nine, she dragged herself out of bed and into the shower. She stayed in longer than she'd have chosen, out of principle, and when she came out she used the highly effective drying method of lying on top of her duvet and waiting. As she lay there, she glanced over at her half-full suitcase and still-packed rucksack and box. She'd got used to living out of them, she knew she still wasn't ready to put up any photos of her loved ones, and there was some comfort in knowing it would take less time to pack then unpack. However, if she didn't do it soon, her clothes would be unwearable. She turned moodily away from them and lay curled up on her bed, drying.

When she was sure she was as dry as she could possibly be, she decided what to wear while hanging up a few of her favorite outfits and everyday necessities, careful not to use the word "unpacking" and trying to look the other way while doing it. Afterward, her rucksack and box were surrounded by most of their contents, her suitcase was wide open and the entire floor was covered with her clothes. It made her feel that the room was truly becoming hers.

Finally, she went into the kitchen.

"Hi!" exclaimed Vanessa.

Jo gave her boss a timid smile.

"Fancy a coffee?" sang Vanessa. "I'm grinding!"

"No thanks," said Jo. "Another time."

"We were just watching *Bewitched*," explained Vanessa, busying herself with dark rich weekend Costa Rican coffee beans. "Want to join us?"

"Actually," said Jo, more timidly than she would have liked, "I'm meeting a friend in the village at eleven. I'll be out all day. I'll have to start walking soon or I'll be late."

Vanessa stopped what she was doing. "Oh," she said.

"I'm not paid for today, am I?" asked Jo suddenly, worried.

"Oh no," rushed Vanessa. "You—you're not. I just thought . . . of course—"

"God, I'm really sorry," said Jo, moved by Vanessa's disappointment more than she expected. "I assumed today was mine. I met this girl at Tallulah's nursery. She's a nanny. We sort of made plans, but if you need me . . ."

"No, of course, the day is yours, and I'm glad you've met someone," said Vanessa. "Good for you. Hope you have a nice time."

There was a moment's silence. Vanessa went to sit on the sofa with the children. "By the way," she said suddenly, turning back to Jo. "Dick and I are planning to go out on Thursday evening. Would you mind babysitting? If you're able to? Otherwise, I'll get the baby-sitter. Or see if my mum can do it."

Jo nodded slowly, as if considering. "Thursday should be alright," she said. "I'll go and put it in my diary."

She went into her bedroom and sat on her bed, a slow grin beginning to form on her face.

By the time Jo arrived at the café on Highgate High Street, she was in high spirits. Just having someone to meet had settled her enough to feel able to investigate her new village. She'd turned off the main street and wandered up through Waterlow Park, where she'd gazed in awe at the view over central London. Then she popped into shops that took her fancy—she spent half an hour in one before even realizing it was a charity shop—and strolled round the picturesque, tiny green. In some ways it reminded her of home, but in other ways, it was vastly different; her village didn't have a shop full of different-flavored chocolates, a grocer's with genuine Italian delicacies, a beautician, a Chinese herbalist, and all manner of foreign restaurants and cafés. And all this on only one, quaint village street.

She popped back into the park to phone Shaun. He was at work.

"It's me!" she greeted him.

"Bloody hell! They let you have a five-minute break, eh?"

She laughed. "I'm in one of the most beautiful parks I've ever seen and I'm meeting a new friend in ten minutes."

There was a fraction of a pause.

"Right," he said. "Well, I won't keep you."

"I-I just—"

"How are you?"

"Fine!"

"Enjoying it yet?"

"The children are lovely," she said. "Really lovely."

"Good."

"How are things in Niblet?"

"Hectic. I'm on-site now."

"Thought so."

"But it's not that bad."

"Will you be able to pop down and see me?"

"Well, you know what they say, if Mohammad won't go to the mountain . . ." She knew he was smiling.

"Sorry, I'm just exhausted by the weekend."

"It's alright. Once I've got a couple of things sorted out, I can spend at least one night away."

"Oh great!"

"One of my suppliers is playing silly buggers, and they said they'd be here at ten. I'm going to have to phone them soon. In fact I'd better do it now."

'Okay.'

"Have a good day. I'll try and get down there next weekend—if not the one after."

"Fantastic! Good luck with the suppliers."

"Thanks, babe."

There was a pause.

"Right then," he said. "Speak soon."

"Thanks for coming."

"I haven't yet."

"You know what I mean."

"Yeah."

Another pause.

"See you soon then."

"Yeah. See you soon."

Another pause.

"Right," she said.

"Right."

Another pause.

"Bye then, babe."

"Bye then," she said, and clicked off her phone.

She walked back up the hill without breaking into a sweat. At the café door, she scanned the room and saw Pippa in the back corner, sprawled on a sofa, her eyes shut, two mugs of steaming coffee on the little table in front of her. Jo walked past the armchairs and sofas, intrigued by the sight of individuals instead of groups, leisurely reading their Sunday papers while drinking coffee and eating croissants as if they were in their own homes. She was growing used to the fact that no one glanced in her direction as she passed them, although half of her still expected to see a face she recognized from kindergarten.

She beamed down at Pippa. "Did I wake you?"

Pippa opened one eye and slowly grinned. "Not really." She yawned and made room for Jo on the sofa. "I got you an Americana," she said.

"Thanks," said Jo, "but I've already got a boyfriend."

"It's a coffee."

"Oh, right."

"So." Pippa looked her squarely in the eye. "How's it going?"

"You were so right about this morning," Jo started.

"Of course," said Pippa. "I'm a pro."

Jo bowed her head. "I have traveled a long way to be your pupil."

Pippa bowed her head in response.

An hour later, Jo's head was buzzing. She bought breakfast and another coffee for her and Pippa, and was then tested on all she had learned that morning.

"Who brought up every monarch this country has ever had?" asked Pippa.

"The nanny."

"Correct. Who won us the Second World War?" asked Pippa.

"Churchill's nanny."

"Correct. Who saved the Von Trapp family from extinction and originated the first national post-Christmas-Day lunch experience?"

"The nanny."

"Correct. What was the name given to the family dog in *Peter Pan* to show how much he was loved and respected by everyone?"

"Nana."

"Correct. What is the name given to a government seen to be all-knowing and all-controlling?"

"The nanny-state."

"Correct. Who has helped the cause of women's equality in the workplace more than any politician?"

"The nanny."

"Correct. You are at a party. A pompous twat approaches. He asks what you do. What do you say?"

Jo stuck her chin out proudly. "I am the lynchpin of the modern family. I make it possible for today's woman to fulfil her potential whatever that might be, while enabling her to enjoy the perks of a family life that her partner enjoys guilt-free. I give today's children belief in themselves, teach them discipline in the context of a fun, warm, loving home, and provide them with a healthy, balanced diet. I'm a diplomat, a listener, an enabler, an organizer, a juggler. I come up with fresh, new ideas every day to keep the toughest audience in the world happy. I please a stressed mother, I accommodate a tired father, I love every child. I cook, I clean, I iron, I wash, I tidy—but I am no one's slave because I do it for a wage."

"What are you?"

"I'm a *nanny!*"

Pippa smiled. "God I'm good."

"Blimey," said Jo. "I never realized how brilliant I was."

"Well don't forget it now you know."

"Okay."

Pippa looked at her watch. "I said we'd meet the girls over at the Flask at one."

"Oh. Right."

"We usually have lunch and then at about four, we go to the pub up the road where we drink ourselves stupid. It's a tight schedule, but we manage."

"Who are the girls?"

"Rachel and Gabriella. They're lovely. Bet you miss your friends from home."

Jo smiled, tucking her legs under her on the sofa.

"Yeah, my best friend, Sheila, and my boyfriend, Shaun. I haven't had that many chances to phone them."

Pippa nodded.

"I remember not being able to phone my boyfriend for about six weeks after I moved here, even when I did have the time."

"Actually, it is a bit like that," admitted Jo. "I have to steel myself to do it, I don't know why."

"Homesickness. You can't confront how much you miss them, and you don't want to confront how much you don't miss them," Pippa replied.

Jo blinked at Pippa.

"Blimey," she said. 'That's it exactly.'

Pippa gave her a kind smile. "It's just that we all go through that phase. If you didn't, there'd be something wrong with you. It's hell but you'll get through it."

Jo let out a big sigh and leaned back on the sofa. "God that makes me feel so much better."

"Good."

"Thanks, Pippa."

"My pleasure. In return I want to hang around with you so that boys look our way. I don't believe in altruism. I'm an underpaid nanny, after all."

"What happened to the boyfriend you didn't call for six weeks?"

"Left me after three. Just didn't bother telling me."

"Oh no."

"It was fine. By the time I was ready to call, I was ready to call it off."

"Oh," said Jo quietly.

They finished their coffees in silence.

"So why did you become a nanny?" asked Jo.

Pippa shrugged. "I didn't have the airfare for Hollywood. But thanks to my nannying I should have it by 2020, no sweat." She stood up. "Right. While I get the last coffees in, you prepare the Shaun and Jo story."

Jo watched Pippa queue at the counter, wondering where on earth to start, unaware that she didn't need to worry.

"Where did you meet him?" asked Pippa as soon as she'd sat down again.

"Kindergarten."

"You're kidding?"

"Nope," said Jo. "I was his very first crush."

"What? And you've been with him ever since? Is that healthy?"

"He bought the company my dad worked for about seven years ago."

"Wow!" said Pippa, taking a break from blowing her coffee.

"Not as impressive as it sounds," said Jo. "Small company, long hours, lots of worry."

"So how did you actually get together? Were you picking up your dad on your pushbike and there he was in his posh sports car, and he spotted you and thought, *I must have that girl*?"

"My dad set us up."

Pippa let out a gale of laughter. "Way to go, Dad."

"Actually, it was very much in character. He's a bit of a control freak. I'm an only child, so my parents are . . ." Jo thought for a while. "Attached."

Pippa snorted coffee up her nose. "Excellent word for it," she said. "And they approve of boss boy?"

"They *adore* him," moaned Jo. "Sometimes I think . . ." She stopped. "They want us to marry. They think the reason I came here was to frighten him into proposing."

Pippa's eyebrows almost collided with her hairline.

Jo shook her head. "I said no actually," she whispered.

Pippa gasped.

"Three times." She held up three fingers to emphasize the point.

It felt so good to laugh about it. To really cackle about it. Make people stare. Snort coffee up her nose and everything. And it felt wonderful not to feel like some sort of emotional runt about it.

"I feel like," she said, when she'd calmed down, "I feel like I must be missing some girl gene for not wanting a romantic proposal from such a catch."

Pippa laughed.

"I mean," continued Jo, thinking out loud, "It's like I'm some social, genetic failure to not be able to come to an emotional climax with him."

They giggled.

"What do your friends think?" asked Pippa.

"Um," started Jo. "Well my best friend, Sheila, she . . ." Jo played with her mug a bit. "She's never liked Shaun. Thinks it's quite seedy to go out with your dad's boss."

"Sounds difficult."

Jo shrugged. "I've just got used to it. Doesn't really bother me that much anymore. Sheila's boyfriend James knew Shaun from school, so we're a bit of a foursome."

"Right."

"In fact Sheila had met Shaun a couple of times before he and I had started dating, which means that . . . well . . . it means that sometimes she makes me feel that she knows him better than I do. She doesn't do it on purpose. It's like she understands him better than I do because she knew him when he was single. It can be a bit annoying actually. Sometimes. So we just don't talk about it really," said Jo. "It's the one subject we steer clear of. Everything else is great. We've been best friends since we were fifteen."

No wonder you miss her," said Pippa.

"I—I do love Shaun," Jo said eventually.

"Of course you do," said Pippa. "Just not enough to wash his pants for the rest of your life. Makes perfect sense to me."

Jo gave Pippa a big smile.

"I suppose we'd better make our way over for lunch," said Pippa. "Otherwise, all the best nooks get taken and we end up with the crap crannies."

They drained their coffee and made their way to the pub.

"So what about you?" asked Jo, as they waited at the crossing. "Anyone in your life at the moment?"

"Nope," said Pippa. "If you find anyone, just flick him my way."

"Okay." Jo smiled, making a conscious effort to remember to do so.

Walking into the pub was like entering the world of Dick Turpin. Dark wood beams and uneven floors transported her back to another time, and she wondered why she'd imagined London would be soulless. Pippa cried out and waved to two girls sitting in the corner of the furthest nook. Rachel was heavy-boned and short, but almost pretty from quite a few angles; Gabriella was an olive-skinned beauty. Rachel was nanny to Ben, Tom, and Sam: "I think they wanted Labradors"; Gabriella was nanny to Hedda and Titania: "Ees harder than my Ph.D., but ees good to be in England."

Jo listened to them give each other intensive therapy over the week that was and found it quite extraordinary to see how much time and energy they focused on each other's problems. When it came to her turn, she surprised herself by talking more about Josh's phone calls than any other aspect of her life at the Fitzgeralds. After detailed interrogation, dissection, and analysis, the others dismissed him as a spoiled rich boy, visualized him as having fat thighs and a double chin and renamed him Josh the Posh Dosh. Jo decided she'd need these sessions every week. By four o'clock, she was happier than she had been for a long time.

"Actually," she confessed over their first postlunch glass of wine, "I was seriously considering giving it all up and going back home."

There was a pause.

"You know why that was, don't you?" asked Pippa.

"Why?"

"Because you hadn't met us yet."

And, as was proving to be par for the course, Pippa was right.

By the time Jo got home that night she felt on top of the world. Except when she fell over her suitcase and landed in her rucksack, when she felt below most of it. She crawled onto her bed and told herself that she'd definitely unpack the next day.

Chapter 8

When Jo's head hit the pillow, she was out for the count. The crash, however, woke her instantly. Once awake, her body flew into action pumping blood away from her extremities to her heart. Her body knew it was terrified before her brain did, but her brain cottoned on fast enough.

Someone was trying to get into the house through the kitchen window.

As her heart thumped uselessly against her rib cage, the noises from the kitchen intensified so much they hurt her already pounding head. The metallic taste of fear at the back of her throat almost made her gag. She understood what they meant about your whole life flashing before you. It wasn't so much a list of events as a new perspective, a finished context.

Instinctively, Jo knew that if the intruder came into her room, he'd sense in moments that she was wide-awake, because her brain was so alive it was practically humming. She held her breath and closed her eyes in the dark. When her head started spinning she opened them again. She could now, without any doubt, hear the heart-clenching sound of the slatted windows over the kitchen sink being slid out of their holdings one by one and being leaned neatly against the garden wall. Then there was silence. She allowed herself some deep breaths. Had he got what he wanted and left?

Then, suddenly, a loud bang as the glass was kicked and some of it shattered against the wall. Then real terror as she heard the intruder's hissed swearing. She was trembling.

It suddenly dawned on her that no one upstairs would be able to hear the intruder. She was the only one who would be able to stop him doing whatever he intended to do. And her job—her well-paid job that came with a Clio—was to protect the children. While most of her brainpower was spent on interpreting what she could hear, a part of it veered off into wretched musings. No wonder they gave her the downstairs suite. Maybe this was why the other nannies kept leaving!

She bit her lip and screwed her eyes shut. A touchy sea monster chose that moment to wake up in her stomach. She realized she had drunk too much the night before. Half of her brain regretted it, half was glad, and the other half rationalized that it didn't much matter as she was about to be murdered anyway.

But what was she thinking? This was no time for musings about musings! The Fitzgeralds' lives were at stake. She needed to be strong. She needed to take control. She needed courage. But most of all she needed aspirin.

She inched her head over to one side of the pillow, noticing for the first time how loud it sounded. She could now see the phone on her bedside table. As she stared at it, willing it to float toward her, she heard a muffled sound, as if the attacker was climbing in through the window. Then a loud crash and a muffled yelp as he fell onto the bread maker.

Jo grabbed the phone and dived back under the duvet. Once under there, she fought the temptation to phone her mother and instead tried to dial 999. Unfortunately, her hands were shaking so much it didn't matter that she couldn't see anything.

Slowly, silently, she turned the top of her duvet over, leaving the phone and her hands outside it. She focused all her attention on her hands, trying to stop them shaking long enough to make the call, while the sound of a man treading softly round the kitchen outside her bedroom door sent her heart shooting into her mouth.

"Emergency, which service do you require?"

"Police."

A click, a pause.

"You're through to the police. How can we help?"

Jo could now clearly hear a ten-foot man treading stealthily round the conservatory, near the television. Jo tried to speak, but no noise came out.

"How can we help?"

"I'm in the bedroom." She started to cry.

"Keep calm and tell me your address."

Jo stuttered out the Fitzgeralds' address.

"Well done. Now keep calm and tell me who you are."

Jo tried to cry calmly.

"I'm Jo."

"What's happening, Jo?"

"He broke in . . . through the kitchen window."

"Keep going."

"I'm in the bedroom, near the kitchen."

"Have you seen him?"

"Downstairs. I mean next to the kitchen."

"Have you seen him? Do you know what he looks like?"

Jo shook her head at the phone.

"Do you have reason to believe this is a sexual intruder?"

Jo couldn't answer, as she was suddenly preoccupied with the fact that her limbs seemed to have frozen.

"Hello? Jo? What's happening now?"

"He's gone away again. No I haven't seen him. Maybe there's two of them."

"Stay on the line. There'll be someone there as soon as possible."

Jo stayed on the line, burrowing down beneath her duvet, feeling stronger just having the phone in her hand, connecting her to the police.

A mile away, Nick and Gerry, two extremely bored CID officers from the neighboring district, were patrolling the area on a burglary initiative. Nick was leaning against Gerry, wiping dog crap from his trainers.

"Jesus," he was saying, "this isn't dog crap, it's human."

"Shut up and wipe before I gag."

They were interrupted by a radio message.

"EK2, 45 Ascot Drive, Highgate, suspect's on the scene, informant is female resident. Graded I, India."

"That's near here," said Nick.

"You're not wrong, my friend," replied Gerry.

"Think we should help out our uniformed friends, Gerrard?"

"Wouldn't be able to sleep at night if we didn't, Nicholas."

"You're all heart."

"And it would get me away from your shoe."

They got into their car and sped off to the house, the windows wide open.

Meanwhile, a police car waited by the curb. Inside it, two constables waited for the longest shift ever to drag itself to an end.

"My point is," repeated the driver, "I wouldn't want to be plain clothed even if you paid me to be."

"No one *will* pay you," yawned his partner. "That's *my* point."

The radio cackled into life, and the driver jumped into action.

"Yeah, received by EK2," he barked, put on his blue flashing light, started his siren, sped off down a dead end, cursed, stalled, spun round, and sped off again.

Nearby, two Flying Squad officers stood staring at an Oxfam shop, which was underneath a flat they were about to visit. It was the tenth tip-off flat they'd been sent to that night for the Urban Bomber. The ninth flat they'd been sent to had been a little old lady, who'd opened the door to them, taken in their tatty jeans and leather jackets, and promptly had a heart attack. They'd had to call an ambulance for her.

They stared at the Oxfam storefront in silence.

"That's a nice top," said one eventually. "You'd look good in that."

"Fuck off."

Their radios crackled into life. They listened to the message and looked at each other.

"We can try here and probably kill someone else's nan, or go for the intruder two minutes away and save a female resident."

They got in their car and sped off.

"I can hear the sirens," whispered Jo into the phone, feeling calmer. Then she saw her door handle turn and almost wet herself.

"He's at my door!" she hissed under the duvet.

"It's okay. They're coming."

A car screeched to a halt outside 45 Ascot Drive, and Nick and Gerry rushed to the front door. Two minutes later the constables arrived.

"She said there may be two of them," whispered a constable.

"Why you whispering?" asked Gerry. "Siren make you go deaf?"

"What's that smell?" asked the constable.

"Shit," groaned Nick, looking at his shoe. "That's me. Sorry."

Meanwhile two Flying Squaddies flew to the back garden and made their way to the kitchen door. One found the broken slatted windows by the wall, saw the man-sized hole in the window, and peered round the kitchen door to see a tall, dark figure hunched up at a door in the back corner of the kitchen, listening intently, his hand on the handle.

He whispered into his radio.

"Intruder's about to enter informant's door."

As he spoke, the front door was kicked from outside. He jumped through the window, followed by his partner. By the time they arrived in Jo's dark bedroom, they could vaguely make her out, standing by her bed, in a most becoming T-shirt and knickers, brandishing an encyclopedia at a tall young male intruder.

Suddenly Nick and Gerry appeared, followed closely by two constables. The intruder held up his hands and Jo screamed, dropping the encyclopedia on her head. The intruder then launched himself at Nick, Gerry sprang at the intruder, and the constables attacked the Flying Squaddies. Meanwhile Jo crouched on the floor finding God.

The intruder wrestled himself away from Nick and Gerry, bolted for the door of Jo's living room, ran straight into her box marked FRAGILE, collapsed knee first onto a sharp edge poking out of it, dived sideways onto the metal framework of her rucksack and catapulted himself head-first into her door frame, from where he executed a stunning backward triple toe loop onto a different, larger, sharper edge poking out of her box marked FRAGILE, all the while emitting a warlike howl. Finally, he crumpled facedown in her suitcase, a resigned and changed man.

Everyone heard the trumpet before they saw it and when the bedroom light was flicked on, they froze, like children caught with crumbs all over their faces. Gradually, one by one, they noticed Vanessa and Dick, who were standing outside the room, wearing one set of pajamas between them and each with a hissing cat by their feet. In the following silence, they took in the carnage, trying to make sense of everything.

After a moment, the Flying Squaddies looked at the constables they were garrotting and let go, only to be pounced on and half-nelsoned by Nick and Gerry.

Vanessa blew the child's trumpet again.

"Right!" she shouted. "I'm not afraid to use this!"

Dick brandished his mobile phone. "I've called the police."

"We *are* the police," said Gerry.

This took a moment to sink in.

"So are we," said someone in a half-nelson. "Flying Squad."

This took another moment to sink in.

"So are we," said one of the constables. He hated to be left out.

"No shit, Sherlock," said Gerry. "We thought you were strip-a-grams."

"Convince me you're Flying Squad," Nick ordered the man underneath him.

"*Let go or I'll fucking geld you.*"

Nick let go. He knew the Flying Squad tone. Gerry was persuaded to do the same with the man beneath him.

Vanessa and Dick tried to take in the situation as quickly as possible.

"What are you all doing in my house?" asked Dick eventually.

"*Our* house, darling."

Three children appeared behind him in the kitchen. "*Go back to bed!*" yelled Vanessa. Everyone jumped.

"What is that awful smell?" she asked.

"Oh shit," said Nick. "That's me. Well it's not *me*—"

"There's an intruder," sobbed Jo.

"There are six intruders," corrected Vanessa. "One who seems to have filled his own trousers."

"It's a *dog crap*, I haven't—"

"He's the intruder!" shouted Jo, pointing at the intruder, who was lying in her suitcase, his nose in her favorite lace thong.

"I'm not an intruder," he whispered.

"You look like an intruder to me, mate," said Gerry, taking the opportunity to half-nelson him.

"Well, I'm *not!*"

Gerry pulled his arm tighter behind him.

"*Ow!*" yelped the intruder.

"What would you call yourself then, mate?"

There was a long silence, as the intruder wiped his tears angrily on Jo's underwear.

"I'm an accountant," he hissed.

"Right," Nick told Gerry. "Cuff the comedian."

Then to everyone's surprise, Dick rushed forward and collapsed on the floor next to the intruder, his arm round his shoulder.

"Oh my God!" he cried. "It's Josh!"

"Where?" asked Gerry. "Who's Josh?"

"My son!" cried Dick. "Get off him!"

"Are you sure, sir—"

"Get off my son!"

Slowly Gerry let go of the intruder's arm and let it fall limply in Jo's undies. There was a very long silence. Eventually, the intruder squirmed painfully into a small fetal ball facing Dick.

"Hi, Dad," he said weakly. "I like the new TV."

Jo blinked as Gerry stepped away from Dick's eldest son. Painfully, slowly, Josh opened out the full length of his body and lay on his back in her open suitcase, breathing shallowly. As Jo frowned down at him, Josh Fitzgerald slowly came into focus.

He had his father's tall, boyish figure and thick, wavy dark hair. A bruise was just beginning to show between liquid brown eyes that were heavy with thick, wet eyelashes, a fresh cut emphasized high cheekbones, a line of blood trickled toward full lips and a firm jaw, and his chin, complete with dimple, was trying hard not to quiver.

She stared at him, dumbfounded. Did he really have her thong wrapped round his left ear, or was she still drunk?

"It's Josh!" yelled Zak suddenly, eyes bright, racing into the room. "With blood all over his face! And lots of policemen!" He bounced up and down, holding his willy. "Mummy," he begged. "Can Toby come and play?"

Cassandra and Tallulah stayed behind their parents.

"Why have they hurt Josh?" asked Tallulah. "Did he take a biscuit without asking?"

Everyone turned to Jo.

"He–he–I–I . . . He. He–he–I . . ." she explained, vaguely conscious that that wouldn't stand up in a court of law. She pulled herself up straight and managed not to lose her balance. "I thought," she spoke very slowly and nearly clearly, "that *heee* was a big, axey murderer."

They turned to Josh, who was now quivering.

"Yes," said Vanessa. "An easy mistake." She knelt down next to Josh. "The doctor will be here as soon as possible."

"Hi, Vanessa." He breathed with difficulty. "Alright?"

"Why didn't you ring the doorbell?" she asked him gently.

"Lost my key. Didn't want to wake you."

Vanessa smiled. "Oh, we have missed you, Josh. You do liven things up."

She turned to Jo, who was now holding her head.

"Jo," she said, getting up, "You appear to be in some pain."

Jo nodded, then stopped.

"Did someone hit you on the head?" Vanessa came toward her.

"Yes," explained Jo, pointing at the encyclopedia on the floor. "I did."

Jo was surprised at how little sympathy she got.

"I thought he was an intruder," she said, a quiver in her voice.

Vanessa was about to answer when her senses were suddenly overpowered. She froze, her eyes watering, her throat spasming. She wasn't the only one. Everyone suddenly started to shuffle away from each other, their eyes averted in embarrassment.

Vanessa's jaw dropped as she pointed in horror at Jo's bed. Has someone crapped on the duvet?" she said, holding her nose.

"Oh shit, yes, that's me," groaned Nick. "Well it's not *me*, obviously, it's dog crap."

"So let me get this straight." Vanessa smiled slinkily at the Flying Squaddie. "You're a policeman, but you're in plain clothes."

"That's right." He grinned.

"Very plain clothes."

He nodded. "Right again.'

A constable slouched behind Vanessa and her squaddie, punctuating their conversation with the occasional *sotto voce* "tosser." Now he remembered why plain clothes thought they were better than uniform. Because women did.

Meanwhile Nick and Gerry took a statement from Jo and tried to calm her down. They failed, especially when they suggested that she put it down to experience as a dry run.

Later, as Vanessa saw six policemen off the premises, answered their questions and gave details, all without any pajama trousers on, Dick poured Jo some brandy in the kitchen and the doctor saw to Josh in her suite. There was no internal damage and no broken bones, just broken pride, a badly twisted ankle, and some very nasty bruises. Josh finally shuffled out into the kitchen and sat down slowly opposite Jo, and both sat in silence while Dick whispered to the doctor by the door. Jo felt almost as self-conscious about her naked legs under the glass table as she felt wretched for what she'd done.

Eventually she spoke to Josh.

"I-I'm sorry," she whispered. "I thought you had an ax."

He gave her a sardonic smile. "I've never heard it called that before," he whispered back.

"Well well," said Dick from the kitchen. "You'll both laugh about this someday."

"Absolutely," agreed Josh. "If I live that long." He glanced up at Jo through thick eyelashes, a glimmer of a smile on his lips. Jo wanted the ground to swallow her up. Then she wanted the ground to throw Josh down on top of her.

"I thought I was protecting the family," she repeated in a monotone.

"Dad," said Josh, eyes still on Jo, "please tell Inspector Clouseau here that I *am* family."

Jo felt stung.

"Dick," she said, ever so politely. "Please tell the Milk Tray Man here that climbing through someone's window at night and skulking around their house is not big. It's not clever, and it's not . . . big."

They stared at each other for a moment.

"Now now now," soothed Dick, handing them both mugs of hot, sweet tea. "It was a simple case of mistaken identity. You both scared each other, and you're both sorry."

Jo and Josh eyed each other over their mugs.

"All friends?" asked Dick.

"I thought he was going to attack me," Jo murmured over her mug.

Josh stayed staring at her over his mug, and Jo couldn't tell if he was smiling at her behind it.

"The night is yet young," he said quietly.

Chapter 9

Jo's head hurt so much the next morning that her first conscious thought on waking was that her brain must have outgrown her skull. Then she remembered what she'd done in the middle of the night and concluded that that an oversize brain was clearly not her problem. Her head must have shrunk.

When she opened her eyes, a piercing pain proved this. She closed them again and waited for the throbbing to subside. She resigned herself to her fate. There was absolutely no way her body would ever be able to get out of bed again. She felt strangely peaceful as she waited for the tunnel and bright light. Then her Mickey Mouse alarm clock almost hit the roof and she found herself on her feet.

When she entered the kitchen she faced a chaotic breakfast scene. Dick was moaning about how tired he was, Vanessa was saying, "Now you know what it's like," and the children were squabbling. No one seemed to be eating much except Josh. He turned slowly to greet Jo, wincing in pain as he did so.

"Ah!" he said, postwince. "The bare-legged inspector!"

She was greeted merrily by all, and to her surprise, instead of Dick and Vanessa firing her there and then, they seemed genuinely concerned for her welfare. Dick made her coffee and toast, which was a nice thought even though she didn't have time to eat it. She took a gulp of the coffee while Vanessa got the children into their coats. With a brief but warm smile, Vanessa said, "Don't worry about walking Tallulah to nursery today. There won't be time," then left for the office.

In the car on the way back from the school, Jo's mobile phone rang. In her usual responsible frame of mind, she'd have pulled in to take the call or ignored it. Today she took the call and revved. It was Shaun.

"Hi, babe."

Jo took a deep breath. "I got their son beaten up in the middle of the night!" she rushed. "I thought he was a burglar! Six policemen came! I thought he was going to attack me—oh wait, I have to turn right . . ." She put the phone down, turned right and picked up the phone again. "I've never been so terrified in all my life! Six policemen! We were up till three!"

She took another right turn.

"Shaun?" she asked.

"Yes."

"Did you hear what I said? I got their son attacked."

"Are you drunk?"

"Um." Jo thought. "I don't think so. But I was last night. I'd been out with Pippa and the girls. Oh Shaun, it was terrible."

"Bloody hell, Jo. What the hell did you think you were up to?"

Jo fought the sudden urge to cry. She couldn't speak.

"If one of my men was drunk on the job," continued Shaun, "I'd sack him immediately."

"I wasn't drunk on the job, it was a Sunday," she said, jumping with shock as she clipped her side mirror on a parked car. "I am allowed a night off, you know."

"Well it obviously affected more than your night off, didn't it?"

Jo parked the car outside the Fitzgerald house. "You know, a bit of sympathy might be nice," she tried.

"Too right," said Shaun. "That family has my every sympathy."

Jo sat motionless in the car. "I have to go now," she said finally.

"Okay," said Shaun. "Oh, before I forget. I can come down the weekend after next."

"Great," said Jo. "Bye." She clicked off her phone.

Meanwhile, inside the house, Dick and Josh were talking at the kitchen table. "I could have sworn I heard her car," repeated Dick. "Ah well, I'm sure it will be alright, but we'll ask just in case."

"Do you think she's the type to mind sharing a bathroom with a stud like me?" asked Josh.

"Funnily enough we didn't ask her that at her interview."

Josh yawned. "I'm sure it will be fine," he said. "She's not remotely what I expected."

"No, but she is very conscientious."

"Except when it comes to unpacking," said Josh. "I nearly ruptured my spleen on her rucksack."

They heard the front door open and lowered their voices. "It's a good sign though," said Dick. "It means she hasn't even moved into the room you'll be moving into."

"But I will have to walk through her room to take a piss and, of course, visit the rest of the house."

"Well, I'm sure if you knock every time . . . '

"Of course."

"Have you called the office?"

"I'll call them when you talk to Jo."

They listened for Jo to come in. What they didn't know was that Jo had gone to the downstairs bath to wash her face and had then stood in the hall for a bit, concentrating hard. She couldn't actually remember any of the drive back home. Not great when it's not your car you're driving.

"Jo!" Dick called out from the kitchen.

"Yes!"

"We're in here."

"Okay!" She gave her head a violent shake, as if to get the fug out of her brain, and went into the kitchen. As she opened the door, she saw Josh slip through the French doors into the garden. She was grateful to have a bit of extra time to return to normal. As she went to take out the ironing board, she was aware of him standing on the patio with his back to her, making a call.

"Um, Jo," said Dick. "Do you have a minute?"

Not really, thought Jo. *I have all your son's pants to iron.* "Of course," she said.

Dick tapped the table in front of him. "Come and join me."

Jo sat down opposite him. She smiled at him. He smiled back at her.

"So you've met Josh then," he said.

"Yes."

"Obviously," he began, "it's hard to make a first impression from last night, and it's going to be hard to know how you feel at this stage, but I just wanted to know, and be honest with me, of course, but we were wondering, well, Josh was wondering, well no, *both* of us were wondering . . ."

Jo was all ears.

"Vanessa, of course, doesn't know yet . . ."

Jo leaned forward in her seat.

"Yes?"

"Well," said Dick, sighing, "here's the thing. How would you feel about Josh moving in?"

"Oh," she gasped.

"Here. With us."

"Oh."

"He's had a bit of a problem with his flatmates. They've buggered off basically, with no notice, to go traveling round the world and he couldn't find any replacements at such short notice so he lost his lease.

"Oh."

"Yes. Shame."

"Where would he stay?"

"In your room."

"My room?"

"Yes."

"Oh." She stood up suddenly. "Gosh it's hot in here, isn't it?"

"Well not your bedroom, obviously," corrected Dick. "Your living room. Seeing as you hadn't actually properly moved into it, we didn't think you'd mind that much—"

"I don't mind at all—" said Jo, standing by the boarded-up gap in the slatted windows above the kitchen sink.

"I mean," continued Dick, "you'd have to share the bathroom, of course—"

"That's fine—" She turned away from the patio.

"But he's very well housebroken," continued Dick. "You'd hardly know he was there."

She glanced back at the patio. "Mm."

"And he's out at work all hours. When he's not out living it up, of course. Not like us old marrieds."

"Oh."

"So, what we, that is Josh and I—Vanessa doesn't know yet, obviously— what we wanted to know was do you mind if Josh moved into the room next to yours?'

Jo turned back to Dick. "No," she said.

"Or . . . or would it be okay?"

Jo frowned. Just before she thought Dick was going to ask her again, the french doors opened behind her and Josh came in. Her greeting stuck in her throat. He didn't greet her, and she watched his slow and painful progress with increasing wretchedness.

"My boss says I can work from home for the next week," Josh told Dick. "Luckily I brought my laptop home with me last night."

"You're sure they don't mind?" asked Dick.

"Josh shook his head. "With my doctor's note I should be off completely, so they know they're getting more out of me than they should."

Josh leaned against the curved work top opposite Jo and crossed his arms.

"All the children off to school then?" he asked her.

She nodded.

"Jo doesn't mind you moving in next door to her at all," said Dick. "Do you, Jo?"

Josh gave her a serious look. She blinked.

"No of course not," she said.

"You don't sleep in the nude or anything I should know about?" asked Josh.

"No." She went to get the ironing out of the utility room.

"Oh. Okay. It's just me then."

Jo gave a short laugh.

"And I promise to knock," he added.

"Great."

"Unless I forget of course."

"Right."

Josh turned to Dick. "Looks like it's all sorted then."

"Now all we have to do is tell Vanessa tonight," said Dick.

A shiver seemed to go round the room.

"Better let you get on with the ironing," said Dick quietly. As he passed Jo, he leaned in to her, gave her a wink, and said, "Don't let him disturb you."

"Oh, he disturbed me quite enough last night." Jo tried to laugh.

"I thought perhaps you were already disturbed," said Josh pleasantly.

At lunchtime, Dick was at work, Josh made calls to his office, and Jo picked up Tallulah, the ironing half-finished. Meanwhile, Vanessa was in the thick of Soho at the Groucho Club.

Members of the club sat in the bar in small, self-important groups, discussing small, self-important ideas as Max led Vanessa, Anthony, and Tom through into the restaurant beyond. Unfortunately there was no one famous in at the moment, which made everyone feel rather less impressed with themselves than they'd have liked. This particular small, self-important group sat in the corner, Vanessa facing Anthony, Max facing Tom. Because of scheduling problems with VC their big meeting had been postponed, but now it was finally time to get down to business.

Vanessa was feeling slightly shell-shocked from a combination of lack of sleep and the terror that Jo might leave. If she went home tonight to discover aliens conducting experiments on her family, she knew her first thought would be "Don't take the nanny." And she was having one of her wretched days where she felt uncontrollable hostility toward her husband, which manifested itself in sudden rushes of anger every time she thought of him. It wasn't anything specific he'd done, it was just everything—the sight of him calmly pouring a brandy for Jo while she saw all the policemen off, the sight of him then pouring Josh a brandy while she put the children back to bed, the thought of him moaning about lack of sleep, then taking the morning off. Nothing and everything.

Anthony and Max were in high spirits, full of optimism and swaggering confidence—Max because he had all the joy of delegating every last aspect of this job to everyone else and Anthony because he was desperately trying to hide Tom's natural pessimism. He was smiling so much he was beginning to fear the onset of lockjaw.

"We're gonna knee McFarleys so hard," exclaimed Max over coffee, "their gonads are gonna shoot out of their mouths."

"What a beautiful image," said Tom. "I'll see what I can do with that."

Max laughed, and Anthony impressed them all by widening his grin further still.

"So! Guys," said Max, in a tone Anthony and Tom had been dreading all meal. He raised his elastic eyebrows high up on his ever-expanding forehead. "Any ideas?"

The best creative team in the agency stole themselves a few precious seconds by looking at each other, then looking back at Max.

"Well," said Anthony finally, "we did have a quick brainstorm before lunch. So we have got a few ideas."

Max gave Vanessa a wide grin. "See what I'm saying? Geniuses, these guys. *Geniuses.*"

Anthony didn't feel the need to explain that the best idea they'd come up with was a dwarf dressed as a telephone and the only slogan they'd come up with was "Competition's dwarfed by VC."

"I'm getting together with the planner on Wednesday," said Vanessa, "to develop the strategy, then meeting up with VC Friday A.M. I'll brief you guys ASAP."

"When's the pitch?" asked Anthony.

"A fortnight today."

"Shit!" cried Tom. "We've only got two weeks?"

"Yup," said Max, relighting his cigar. "That's why we brought in the best."

Tom and Anthony both finished their wine.

After lunch, they all walked back to the office, Anthony naturally falling into step beside Vanessa.

"Tom's a bit tense, isn't he?" she asked after a while.

"All the better to be creative with," answered Anthony.

"You sure he's up to this?"

Anthony turned to her, and she had to move back slightly to stop bumping into him. He was so short, she could look into his eyes without even tilting her head. "Vanessa."

"Hmm?"

"This is the man who *created* Bobby the Baboon."

They locked eyes.

"You're right," she said. "I'm sorry."

"Hey, I understand," said Anthony. 'That's the "suits" jobs—to worry. And what a job you do. Don't know how you do it, to be honest. Rather you than me.'

They set off again, and, walking beside him, Vanessa pictured Dick saying the same to her about her contribution at home. She felt her blood start to simmer almost instantly.

"But it's our job to create," Anthony was saying. "So you just leave that to us."

She smiled a wide, relieved smile and wished she could feel so confident in her husband's abilities.

Back at the office, standing in front of Anthony in the lift, Vanessa could see him in the mirrored door collecting visual data about her body to be downloaded later. Eventually, his eyes met hers in the mirror, and he pulled a shamefaced schoolboy grin. She tutted inwardly. He must think she was born yesterday. She imagined Dick catching sight of her being ogled and smiled to herself.

The doors shut slowly behind her and Max. Finally, the boys were alone. They let out deep, grateful sighs.

"Bloody suits," moaned Tom.

"Mm."

"Bloody bloody suits."

"Mm."

"Think they know everything."

"Mm."

"While we have to create a masterpiece in two bloody weeks."

"Mm."

The lift door opened onto the penthouse floor, and they walked over plush carpet to their office-with-a-view.

"I'm not sure she's all bad," said Anthony.

"Bollocks. She's one of the worst."

Anthony shrugged.

"You've just got to know how to play her," he said, shutting their office door behind him.

When Vanessa got home that evening, the kitchen was buzzing. Jo tidied while chatting to Tallulah, Dick helped Zak with his homework, Cassandra practiced her recorder in the living room, and Josh sat at the table, tapping into his laptop, occasionally shooing off the cats, who had decided his keyboard was their activity center. Vanessa felt a rare moment of contentment.

'Hello, darling!' greeted Dick. "Josh is moving in."

And lo. The moment was over.

Once the children were all in bed, Dick and Josh assembled a dinner of salads, cheeses and breads and Vanessa opened the first bottle of wine. She insisted Jo join them.

"I suppose it just would have been nice to have had some notice," Vanessa told Josh.

"I kept thinking I'd find someone to replace them," said Josh, shrugging. "But no luck."

"Even in Crouch End?" she said incredulously.

"Yep. Even in Creche End. Too many bloody babies in that place. You can't even have a decent pint without some bloke coming in with a baby strapped to his front, talking about how little sleep he's getting, like he wants a medal for it."

"I suppose your ideal flatmate would have been Claudia Schiffer," muttered Vanessa.

"I'm not quite that shallow," said Josh, casting Jo a quick glance. "I'd have coped with Yasmin le Bon."

"Well, it's okay with me," said Vanessa, "as long as Jo's happy sharing her suite with you."

"So, Jo!" he said. "What's it like having Vanessa care what you think? I've never known."

"Well, if you helped with the children occasionally," retorted Vanessa, "I'd care what you thought, too."

"I didn't know that was my role in life," said Josh calmly, buttering some bread. "To look after my father's second family after he left mine."

There was an ugly pause. Jo stared at her unfinished meal.

"Come on, people," whispered Dick eventually. "Come on."

Jo noticed that Josh didn't eat his bread.

Over freshly ground evening coffee and Chinese green tea with fresh mint from the organic grocers, Josh explained to Vanessa why he'd be spending his days at home for the first week or so of the new arrangement, until he felt well enough to go on the tube.

"Rush hour's a nightmare at the best of times," he said. "This way I do my annual homework leave time and don't get my already-twisted ankle and already-crushed bones damaged even more on the tube. The doctor said I should keep it up for two weeks. So to speak. But I can't afford two weeks off. Anyway, it'll be fun working from here. Sharing an office with your incredibly efficient nanny."

Dick and Vanessa gave him a pointed look.

"Hey! Don't look at me," he said. "It's not my fault my body's black-and-blue." He toasted Jo, with a wicked glint in his eye. "You can thank Nanny Psycho for that."

Vanessa took a deep sigh and put down her wineglass. Jo could almost hear Dick's buttocks clench.

"Joshua," began Vanessa. "I think we need a little talk." She spoke to Josh as if he'd just done a poo in her shoe. "Dick and I feel genuinely wretched that you have been hurt in our home, and I think it is safe to say that Jo feels the same." Dick and Jo nodded vehemently and attempted some half noises of assent.

"But," continued Vanessa, "if you honestly think we'd rather have a nanny who slept through a man breaking into our home than a nanny who fought her terror and called the police, you are more of a fool than you look."

Josh's already-stiff body stiffened some more.

"Now, now—" started Dick.

"Richard!" shot Vanessa, as if her husband had picked up the shoe with the poo in it and eaten it. "I am handling this, thank you very much."

If there had been any doubt before, all was now squashed.

"As far as we're concerned"—Vanessa turned her attention back to Josh—"you gave Jo here a unique opportunity to prove to us just how much of an addition she is to our family and"—she left a pause so dramatic even the goldfish tensed—"exactly how much you are not." Jo winced. "Any more snide comments about our nanny, who after her heroics last night has proved herself clearly underpaid, will simply not be tolerated under this roof."

The silence following this little speech was interrupted only by Molly and Bolly, who chose this moment to lift their right hind legs in corps-de-ballet synchronicity and conduct a thorough investigation of their bottoms.

"Am I making myself clear, Joshua?" asked Vanessa.

There was a pause.

"Crystal," said Josh quietly.

Vanessa turned to Jo and spoke in the tone of Cinderella addressing her favorite fluffy kitten.

"In fact, Jo, we haven't discussed it yet, but I know Dick would agree with me. We'd very much like to offer you a raise."

Jo was so shocked she didn't even notice Dick's and Josh's reactions.

After dinner, Jo had to move the few things she'd put into her dressing room out of it, while Josh moved his stuff in. That day, Dick had gone to IKEA and bought Jo a fabric wardrobe and a tiny table which was to act as her dressing table. It suited her fine.

Surveying her packing with a dismal air, she quickly plaited her hair out of her eyes and then started when she realized Josh was standing in her doorway, surveying her in a somewhat similar vein.

He suddenly held up a bottle of wine and two glasses, and managed a smile that Jo imagined cost him a great deal. "Fancy a cheeky little Italian?"

"Oh," she said.

"To relax us both after our adventures." She nodded very slowly and thoughtfully, as if her head was trying to make its imprint in treacle, and Josh commenced pouring, a tad erratically. "And to help me forget that my father's wife hates me." He stretched out the full glass of wine toward her, and she extended her arm to take it. As her hand clenched the glass they locked eyes.

"Thanks."

"And of course," he smiled, before letting go, "to dull your senses. We don't want you phoning the police if I make any sudden moves."

Jo heard herself let out a sudden laugh. "That's not fair," she said quietly, not daring to pull away the glass. "You really scared me."

"Did I? Sorry about that," he said, and allowed her to take the wine. She gulped it down.

'Forgiven,' she said lightly, turning away.

They unpacked in silence, apart from Jo's gentle humming. When her mobile phone rang, she picked it up, saw it was Shaun, and turned it off angrily. She didn't feel like being told off again, especially in front of Josh.

It didn't take either of them long to unpack. Afterward, Josh hobbled into Jo's room and sat down slowly on her bed, putting the wine on the floor between them. He smiled pleasantly enough at her but she wasn't convinced. Warily, she sat against the wall, strands of her plait falling round her face.

"So," he said. "How are you enjoying working for the Munsters?"

"It's fine," said Jo carefully.

"Oh come on," said Josh. "They're bloody mad, the lot of them."

Jo forced what she hoped was an easy smile. "It's hard work," she confessed. "But the kids are lovely."

"Yeah," agreed Josh, the corners of his mouth curving up a fraction, as if keeping a secret. "They are."

They both nodded and smiled for a bit.

"Yep," he added, taking some more wine. "If your dad's gonna upsticks and start again, you couldn't hope for a nicer brood."

Jo's brain scanned all the possible things to say in response and then stopped. She decided to change tack.

"Has your mum remarried?"

As Josh shook his head, Jo scoured his face for any hints of the woman with the hard eyes and dry voice who had dropped Toby off.

"So is this the first time you've left home?" asked Josh.

Jo pushed some loose strands of hair behind her ears. "Is it that obvious?"

Josh shrugged and she felt compelled to fill the silence. "I suppose it is all a bit scary," she confessed. "Everything's so different." Josh didn't answer. "Maybe that's why I overreacted last night." She took some more wine. When she looked back at him, Josh was staring at her with an intensity that made her feel aware of the hairs on her skin. She glanced at the grains in the wood floor.

"I think you were very brave," he said.

"I phoned the police from under my duvet," she grimaced. "I could hardly dial for shaking."

Another pause. This time Jo braved it out.

"Exactly," said Josh eventually. "You were terrified and you still did it."

Jo took some more wine and felt its warmth ooze through her body.

"People don't like it when you're brave, do they?" she asked suddenly. "It's as if they want you to be scared, because it permits them to not have to take any risks either."

Josh tilted his head at her, his forehead puckering.

"My decision to leave home wasn't exactly a popular one," she explained, taking another sip and wondering if she'd had enough to drink.

"Ah," he said. "With anyone specific?"

Jo re-heard Shaun telling her off and shrugged her sudden anger away. "Just everyone," she said grumpily.

"Really? Wow," said Josh.

Jo eyed him suspiciously, convinced he was mocking her. But his face showed no signs of mockery.

"You must have been very strong to have gone ahead with it then," he continued.

She tried to speak, failed, so shrugged and drank some more wine instead.

"Between you and me," Josh went on, "I wish I could be that brave."

"You'd like to move away?" asked Jo.

He shook his head. "I'd like to change career. But I don't know what I'd like to do instead and both my parents would kill me."

Jo gasped. "Tell me about it," she said with feeling. "Guess whose idea it was for me to be a nanny?"

"Your parents?"

"Ten out ten."

"What did you want to be?"

"Oh noth—It's stupid—"

"Go on."

"They were probably right."

"Tell me."

Jo took a deep breath. "I wanted to be a . . . don't laugh—"

"I won't—"

"I wanted to be an anthropologist."

She gulped down more wine.

"Wow," said Josh. "Brilliant."

Jo shrugged. "When you're young you're full of silly ideas."

"What's silly about that?"

"Anyway, I'm a nanny. And it was hard enough being a nanny who'd moved away from home."

Josh leaned toward her and poured more wine into her glass.

"No thanks," she said, when he'd finished.

"So how come you did it anyway?" he asked.

She cushioned each word with a thoughtful pause. "The need to know that my choices so far in life weren't just the easiest ones."

They locked eyes, Josh nodding thoughtfully. "Yeah," he whispered. "I know what you mean."

Most of her hair slipped out of the plait and she put down her glass, shook the rest loose and looped it into a lazy ponytail. When she finished, she glanced all round the room and eventually at Josh and again found him scrutinizing her. She was just about to announce that she really needed to get some sleep when he gave her a big, warm smile and held up his wine glass to her.

"So," he murmured. "To the right choices."

She felt vaguely conscious that she'd just witnessed a decision being made. She picked hers up, returned his smile and they clinked glasses. "To the right choices," she agreed and finished her wine.

That night she fell asleep to the sound of Josh's slow padding round his room and slept right through till morning for the first time since she'd arrived.

Chapter 10

Over the next week, Jo discovered that the average accountant does approximately half the amount of work that an average nanny does. Josh would get up early and do two hours before she got back from dropping all the children off at school. Then he was ready for a two-hour tea break. They soon got into a routine where he'd make them both a cup of tea and, while idly tapping away at his laptop, chat while she ironed. At first she found his presence intimidating, but gradually the conversational pauses grew shorter and the tension evaporated until she didn't mind at all. In fact, she was amazed at how much difference it made to her life having someone to chat with during the day.

After a while, he stopped asking if she was going to phone the police every time he stood up quickly and stopped asking when the laptop dancing was due to begin. He'd also started hobbling around after her as she tidied the children's rooms—"good practice for my foot." She didn't mind slowing down for him to keep up, especially as part of her still felt guilty that she had been the cause of his obvious pain. And it certainly wasn't a hardship as it meant she spent most of her time laughing. One morning, she didn't know how it even came up, they ended up talking about how Josh's parents had split up. It turned out Dick had had an affair with his secretary, and Josh's mother had been unable to forgive him.

"What a waste," he said. "A family dissolved forever—he clicked his fingers—"just like that."

"How awful," said Jo.

"I was bitter for a long time," he said with a nod. "Fourteen's not a good age to lose your dad."

"But you're friends now, aren't you?"

Josh seemed to consider this.

"Yeah, we're cool. And these things happen."

Jo nodded.

"You've got to move on," he continued. "But it has made me realize how damaging infidelity is. Trust is everything," he said quickly before changing the subject.

The more they talked, the more conscious Jo became that Shaun had never come up in conversation. Over the days they managed to talk about pretty much everything, but somehow they never talked about their love lives. It was like an unspoken code, but the more they chatted and the closer Jo felt to Josh—and she felt increasingly close to him— the more she felt she was somehow misrepresenting herself. Yet she could never find the appropriate moment to mention Shaun without feeling that it might come out sounding gauche and pointed.

She brought this up at her weekend therapy session with the girls.

"So let me get this straight," clarified Pippa. "You've managed not to even *skim* over the fact—even in passing—that you've had the same boyfriend for the past six years. And still very much have him."

Jo nodded.

"I keep waiting for the right moment," she insisted, "but it's hard to say 'Pass me the dishcloth, I've got a boyfriend.'"

"But if you're just friends," said Rachel, "surely it comes up in conversation?"

"I know," agreed Jo, "you'd think so, but somehow every time I want to say it, I feel like it would look like I'm trying to put him off or something, which would make me look really arrogant."

"*Are* you just friends?" asked Rachel.

"Of course," insisted Jo.

"Hmm," said Pippa. "How come you didn't seem to have any problem finding the right moment to tell me?"

"You asked," said Jo.

"That's true."

"And I didn't fancy you."

"*Aha!*" exclaimed the girls.

Jo grinned. "He hasn't even asked if I've got a boyfriend," she said, "so he's obviously not interested."

"Would it make a difference if he did ask?" asked Pippa.

Jo thought about this. Then she thought about Shaun. She shrugged miserably.

After a pause, Gabriella had a question.

"What does theez Josh the Dosh loook like?"

Jo closed her eyes. "Ioan Gruffudd."

The girls took a moment to show their appreciation.

"Oh my God!" cried Pippa. "You're living with Hornblower?"

"Yes," confessed Jo. "Without the breeches. And a bit more sultry."

There was a long silence.

"Well," said Pippa. "I think it's all very simple. As soon as you start blowing his horn you chuck Shaun."

"Oh God!" Jo said through the laughter. "I've got a boyfriend! A boyfriend who's coming to stay."

"Looks like that's when Josh will find out then." Rachel grinned.

Jo winced into her wine.

"Don't worry," said Pippa. "You've got days before Shaun gets here. You're bound to find an appropriate moment."

For the first time in their short acquaintance, Pippa was wrong. During the next few days with Josh, the subject was on the tip of Jo's tongue many times, but every time she could see the conversation veering in that direction, it somehow directed itself elsewhere. The last thing she wanted to do was offend Josh. And the thing just before the last thing she wanted to do was put him off, just in case he was interested.

The longer she left it, the harder it got, because every time she thought of Josh's belief that trust was everything she felt even more unable to tell him. She was caught in a stalemate and didn't know how to get out of it.

She started making all her calls to Shaun in the car and told herself it was because it was the only place she got any privacy. In many ways that was true. Josh was in and out of her room all the time; in fact they left the door open between their rooms until bedtime.

She hadn't really forgiven Shaun for acting like her teacher instead of her boyfriend when she'd told him what had happened the night Josh had arrived, but they'd reached an unspoken truce. He'd said he missed her, and she'd said she was looking forward to his visit. And she was sure it would all be better when she saw him. She started counting the days with nervous anticipation.

One evening, when Vanessa was out working late and Dick was asleep in the lounge, Jo sat watching television in the conservatory wondering how long Josh would be in the bathroom. When the doorbell rang, she heard Dick answer it. She was very surprised when he came in and presented her with one of the policemen from that night.

"Look who I found on the doorstep!" said Dick. "One of those nice men who attacked my son."

"Oh yes," said Gerry. "Sorry about that."

"Not to worry," said Dick. "He'll be over it in, ooh . . . months. Tell me, were you the one who smelt of dog crap or were you the other one?"

"I was the other one. Definitely the other one."

"Excellent. Excellent."

He looked over at Jo, said "Well, I'll leave you both to it," and did so.

"Hello," said Jo, baffled.

"Hello there," said Gerry, walking a couple of steps toward her. "I just wanted to see how you were. You seemed in rather a bad way the other night."

"Oh God I know. I'm so sorry about that. I'm fine now. Thanks ever so much." She started fiddling with her hair.

"I've got this for you." He produced a card. "It's Victim Support. Sometimes people get a delayed reaction to shock."

"Oh," said Jo. "Thank you."

She took the card and smiled at Gerry. He smiled back at her and stepped forward to lean against the counter near her. She read the card and nodded several times. When she finished reading it, she started reading it again. Then she filled the little pause that followed with a few more nods.

"So, no more bumps in the night?" asked Gerry.

"No. Thanks."

"Good. Good. And you feel easy in your bed?"

"Yes—"

"At night?"

"Yes. Thanks."

"Anyway, the thing is, I was just wondering—"

The door from Jo's bedroom opened and Josh walked in. As soon as he saw Gerry, he seemed to freeze. Gerry seemed to freeze, too. They both froze. Jo had frozen a while ago.

"Look!" she told Josh. "It's . . . from the other night . . ."

"Ah yes!" exclaimed Josh. "The nice man who beat me up."

"Gerry," said Gerry, putting out his hand. "Call me Gerry."

"As in Tom and Jerry?" asked Josh, shaking his hand.

"No," said Gerry, "with a 'G.'"

The two men nodded at each other and continued to shake hands very firmly and with great determination. When they stopped, Gerry took a small step away from Jo. "I was just asking Jo here if she was alright," he said casually. "And if she felt safe," said Gerry.

"Oh I see!" exclaimed Josh suddenly. "Like customer relations! Wow! I never knew you guys did that."

"Well, we don't do it as a rule—"

"But you're a maverick are you?" asked Josh. "A bit of a rebel, eh? You don't give a damn who you hurt, you're gonna do this customer relations shit."

Jo stifled a laugh. She watched the two men stare each other out. She'd never seen two men confront each other after fighting.

"I just gave Jo a Victim Support card," said Gerry calmly. "Sometimes people get a delayed reaction to shock."

"Really? I didn't," said Josh. "Mine happened right while I was being attacked.

"Ah yes, sorry about that," said Gerry. "Genuine mistake."

"Thank you. That'll help my genuine pain."

Gerry turned to Jo, almost turning his back on Josh.

"My number's on the card too," he told her. "If you ever need to chat, just call.'

"Thanks ever so much," Jo said quickly.

"Not at all," said Gerry. "And if you ever fancy a night out sometime . . ." he coughed over Josh's snort. "Unless"—Gerry suddenly turned to face Josh and pointed to both of them— "you two . . ."

"God no!" said Jo and Josh together. Jo noticed Josh said it far more loudly than her.

Gerry smiled at Jo. She grimaced. Now was the time to tell him she had a boyfriend at home. A boyfriend she'd been with for six years. Who was coming to stay. There was even a pause for it.

And there was still a pause for it.

But how would it look to Josh to mention Shaun now? What a horrible way for him to find out. And would it make her look callous to let Gerry down so heavily, when he was probably just being friendly? Or would Josh think she was lying to Gerry and there was no boyfriend and she was therefore a detestable untrustworthy woman? Either way, she'd have to fill that pause somehow.

"I have some girlfriends," she heard herself say, "who'd love to meet some . . . friendly guys . . ."

She saw Gerry visibly droop.

"So if you have some friends . . ." she said, her heart going out to him.

"Oh great!" said Gerry. "The more the merrier! Well, I've got your number from the other night."

Jo nodded, looking at the floor, and flicked her hair back off her face.

"I'll see myself out," said Gerry, making to leave.

"Well you saw yourself in," muttered Josh, as Gerry passed him.

"As I recall," Gerry muttered from the kitchen door, "so did you." He turned to Jo and gave her a big smile that made him look almost handsome. "Bye then," he said. "Speak soon."

Jo and Josh listened as Gerry walked down the corridor and shut the door behind him.

Jo decided suddenly that it was the perfect time to mention Shaun, the moment she'd been waiting for! She could say how awkward that was because of her boyfriend, who she'd been with for six years, who was coming to stay, who was called Shaun. Had she really not mentioned it? Gosh. Funny that. She could have sworn she had—

"Well," said Josh. "Wasn't that decent?"

Before she had a chance to answer, he'd vanished back to his room.

Chapter 11

Vanessa sat in the Monday morning status meeting hunched over her coffee, wondering why they didn't sell it in pints. Tallulah had woken her twice in the night, once at four and once at six, and it had taken her an hour to get back to sleep both times. Unlike all the other passengers in the train that morning, she'd been grateful when it stopped for ten minutes between stations because it gave her a clear run to do her makeup, catch her breath, and remember her name.

She'd sat opposite a teenager who was obviously on her way into town for a shopping day. She'd been unable to tear her eyes away from the young girl, trying to remember the teenager she'd been, able to do things purely for her own happiness in blissful ignorance of how selfish that would one day seem. It was as if the minute she'd become a mother, the definition of the word "selfish" had become gender-specific. A man could play golf all weekend and still be a family man. A woman could earn money all week, spend every spare moment with her children, and be selfish because she wanted both. One day she'd write a tome on the subject. When she had time.

"And that's it," finished Tricia, Vanessa's junior. Vanessa stared at Tricia and was only a little surprised to find Tricia staring back at her. The girl must have finished updating.

"Thank you, Tricia," said Vanessa, and proceeded to update everyone on the VC project so far. She was so tired she failed to notice an increasing intensity in Anthony Harrison's stare. And she was completely unable to surmise that he was matching up certain key facts about her to certain key facts about his dream last night.

"So," she concluded, "I'll be seeing Miranda Simmonds, the marketing director for VC, again tomorrow, and after we've chatted, I'll be able to brief the creative team. Shall we say nine A.M. Wednesday?"

"We can't do nine, I'm afraid," said Tom. "We've got a meeting with Happy Kids."

"Afternoon?"

"Elephant plasters."

Vanessa sighed. They had to get the ball rolling soon.

"How about 5:30?" asked Tom. "That way we don't lose another day, and I get to miss bathtime with the twins. So everybody's happy."

Vanessa managed a tight smile.

"And we can go for a quick celebratory drink afterward," added Anthony.

Vanessa didn't have the energy to argue. She made a note to tell Jo that she'd have to pick up Cassie from choir practice.

After the meeting Anthony caught up with her in the corridor. "I look forward to being briefed by you." He brushed past, his hips almost touching hers.

"Oh. I'll look forward to giving it to you. I mean—"

"Terrific."

Jo ironed happily, humming to herself while Josh read some notes, his foot resting on the kitchen table, a cat nudged up against his heel. When her mobile rang, Jo went into her bedroom to answer it.

"There you are!" shrieked Sheila. "I thought they'd eaten you!"

"Sheila!" screamed Jo, coming back into the kitchen. "Oh my God, how are you?"

"Neglected, you old bitch."

"God, sorry. I've just been so busy."

"Obviously. Far too busy to phone me." Jo could sense a steel rod beneath the fluffy tone.

"Sorry, Shee."

"So! I hear you've got a new friend."

"Eh?" Jo tucked the phone under her ear as she continued with the ironing.

"Shaun told me. Some bird called Pippa. Does that mean I'll be getting even fewer calls now?"

Jo stopped ironing. "Shee, please. Don't give me a hard time. It's not been easy. I—"

Jo was interrupted by the doorbell. She looked over at Josh. He glanced up and started moving his foot off the kitchen table. When he had to hide a wince, Jo motioned for him to stop trying.

"Shee," she said, "I have to go. There's someone at the door."

"Right," said Sheila. "Bye." And she'd gone.

"Sorry," said Josh. "This bloody leg."

The doorbell interrupted again and Jo rushed to the door. She opened it to Agnita, the smiling Polish au pair who worked nearby and who came to the Fitzgeralds' twice a week to do any ironing that wasn't the children's. Jo was convinced Agnita never wore knickers and today, as she followed her down the hall, it was more than usually obvious because she'd chosen to wear skintight white leggings. Jo found herself drawn to her amazingly pert, round bottom and scolded herself for being grateful that Agnita's face had the bone structure of an archaeological find.

She glanced at the clock and saw that she had ten minutes to spare before picking up Tallulah. She imagined what Pippa would do in the same situation. She went into her room and and dialed Sheila's number. Damn. Busy. She left a message explaining that she was terribly sorry she hadn't been able to talk and she had loads to tell her. Then she tried Shaun. Damn. Also busy. She left a message telling him that she couldn't wait until he came and visited. Then she paced round her room and went back into the kitchen. She wasn't surprised to see Josh's fingers hovering above his keyboard, his eyes fixed on Agnita's bottom.

"Busy?" she asked pointedly, making sure he saw her smile.

He grinned. "Oh yes."

Unaware, Agnita smiled pleasantly up at Jo, and Jo smiled extremely widely back.

"Right," she told them both. "I'll be off to get Tallulah." She turned to Josh. "Don't do anything I wouldn't do."

Agnita smiled, and behind her Josh looked ostentatiously despondent. Jo slammed the front door behind her, wondering what the definition of "flirting" was.

As he heard the door slam, Josh sighed heavily. With some effort, he lifted his foot off the kitchen table and limped out into the back garden, where he settled himself on a bench. After a moment, he took out his mobile and dialed his father's number at the shop.

"Hello?" said Dick.

"Dad, it's me."

"How are you feeling?"

Josh gave himself a moment.

"Impotent. You?"

"Resigned."

"Don't say that. You took a risk, and it didn't pay off. I'm still going to try and help."

"How?"

"Just leave it to me."

Dick sighed. "I can't believe I got myself into this mess."

"Dad, stop torturing yourself."

There was a pause.

"It would have all been okay," said Josh, "if it wasn't for that screw up that night."

"Why couldn't you have just used your key?" asked Dick.

" 'Cos someone forgot to tell me the nanny lived off the kitchen, didn't they? I thought I was going to be beaten to death."

"Well where do you think the nanny lives?"

"I don't know! Under the stairs? We don't have nannies in bachelor pads. More's the pity."

Dick let out a sigh.

"And then," continues Josh. "Vanessa goes and gives her a raise! Don't get me wrong, I don't want the girl to starve, but—"

"I know. It's not ideal, Josh, and I'm sorry. After everything you've—"

"No, Dad, I'm sorry. I just . . . wanted to help. I messed up again."

"Josh, you're helping by just being there."

Josh stayed silent.

"Son, you are not responsible for my . . . for this."

More silence.

"I better get back now," said Dick. "Bye, son."

In the record shop, Dick put down the phone, picked up his jacket, and locked the door behind him for the third time that morning. Josh wiped his face furiously on his sleeve, limped back into the kitchen, and resumed his work.

Chapter 12

It was teatime and Jo had invited Pippa and Georgiana over to play. Sebastian James joined them because his mother was at a vital Pilates lesson. Jo was obliging Zak by wearing a cat outfit, which consisted of a black-and-white furry cat hat with cat ears, cat mittens, and a proud black-and-white cat tail, while he painstakingly drew her. Over tea and Marks & Spencer chocolate squares, Zak filled in his drawing of Jo as Catwoman, Jo filled Pippa in about Shaun's visit, and Sebastian James filled his nappy.

"Where shall I take Shaun?" asked Jo. "I'd ask Gerry, but I don't feel it's appropriate."

"Ooh," said Pippa. "So you *do* like Gerry?"

"No." Jo frowned. "Not like that."

"So why are you keeping him interested?"

"For you! He might have a friend."

"Uh-huh."

"Oh God," said Jo. "I'm so confused."

"Why?"

Jo looked at Zak. "You know . . ." she said. Zak didn't even look up. He was filling in Jo's cat tail.

Pippa mouthed, "Josh," and Jo nodded.

"Told him yet?"

Jo shook her head, and Pippa tutted, then dunked her chocolate square in her tea and sucked contentedly.

"How's the picture of Catwoman going?" Jo asked Zak.

Zak didn't look up from his drawing. "Fine."

"Pippa," said Jo, turning back to Pippa, "either Sebastian James needs changing, or you've got a serious problem."

"I know. I was seeing how long I could leave it."

"Well, give it another ten minutes and I'll be sick."

Pippa looked at her watch. "Okay."

Five minutes later his picture was finished, and while Pippa changed Sebastian James, Zak performed the unveiling ceremony in front of Jo.

Her ears were a bit big, one arm was longer than the other, and she only had one leg, but apart from that it was an uncanny resemblance, especially the bouncy tail, which seemed to defy gravity.

"That's fantastic, Zak!" she cried. "Look! I've got a tail!"

"Of course you've got a tail," said Zak. "You're Catwoman. Can I have my Fruitellas now?"

"Not till after tea."

When the mummy of Sam, one of Zak's best friends phoned, Jo answered it happily. "I'm not accusing him of anything," said Sam's mum wearily over the phone. "It's just that Sam can't find his tortoise anywhere, and he's distraught."

"Of course I'll ask," said Jo. "I'll call you straight back and let you know."

She clicked off the phone and sat next to Zak, swishing her tail deftly out of the way.

"Zak," she said.

"Mm."

"That was Sam's mummy."

Zak went quiet.

"Sam's very upset."

"Mm?"

"Because he thinks he's lost his toy tortoise."

Zak shrugged.

"Do you want to go upstairs and have a good look and see if you didn't bring it home accidentally?"

For a few seconds Zak's body seemed to fight itself, but finally the part that knew there was no point in arguing stomped upstairs, furious that the other half of his body hadn't been stronger.

"*I can't find it!*" he shouted immediately.

"*Do you want me to come up and help you look?*"

"*Found it!*"

Jo crossed her arms.

Zak came downstairs and produced a tiny plastic tortoise for her to inspect. A deep flush had spread all over his cheeks and he couldn't look her in the eye.

"I'm not pleased, Zak," said an unimpressed Catwoman.

"I just FOUND it."

"Don't lie to me, Zak," said Jo firmly. "If there's one thing I cannot bear, it's lying."

Zak felt surprisingly icky.

"I'm going to phone Sam's mummy," she said.

"It was an accident!"

Once the call had been made, she went upstairs and found Zak sitting on his bed.

"It was an accident!" he repeated, though with decreasing vehemence.

Jo sat down on the bed, her tail perkily behind her.

"Zak. How would you feel if Sam came here and took home your cyberdog?"

Zak's foot started tapping and he took in air like a fish out of water, a useless displacement activity his body did to stop tears coming. "It was an accident," he whispered, but the tears gave him away.

"You've stolen something, then lied about it," said Jo sadly.

Zak fell facedown onto his pillow as she left the room.

After changing Sebastian James's nappy, Pippa helped Jo compile a list of the top London clubs, wine bars, and restaurants to introduce Shaun to and help make the weekend go with a bang, " 'Cos it doesn't look like there'll be much other banging going on," she told Jo.

Tallulah entered.

"I need to do a poo," she announced with great aplomb.

When the doorbell rang, Jo grimaced at Pippa. "That's probably Josh back from his walk, forgotten his key again. You don't mind getting it do you? Tallulah and I have a prior engagement."

"Course not," said Pippa. "Can't wait to see the famous Joshua Fitzgerald."

Pippa went to answer the door, holding Sebastian James in his car seat against her hip. The sun shone on her blond hair, showing up the hazel flecks in her eyes, as she grinned openly at the two tall men in suits standing at the door.

Nick and Gerry looked at her keenly and, thanks to years of undercover training, remembered not to pant.

"Hello!" said Pippa to Nick.

"Hello!" said Nick and Gerry.

They all grinned happily at each other.

"Can I help?" asked Pippa.

"We just came to pop in on Jo," said Gerry.

"Well, *he* did," explained Nick. "I just came along for the ride."

Pippa and Nick smiled at each other. "Well," said Pippa, as seductively as she could, "Jo's just wiping Tallulah's bottom, would you like to come in?"

"How could we refuse?" answered Nick, and the two men entered the house.

When Jo and Tallulah came into the kitchen a while later, they found an intriguing sight. One CID officer was reading *How Much Do I Love You?* to Sebastian James at the kitchen table, the other sitting in the conservatory armchair with Georgiana on his lap, reading *Whatever Next?*

Nick and Gerry also found an intriguing sight. Jo stood long-limbed in front of them, wearing a furry cat hat with pointy ears, mittens, and a bouncy tail. The sun that had done such favors for Pippa's hair was making Jo's dark blue eyes look all the more feline.

"'Allo, 'allo, 'allo," greeted Nick. "Looks like we've found our cat burglar."

"Do you think we should take her away for questioning?" suggested Gerry.

"You brought your dog-crap friend!" Jo laughed.

"Well, actually—" started Nick, glancing at Pippa, who grinned back at him.

"They've been reading to the children," said Pippa. "Looks like our work here is done!"

Tallulah, yet to learn the complex ways of feminine guile, ran up to the nearest man in the room. "I did a poo!" she exclaimed.

"Did you?" asked Gerry. "Uncle Nicholas likes those."

Tallulah turned to Nick obediently. "I did a poo!" she told him.

"Well done!" he said sincerely. Truth was he never failed to be impressed by those. The lads at the station would understand ("I just gave birth to a seven pounder . . ." "That's nothing, mate, I needed stitches last Tuesday . . ." "Bollocks. Until either of you get a nosebleed, I'm still King of the Craps," etc).

"It wasn't as squidgy as yesterday," continued Tallulah.

"Really?" asked Nick. "Excellent."

He then looked at Jo apologetically. "Did you get it off the duvet?"

Tallulah let out a gale of laughter. "I didn't do it on the duvet, silly!" she giggled. "He's being silly!" she informed Jo.

"Yes, thanks." Jo grinned at Nick. "First wash."

"Just let me find that dog in a dark alley," said Nick. "It'll be crapping sideways for a month."

"Ooh," quivered Pippa. "Sexy."

Tallulah giggled so much she almost fell over. The laughter caught her body unawares, and she let out a neat little trumpet.

"I did a *fart!*" she cried gleefully.

"Well done!" congratulated Nick and Gerry, genuinely impressed. At last, a female they could talk to.

"I'll tell you what you can do to make up for it though," teased Jo.

"Dinner for two?" asked Gerry.

"No. You can show a good little six-year-old boy your badge."

"I didn't do a poo on the *duvet*, silly!" repeated Tallulah, climbing onto the lap of the nearest man. But he seemed far more interested in the sight of Jo wandering off with a pussycat tail bouncing up and down on her J-Lo bottom.

While Jo went upstairs to tell Zak the exciting news, Pippa, Tallulah, and Georgiana made the men a cup of tea. Alone in the room, the two men exchanged meaningful glances.

"I'd rather show her something else than my badge, Nicholas, if you know what I mean," Gerry whispered.

"Shh!" said Nick, putting his hands over Sebastian James's ears. "Not in front of the littl'un, Gerrard."

"Sorry, Nicholas. Wasn't thinking."

Jo put her head round Zak's door.

"Zak," she whispered.

Zak was perched on the edge of his bed, head tilted slightly, feet crossed at the toes, eyes wide, watching Buffy about to kick the hell out of a vampire. He pressed the PAUSE button and pointed at the screen.

"Look!" he said. "She's about to boff him!"

"Ooh! Lovely! I've got a surprise for you."

Zak's eyes doubled in size.

"What?"

"Guess who's downstairs!"

"Who?"

"You'll like it," she said.

"Batman?"

"No."

"Spider-Man?"

"No."

"Yoda!"

"This may take some time."

"Daddy?"

Jo thought she'd better tell him before it became too much of a bitter disappointment.

"Two real live policemen."

Zak gasped in horror, his face turning purple.

"It was an accident!" he shrieked, backing away against the wall. *"I'm not going to prison!"*

Jo realized her mistake, but not before Zak had gone through the terror barrier and come back again.

He got his Fruitellas early that afternoon.

During the afternoon with Nick and Gerry, Jo managed to mention Shaun casually a few times, helped by prompts from Pippa, and she felt sure that Gerry clearly received and understood the message. In fact he seemed to have taken it very well. So when both men invited her and Pippa out in a foursome to the cinema the following Saturday, the weekend after Shaun's visit, she felt confident that it was all aboveboard.

Unfortunately Josh got home from his slow ankle-strengthening stroll round Waterlow Park before the men had left, after Pippa had gone and before she'd taken her outfit off.

When he entered the kitchen, she was reaching up, blu-tacking Zak's picture of her to the top of the fridge door. She felt the atmosphere change and swung round, her tail bouncing behind her. Josh was standing in the doorway looking at Nick and Gerry. Then he turned to her, paused in what looked like midthought, and blinked. She stood tall while he slowly took everything in. Her hand shot to her curvy tail and rested on it defensively as Josh's eyes went to her black-and-white furry hat and fluffy ears, and then slid downward. She tried to smile, then tried not to. Eventually, he looked back at her eyes.

The room was silent.

Josh lifted his eyebrows. "Coppers follow your tail then?" he queried quietly.

Gerry laughed, and the room seemed to breathe out. "Too right, mate."

"Hello," said Josh, in a faux-cheerful tone. "It's Maverick and Dog Crap. Back again?"

"Looks like it," said Gerry, just as cheerfully.

Josh glanced at Jo before turning to Gerry. "Have a nice time." And with that, he went into the living room.

Jo raised her eyes heavenward and caught a glimpse of the clock. With a start, she realized she was late for Cassandra's pickup from choir practice. Within five minutes, she'd got the policemen, Tallulah, and Zak out. She drove like a maniac to find the little girl sitting miserably on the school wall. Not even the sight of Jo wearing cat ears cheered her up.

"Right, let's get started," Vanessa told Anthony and Tom, crossing one stockinged leg over the other.

Anthony coughed quietly, lowering his face into his hand.

"I've spent a fascinating morning with VC, and here's what they want," she began.

"They want fast, they want funny, they want friendly."

"Right," said Tom, making to stand up. "We'll get on to it."

"I haven't finished."

"How did I know that?" He sat down again.

"They want bubbly, clean-cut, clean-shaven, clean-living, white, heterosexual, happy, family-loving, new Labour-voting but growing cynical, preferably with blue eyes."

"Right."

"The key thought is 'Takes you to another world.'"

Tom and Anthony wrote down all this information.

"What color underwear would they like?" asked Tom.

Vanessa sighed. "VC are fascists. I'm not apologizing, I'm just telling you."

"We were hoping to get a dwarf in the ad" said Tom, for the hell of it.

Vanessa smiled. "I was hoping I'd get a holiday before the summer," she said. "Life's a bitch."

Anthony laughed.

"It looks like their marketing director is the biggest cow in the world," she continued.

"I swear these people have How to Be a Bastard training weekends. There's just no point trying to fight it."

Anthony nodded. No point indeed. He kept his eyes on Vanessa.

"Have you ever tried to create anything, Vanessa?" Tom asked quietly.

Vanessa tensed. "Three children, a happy home life, and a career path," she said. "Besides that, nothing much."

"I mean really *create* anything?" repeated Tom. "Something from a key thought—spun magic from a shopping list of requirements? Something unique, memorable, clever, original from nothing but your own ideas . . . your own imagination . . . your, your innards."

Vanessa looked at him. "Ooh! Listen!" she suddenly exclaimed. Tom and Anthony listened.

"What?" whispered Anthony.

"Warning bells," said Vanessa wryly. "Bloody deafening."

Tom sighed loudly.

"No, Tom," she told him. "That sort of creativity is your job. My job is to squeeze your enormous talent into the small mind of a marketing director."

Tom's frame expanded. "It's a tough job." He grinned. "But someone's gotta do it."

They all smiled at each other. *Wow*, thought Anthony. *Three children, and she still has that body.*

After the meeting, he hung back, fiddling with his papers while Vanessa packed up all her notes. As she left, he fell into step beside her.

"Coming for a quick drink?" he asked her. "We're only going downstairs."

"I should get back home. I have a husband to be bitter at."

"Oh go on." He smiled. "It's vital to work up a good relationship with us. I think Tom would appreciate it."

Vanessa paused. "You think I was a bit heavy with him?"

Anthony smiled, and Vanessa admitted that if you liked blonds, he really was a stunner.

"I think it wouldn't go amiss to show willing and buy him a quick drink," Anthony confided.

Vanessa looked at her watch. Cassie would have been picked up. And it wouldn't do her career any harm to build up a relationship with these guys. If they genuinely liked her, there was more chance they'd work well for her, which meant there was more chance of a great Christmas bonus for them all. She'd be doing it for her family.

"Alright." She smiled. "Just the one."

Four hours later, Tom was the first to go home.

"One for the road?" Anthony asked Vanessa.

"Why? Does the road need me semiconscious?"

"You tell me," said Anthony quietly.

Vanessa giggled and shoved him playfully on the arm. She picked up her handbag.

"I really must go," she managed. "I have an entire family to heckle."

"Sounds wonderful."

With considerable messing about, they collected all their belongings and pushed their way out of the by then heaving wine bar. Outside, the fresh night air sobered them up enough to feel slightly self-conscious.

"Are you getting a cab?" asked Vanessa.

"Nah. Where you going?"

"North. Highgate. You?"

"Notting Hill. I'll catch the tube."

A cab appeared, and Anthony waited contentedly by its door, watching Vanessa lean into the window to give her address to the driver. Before opening the door, he stepped an inch toward her. They were eye to eye. She could smell the mingled aroma of smoke and aftershave.

"Night then," he smiled.

"Night then."

It started off as a fairly friendly good night kiss, perhaps a tad unnecessary for a business meeting, but pleasant nonetheless. It ended up, however, as something very different. Before the cab had rung up a fiver, Anthony had mastered most of the curves that had been preoccupying him of late and Vanessa had transformed into the woman she once was. It was as much of a discovery for her as it was for him.

Eventually, they stepped apart for some air. Vanessa leaned against the cab door, catching her breath. Her legs were trembling.

"Night then," she mumbled, turning without looking back.

"Night then," whispered Anthony, drawing himself back into the cold.

Vanessa stumbled into the cab and sat down heavily, her lips hot and stinging, her stomach liquid acid. As the cab driver put down his sandwich and set off, she was thrown into the back of the seat and started to feel very sick indeed.

When she flicked on the kitchen light, Vanessa found Jo sitting at the kitchen table.

"Oh!" she jumped. "What are you doing? Spying in the dark?"

Jo gave a little smile. "Josh is showering. I thought I'd give him some privacy."

"Oh God," moaned Vanessa, making herself a nightcap. "I'm so sorry you've got to put up with him. It's ridiculous I know. Homeless in Highgate, living rent-free in his father's house, age twenty-five. I ask you. Dick hasn't got a clue."

Jo's jaw dropped. "Rent-free?" she breathed.

"God yes. Poor little rich boy."

"I-I had no idea. He pays . . . absolutely nothing?"

"Absolutely nothing."

Jo couldn't speak. She thought of how young she was when she'd started paying rent to her parents. She thought of how hard Shaun worked. She thought of the holidays Sheila had missed because she hadn't worked enough on weekends. It was as if someone had deflated the bright balloon that was Josh.

Vanessa went to the drinks cabinet and took a long look at Jo.

"Don't go falling for the famous Josh Fitzgerald charms," she said kindly. "Twenty-five going on fourteen. Of course," she added, tapping her nose with her finger and spilling some whiskey on the floor, "that's all between you and me."

"Of course," whispered Jo.

After a swig of whiskey, Vanessa started up again.

"I suppose Dick's been watching television all night again?"

Jo tried to think what Dick had been doing.

"Of course he has!" Vanessa answered her own question. "I'm the only one who works around here. My husband's job is to have fun. My job is to make it possible for him to have fun. And you know what the funny thing is?"

Jo shook her head, preparing herself for something very unfunny.

"The funny thing is that my husband thinks he works hard!" Vanessa came and sat at the table. She leaned forward. "I'm so sick of my job I could puke. I hate it. It's exactly the same at my office as it is in my home. My job . . . my *job* . . . a job with its own title and a salary . . . is to make sure that everyone else gets to have all the fun and all the kudos."

"Oh dear."

"*And!*" she said, "And . . . it's not as if I get support from my husband. Oh no! He resents me. He resents the fact that I work my arse off to support our family. Hard to believe isn't it?"

Jo nodded.

"I spend every minute of every day working, supporting our family while Dick's doing God knows what—probably dallying with some woman for all I know, 'cos he sure as hell isn't selling any fucking records—and . . ." she worked herself up to a crescendo, "he *resents* me for it!"

"Oh dear."

"You know what my title should be?"

Jo shook her head.

"Shitwork manager. That's what I do. Manage all the shitwork. At home and in the office. All the invisible, dirty, thankless shitwork. I'm the eternal housewife of the operation. I spend every minute of every day massaging the geniuses' egos while making sure they work to deadline, brief, and budget, making sure the client doesn't know how much everyone hates them, and making sure a thirty-second ad is made at the end of it. And then I come home and do exactly the same here. Except without the ad, obviously. In fact, my job, by its very nature, is totally invisible. You only notice my job when things go wrong. In *fact*," her voice was rising, "the better I do my job, the more invisible it becomes. I *mean*," she was now ranting, "when the cogs are well oiled everyone assumes it must be easy to oil bloody cogs. Don't they?" She was now shouting. "But it's not! It's *impossible* to oil buddy clogs." She stopped, and said slowly and carefully, "*bloody cogs*." She paused. "I just do it bloody well."

In the pause that followed Vanessa drained her drink and walked precariously to the sink. "Bloody well," she repeated, "for not enough money and absolutely no kudos." She added her tumbler to the others in the sink.

"Oh," she exclaimed politely, staring into the sink. "We seem to be behind on the dishwasher schedule."

"I was just going to fill it and put it on after I'd finished my drink," said Jo.

"Ah good," said Vanessa, leaning against the sink and looking at the floor. "And I think I may have spilled some drink too." She looked back up at Jo. "What would we do without dishwashers eh?" she winked, woman to woman, then gave the kitchen a once-over. "Perhaps you could give the place a little tidy while you're at it. Right then. Better get to bed. I'm knackered. No peace for the wicked eh?"

Jo smiled.

"Do you want the light off again?" asked Vanessa. "Or will you need it on to finish up?"

"On please."

"Okay then," Vanessa said. "Sleep well."

Jo yawned as she watched her boss walk down the corridor and turn to go up the stairs.

When Jo heard Josh leave the bathroom and pad through her bedroom into his, shutting his door behind him, she got up, poured her unfinished drink down the sink, and started to transfer Vanessa's and Dick's evening tumblers into the dishwasher.

Meanwhile, Vanessa tiptoed up to Zak's room, hitting her forehead on the giant plastic dinosaur hanging from the door to scare robbers, and kissed him softly on his face. She sat on his bed and watched him sleep for a while. She went into Cassandra's room and found her, boiling hot, lying upside down on her bed. She swept her daughter's sweaty hair away from her face and kissed her on her unusually flushed cheek. Then she sat on her bed and watched her sleep. Finally, she entered Tallulah's room, where the little girl was breathing heavily, her eyelids flickering. She watched her sleep for a while. Eventually she crept into her own bedroom. Dick lay fast asleep, dead to the world.

She looked at him for a moment, then looked away. She got into bed and lay there, her body still reeling from Anthony's unexpected, expected kiss. Every time she closed her eyes to allow the familiar, trusty Harrison Ford to calm her anger and help her sleep, she got Anthony instead. His image seemed to be imprinted on her eyelids.

She opened her eyes and stared into the dark. Why wasn't her life simple like the rest of her family's? She lay awake for what felt like hours, reliving her secret like a naughty schoolgirl until the early hours.

Chapter 13

Shaun was visiting that weekend, so Jo would be unable to spend her Sunday with Pippa and the girls. They'd planned to all meet up on Saturday night, but her Friday night, Saturday, and Sunday were strictly reserved for him and him only. Which meant she had to make up for it on the Thursday night.

"That's brilliant," said Rachel. "Thursday night is ladies' night at the club."

"Fantastic," said Pippa. "Now all we need is to find some ladies."

They all shrieked with stupid laughter.

As they turned up at the club, Pippa gave Jo a little nudge.

"So," she said. "Shaun's coming tomorrow, eh?"

"Yup."

"Does Josh know he exists yet?"

"Nope."

"Never mind," said Pippa. "I'm sure he won't even notice."

"Mm. Thanks."

It was a brilliant night. Rachel and Gabriella decided that as they got in for free, they had to make up the difference in tequila slammers. Gabriella confessed that she fancied her boss's husband and thought he fancied her and proceeded to give all the tiny sordid details, and Pippa had a shocking story about a friend of a friend who had been caught wearing her boss's clothes. For Jo's part, she made a mental effort to forget all about Shaun, Josh, and Gerry and when it didn't work, got rat-arsed.

And after that, the evening just got better and better. In fact, when Jo got home and fell over Tallulah's Barbie tricycle in the pitch-black hall, it was undoubtedly one of the funniest things that had ever happened to her in her entire life. And then, when she tried to get up but fell down again, landing on her knee because her heel was caught in the wheel, she thought she was going to asphyxiate from laughter.

Ten minutes later, she crawled into the kitchen, exhausted. She had to wash her knee. Easy. She climbed onto the kitchen worktop, turned on the tap, soaking herself in the process and then, positioned on all fours over the sink, put her knee in it. She hiccuped as her long hair cascaded over her face into the sink.

"Bugger," she said. "Can't reachy reach. Can't reachy reach."

She really couldn't be bothered to get all the way off the work top, so she pushed one leg off the sink and tried to put the other one further in. Good thing she had such long legs and was wearing such a short skirt. Once her knee was wet enough, she tried to get the leg it was attached to out of the sink. Slowly but surely, she lowered the leg not in the sink, until eventually she had one foot on the floor and the other leg now at an uncomfortable angle on the worktop. She stood, breathing heavily.

"Oh deary deary dear," she said to herself. "Who's in a pick—" Hiccup. "Pardon. Who's in a pick—" Hiccup. "Pardon. Who's in a pick—" Hiccup. And then she laughed so much she almost fell over.

"Do you want any help?" someone said in the dark.

The shock of hearing Josh's voice from the kitchen table made her jump.

"No thanks," she said in a small voice, then swiveled her leg down and fell flat on her face.

There was a pause as a wave of humiliation washed over Jo's previous hysteria. As the pause continued, certain parts of her body began to hurt. She hoped that she'd imagined Josh's voice and the increasing pause convinced her of this. In the silence, she could just make out the pitiful sound of a drunk female starting to cry.

"Are you alright?" asked Josh, with a smile in his voice Jo could detect even through the haze that was her brain. "Don't panic," he said. "I'm coming." She heard him heave his leg off the kitchen table. "I'll be with you any hour now."

"Ow, ow, ow, ow, ow, *ow*" she explained, now weeping uncontrollably.

She couldn't understand where the tears were coming from, she just knew she couldn't stop them. She didn't know how long she was there before Josh was crouched next to her.

"I'd pick you up," he whispered, "but I can't pick up a teaspoon at the moment."

Jo hid her face in the floor. "I got you maimed," she whimpered.

"Please don't cry," begged Josh. "I'm a bloke. I don't know how to cope."

Jo mumbled something incoherent, which seemed to upset her even more.

Josh leaned in close and was almost intoxicated by her breath. "What's that?"

She mumbled it again.

He came in even closer. "I didn't quite catch—"

"I miss my mum and dad," She yelled into his ear. She started sobbing.

"Come on," whispered Josh. "Up you get, you'll be fine. Lean on me."

With considerable effort on both of their parts, Jo got up and leaned on him.

He flinched. "Not that hard."

Jo jumped away and was about to lose her balance when Josh gripped her firmly round the waist. They both fell against the worktop, their faces inches apart, their hips touching. Jo could feel Josh's breath on her lips. She closed her eyes. The room spun. She opened them again.

"Alright?" he whispered.

'Mmhmm,' she murmured, her bones softening. She let her body pour in toward his and steadied her head against his chest. Everything felt better now. She didn't dare move. Perhaps she could stay here forever. No, that was impossible, she had work tomorrow, and anyway, Shaun was coming to stay . . .

Her eyes opened suddenly. Shaun. Her boyfriend. Whom she had yet to tell Josh about. She was paralyzed. She was a wicked, bad person and she was paralyzed.

"Jo?" She heard his croak in her hair. His voice seemed to flow through her veins and it took every effort of willpower to pull herself away from him. Her throat was dry.

To her delicious horror, Josh's body followed her, his face leaning in toward hers.

She gasped.

He gasped.

She stared at him in the dark.

He stared back at her.

She tried to speak.

He inched toward her.

"Josh?" she whispered.

"Yes?" he whispered back.

She felt tears in her eyes. "I—"

"Yes?"

"I have a boyfriend."

Josh stopped.

"What?"

"Shaun. He's coming to stay tomorrow, we've been together for six years, he's proposed three times, he works in the construction industry."

Josh moved away, and she almost fell over.

"Right," he said, all warmth gone from his voice. "Let's get you to bed."

He guided her out of the kitchen, his had barely touching her.

"I'm so sorry, I should have told you—" the tears began again.

"Don't talk daft—"

"I just couldn't find the right time—"

"Now was perfect—"

"You hate me." She tried to turn toward him.

"I don't hate you." He gently moved her away.

"You do, you hate me."

"I don't hate you."

"You do, you hate me."

"Shut up, Jo."

Friday morning started fine and bright, which Jo could really have done without. She lay in bed torturing herself with regret. How could she have got so drunk? How could she be hungover the morning she was due to pick up Shaun? How the hell had she got into her nightshirt? She suddenly remembered what had happened when she got in last night. She cringed at the memory. The change in Josh's personality had totally unnerved her. She wondered if he would be back to normal today. Her stomach churned. Oh God. She couldn't face him. And she couldn't face Shaun. She wanted to die.

Talking of which, her body could see her point. Some breed of farmyard animal had nested in the roof of her mouth during the night, and from the feel and sound of it, her brain was escaping out of her ears. It took her a good few minutes to realize that the sound was actually Josh in the shower.

She heaved herself up, sat on the edge of her bed, and looked at her bedside clock. Mickey Mouse's long hand was nearly pointing at the twelve, which might have been why she found his smile particularly annoying this morning. She sat there for another five minutes before deciding that she was going to have to knock on the bathroom door.

She tapped gently. Nothing. She tried again. Nothing. Then just as she was about to hammer, the door opened and Josh stood there, a towel round his waist, water dripping off his torso. Her head jerked back in shock, which made it throb. "Yes?" asked Josh and then his eyes drifted to her chest. "Nice T-shirt," he said tightly. "Wile E. Coyote was my favourite, too."

She looked down at her T-shirt and frowned. Her head was not impressed by either action and let her know it in no uncertain terms.

I have to get in the shower," she croaked, "or the kids will be late for school."

Josh opened the door wide, letting it bang against the wall. "Don't let me stop you," he spoke loudly and walked past her. He was like a different person. To the sound of his door shutting, she stepped gingerly into the bathroom. She turned on the shower and stared at the falling water, wondering what she could have possibly drunk last night to make her feel this soul-destroyed.

Josh stood in his room, his body tense as he listened to Jo's shower. He lowered himself onto his futon. Then very slowly, he inched himself down so that he was lying on it. He was absolutely knackered. He'd hardly slept a wink all night. It wasn't so much the physical pain, which was making sleep hard enough, as the return of old prepubescent anxieties. He'd thought he was stronger than this. Everything, was so much easier when you had distance. He touched his forehead with his hand, then quickly moved it away again as soon as it made contact with the bruise between his eyes. He shifted into a more comfortable position.

But layered finely on top of those deep, familiar anxieties was a whole new set of fresh ones. He felt a strange, sick sense of confusion whenever he thought about last night. Jo turned out to be exactly the opposite of what he'd dared hope she was. And then, while a pattern of hateful, reassuring thoughts had made themselves at home in his head, he'd had to soothe her as she poured out her heart to him: She was terrified that her dad would die of a heart attack and her mum would die of loneliness. Oh yes, and by the way, she'd forgotten to mention she had a boyfriend. So could they just pretend that all the flirting and teasing and long lingering looks and that full-body hug and come-to-bed look and neck-nuzzling hadn't happened, because by the way, that boyfriend she'd just mentioned? He was coming to stay. And then she'd instructed him to turn his back and wait for her to change, which took another half an hour because for some bizarre reason she was all fingers and thumbs.

It had been three before he'd got to bed. And once he lay there in the dark—on his own, out of Jo's presence—everything became clearer. It was much easier to see the harsh truth when it wasn't couched in a honey-limbed, aqua-eyed package.

After a night of not much sleep, he'd woken with a start at six this morning, and had had an immediate sensation of gut rot. It would pass, he told himself. It was a necessary stage, and it would pass. In too much discomfort to toss and turn, he'd had no choice but to walk through her room to the bathroom. He'd cracked open the door between them and sidled into her room. All was still. He'd tiptoed slowly across the floor, keeping his eye on the sleeping form in bed to check that it didn't wake and do anything untoward like call six policemen to beat him to a pulp.

His eyes were accustomed to the dark by the time he reached Jo's bed, and he stopped midtrack as he looked down at her.

Her long dark hair was fanned out against the pillow, her skin flushed with sleep, her lips parted in a half smile, and although those wide, almond-shaped blue eyes were shut, he noticed that the thick black lashes were gently fluttering. Soft sleep noises whispered out of her mouth, and before he knew it his mind had escaped and was wondering what she was dreaming of.

His gaze moved slowly downward. The duvet was twisted round those endless legs, and the mischievous face of Wile E. Coyote, lying snugly between her gently rising and falling breasts, winked up at him, man to man. He took one last glance at her innocent-looking face and proceeded into the bathroom, where he had a considerably colder shower than usual.

By the time Jo was out of the shower, he had dried, dressed, and made it into the kitchen. The children were all there with Vanessa and Dick, Dick cajoling Zak to eat his cereal, Cassie tying Tallulah's shoelaces instead of eating breakfast, while Tallulah waved her pink glittery wand over the proceedings and Vanessa jotting down notes for Jo, issuing orders for all. Josh hardened himself to the image.

"Morning all!" he greeted them. "Who wants coffee?"

"Josh!" greeted Zak. "Will you play Batman with me after school? You can be the Joker."

"*Zak!*" yelled Dick. "Sit down and eat your cereal. I'm not going to tell you again."

"Good," said Zak. Parents were so thick sometimes.

Josh started putting the coffee on, hardly limping, but still moving slowly. When Jo finally came into the kitchen, he ignored the fact that she was paler than usual. Holding her head, she edged her way into the kitchen and apologized profusely for waking up so late. No one answered, and Vanessa, without looking at her, started giving her notes for the day. Jo nodded at them all, her eyes on the floor.

"Oh and I've got another meeting this afternoon," continued Vanessa, "and I don't know when it's going to end, so can you pick up Cassie from her extra drama class? You haven't got anything on have you?"

Jo's face fell.

"Oh God," she said. "I'm so sorry but I can't. Shaun's coming up today, don't you remember? I told you last week."

Josh leaned against the counter and started eating his cereal.

"Shit," muttered Vanessa.

"Shit," said Tallulah, waving her pink glittery wand over Zak's head.

"I'm really sorry," said Jo.

Josh tutted. "Why the fuck are you sorry?" he muttered through his cereal. "You're allowed to have a boyfriend."

"Fuck!" cried Zak, as Tallulah poked him in the eye with her pink glittery wand.

"Josh!" yelled Dick and Vanessa.

"Whoops. Sorry guys."

"If you can't keep a civil tongue in your mouth in front of the children, perhaps you could just not talk at all," said Vanessa.

"I said sorry!"

"I'm sure it was an accident, darling," said Dick. 'Much like your eloquent "shit." '

"Shit!" repeated Tallulah, as Zak threw cereal in her face.

Josh turned to Jo.

"You need to stop apologizing for your personal life, you know," he told her. "I hate to break it to you, but no one here gives a damn."

"Thank you, Josh," snapped Vanessa. "I don't think we need your help here."

"Well you need someone's help," countered Josh, "or you may end up with a child who feels abandoned, which can have nasty long-term effects."

"I'll do it," said Dick quickly. "I'll come home from work early. No problem. It'll be nice to spend some quality time with Josh, too."

Josh smiled. "There, that's all sorted then. Cassie won't feel abandoned, Dad and I get to spend time together and Jo gets to do whatever the hell she wants to do in her own personal life. Everyone's happy."

Jo blinked hard.

"Josh," said Vanessa. "Please try not to use the 'f' word in front of Cassie."

"Why?" asked Cassandra. "It's not as rude as the 'c' word. Even though that refers to a perfectly natural and beautiful part of the female body."

There was a moment's silence.

"Zak!" screeched Dick suddenly. Zak nearly fell off his chair. *"Eat your cereal! or Daddy's going to get angry!"*

When Jo sat in the Clio on her way to pick up Shaun from Highgate Station, she paused and took stock. This was her private space—much more so than her room, which almost felt like a shared room with Josh. She'd put her collection of small, cuddly toys in it as her lucky talismen and stared at them now to try and stabilize her thoughts.

It was the first time she'd been on her own for weeks and she was about to see Shaun for the first time in over a month, in just five minutes. And her head was jam-packed full of Josh. She wanted to apologize to him, but she wasn't sure which bit of her behavior she was apologizing for. And anyway that hadn't seemed to work last night. It was all so disconcerting—not just his Jekyll/Hyde turn, but how much she was letting it upset her.

She looked at the car clock. She was going to be late for Shaun. She tried staring at her cuddly toys again. They stared right back at her. None the wiser, she started the engine. As she drove down the steep slope toward Highgate Station's entrance, she wasn't surprised to feel a knot of tension in her stomach. And then she spotted him, sitting on the wall, reading a magazine.

Cheekbones like ice and eyes that matched his denim jacket and jeans. He'd washed his hair too. *Goodness me*, she thought. *Ambassador, you are spoiling us.* He didn't spot her for a while, and she parked nearby and watched him. After a moment, he looked up. They looked at each other for a second, and then both grinned as familiarity slowly seeped back into their lives.

As he got up and walked toward the car, Jo's breathing calmed. Everything was going to be alright, she was safe again. He opened the car door and leaned in, eyes twinkling in the sun.

"I wondered who that gorgeous girl was in the posh car." He grinned. "And then I realized it was my gorgeous girl."

To her surprise, Jo felt a wave of emotion wash over her, and she started crying.

Shaun quickly put his bag in the back and got into the car. "What's wrong?" he asked, looking straight ahead.

Jo flung her arms round his shoulder. "It's good to see you," she said, hugging with all her might.

Shaun closed his eyes, then held her tight until someone began hooting.

Jo really didn't want to take Shaun straight back to the Fitzgeralds', but she had the ironing and tidying to do, and Shaun said he didn't mind at all. Thank God Josh had gone out.

As it transpired, what Shaun meant was that he didn't mind seducing Jo while she tried to do the ironing. She finally gave up and they had a quick catch-up session in her bedroom. It had been nice, but she'd have preferred it if she hadn't been listening for the door with one ear, worrying about the ironing with half her mind and thinking of Josh with the rest of her body. She did enjoy the novelty aspect of making love to Shaun after such a long time. Even though they followed their well-practiced technique, it didn't feel predictable, it just felt safe and comforting, like coming home. *Or rather*, she thought, *coming at home.*

As soon as it was over, she leaped out of bed, dressed, and started the ironing again.

After ten minutes, Shaun joined her in the kitchen, pulling his shirt over his head.

Half an hour later, he watched her iron her fourth Barbie vest with impressive speed. He looked up at the kitchen clock occasionally, sipping his tea.

"There's something wrong with this tea," he said.

"It's leaves. Proper tea leaves."

"Tastes like shit."

"You get used to it. I'll get some PG Tips in."

"Thanks, babe."

He stared at the tiny items of clothing that Jo still had to iron. Eventually, he got up and washed his mug in the sink. He'd seen taps like this in some of the new houses his teams had been commissioned to build. He mastered how the tap worked in only a few minutes. Afterward, as calmly as he could, he tore some kitchen towels off the chrome holder on the wall and wiped his groin.

He turned and watched Jo.

"Why are you ironing the boy's pants?" he asked.

Jo glanced over.

"Can you take the paper off your groin while you talk to me, please?"

He grinned. "Come here and say that."

"I'm ironing them because he won't wear them otherwise," she answered. "It's difficult enough to get him to wear them when they are ironed. Downright impossible if they're not."

Shaun shook his head wearily. "What's wrong with kids today?" he muttered. "What he needs is a good clip round the ear. He'd wear them then."

"Mm," agreed Jo. "And a woman's place is in the home."

"If he was your own kid, you could do it. No child of mine would ever expect his nanny to iron his pants."

Jo put Zak's pants on the table and picked up the Tweenies pillowcase. "But then no child of yours would have a nanny would they?" she asked. They'd been through this so many times, but today they were both saying it with half a smile on their faces. It was nice to know that some things never changed.

"Nope," he said, adopting the tone of a Texas cowboy. "I'd find me a real woman who could be a real mother."

Jo stopped ironing for a split second and looked up at him. "You mean you'd expect her to do all this for no money?" She grinned. "Tell me, Shaun—"

"Oh dear—"

"—do you think the child's father isn't a real father because he's not ironing his son's pants? Or is it just the mother who's fighting her genetic programming by not ironing?"

"Don't start," said Shaun. "You know what I mean."

"Oh yes," said Jo. "I know exactly what you mean."

"I mean a nice, happy family."

"Where the woman's life gets shrunk to fit her home, and the man's expands—"

"Where the man earns the money that puts the roof over their heads, that's what I mean."

"Ooh," said Jo. "It sounds lovely. Just like in *The Waltons*."

"That's right."

"That anachronistic fictional escapism. For children."

"You know, you don't need to use posh words to impress me. Your arse is doing a good enough job already."

Jo smiled. "Oh you sweet-talker, you."

Shaun came and stood behind her and kissed her gently on her neck. Then he gave her another, even softer kiss further down her neck. Then he twisted her body round to face him and softly brushed his lips over her front. Then he pushed her up against the ironing board and started messing up the ironing. Then Josh came home.

"Don't mind me," called Josh, and they both jumped. As it happened, they both minded him very much. Jo spun back to her ironing, her face burning. She could hardly bear the new coldness in Josh's eyes. She felt like some scarlet woman in a bad movie. Shaun waited a moment before stepping forward to Josh.

"Shaun Casey," he said, holding out his hand. "Jo's better half."

"Josh Fitzgerald," said Josh, shaking his hand firmly. "Half brother, half human."

"Oh right," grinned Shaun. "So not one of her charges then?"

"God no."

"So she isn't tucking you up in bed, too?" he laughed.

Josh let out a short sharp laugh. "Nope. If anything, it's the other way round."

The laughter stopped. Shaun looked over at Jo.

"I-I got a little drunk last night," she explained.

Shaun tensed. "Right," he said between his teeth.

"Then she got a little homesick," explained Josh, "you know the thing, missing her mum, missing her dad, missing"—he gave a little shrug—"her mum and dad."

Shaun nodded. "Right," he said slowly.

"Anyway," said Josh tightly, "don't let me interrupt what you were doing. I know Jo always puts everyone's needs before her own. Nice to meet you, Saul."

"Shaun."

"Shaun."

And Josh left them to it.

Jo ironed three pairs of Zak's pants before Shaun spoke.

"What the hell was all that about?" he whispered.

"What?" she answered innocently.

"Don't play games, Jo."

Jo sighed.

She spoke very quietly. "I don't know what he's talking about. I got drunk last night and told him all about you. That's all. It must be hurt ego. Probably expected me to fancy him, you know, poor little homesick nanny."

She wondered who she was turning into as Shaun settled back down to watch her finish the ironing. After five minutes, they heard the front door slam shut. Josh had gone out for his afternoon walk.

"So why's he at home then?" asked Shaun.

"I got him maimed because I thought he was going to kill me with an ax, so he's been working from home to avoid getting his twisted ankle broken in rush hour. He's back at work soon, thank God."

"No I don't mean that. I mean why's he living here at all?"

"God knows."

"What does he do?"

"He's an accountant."

Shaun sucked in a vast amount of air between his teeth, a trick he'd learned from years in the building trade.

"So he's loaded, right?"

Jo shrugged. "No idea." She finished the laundry and put the ironing board and iron away in the utility room. "Apparently his flatmates went traveling," she called out. "Left him homeless."

"They must all be made of money," shouted Shaun. "If I had that sort of money, I'd be putting it into the future. Put a deposit on a house. Invest it."

Jo loaded the washing machine.

"Maybe they can do both," she said quietly.

"I bet that's not the real reason he's here," shouted Shaun.

Jo came back into the kitchen, put down the empty laundry basket and started filling it with piles of neatly folded ironing.

"What do you mean?"

"I don't trust him."

"I told you, there's nothing to worry about. I just got drunk—"

"Not about that," interrupted Shaun. "Just generally. His eyes are too close together."

"They look fine to me," said Jo quickly. "I'm going upstairs, follow me."

Shaun followed her up the stairs into Tallulah's bedroom, and leaned against the doorframe as she tidied up the child's toys. Jo picked up the orgy of naked Barbies and Ken and dressed them all. Then she placed Tallulah's Barbie Doctor, Barbie Civil Servant, Barbie Social Worker, and Ken Architect in their allotted space underneath the stationery shelves, checking that the 0.6mm lilac pens abutted the 0.6mm purple pen and not the 0.8mm blue.

"Why would a grown man," continued Shaun, "with money to burn, come back home and live with Daddy and Daddy's new wife and precocious kids if he could afford not to?"

"They're not precocious," she said, returning the dolls' house figures to the library by the Dickens classics.

"I think," said Shaun slowly, "that our Josh is a bit of a sponger. I take it he's not paying rent?"

"No," said Jo. "Vanessa said he was rent-free. How did you know that?"

Shaun laughed. "I've done up houses for blokes like him. So spoiled they don't realize they're grown-ups."

Jo looked at him. "Follow me," she said, and went up the next flight of stairs.

"Bugger me," said Shaun. "How many floors does this house have?"

"This is it."

Shaun followed her into Zak's room and stopped at the door. He gave a slow, appreciative whistle at the toys.

"Shit," he said. "I could be very happy in here."

A top-of-the-line scooter sat beside the myriad robots, signed Arsenal football memorabilia, dinosaur collection, and racetrack. Gameboys littered the room. Above the bed hung a hammock full of more toys. In the corner was a small television and some more Gameboys. Shaun tore his eyes away and got back to the point.

"I've got it!" he cried.

"Well don't come near me," muttered Jo from under Zak's bed, "I can't catch it. Can't take time off."

"Josh knows something about Daddy that Daddy doesn't want new wifey to know. And in return for keeping the secret, Josh has wheedled free rent and food from Daddy."

Jo stopped folding Zak's track suit bottoms.

"You think Dick's having an affair?"

Shaun shrugged. "Or had one in the past. He had one when he was married to Josh's mum, didn't he?"

"That's a horrid thought," murmured Jo. She gasped. "Mind you, Vanessa did say she thought something was going on. And he does come home very late. Bloody hell."

"I dunno," said Shaun. "I just think there's more to Joshua than meets the eye. How old was he when Daddy left?"

"Fourteen. Vanessa told me it was an awful marriage. They were rowing all the time." Shaun shook his head and sucked in his breath again. "Bad age. Bad age for your dad to leave."

Jo decided not to tell Shaun that's exactly what Josh had confided to her. Anyway, it was beginning to strike her that maybe Vanessa was right about Josh. He seemed able to switch the charm on and off like a light.

"Bet you never get over that." Shaun was still talking. "And it was rarer then, wasn't it? Bet he was teased at school. Poor bastard. Must be really fucked up. Watching Daddy with his new kids all the time. It's sick."

Jo sat down on Zak's bed. "Yeah, suppose it is."

"So," continued Shaun, "he can't exactly like his stepmum much can he? Or his stepbrothers and -sisters?"

"He said . . . he mentioned briefly that he did."

"Well of course he's going to say that, isn't he?" said Shaun.

"Yes. S'pose so."

"And yet he's chosen to live with them instead of finding his own place."

They stared at each other.

"Maybe . . ." said Shaun, "he's spying for his mum?"

Jo shuddered. "She's a bitch. Big-time."

"Ah!" said Shaun. "But I bet Josh loves her."

"Of course he does."

"Well there you go! She's got Josh to sponge off the dad who left him, while spying for her at he same time."

Jo sat motionless on the bed. Maybe, just maybe, that would explain why he was so friendly to her so quickly. Come to think of it, he'd plied her with drink and then he'd started confiding in her the first night they met—maybe he was trying to ingratiate himself with her so that she could help him spy on Vanessa? She thought back to that first conversation. How he'd been so insistent to know what she thought of them all. And how he'd given away so much about himself. She thought back to Dick telling her that Josh was a ladies' man and Vanessa warning her not to fall for the famous Josh Fitzgerald charm.

After a moment, she shook her head, utterly confused and feeling increasingly depressed.

"I don't think so—"

Shaun shrugged. "I dunno. I'm probably just imagining it all.

"We shouldn't be talking like this," said Jo suddenly. "They probably have a video cam up the cyberdog's nose."

Shaun laughed. "How does he smell?" he asked.

"He doesn't," replied Jo, scanning the tidy room. "He's not real. Follow me."

"Haven't you finished yet?"

"No. And the quicker I do it the sooner we can go out." She walked back downstairs and started tidying the kitchen.

"You have to admit the boy's good-looking," said Shaun.

"Who?"

"Josh."

"Are you still going on about him?"

"I'm not going on about him, I'm just saying you have to admit he's good-looking."

Jo let out a wry laugh. "I don't have to admit anything," she said, filling the dishwasher. "I want my lawyer."

"Oh come on," said Shaun. "You must have noticed. If you like the poncey, public school type."

"Never occurred to me."

"Oh come on."

"Alright," she said, putting her hands on her hips. "He's good-looking."

Shaun didn't answer.

"Perhaps you could actually help instead of just pestering me," she said.

"Right," said Shaun, joining her in loading the dishwasher while reminding himself to quit while he was ahead next time.

Jo knew exactly where to take Shaun on Friday night. Saturday night the girls were taking them both up to a great nightclub in town, so tonight she wanted to keep it local. She'd spotted a tiny French restaurant on Highgate High Street, which looked adorably cute. Shaun loved French food, and she'd booked ahead.

"We've only got two hours there," she told Shaun as they walked up the hill.

"What do you mean?" he asked. "They chuck you out?"

"Not exactly, but they use the table twice in one evening. You can't book it for the whole evening."

"Bloody hell."

"It's a tiny restaurant."

"And that's *our* problem?"

"No, it's just—look, it's special."

"What, as in 'special needs'?"

She linked her arm with his.

"Come on," she coaxed. "Don't spoil it, we've only got one night alone."

Shaun unlinked their arms and put his arm round her shoulder, squeezing her tight as they continued up the hill. He stopped at every estate agent they passed, which took considerable time as there were more estate agents than newsagents on Highgate Hill.

"Jesus Christ!" he exclaimed. "Look at the prices!" He started laughing. "And Londoners think they're better than us!"

"No they don't."

"Look at that one! And it's only a two-bed flat. We could get a mansion for that at home."

"Yes," but you wouldn't be in London."

"I know!" he cried. "Brilliant!"

When they finally reached the restaurant, Jo led Shaun to the tiny window and made him peer in.

He smiled down at her, and she felt a weight lift from her shoulders. "Very nice," he said. They walked down the narrow covered pathway to the side entrance and were led to the one table in the restaurant window. The waitress handed them their menus.

"Jesus Christ!" whispered Shaun. "Look at the prices!"

"*Shaun!*" hissed Jo, flushing.

"No wonder the Fitzgeralds pay you so much."

"Shaun," asked Jo. "Why are you spoiling this?"

Shaun looked up at her. He held her hand over the table. "Am I? I didn't realize," he said. "Sorry. It's all just a bit new to me, that's all."

"I suppose I've got used to some things."

Shaun gave a twitch of his eyebrows, which Jo pretended not to see.

When the waitress came over, Jo was about to order, when to her amazement, Shaun ordered for them both.

"What are you doing?" she interrupted.

"I'm ordering. What do you think I'm doing?"

"How do you know what I want?"

Shaun frowned. "You like it when I order for you."

"I do not."

"Yes you do, you always say you can't make up your mind."

"Well," said Jo uncomfortably, "I can now."

The waitress stopped writing. "Shall I come back?" she asked.

"Yes," said Shaun.

"No," said Jo. "We both know what we want, thanks."

When Jo made her order, she looked straight at the waitress. Shaun ordered his usual, French onion soup and rack of lamb. When the waitress left them alone again, they looked at each other.

"So, since when did you like gravlax?" asked Shaun.

"Since I tried it."

"What is it when it's at home?"

"Dry-cured salmon marinated in herbs."

Shaun tutted and shook his head.

When their food was brought to them, Shaun eyed Jo's suspiciously. "Looks like leather."

Jo gave him a look, and he shut up. They ate the rest of their meal in silence, occasionally interrupted by Shaun remarking how tasty the food was.

When they walked back, Jo started to tell him about the new friends she'd met and ignored the lack of enthusiasm in his responses. She supposed it was a bit unsubtle, telling him how happy she was, so she stopped. Instead, she began to describe the kids. When he started sighing at her tales of how much work she was expected to do and told her to have a word with her boss, she stopped. She was relieved when they got home.

Dick and Vanessa were in the lounge with the door shut, so they were able to tiptoe unnoticed into Jo's room.

Half an hour later, Shaun rolled away from her and fell asleep. She lay in bed wondering if Josh had heard anything.

Chapter 14

Saturday morning, Jo woke early. She listened intently for any noises coming from Josh's bedroom. If he was in bed, they would have to be quiet. If he wasn't, it meant he'd seen them in bed together on his way through her room. This was beginning to feel intolerable. Then she heard a very loud yawn and knew that Josh was still in bed. Worse, he was letting them know he was in bed. Even worse, if she could hear him yawning, he would have heard last night's noises.

She got out and went into the bathroom for her shower and took her clothes in with her to change. She'd hoped Shaun would have woken up by the time she returned, but he was absolutely fast asleep. She knew Josh would want to get dressed, but was trapped until he knew they were both finished. She shook Shaun. He grunted. She shook him again. He grunted again. She whispered his name in his ear. He smiled. She whispered it again. He grabbed her round the waist and pulled her onto the duvet. When he realized she was serious and not coming back into bed, he opened his eyes. "Crikey, you're dressed," he said. "What time is it?"

Jo looked over at Mickey Mouse, whose grin seemed frustratingly knowing. "Eight."

Shaun moaned. "You mean we don't get a lie in?"

"We can't."

"Why?"

"Because he can hear everything."

"Who?"

Jo pointed her head at Josh's door. "Josh."

"His room's there?"

She nodded.

"Bloody hell."

"He'll hear everything."

"Good," he said, and tried to grab her again.

"No, Shaun."

He started tickling her and despite herself, she started giggling. Shaun always knew exactly where to get her.

"Stop it!" she shouted eventually. "Leave me alone!"

Shaun stopped it and left her alone."

"I'm going to put on some coffee," she whispered. "Get in that shower immediately or I'm going out without you."

Shaun grinned up at her. Anything you say, sexy," he said at full volume.

"Shhhhh."

As soon as Jo shut the door behind her, Shaun yawned very loudly and started whistling the theme tune to *The Italian Job*.

Jo opened the door and shushed him again, nodding toward Josh's room again. Shaun stopped.

"*Oh yeah!*" he hissed loudly enough to be heard in Niblet. "*Sorry.*"

They spent the afternoon wandering round Covent Garden, watching the buskers and eating ice cream. The weather was idyllic—it was turning out to be a beautiful spring—and it reminded Jo of their first few months together all those years ago. And yet, she couldn't seem to get rid of a nasty feeling of guilt. As she watched a juggler while Shaun made a work call on his mobile, she retraced her steps, waiting for the guilt to reappear. She pinpointed the feeling back to her bedroom, but Shaun was the only person who'd been in her bedroom, and she didn't think she'd said anything to hurt him. Or had she? He didn't look hurt, he looked very busy behind his shades, eating his ice cream and chatting on the phone. Good.

Later that evening, they made their way to the nightclub where they were to meet Pippa, Gabriella, and Rachel. Jo found them already in the queue.

"Hiya!" she called out. "This is Shaun." She held him forward on her arm and basked in their appreciative gazes.

"We've heard so much about you!" greeted Rachel.

"Lovely to meet you," added Gabriella, taking his hand in hers.

Jo was extremely grateful to her friends.

Pippa stretched out her hand. "Hi." She grinned. "I'm Pippa. Really glad to meet you. Jo talks about you all the time."

Once they were inside, Pippa came up beside her.

"You're a dark horse, aren't you?" She grinned.

"Am I?"

"Yes, he's gorgeous!"

Jo smiled. "Mm."

"How's it going?"

Jo nodded slowly quite a few times before answering.

"Fine thanks," she said. "Yeah. Fine."

Then she spotted Shaun chatting to Gabriella and stopped nodding.

"Come on," said Pippa. "Looks like someone needs saving."

"Yeah," said Jo. "But which one?"

When they got there, Shaun gave them both a great big grin.

"Hello there!" he said. "Gabriella was just telling me all about being a nanny."

Gabriella gave a little smile. "Aiy was telling 'eem all abowt Joshua," she said, "and 'ow mush wee all luff about 'eem."

Pippa gave Jo a sympathetic glance.

"Oh yeah, that might have come up," said Shaun, eyes on the dance floor. "Wanna dance?"

When they got home, he collapsed into bed. "God I'm knackered," he said loudly into his pillow.

Jo sat down on the bed and looked at him. Was she a terrible woman? She wanted to say something, but she couldn't think of anything, so she went to sleep instead.

Sunday was a lazy day. Jo and Shaun woke to the smell of brewing coffee and warm brioche.

"Blimey," mumbled Shaun, rubbing his stubble against her neck. "How the other half lives, eh?"

Josh wasn't up yet either, so Jo spent another morning shushing Shaun, who seemed unable to lower his voice. Unsurprisingly, Josh appeared in the kitchen half an hour after they did. Jo was unable to meet his eye.

She was determined that Shaun meet all the Fitzgeralds, because she felt it was the right thing to do. Toby was there for the weekend as usual, so after Shaun had finished his calls, he was treated to Sunday lunch with the family.

"What's wrong with normal tomatoes?" He smiled at Vanessa when he'd found sun-blushed ones in his salad.

"Nothing at all," replied Vanessa. "We're just rather addicted to sun-blushed ones."

"Addicted?" he smiled. "Gosh, that sounds serious."

"What do you mean?" asked Tallulah, giving him an intense stare from across the table.

"I'm just joking with your mummy." Shaun winked.

"Why?" she asked.

"Because, sweetheart," said Josh, "he's trying to be funny and superior at the same time."

"Now now," said Dick. "Shaun's a guest."

"He's not a guest of ours," said Toby. "He's a guest of Jo's. Because he's having sex with her. Josh heard them last night."

"Oy, mate," rushed Josh. "That was a secret."

"You said Shaun sounded like a car with a flat battery," snorted Toby. Jo stopped eating.

"I like your goldfish," Shaun said.

"What's a flat battery?" asked Tallulah.

"He's called Homer," Cassandra told Shaun.

"What shape should a battery be?" asked Tallulah.

"After the writer of *The Odyssey*," added Jo quickly.

Shaun looked at her. "Thanks."

"So," said Dick. "Back at work tomorrow eh, Josh?"

"Mm," said Josh. "Can't wait."

"Ready to brave the tube then?"

"Mm. Well, I'll have to see. I'll walk to the bus stop and if it hurts too much doing that, I'll take the bus all the way in instead of getting it to the tube. It will take much longer, but it won't cause complete agony."

"Don't be ridiculous," said Vanessa. "Jo will give you a lift to the station and pick you up when you come home. She drives past it all day long with the kids in tow."

"No need," said Josh. "It's fine."

"Jo," said Vanessa. "That will be okay, won't it?"

Jo glanced at Shaun, who stuffed some brioche into his mouth while watching her.

"Of course," she said dully.

"No need," repeated Josh.

"Don't be a martyr, Josh," said Vanessa. "It doesn't suit you."

There was a pause.

"Okay," Josh agreed. "Cheers."

"Jo, will you be able to take him until his ankle's completely better?" asked Dick.

"Mm," said Jo.

"Won't be long now," mumbled Josh into his brioche.

"No problem," whispered Jo, who concentrated on her breakfast.

And then the children got very excited about the thought of Josh joining them on the school run, and any sense of decorum they might have enjoyed up until then was abandoned.

Shaun and Jo weren't alone again until she was driving him back to Highgate Station that evening.

"So," he said.

"So."

"Scrounger boy gets driven to school by nanny, just like his baby brother and sisters."

Jo grunted. "Does seem a bit rich, doesn't it?"

"What the hell's wrong with him taking the bus? Anyone would think he was still in short trousers."

"At least Vanessa made it so that I don't have to go too much out of my way or leave earlier. And I suppose it was all my fault."

"How d'you figure that?"

"Well it's because of me that he got so battered and bruised."

"And it's because of him that you got scared out of your wits!" exclaimed Shaun.

"What the hell did he think he was doing, breaking in like that? What he did was moronic."

There was a pause.

"That's not what you said when I first told you. You told me off."

"Yeah, well, I've had time to think. And I've met him."

"It never even occurred to me to be annoyed with him for scaring me so much."

"Well it should have. Dick and Vanessa have shown you that they think you were right, and he was wrong. And he's a tosser for giving you the cold shoulder for giving his ego a knock."

She looked down at her hands. "Yeah. Maybe you're right."

"You know I'm right."

"Thanks." She smiled. "You protect me."

"Course I do," said Shaun. "I'm your man."

Jo smiled as she parked at the station. Shaun turned to her.

"Well."

"Well."

"It's been a gorgeous weekend, gorgeous."

"It has, hasn't it?"

He kissed her, and she gave him a hug. "I'm going to try and come home the weekend after next," she told him.

"Try?"

"I'm just so tired by the weekend I haven't got the energy to travel."

"Right."

As she hugged him, he whispered in her ear, "Don't let the buggers get you down," and they hugged a bit tighter.

Then Jo watched him walk toward the station. When he reached the top of the stairs, he turned round and gave her a wave. She waved back, suddenly feeling lower than she had since she'd first arrived in London.

Chapter 15

Jo woke early on Monday morning, aware that Josh would need to get into the shower soon for his first day back at work. Mickey's long arm was not even near the six, let alone the twelve and she thought disturbing thoughts about both Mickey and Josh until it was time to get up. She tried to pretend Shaun was still there to make her feel better, but it didn't work.

She got ready in half the usual time and was preparing Tallulah for the spring rain when Josh appeared in the kitchen.

"Morning." He yawned.

"Look!" instructed Tallulah. "I'm wearing my wellies. They've got pink flowers on. Look."

"Well done," said Josh, walking to the fridge.

"Wait!" cried Tallulah. "You haven't seen the ones on the back."

"Gosh, sorry," said Josh. "Wow. Wow. Wowee. Those are ay-mazing flowers."

Tallulah smiled. "Told you," she said quietly.

Josh opened the fridge door.

"Blimey," he muttered. "Six pints of milk. Have they ever thought of investing in a cow?"

He turned to them and saw Jo looking at Tallulah's feet.

"Popsie," she said in a soft voice. "You've got them on the wrong feet."

Tallulah stared at her feet and frowned.

I haven't got any other feet," she said, worried.

Jo laughed and took Tallulah's little face in her hands.

"I adore you, piglet"—she kissed her on the cheek—"but you need to swap them over quickly like a big girl, or we'll all be late."

Josh watched as Jo collected Tallulah's packed tea break that she'd prepared earlier and put Zak's football and recorder in his schoolbag. Jo looked over at him.

"Ready?" she asked.

"Yep."

She looked at Tallulah's feet again. Sweetiepie, you've done it again."

Tallulah studied her feet. Then she looked up at Jo, mild panic surfacing on her little face. Jo was busy looking for the car keys.

"I'll do it," said Josh, and slowly crouched down to help Tallulah with her boots. When he finished he looked up at her and found her staring at him intensely. The look seeped through his skin.

"Right, we're off," called Jo. "Are you ready, Josh?"

"I've been ready for an hour, miss," he said. He looked back at Tallulah. "She's scary isn't she?" he whispered.

"Not when you get to know her," answered Tallulah, putting her hand in his and leading him to the front door.

"Right!" yelled Jo to the others. "Come on!"

After Zak and Cassandra had been deposited at their schools, Tallulah fell asleep and snored magnificently. Alone with Josh in the car, except for Snoring Beauty in the back, Jo felt Shaun's disapproval as plainly as if he were another presence in the car. After a while, she decided the air needed clearing and forced herself to speak.

"Listen," she started. "I'm sorry."

"What about?"

"That night. When I got drunk."

"You're sorry about getting drunk?"

"No." She sighed. He was going to make this difficult. "I'm sorry about the way I told you about Shaun."

Josh snorted. "Jesus, I'd forgotten about that."

"Well I hadn't. And I'm sorry."

"D'you think you've broken my poor little heart or something?"

"No, I just—"

"You just what? Thought I was going to make a play for you?"

"No—"

"Listen, if it's on tap, of course I'm going to go for it. What bloke wouldn't? And you were certainly on tap that night—"

Jo gasped in shock.

"But anything more than that, and you're living in some little chicklit fantasy world. You've seen too many Hollywood films. Sorry to disappoint you."

Jo bit her lip and blinked hard. She didn't trust herself to speak again.

They reached Highgate Station in silence. Josh opened the door and slowly heaved himself out of the car.

He stood in the door. "So," she heard him say in the same infuriatingly happy tone. "I'll see you back here as arranged."

"Fine," said Jo, staring ahead of her.

"By the way," he said. "You didn't sound anything like a car with a flat battery." And he slammed the door.

Jo sat for a while, watching him hobble off, tears stinging the back of her eyes. At least she knew where she stood. She'd let her imagination run wild like the complete girl that she was, and now she'd made an absolute fool of herself. She could kick herself; it was the oldest trick in the book and she'd fallen for it. The minute he discovered that he wasn't going to get into her bed, he'd simply dropped the charm offensive and turned into the real Josh—a rude, arrogant bastard. The kind of bloke who'd call a new nanny on speakerphone to laugh at her with his office colleagues. Thank God she'd found out before making a big mistake.

Josh felt strangely vulnerable on the tube. People sat so near to each other, his arm was actually touching the arm of the man next to him. He'd forgotten how invasive it all was. From Highgate, the journey was more straightforward than from Crouch End, but far uglier. He was used to buses and overland trains. On the underground, even outside rush hour, people were a different, harder breed, as though all traces of humanity got suffocated in the dark.

The thought of changing from the Northern Line at Tottenham Court Road onto the Central Line, getting off two stops later and still being further away from his office than he was used to, tired him, both physically and mentally. As people rushed past, he felt the need to hold out his arms so that they didn't bump into him. If he could, he'd have worn an L-plate.

As he progressed, increasingly slowly, toward his office, he felt a familiar depression start to loom. He then realized that he hadn't felt this bad all the days he'd been away from the office. Then it dawned on him that before he'd spent time off from work, he'd felt this bad every single morning. He'd just got used to it.

As he turned into the street where his office block stood, he vowed that he wouldn't let himself get used to feeling this bad again; he'd harness the emotion of last week and use the memory of it to inspire him to change his life.

As he reached his office, he savored his last few minutes of freedom and sunlight. The next eight hours were not his own. He'd sold them to the highest bidder. With a sinking heart, he climbed the grey stone steps to his office.

By lunchtime Josh had got back into the stride of things. The cliché was true, it was like riding a bike. True, he still felt tired and a tad excluded from the office politics that were usually the only fun of his job, but he knew that would only be a matter of time.

When Sally appeared at the corner of his desk, ever so slightly arching her back while assuming a coy air, he looked at her as though she was from another planet.

"Welcome back," she purred.

He smiled at her from behind his desk. It was a very distinct smile, a smile many had made before and many would make again. It said loud and clear, "I am a coward. I do not want to openly tell you It's Over, because that would mean a) making a decision and b) taking control. But you'll get the message and make the decision for me. I thank you."

"I've missed you," she said with a coy air, while arching her back a little more.

Josh made a mental note to work on his smile, while wondering what on earth had possessed him to possess this woman. He felt as though a switch that had once been clicked to ON inside his body—the switch that connected every single nerve fiber to his brain with the compelling message "Sally Is a Fox; Must Act"—had been clicked to the OFF position. There was nothing he could do about it. It was an animal thing.

"Wanna show me your bruises?" she was now whispering.

With some horror, Josh realized showing anyone his bruises was not something he'd ever feel up to doing, least all to this woman. The last thing his bruises felt like was sexy. In fact, he could feel most of his bodily organs shrinking just remembering how he got them. His phone rang, making him jump, and with an apologetic glance at Sally, he picked it up on the first ring.

"Josh? It's Toby."

"Josh put all his energies into sounding relaxed and chirpy as Sally slowly—and if he wasn't mistaken, coyly, while arching her back—walked away.

"Hiya, how are you doing?" he said into the phone.

There was a long pause.

"Fine," squeaked Toby.

With Sally gone, Josh could focus his mind on the call. He realized his kid brother was trying not to cry, which was making his voice go up by about two octaves.

"What's the matter, mate?" he asked softly into the phone.

Another pause.

"I'm a bit . . . down," squeaked Toby.

"Course you are, mate. You're thirteen and you're at school. Life's shit."

Toby snorted.

"Mind you," Josh went on. "Life doesn't get much better when you're twenty-five and at work, but at least they pay you and you've had sex."

Toby made a strange guttural sound, which almost became a snort of laughter.

A group of fellow schoolboys ran past Toby at the pay phone and he turned himself to face the wall. After they'd passed, he put his elbow up on the phone and rested his head in the cup of his hand, hiding his face from the stairs leading to the science labs behind him.

"Are you gonna be at Dad's this weekend?" he sniffed.

"Yeah, I live there now full-time," said Josh. "I told you last weekend, but you were more concerned with pulling Tallulah's hair, as I recall."

"What are you doing Saturday?"

Josh paused before he spoke. "Spending the day with my favorite kid brother, that's what."

Another long pause.

"Thanks," squeaked Toby.

"Now, go and wash your face, take a brisk walk, then gratuitously pick on someone smaller than you."

Toby wiped his eyes furiously with his hand.

"See you Friday night," said Josh. "Think of what you'd like to do on Saturday."

When he heard the phone ring off at Toby's end, Josh sat brooding on a familiar theme for a while. He hated Toby's school with a vengeance. If he had the money, he'd gladly pay for his kid brother to be at a better one.

He picked up a pencil and started chewing its end. Dick's disappearance may have been more emotionally scarring for him at fourteen, but for Toby, at two, it had had far more serious implications. Josh had already started his "O" level syllabus at his private school, so Dick's alimony payment had included that. By the time Toby had been ready to start secondary school, Dick had been long gone and his once generous alimony didn't stretch nearly as far, private school fees had soared, and their mother still had no new man on the horizon to help bolster up her income. She'd asked Toby whether he wanted to go to a private school or have annual holidays abroad. To nobody's surprise but her own, he chose the latter. Now he went to a school where the teachers were frightened of the kids and the kids were terrified of each other. All Josh remembered being scared of at school was exams.

When someone approached Josh to ask him a work query, he took the pencil out of his mouth, concentrated hard, and brought his mind back to the present. He'd almost chewed the pencil end away.

While Josh was dissecting the disturbing facts about Toby's school life for the hundredth time, Toby was putting the phone down and walking, head down, to the toilets. He washed his face with very cold water, stood by the window and waited until it stopped looking like he'd been punched in the eyes by a sixth former. A first year walked in and did a double take.

"What?" demanded Toby gruffly. "Wanna black eye?"

The first year shook his head violently and changed direction sharply from the urinals to a cubicle.

Toby's eyes watered again, and, as he put his face back under the cold water, the first year stood terrified in the cubicle, unable to move and completely unable to perform.

Vanessa was also having considerable problem. Creatives still hadn't called, Max was getting hot under the collar, and she didn't want to think about where she was getting hot.

When the call finally came, she was not best pleased.

"Do you think you're ready for me?" Anthony asked slyly over the phone.

"Do you have some scripts?" she cut in.

It was the first time she'd spoken to Anthony since that night. And she was very angry with him. She'd gone into work the next day not sure whether he'd call her or appear at her office door. Either way, she'd simply have to explain to him firmly and conclusively that what had happened between them had been a drunken mistake and was never going to happen again.

When he hadn't appeared by three o'clock, she started facing the almost inconceivable possibility that he wasn't going to appear at all. Around the crucial ten minutes of 4:50 to 5 P.M., her confusion, shock, and humiliation merged seamlessly into anger. By 5:30 P.M. she was livid.

When he didn't even get in touch the next day, her healthy anger turned into an unhealthy preoccupation, the implications of which were beginning to scare her. She knew she'd have to call him that afternoon at the very latest. Unfortunately, by then she felt so hostile and defensive with him that she knew their relationship was turning into something more tortured and political even than a professional relationship. He had manipulated her emotions, as he had done with so many before her.

She banged her desk suddenly. What the hell was she thinking? She was a happily married woman. Or at least, she was a married woman, and it amounted to the same thing. She loved Dick. That didn't mean she didn't hate him a lot of the time, but that was just marriage, wasn't it? Marriage meant children you adored and pairing your husband's socks in return for memories of the sweet nothings he used to say that you pretend you'll hear again before you die. And she didn't want some office Romeo coming in to break all that up, thank you very much. There was silence on the other end of the phone. Did he have the script or not?

"Or is this a social call?" she asked him, her sarcasm so acidic it could have burnt the phone line.

"Um, yes," said Anthony, all slyness gone from his voice. "We're ready for you."

They arranged the soonest available time for everyone to meet and rang off.

After the call, Anthony stared into the middle distance biting his lower lip for a full five minutes.

This was exactly what he'd been dreading. Vanessa's brittle tone told him she was not happy. But was that because he'd kissed her, because he'd been late with the scripts, or because he hadn't called her after he'd kissed her?

The day after sharing with Vanessa Fitzgerald the kiss that had shot up to joint Number 1 on his all-time earth-shattering kiss list (together with the one he'd shared with Lucy Spires from first year round the bike sheds when he thought his body was literally going to explode) he had felt great. His ideas came thick and fast, and he and Tom had worked furiously on the campaign.

He was on such a high that the last thing he could do was call Vanessa. It was too big a risk. (Lucy Spires—raw, fearless Lucy Spires—had gone into school the day after the magnificent bike shed experience and magically rechristened him All-talk Anthony. How the hell was he supposed to know she'd take it personally that he hadn't let his body explode? Why didn't anyone just tell you the rules?) He couldn't face that experience again.

The longer he left it, the more the kiss with Vanessa became a pure fact, uncomplicated by afterthoughts, regrets, or apologies. He hadn't wanted it ruined. And now it would all be ruined. He would have to see Vanessa again, hear her icy tone, feel her indifference. At least he had one thing on his side, he thought gratefully. Thank God he'd be in a six-foot-tall bunny suit.

Vanessa buzzed Tricia, who had to then humiliate herself by canceling an important meeting with another big client. The two women stood together in the lift. Vanessa smiled at her junior. She knew it wasn't fair that Tricia had had to look an idiot in front of the most notoriously awful clients, just because the Creatives chose this moment to be ready.

"Were they awful?" Vanessa asked her.

"They called me a lying whore."

Vanessa gasped. "You're joking?"

Tricia shook her head.

"Don't worry, I'll have a word with Max," said Vanessa. When Tricia's chin started quivering, she added. "Come on, chin up. Think bonuses. I'll see what I can do for you."

Tricia managed a smile.

"But of course I will have to know one thing, purely to back up our case," said Vanessa, in a matter-of-fact tone." *Are* you a lying whore?"

By the time the door was opening, Tricia was managing a smile.

Vanessa had already had to have soothing words with Max, who was getting jittery and was now popping into her office on average four times a day. Of course, he'd never bother Creatives—they were far too precious to bother—so he'd shouted at her instead. He was on his way up to the meeting—he'd been called out of a working lunch.

Oh boy, she thought, *this presentation had better be good*. She had butterflies. *Oh boy*, she thought, *this had better be because of the presentation*.

She and Tricia walked into the office and found a six-foot-tall white rabbit drinking a cup of tea, pinkie daintily held out. He stood up when he saw them come in and made a deep, majestic bow.

"Welcome . . . to *Wonder*land," came Anthony's warm, sexy voice from inside the rabbit costume.

The backs of Vanessa's knees went spongy.

"I love it!" bellowed Max. "*Love* it!"

Anthony watched Vanessa and Tricia smile at Max from behind his outfit.

"*Rabbit* on the phone! *Rabbit* on the phone! *A Wonderland* of communication! I love it!" repeated Max. "Fucking genius!"

Anthony was sweating like a pig in his rabbit outfit, but it had been worth it. It was unheard of for Creatives to get dressed up for anything other than the actual pitch before, but he and Tom had been so nervous they'd decided to go ahead anyway. And it had worked. Not only that, but the bunny outfit made him feel strangely braver.

After the meeting, he swiveled his head inside the costume and watched Vanessa slowly and carefully tidy her pens and notebooks while the others left the room. Suddenly, he leaned across the table and rested his big white paw on her hand. She jumped slightly. So did he. He watched her look up into his eyes.

"Please take that outfit off, Anthony," she said.

"How are you?" he asked, hearing his muffled voice echo back to him.

"Fine!" she exclaimed. "Why wouldn't I be? I'm in Wonderland."

He followed her out of the office. Max, Tricia, and Tom were already out of sight. As they came to the door of one of the stock cupboards, Anthony spotted that Vanessa's head turned fractionally toward it. Without pausing for thought, he grabbed her round the waist, pushed open the door and tumbled her into the cupboard, slamming the door behind them.

They stood, breathing heavily, in the pitch-black silence, surrounded by four thousand Silly Nibble chocolate biscuits.

"What the hell am I in here for?" whispered Vanessa, her voice trembling.

"Well, rabbits are known to excel at one thing in particular," he said, edging her away from the door.

"Let me out," she whispered, backing away from the door.

"Okay," he said, kissing her.

Five minutes later, Vanessa pushed her way out of the Silly Nibble cupboard door, straightened her hair, did up her top button, and rushed to follow the others.

Chapter 16

By the time Jo was rounding up the children for the fourth time that day to collect Cassandra from school and Josh from work, she was exhausted.

Tallulah fell asleep the second Jo strapped her into her car seat, snoring so loudly that neither Jo nor Zak could hear Zak's favorite tape. By the time Jo had eventually found a parking space in the limited Hampstead spaces, put her sticker on the window, and dragged Tallulah out of her seat, the little girl had been deeply and happily unconscious. Naturally, as anyone would be after being dragged out of an idyllic slumber, Tallulah was grumpy. So grumpy, in fact, that if she hadn't been four years old, Jo would have assumed she had PMS.

"Don't sing that song, Zak," whined Tallulah, as Zak hummed the tune on his tape that he'd been trying to listen to on the way there.

"Stop walking ahead, Zak," she whined. Zak and Jo exchanged quick knowing looks and kept as quiet as possible.

When Tallulah dropped precariously off to sleep in Jo's arms, Jo gave Zak a quick wink, and whispered, "Good practice." He didn't know what it meant, but he grinned anyway.

Tallulah refused to walk, so Jo had to carry her all the way to the school gates. A deadweight four-year-old is heavy at the best of times; a deadweight four-year-old with PMS is somehow far heavier.

Jo walked up the steps to the playground where the children milled around waiting to be picked up. Cassandra, as usual, was standing to one side with her little friend Asha, who somehow always made Jo want to say very kindly, "I am not going to abduct you."

"Do you want to sit in the front until we pick up Josh?" Jo asked her when they got to the car.

"Alright," said Cassandra.

None of the children talked to each other on the walk back to the car, and Jo let them be. She knew that sometimes you just want to be alone with your thoughts, especially after a hard day.

By the time the prepremenstrual post-toddler was strapped safely in her seat, Zak and Cassandra were already arguing. Their rows could flare up faster than a rocket up a cat's tail. One second they could be giggling together, the next trying to kill each other, then back to giggling. Jo was firm but fair. It was Cassandra's turn to listen to the music, Zak had listened to his on the way there. Zak soared into an apoplectic fury because he hadn't been able to hear his tape thanks to Tallulah's snoring, until Tallulah sorted out the situation by snoring so loudly no one could hear Cassandra's music either.

By the time they got to Highgate Station, the evening had turned fine, and Josh was waiting in the sun, his tie loosened and a smooth olive-skinned collarbone just peeking out of his navy blue shirt. Jo took a deep breath, beeped her horn, and turned away when he looked up. He grinned at his family and tousled Cassandra's hair as she got out of the front for him and moved into the back. Cassandra grinned ruefully, the dark netherworld of school already diminishing to the background of her real life, where she was Number 1 child with a pretty nanny, a fun half brother, and a mummy and daddy who'd be home soon.

Josh got into the front seat.

"How's the family?" he asked, in a particularly friendly voice. Jo's spirits rose.

"Fine!" they all shouted.

"I meant these ones," he said, pointing to Jo's cuddly toys on the dashboard. "Daffy, Duffy, Dozy, and Dud."

Jo tutted. "Huh. I won't leave you to name the children."

Damn. That had sounded different outside than in. She wanted to counter it with some pithy, pointed backstitch comment but was preoccupied by her skin shifting and resettling. And, anyway, Josh had either not heard it or ignored it and was turning round already, teasing the children.

"*Josh!*" bellowed Zak, as if Josh was still in his office and deaf. "Will you play cricket with me when we get in?"

"Jo! After my homework, can I do your hair?" asked Cassandra.

Tallulah snored like a rhinoceros in the back, and they all laughed.

Jo concentrated on driving without grinding the gears as much as her teeth. She couldn't tell what she wanted to do most—apologize again to Josh or hit him very hard on his bruises.

Josh settled into his seat. "Another day another dollar."

"For some," said Jo pleasantly. "My day's only halfway through."

"Good thing it's an easy job then." Jo almost stalled.

Later, as the children galloped ahead into the house and Jo and Josh bent down to pick up the new yellow pages outside the front door, Jo told him quietly but firmly, "I think Cassandra had a horrid day."

He caught her eye. When their knees touched briefly, they both acted as if they'd got an electric shock.

"What makes you say that?" he asked.

Jo shrugged. "I don't know." She looked ahead at Cassandra, already inside the hall. "Just . . . be gentle with her."

"Thank you," he said. "Until you came along, I always treated Cassandra with a rod of iron." And he walked into the house ahead of her.

She locked her jaw as she stood up and followed him.

It was a long evening. Jo and Josh divided responsibilities without conferring, Josh playing with Zak in the garden and Jo playing with Cassie and Tallulah in the conservatory. Jo found it hard to believe that only last week she would have found it more fun for Josh to be indoors. She hoped Zak was tiring him out in the garden.

Meanwhile, in the garden, Zak was tiring Josh out, winning at cricket with all the grace and goodwill of a six-year-old boy.

"I'm winning!" he yelled inside to Jo. *"I'm killing him!!"*

"Good boy," said Jo. "I'm proud of you."

Zak, giggling, raced back outside to thrash his half brother. He hoped Josh would never leave.

"I don't think I want to bowl anymore," said Josh, pulling his shirt out of his trousers and flapping it to give himself some air.

"But I'm in bat," said Zak nonplussed.

"Oh."

"You can be wicketkeeper," offered Zak magnanimously.

"Wow!" exclaimed Josh. "You mean I get to keep your wickets? Forever?'

Josh enjoyed the delicious sound, like water trickling off rocks, of a boy unable to control his giggles.

"No!" said Zak, when he was able to speak. "They're *my* wickets!"

"That's awfully good of you," continued Josh. "I'd have thought you'd want to keep them."

Zak tried to get a grip.

"No," he gasped, "that's not what wicketkeeper *means!*"

"How long can I keep them for?"

More water trickling off rocks, then some serious cricket and half an hour later, after Josh had been thrashed good and proper, he pretended to collapse, which took longer than he'd hoped, given the bruises. He lay on the grass, blinking up at the sky. "I'm dead," he said gravely. "The shock of losing to a four-year-old."

Zak became hysterical with laughter again, jumping from foot to foot. "I'm *six*!! Not *four*!!"

"Sorry. *Five*-year-old."

"*Six!*" managed Zak.

"I'm going to heaven now," said Josh, getting up slowly. "In the kitchen. Look after my plants."

Zak followed Josh inside, yelling, "*I won! I beat him!*" He overtook him, barely noticing Josh stop still in the doorway.

Jo was motionless, sitting cross-legged on the floor by the conservatory window, her back elegant and straight. Her thick dark hair was being meticulously plaited by the two silent girls, who were draped around her. Tallulah was sitting on Jo's lap, Cassie kneeling behind her. Six limbs were intertwined and every now and then, soft whispers of encouragement from Jo caused flickers of half smiles. Occasionally, Jo stroked Tallulah's head, and Cassie hugged Jo. The sun was coming in through the conservatory doors, and a deep glow of blue seemed to lighten the strands of Jo's hair that Tallulah kept dropping.

Josh stepped inside the room slowly, like a swimmer hauling himself out of water.

"*I beat him!*" repeated Zak.

Jo spoke without moving. "Well done, Zak, just in time for tea."

Zak found little to engage him with the girls and joined Josh back at the garden door.

"Mate," said Josh with a knowing wink. "The ladies don't like it when you hold your ding-dong."

Zak became temporarily speechless with laughter.

"The ladies! My ding-dong!" He giggled eventually, then stopped suddenly. "What's for tea?" he asked.

Jo pointed to the oven and hob, where some vegetables were steaming and some fish fingers were grilling.

"Fish fingers, chips, broccoli, and peas," she said, handing Cassie a hairband. "Are you going to be a good boy and lay the table?"

"Alright then," said Josh. "But only because you called me a good boy."

The children had hysterics. Jo handed Tallulah the other hairband.

The girls had finished her hair. She stood up and twirled for them to appraise their handiwork.

"Tallulah's is lower than mine," said Cassandra. "She looks awful."

"No she doesn't," said Tallulah. "Does she, Josh?"

Josh crossed his arms and made great play of studying Jo. She was wearing three-quarter-length trousers and a T-shirt with a picture of a little pink heart on her chest. She'd been studiously copied by Cassandra and Tallulah down to the color and style of their hairbands, the only visible differences being that they both had nail polish on and no breasts. The three of them stared defiantly back at him.

"Hmm," thought Josh out loud. "Does Jo look awful? Let. Me. Think."

After a while, Jo moved to the oven to start preparing tea.

"She looks like a ten-year-old," Josh said eventually, joining her at the hob.

"Well," muttered Jo, her head half in the oven. "Better than acting like one." She took her head out of the oven and found Josh staring at her with an inscrutable expression on his face. Had she gone too far? Flushed, she remembered what Shaun had said about Josh being a spy for his mother. Could he get her into trouble?

"Where are the forks?" asked Zak, suddenly behind them.

When Jo's mobile rang, and it was her mum, she made a point of asking Cassandra to finish the tea, instead of asking Josh.

"I'll do it," said Josh quietly.

"No, it's fine," said Jo.

"I can do it," said Cassandra.

"I don't mind," said Josh pointedly. "I'm not a child, I can look after my own family."

Jo stared at him. Then said into the phone, "Mum, can I phone you back—"

"Don't be ridiculous," interrupted Josh, his voice rising. "Speak to your mother, I'll finish doing the tea." As she went into her bedroom, she heard him muttering, "No one's indispensable."

She shut the bedroom door behind her.

"How's Dad?" she asked.

"He's got a checkup next week," answered Hilda. "I'm terrified. He hasn't been looking good lately."

"He hasn't been looking good for the past fifty years," said Jo. "But we still love him."

There was a pause. "How are you there, love?" asked Hilda.

"I'm fine, Mum. How are—"

"They feed you properly?"

"Well, they feed me, but most of their food's really weird."

"They're not Asians are they?"

"Mum! No, they just eat differently."

"You're getting your meat and two veg?"

"Yes, Mum. I— Would you like me to come home?"

"Course not!" exclaimed Hilda. "What d'you want to come home for?"

"To see you, silly."

"What d'you want to come home to see me for?"

"Because I miss you!"

"Don't be ridiculous. You're far too busy. Can't go rushing off all the time—what would they think? Mind you, I think your dad misses you a bit."

"I'll come next weekend."

"Ooh, lovely!"

"Oh no! I can't. The weekend after."

"Smashing."

"I'd better go."

"Right."

"I've got to give the kids tea. Their half brother's with us, and I think he may be checking up on me."

"Oh dear."

When Jo returned, she found the children seated politely at the table, eating quietly. She started tidying the kitchen up around them.

"I know what I want for my birthday," announced Zak, milk moustaching his upper lip.

"Do you?" asked Josh. "What?"

"I need a digital watch."

"Didn't Mummy and Daddy buy you a watch last year?" asked Cassandra. "You keep breaking them."

"You're right," said Zak seriously. "Perhaps I should get two."

"How many children do you want when you're older?" Cassandra asked Tallulah gravely, forking her peas.

"Four," answered Tallulah. "How many do you want?"

"Two," said Cassandra.

"Do you want a boy and a girl, or a girl and a girl or a boy and a boy?" asked Tallulah, in between small, pensive mouthfuls of broccoli.

"Boy and a girl," came the rapid reply.

Jo smiled. "I don't think it works like that. You don't get a choice."

The girls thought about this.

"You might get a boy and a *boy*," whispered Tallulah.

There was a long, long pause.

"Tallulah's so lucky," whined Zak suddenly. "She's got more chips than me. That's not right."

"Lula, honey," coaxed Jo, using her soft Tallulah voice. "Do you think you'll be able to eat all those chips?"

Tallulah looked at her plate and considered the question. "Probably not."

"Would you give Zak some?"

Tallulah handed Zak some of her chips.

"Thank you," said Zak, slightly taken aback.

"My pleasure," said Tallulah gravely.

Josh and Jo glanced at each other and then quickly away, before Tallulah crumpled into Jo's body, a heap of anguished regret.

When Dick came home, the children were bathed and ready for bed. It never mattered how tired they were, whenever Daddy got home they found new energy and fluttered round him like day-old butterflies, enjoying their last moments of consciousness. Jo watched Dick come alive in his children's company. She smiled, then looked over to see if Josh was also watching. He was watching, but he certainly wasn't smiling. Maybe Shaun was right about him.

That evening, she made a concerted—and big—effort to phone Sheila.

"Shaun says he had a good time," said Sheila.

"Oh!" said Jo. "Have you seen him then?"

"Yeah," said Sheila. "He had lunch with me and James today."

"How's James?"

"Fine."

There was a pause. Jo didn't know what else to say.

"How is everyone?" she asked.

"What?" said Sheila. "Everyone in the world?"

"No. Your folks."

"Same as usual."

"James?"

"Still fine."

There was another pause.

"It's so knackering here," said Jo. "And this stupid brother's making my life a misery."

"Oh yeah," said Sheila. "Shaun told us all about him. The one who listens to you two having sex."

"Yeah," said Jo, her mouth dry. "That one."

"Sounds like a right saddo."

"Mm."

When Jo got off the phone, she had a quick shower and lay on her bed trying to read. She knew there was absolutely no way she'd manage to get to sleep before Josh came and showered and walked through her room to go to bed.

Three bedtime stories, three last hugs, three big fat kisses, and three sleeping children later, Dick went downstairs, tired but content. It wasn't to last.

He went to the drinks cabinet and poured himself a stiff whiskey, sat down in the conservatory, turned on the TV, then turned it off. He stood up, sat down again and then, very slowly, put his head in his hands.

Vanessa got home at ten and went straight to the kitchen for a stiff drink. Dick was putting a video of *Top Gear* in the machine. He looked up at her briefly.

"Hello, darling, decided to come home have you?"

She watched him as he perched on the edge of the sofa, head tilted slightly, feet crossed at the toes, eyes wide, watching his video. Her stomach lurched. She walked slowly toward him. She was wearing the high heels she knew he found sexy.

Dick pointed at the screen. "Look! It's got a gently kicked-back rear end."

Vanessa stopped. "That's nice. Night, darling," she said, gently kicking back her own rear end. "Don't forget to turn off the lights."

"Mmm," called out Dick after her, eyes still on the screen.

Half an hour later, a knock at the en suite shower door disturbed Jo from her thoughts. She picked up her book.

"Come in!" she called, and immediately felt foolish—Josh didn't want to come in, he wanted to come through. Josh opened the door slowly and

Jo glanced up from her book toward him. She felt heat flush up her chest. He was wearing nothing but jeans, his damp hair tousled. He stood in the doorway drying his hair before replacing the towel on the rail. Jo stared until he looked at her.

"Bruises are going down nicely," she said quickly, turning back to her book.

Josh padded slowly across her room and looked down. "You think?" he asked opening his arms out. She looked up.

He turned slowly round until he faced her again. She was lying on her side, head cupped in hand, legs dangling over the bed, hair cascading over the grinning coyote. He raised his eyebrows at her, as if daring her to answer.

Jo frowned intensely, disturbed by the sight of his bruised back. "Not long now, I suppose," she said, her tone softer.

Josh nodded. "Why, thank you, Dr. Nanny. Can I go now?"

She nodded miserably.

"Night then," said Josh.

"Night."

Jo stared at the open page of her book while Josh left her room. And then, to the murmuring vibrations of him going to bed one foot away from her, she shut her book, lay back on her bed, and closed her eyes.

Chapter 17

Saturday morning, Vanessa woke to feel someone gently stroking her ear. She nuzzled closer. Slowly she opened one eye and saw Tallulah, thumb in mouth, staring deeply at her. Vanessa snuggled up against her baby.

"Hello, Tallulah-mae," she whispered. "What are you doing in here?"

"Watching you," said Tallulah.

Vanessa smiled, inhaling her daughter's smell.

"Mummy?"

"Hmm?"

"Who's Anthony?"

Vanessa opened her eyes and edged away slightly. She blinked a couple of times to clear her cobweb brain. "Oh just some awful person Mummy's having to work with at the moment." She closed her eyes again.

"Were you having a nightmare?" asked Tallulah.

"Mmm," answered Vanessa. "Most probably."

"Is that why you were moaning?"

And, as if by magic, Vanessa was wide-awake. "Is Daddy making breakfast?" she asked her daughter.

Dick always did the early Saturday morning shift. He didn't mind because the TV channels had just woken up to the fact that dads were now involved in child care and so had started to screen sport, followed by children's TV hosted by nubile blond babes. Funny that, pondered Vanessa, curling up round Tallulah. No *Love Boat* and hunky male presenters in the weekdays for mums. *Oh God*, she thought, interrupting her own thoughts. She was so sick and bored and tired of being angry all the time. Why did these destructive thoughts circle like vultures in her head all the time? Why couldn't they just leave her alone? She didn't want to hate Dick. She didn't want their marriage to turn into one long blame-fest. She hugged Tallulah and kissed her baby neck.

"Is Toby up?" she asked, stroking Tallulah's hair.

"Yes," said Tallulah. "He's taken Josh to see the Lord."

"What? He's taken him to *church*?"

"That's what he said. Where everyone wears white together."

"Oh my God. They've gone to a *church*?" Vanessa was completely awake now, no going back.

Dick appeared at the bedroom door with a tray containing a cafetière, half a grapefruit, a bowl of organic muesli with soya milk, a bowl of crunchy nutty chocolatey cereal with full-fat milk and a copy of the *Observer*.

"Breakfast in bed for two of my favorite women," he said, placing the tray on the chair at the end of the bed. "And certainly two of the most terrifying."

"Thanks, Dick," croaked Vanessa. "It would be absolutely marvelous if you could walk it an extra two feet so we don't have to get out of bed for our breakfast in bed."

"Of course, darling," said Dick, stepping back and picking up the tray again. He placed it on the bed. "Would you like me to oil your pillows while I'm here, too?"

"Has Josh taken Toby to a happy-clappy church?"

Dick frowned. "No, dear. To Lords to see the cricket. But I can see how you'd make the mistake."

Vanessa looked hard at her husband. "Thank you for bringing my breakfast and a stomach ulcer, darling. You do help."

"Pleasure, darling. I'll be off to do a hard day's work. Don't worry about me."

"I should think I'll be far too busy looking after all your children, including the ones that aren't mine."

"Bye then."

"Bye then."

Dick shut the bedroom door behind him, and Vanessa shut her eyes tight.

That afternoon Toby and Josh sat in Regent's Park together. Toby was now so tall he almost reached Josh's shoulders. One more growth spurt and he'd easily be taller than his big brother. He would never have the same brooding looks as Josh because he'd inherited his mother's coloring, but he did share Josh and Dick's handsome features, and at times, a fleeting expression—usually of bewilderment—revealed his genetic connection to the male role models in his life.

Josh kept sneaking sideways glances at his brother, trying to remember how he felt at that age. But he kept coming back to the same thing. When he was Toby's age, he'd already started eavesdropping on his father's telephonic trysts with his secretary, and the first signs of insomnia had kicked in.

He tousled Toby's hair.

"Don't!" said Toby, curling his lanky form into a semicircle. If he could, he'd have formed hedgehog prickles on his back.

"Why?" asked Josh. "Too mature for it?"

"Nah. It's budgit, man."

"It's what?"

"Like, lame."

"Like lame?"

"Stupid."

"Ah! Stupid. Right."

Josh watched as Toby groomed his hair back into position. As Toby lay back and raised his face to the sun, Josh noticed a neat constellation of spots round his mouth. He didn't know when or how to approach the subject of Toby's phone call from school earlier that week, if at all. Toby had seemed fine today, and they'd sat together watching the cricket for about four hours without either of them saying anything about it.

"So," he said eventually, as indifferently as possible, "how's things?"

Toby's volume knob went to mute. He turned his head away. "There's this girl," he forced out of his body.

Josh almost had to stop slapping himself on the forehead. Of course! Girls! Toby was thirteen years old—what had he expected? Here he was imagining it would be something between Mum and Dad, something he could perhaps help with, add his expertise to, but no. It was about girls. How could he tell his kid brother that he'd come to the last person on earth who could help him?

"Right," he said seriously.

"She's a ledge."

Josh frowned. A *ledge*? Was that a good thing? Or a bad thing? He racked his brains for what that word might mean, but kept coming back to a window ledge. Did Toby mean she was "on the shelf"? If so, did that mean she was the ugliest girl in the class? Still, it seemed a bit cruel to describe a thirteen-year-old girl as on the shelf.

"A ledge," he repeated thoughtfully.

"Yeah," said Toby. "You know. A ledge. A legend."

"Oh right."

"Like, safe."

Nope. He'd lost him again. "Oh, like, safe," he repeated, hopefully.

Toby sighed heavily. "She's practically famous at school 'cos every boy fancies her."

"Ah, right."

"She asked me out to the cinema."

"Wow!" Josh slapped his brother on the back. "Look at you! My kid brother, eh? Can you give me some dating tips? I always go for the wrong type and am scared I'll end up alone. What do you suggest?"

"And now Todd Carter says he's gonna split my head open."

Josh stopped still. He stared at the grass. He wanted to kill Todd Carter but he knew that the little shit could probably wipe the floor with him. He thought long and hard. "Oh dear," he said weakly.

Vanessa and the children were eating ice cream for dessert. They'd enjoyed a lunch that had consisted entirely of additives, except Zak who had eaten four whole wheat digestives (albeit covered in golden syrup and chocolate buttons). *Oh well,* thought Vanessa. *It's only two days a week.*

She was sitting on the floor with her children, watching a tape of *Buffy* when the front door slammed. Toby and Josh wandered into the room, glanced over and said hello. While Josh went to make a pot of tea, Toby stood behind them, casting a shadow over the happy scene.

Tallulah looked up at him.

"What are those things round your mouth?" she asked, pointing.

"Spots," grunted Toby, eyes on the TV. "You get them if you're good."

"Mummy," whined Tallulah, "I want spots."

"They'll come soon enough, sweetheart."

"I want them *now*."

"And then you'll get your girl's periods," continued Toby, "and you'll go all ugly."

"Thank you, Toby," said Vanessa.

"No you don't," corrected Cassandra. "Some women glow. I read it in a book."

"What book was that?" asked Vanessa.

"Yeah, the *pretty* ones glow," growled Toby. "You two will just go even uglier."

"Thank you so much, Toby," said Vanessa. "Don't you have anything to do, like strangle a hamster or something?"

Having successfully completed his task for the day, Toby joined Josh at the kettle.

Josh wasn't sure if he should say something to Toby about how being loathsome wasn't nice and how it wasn't actually Tallulah's and Cassandra's fault that his parents split up. He often found himself wondering if he should play the father figure or the friend to Toby. Could he be both? If he started telling Toby that sometimes he was a shit, would Toby then have no one to confide in? He decided to merge the two.

"Here you are," he said, handing Toby a cup of tea, "you little shit."

"Cheers." Toby grinned.

The front door slammed again and moments later Jo and Pippa wandered in, laughing and chatting, both in their gym kit. They'd been to an aerobics class at Pippa's gym. Pippa had assured Jo that they would be able to stay at the back of the class and muddle their way through it, but the instructor had insisted Pippa stand right at the front. They'd been compelled to behave and were both knackered.

And then they'd experienced the strangest coincidence. As they'd walked out of the gym, they'd found Gerry standing outside it, reading the timetable, which was pinned to the glass frontage. He appeared just as surprised to see them as they were to see him, and after a few moments' chat, they all went their separate ways. But it had left a nasty taste in Jo's mouth.

"Did you tell Nick we were going to the gym this morning?" asked Pippa.

"No idea," replied Pippa. "Why?"

"No reason." Jo stopped herself from letting paranoia settle under her skin. Maybe even in London, flukes like that did happen.

They'd planned to change here before spending the afternoon shopping in Crouch End together. Pippa wanted to buy something new to wear for their cinema date with Nick and Gerry, and Jo was happy to accompany her. She missed the shopping trips she used to go on with Sheila.

Toby and Josh, sitting at the kitchen table with their mugs of tea, stared openly. Jo had her hair in high, looped bunches, and there were dark patches of sweat in key areas of her body. Her cheeks were rosy, her eyes bright, and her lips ruby red. When Pippa caught Josh's eye, he looked down at his tea.

Pippa grinned. "Well, hell-o!" she greeted, hands on hips. "I love the smell of testosterone in the morning!"

Toby almost died there and then, but thankfully, Vanessa, blissfully unaware of any sort of tension other than family tension, butted in.

"Hiya," she said. "I let them watch *Friend*s."

"Oh, right," said Jo.

"And eat chocolate," called out Tallulah. "One day I'm going to have girls' periods and spots!"

"And ice cream," said Cassandra. "And I'm going to glow."

"Great." Jo smiled. She looked sadly at the kitchen.

"I'll tidy it all up, promise," said Vanessa. "I know how anal you nannies are about your workspace!"

Jo sighed. "We're just gonna use the shower," she replied.

"What? Together?" squeaked Toby.

Josh laughed loudly at this. He suddenly saw all the uses a younger brother could have. He would have pondered the same question, too scared of making a stupid arse of himself to ask. He now fondly handed over the mantle of stupid arse to Toby and considered bringing him along on dates.

Pippa joined in the laughter and approached the kitchen table.

"No, of course we won't shower together," she said, leaning over the kitchen table and whispering. "Then we wouldn't be able to work up such a lather, would we?"

Toby swallowed.

"How old are you, handsome?" asked Pippa.

"Thirteen," Toby mumbled into his mug, wishing Pippa had stayed over there.

"And how old's your gorgeous big brother?"

Toby snorted his way through three octaves.

"Hi!" said Josh, extending his hand across Toby, who seemed suddenly fascinated by the oven. "Josh Fitzgerald."

"Oh, I know who you are. I've heard all about you."

Jo found herself by the drinks cabinet and moved to the kettle, where she got busy making her and Pippa some tea, wishing she was somewhere else and listening avidly.

"So!" said Pippa, looking at Toby's and Josh's somber faces. "What's making the brothers grim?"

Toby snorted again.

"Toby's got a dilemma because he's got the hottest date in his class tonight," said Josh.

"Jo-osh!" whined Toby.

"What's wrong with that?" asked Josh. "It's true. You're too damn hot for your own good."

Toby tried not to smile and failed.

"That true?" said Pippa. Toby grunted.

"Why's that a problem?"

"Can I?" Josh asked Toby. Toby grunted again, the Esperanto of adolescence.

"This tosser in his class is jealous, so he's threatening to follow them and beat Toby up tonight."

"Oh my God," said Pippa. "Where are you going for your date?"

"Dunno yet," said Toby. "I'm gonna call her later. But her older brother is mates with the older brother of the bloke who's threatened to get me, so she's got to keep it a secret from him. Might not be able to 'cos her mother wants to know where she's going."

"So you mean," said Pippa slowly, "that you might be beaten up during your dream date tonight?"

"We were just trying to work out where would be a safe place to go," said Josh. "I might follow."

"*No!*" said Toby.

"From a safe distance," insisted Josh. "Believe me, I don't want to watch. I just don't want you getting into trouble."

"I'll be *fine*," said Toby.

"I've got an idea," said Pippa. "Let me just make a call."

As she went to get her mobile from her bag, Jo finished making the tea.

"Right!" Jo exclaimed. "I'll just have my shower." She noticed that no one answered.

When Jo returned to the kitchen, clean and dry and dressed, she found Pippa on her mobile phone and Toby and Josh grinning identical schoolboy grins at her.

"That's fantastic!" Pippa was saying into the phone. "We'll owe you one." She giggled and winked at Toby, before clicking off and replacing her phone in her bag. "Right," she said. "It's a deal. We'll go to the same film as you and if there's any trouble, Nick and Gerry will kick the shit out of anyone who touches you. Except your date of course, 'cos we *want* her to touch you."

"Wicked!" said Toby.

"And Josh will chaperone us so that his mind is put at rest and so he can drive my date wild with jealousy," finished Pippa, holding up her mug of tea as if to make a toast. "It's the perfect plan!"

Josh held his mug up, too. "Much as I hate the thought of being a gooseberry to three separate dates," he interrupted himself, "—does that make me three gooseberries?—especially with two blokes who've beaten me up, it's all gonna be worth it to see those arseholes who are picking on my kid bro shitting themselves with terror."

"Mine isn't a date actually," said Jo, but no one seemed to hear her.

"So thanks, Pippa!" finished Josh.

"Yeah, thanks!" Toby managed, eyes darting to her before returning to the safety of the floor.

"My absolute pleasure!" grinned Pippa. "And now I must peel these damp clothes off and have my shower," she said as she left the room.

Jo followed Pippa into her bedroom, shutting the door behind her.

"Is he really going to come with us?" she hissed.

"Of course," replied Pippa, brushing her hair. "You don't expect him to stay at home and miss all the fun, do you? Especially when he is sex on legs."

"He's got a very ugly side," muttered Jo.

"They all do," said Pippa. "But I bet it'd be fun looking for his."

"He's putting on the charm," said Jo. "The famous Josh Fitzgerald charm. He can turn it off very quickly if you piss him off. And he's toxins on legs when he does."

"Why? What's he's done?"

"I was too embarrassed to tell you," confessed Jo, plonking herself down on her bed. "It was excruciating, Pip."

Pippa sat down too. "Go on."

Jo sighed. "The night before Shaun arrived, I got home pissed from our night out . . . and . . . I thought we were going to kiss. I really did and so I just . . ."

"What?"

"I blurted out all about Shaun."

"Oh my God. You waited all this time to find the right time to tell him and then told him when he was moving in for the kiss?"

"Yes."

"And there I was thinking it was the nannying you needed help with." Pippa sighed.

Jo leaned forward. "It seemed like the right thing to do. I've never two-timed Shaun, and I actually cared about not hurting Josh."

"So?"

"He just . . ." She shook her head. "It was so weird. Even as pissed as I was, I could feel the atmosphere completely change. It was like the kitchen suddenly had frost. He turned into a different person."

Pippa's eyes were wide. "Blimey."

"He went completely cold and I kept saying sorry and he kept saying it was fine."

"Bleagh."

"He spent the whole weekend being absolutely horrible to Shaun—and me—and hinting that I was easy—"

"Bastard!"

"—which did not help things with me and Shaun. Then I tried to apologize to him again." Jo shut her eyes.

Pippa whispered. "What did he say?"

Jo knew it by heart. She spoke in a monotone. "He said, *If it's on tap, I'm going to go for it, what bloke wouldn't, and you were certainly on tap that night, but anything more than that and you're living in a chicklit fantasy world, you've seen too many Hollywood films, sorry to disappoint you.*"

Pippa's eyes were saucers.

Jo stood up suddenly. "And since then he's been a complete bastard," she continued. "Anyway, he's so immature. He's twenty-five and not paying a penny in rent even though he earns stacks as an accountant. And he goes on about his dad leaving his mum, which was absolutely years ago. My first impression was right—when he spoke to me on speakerphone, with his entire office listening to him take the piss—that was the real Josh Fitzgerald."

Pippa whistled long and low.

There was silence for a while, as Jo started to do her makeup.

Pippa was the first to speak. "It's just so easy to forget when he looks like that."

"Well, it's hard for me to forget because he's a bastard to me."

"He doesn't pay any rent?" asked Pippa.

Jo shook her head. "Nope. Vanessa told me."

"Bloody hell," whistled Pippa. "Life is so unfair, but now we don't have to feel guilty using him to make the boys jealous tonight."

"I don't want Gerry to be jealous of him," moaned Jo. "I don't want Gerry being jealous of anyone. I don't want Gerry, period. I've got Shaun."

"Alright, sorry. We'll just work at Nick being jealous of him then."

"I don't want him coming with us tonight," whined Jo, slumping onto her back. "He makes me a nervous wreck."

"Does he?" asked Pippa. "Why?"

"Because he watches me like a hawk all the time."

"Who said he'll be watching *you*?" quipped Pippa, before sauntering into the bathroom.

While Pippa showered, Jo phoned Shaun. He was out, so she left a message on his voice mail and tried Sheila. She was also out, so she left a message on Sheila's voice mail. Then she phoned her parents. They were also out, but didn't have voice mail. By the time Pippa wandered out of the bathroom, wearing a small towel and a big smile, Jo had given up wondering where on earth everyone could be.

Pippa had had such a hot shower that steam billowed behind her into Jo's room. Loath to open her window on to the building site next door, Jo asked Pippa to open her bedroom door into the kitchen a crack. Pippa did so, but instead of leaving it, she stood, transfixed. Watching her, Jo became transfixed, too. And then Pippa frantically beckoned her over to behind the door.

At first Jo shook her head, but when she thought Pippa's eyes might actually fall out of her head, she rushed to the door and tried to see into the kitchen. Pippa was in the way, so Jo nudged her over a bit and the two of them strained to listen. All the children had vanished, as had Vanessa. Through the crack in the door, they could see Josh and Dick whispering urgently to each other in the kitchen.

"Is that why you're back so early?" they heard Josh hissing.

"Of course it is," hissed back Dick. "Do you think I'd be here other-wise? She just didn't turn up."

"Why not?"

"How the hell do I know? I phoned, but there was no answer."

"You don't think Vanessa might get a little bit suspicious about you coming back so early on a Saturday afternoon? She thinks you're being rushed off your feet in a busy shop every week."

They heard Dick let out a short, sharp laugh.

"Jesus, Dad," came Josh's voice. "You can't keep this double life up for much longer."

"You think I don't realize that?" Dick raised his voice.

"Shhh! She'll hear you!" There was silence. Then, "Dad, you've got to do something."

"I could always leave," came Dick's voice.

"Oh, like last time? Dad, why didn't you listen to me? I told you not to fall for her—"

"Give me a break, Josh. Now's not the time."

They moved out of sight toward the conservatory and started talking louder, confident they were alone.

"Maybe I'm just not cut out for marriage," the girls heard Dick say.

"Dad," said Josh firmly, "just tell Vanessa. Before it's too late."

"Are you mad?" there was real terror in Dick's voice. "And risk losing everything?"

"She'll understand, Dad. She's not that bad. She's not . . . she's not like Mum."

"You've got a lot to learn about women," observed Dick, to the accompanying sound of whiskey being poured into a glass.

Silently, Jo pushed the door to. She'd heard enough. She and Pippa stared at each other, jaws dropping, brains buzzing. They then tiptoed into the en suite bathroom and shut the door behind them.

"Oh my God!" whispered Pippa. "Dick's having an affair!"

Jo put her hands to her head. "Poor Vanessa! She suspected this! And she's working so hard at the moment." She gasped. "And Josh—the man who hates infidelity—is helping his father have an affair! The hypocritical bastard!"

"Maybe he's one of those men who hates infidelity in women only," pointed out Pippa. "But thinks it's all part of being a red-blooded man."

Jo frowned. "But it was his dad's affair that finished Dick and Jane's marriage."

Pippa nodded. "Exactly! And he told you trust was everything! He blames the woman and not his dad! Absolutely typical!"

"But why is Josh telling Dick to tell Vanessa about his lover?" pondered Jo.

Pippa's eyes narrowed. Then she gasped. "Because he wants to ruin his father's second marriage. Of course! He doesn't want to see Daddy happy with another family, does he?"

"Oh my God," muttered Jo, shaking her head. "He told me, the night he moved in, that if his Dad was going to leave his family it might as well have been for a nice one. I knew it didn't ring true! When you think about it, it's really sick coming to live with the family that your dad chose over yours. D'you know, Shaun saw the real Josh—because Josh wasn't putting on the charm for him—and Shaun thought he was up to something. He thought Josh was spying for his mum—but it's even worse than that, he's actually trying to break up his dad's second marriage." She sat down on the closed toilet lid, landing with a thump. "God," she breathed, "and I almost fell for him."

"I wonder if Josh's mother has somehow found out about Dick's affair and smuggled Josh in to make sure Dick doesn't get away with it this time," wondered Pippa. "Maybe they're in it together!"

Jo put her head in her hands.

Pippa stood against the sink and crossed her arms. "What was Josh's story for having to move in here?"

Jo looked up. "His flatmates went traveling. And he couldn't find anyone else to move in at such short notice."

They looked at each other.

"Where was his flat?" asked Pippa.

"Crouch End."

Pippa raised her eyebrows. "He was living in *Crouch End*—an area with its own recording studio, its own private club, its own massage parlor, more cafés than Soho, and the famous Trumpton clock tower—and he *couldn't get* flatmates?"

Jo's head dropped. "I've been such a fool."

"Blimey," said Pippa. "This is knackering. I can see why Sherlock Holmes needed drugs."

"At least I'm not confused anymore," said Jo, thinking aloud. "Bloody hell. I was even considering breaking up with Shaun."

"Well," said Pippa. "He *is* Hornblower."

"On legs," added Jo.

"Tell you what though," said Pippa. "You don't have to worry what he thinks of you now."

"Why?"

"Because he's a shit. And he's too busy screwing up Vanessa's life to really care about you."

There was a knock on the door.

"Coming!" answered Pippa. Jo stood up from the toilet and, as a reflex action, flushed it. Pippa gave her a dumbfounded look, then started giggling. Then she opened the door to Josh.

"Bloody hell," he said, when he saw both of them and heard the flushing toilet. "You really did shower together."

Later that evening, the wine bar was humming. Pippa was wearing new jeans and was arm in arm with Josh. They made quite a pair, and heads turned to see them pass. Jo's heart went out to Nick.

"I thought the brother was thirteen years old," greeted Nick.

"Ooh," said Pippa. "You're not in CID for nothing, are you?"

"It's alright," said Josh, extricating himself from Pippa's clasp. "For the purposes of the evening, I'm a spotty teenager. The real spotty teenager is already there."

Nick frowned at Josh.

"Believe me," insisted Josh, "I didn't want to be part of this date any more than you lot wanted me here, but if it's for my kid brother, I'll do it. Just pretend I'm not here."

Nick and Gerry gave him one smile between them.

"Sorry about the other night," said Nick. "You know, trying to beat you up."

"Trying? I don't want to be there when you succeed."

Gerry made a move to kiss Jo hello and she instinctively leaned backward, into Josh.

They sprang apart.

"Right!" she exclaimed. "Who'd like a drink?"

"I'll come with you," said Gerry. "Give you a hand."

At the bar, Jo made a point of standing at a safe distance from Gerry and focusing on getting the bar staffs' attention. When the drinks were ordered, she led the way back swiftly and surely. The others had found some seats—a sofa and a couple of chairs. She sat on a high-backed chair, leaving Gerry to sit on the other one, the sofa between them. Josh had nabbed the other chair and Nick and Pippa nestled with ample room on the sofa.

"So." Gerry grinned over at Jo. "How was your day?"

"Fine thanks," said Jo.

"Getting used to London?" he asked.

She thought about this for a moment. "Mm," she allowed.

"That doesn't sound too encouraging," said Gerry.

"It's still hard," she said.

"Hard? Why?"

She shrugged and felt her throat close over. "I suppose I still miss everyone from home."

"Ah right," nodded Gerry. "The boyfriend."

Jo stared at the floor, keeping very still and waiting for the salty sensation at the back of her throat to dissipate.

"Yes," she said eventually, in a level tone. "It's still a bit hard."

"Can't be *that* hard, surely," coaxed Gerry. "Otherwise you wouldn't have left him."

Jo stared him straight in the eye, aware that hers were glistening. "No," her voiced seemed to echo. "Some choices are just hard."

She found it impossible not to glance at Josh as her eyes made the scenic route back down to her drink. She thought it must be the first time they'd made eye contact since before he'd dropped the charm offensive. And, oh boy, how the look had changed. It was no longer a warm connection that helped banish homesickness, it was a cold, observing mask. She knocked back some wine.

"Wouldn't be able to understand it myself." Gerry grinned at Nick. "If my girlfriend left town, I'd take it as a pretty bad sign."

"Well," smiled Pippa sweetly. "Maybe that's why you haven't got a girlfriend."

"At the moment," he pointed out quietly, eyes on Jo. In the silence that followed this he finished his pint. "Right! Who wants another?"

Jo shook her head without making eye contact. When Gerry and Nick left for the bar, she turned to Pippa, so angry she temporarily forgot Josh's presence. "I thought I'd made it clear—" she started.

"You did," Pippa told her firmly. "It's not your fault he's choosing not to take the hint." She turned suddenly to Josh. "Is it?" she asked him.

"What?"

"You're an impartial bloke, what's the bloke's view?"

"Um—"

"Jo can't help it if Gerry chooses not to take her very pointed hints, can she? There's not much more she can do than keep reminding him she's got a boyfriend, is there? I mean, she can't help it that he doesn't live in London, can she?"

Jo tuned out of the conversation as much as possible, staring into her drink. She heard Josh take in a deep breath. "I should think after this eve-ning, Gerry'll get the message loud and clear."

"Good," said Pippa. "Our Jo doesn't need guilt from all sides, does she? Come on, Jo, cheer up. It's Saturday night."

Jo managed a perfunctory smile, aware that Josh was still openly observing her.

Josh bought them all popcorn at the cinema, which pissed off Nick and Gerry, who felt this was part of their gentlemanly duty, and riled Jo, who felt it was easy to be generous when you were a city accountant with no rent.

In the cinema, Pippa led the way into the seats, followed sharpish by Nick. Jo followed him and, aware that Josh was nearer to her than Gerry, left them both to it. Gerry suddenly appeared beside her, walking along the row behind, and he nipped ahead of her and jumped over the seat so that he was now next to her and not on the end, next to Josh. She stopped dead in her tracks. Until she felt Josh approach behind her, when she forced herself forward.

Nick sat down, Pippa sat down, Gerry turned back to Jo and sat down. She sat down, crossing her legs away from him, her eyes fixed straight ahead, her body frozen. Gerry offered her some popcorn and she shook her head and turned away. To her surprise, Josh's voice sounded in her ear. "You all right?"

She managed a nod.

"Only," he continued, "you look like you're about to be tortured rather than see a film. You didn't read the reviews, did you?"

Jo let her shoulders relax. "I'm fine thanks."

Immediately Josh swore loudly.

"What?" she asked.

"There's Toby," he said.

"Where?" Jo scanned the cinema.

"There," he pointed with his head. "Right smack bang in the middle, by the front."

They watched him in the dark.

"What the hell's he doing in the front?" hissed Josh.

"Maybe he wants to see the film," pointed out Jo.

"See if you can spot a thug who might be Todd Carter," Josh cut into her thoughts.

"The only thug I can see is Toby," she replied.

"Oh my God, he's holding her hand," whispered Josh. "Is he mad? Todd Carter's gonna kill him."

"He's a fearless young man. You should be very proud."

"He's a horny idiot who's going to get his face feng shuied. If she breaks his heart," he said, "I'll break her fucking scooter."

"You don't mean that."

"No," said Josh, bowing his head. "You're right. They're built to last."

Jo stifled a snort. *The famous Josh Fitzgerald charm*, she repeated in her head. She hoped the film was good. She needed distracting.

The film was shit. Toby completely forgot about the presence of Todd Carter thanks to the close proximity of thirteen-year-old ledge Anastasia Smith, a vision of virginal purity wearing a T-shirt that pressed against her buds of breasts and a wicked nose ring. So carried away was Toby by the proximity of such guileless beauty that he swallowed his chewing gum, got three lengthy snogs and a quick grope, all without spilling his popcorn.

This was more than anyone got in the group behind them. During each of his kid brother's excruciating snogs, Josh squirmed, sighed, and swore so much that people started to turn round and shush him. Every time the film showed a fight scene, Josh sensed that Todd Carter was taking notes for later and made noises about complaining to the censors for giving youngsters bad ideas. By the time they all came out of the cinema, he was a wreck.

"Far too much sex and violence," he muttered. "No wonder the youth of today are such losers."

"Right," said Nick, hand placed round a grinning Pippa's waist. "Which way did the lovebirds say they were going?"

"They were going to go up the back roads to the nightclub," said Josh. "The long way, because they really want me to suffer."

"Right, well let's follow them," said Gerry. He shot Jo a wink. "Now for the evening's real entertainment."

Jo only realized she'd grimaced to herself in the dark when she heard Josh chortle beside her.

They kept a safe distance. Josh would have liked the distance to be considerably less safe, but the CID boys said that if it was, Todd Carter wouldn't pounce. Josh said did they really need him to pounce, couldn't they wait until just *before* he pounced, and the CID boys insisted that no, Todd Carter had to actually pounce before they could do anything. Josh said could they at least use a different word because the word "pounce" was starting to make him feel sick.

At this point Pippa came over and whispered to Jo that Josh was a fantastic actor and if she hadn't overheard the conversation he'd had with Dick in the kitchen earlier and he hadn't been so obnoxious to Jo, she'd have thought he was one of the sweetest, most vulnerable men she'd ever met. At which point Jo realized she'd completely forgotten how much she hated him.

"Look at that!" hissed Josh suddenly, pointing in the distance. "He's got his arm round her!"

"Well it's a date, isn't it?" said Gerry, looking at Jo.

As they approached the end of the wide but dark Princes Avenue, which took them on to busy Muswell Hill Broadway, Toby and his young lady friend stopped. Then Nick, Pippa, and Gerry stopped. Then Josh and Jo stopped. Then they realized that Toby was talking to someone who had been loitering behind the pub in an alleyway.

"Oh look!" cried Pippa suddenly. "Someone's about to beat Toby up."

Sure enough, three tall lads were approaching Toby. Anastasia Smith, clearly a girl of some perspicacity as well as tight little tummy muscles, was moving slowly away toward the Broadway.

"Right," said Nick. "Wait for him to pounce."

Jo heard a soft whimper come from Josh.

And then Todd Carter pounced, Josh moaned, and Jo grasped his hand.

"Right," said Nick. "Let's *go!*"

Nick and Gerry legged it toward the group of boys, who were concentrating so hard on menacing Toby—whom they found strangely fearless—that they didn't hear anything until it was too late. By the time Pippa, Josh, and Jo had reached the group, Nick had one boy in a stranglehold against a wall and Gerry had two lads on the floor. The boys were sobbing in shock and terror.

"Jesus," whispered Josh and half-shielded Jo with his body. She peered out from behind his shoulder.

"Are you upsetting our friend?" Gerry whispered into the ear of the biggest boy. The biggest boy shook his head violently.

"'Cos we look out for our Toby," he whispered.

The boys continued to sob, while Toby ran ahead to look for his girlfriend.

Josh quickly turned to face Jo. "I can't look," he whispered. "Tell me when they've finished."

"Now," said Jo, giggling, as Gerry and Nick let the boys go.

Josh swiveled round to face them and seeing all was clear, gave Jo a little grin. "Just trying to make you laugh there," he confided. "Keep you relaxed."

"Thanks," she said through a smile.

"Don't let us *ever* see you anywhere near him, you hear?" said Nick. "Or we might have to find you again."

"Yeah," said Gerry. "We don't like bullies. Awright?"

The three schoolboys, by then looking like three small thirteen-year-olds, nodded firmly while holding back the tears.

"Well. What you waiting for? Piss off," concluded Nick, and the boys scarpered.

Nick and Gerry looked over at Pippa, Jo, and Josh. Pippa was the only one not wondering when she could run away.

"You're just big bullies, aren't you?" whispered Jo from behind Josh.

"Yum-my." Pippa sighed.

"I don't know how to thank you," said Josh. "But perhaps I could start by offering you my weekly pocket money."

Just then Toby came running back down the street.

"I can't find Ana!" he cried. "She's vanished!"

"So would I if I thought these thugs were your mates," answered Jo. "What made you think she'd be braver than Todd Carter?"

"Oh no!" said Toby, panicking for the first time all evening. "What if she tells her mum?"

"Come on, mate," said Josh, rushing forward to his brother. "Let's go look for her. She's probably gone straight on to the nightclub."

He turned to Nick and Gerry.

"Thanks, guys. You were amazing. It was worth getting the shit kicked out of me for that." He turned to Jo and gave her a wide, warm grin. "Enjoy your evening. Thanks for calming me down." And he put his arm round his kid brother and left her in the cold with the others.

By the time Jo got home, it was midnight. She and Gerry had gone to a pub with Nick and Pippa and then Nick and Pippa had vanished indiscreetly to Nick's place after twenty minutes. Jo then painstakingly told Gerry all about Shaun and tried to ignore the sensation that she was creating a fictional character. Gerry had nodded thoughtfully throughout.

"No worries," he said, sipping at his pint. "We can still be friends. Can't we?"

"Of course!"

"And if it ever develops into something else, so be it."

"I-I don't think it will. Because of Shaun. My boyfriend. It can't, you see."

"No worries," said Gerry, shrugging. "If it does, it does."

When she returned home, all the lights at the front of the house were off. She was glad. She was exhausted. But when she opened the kitchen door, she found Josh and Toby giggling over some beer. They looked up and greeted her like a long-lost friend. "Here she is!" cried Josh drunkenly. "Our savior!"

Jo laughed. "You're drunk."

"Yep," said Josh, pinching Toby's cheek. "And Tobe's got another date."

"Jo-osh," said Toby, trying not to grin.

"Well, what's wrong with telling Jo? She won't tell anyone will she? She's a mate."

They both looked up at her a bit shamefaced. Jo told herself it was the drink that was making Josh's eyes all warm again. Perhaps he should drink more.

"Thanks, Jo," said Toby.

"Pleasure," said Jo. "Anytime you want heavies, you know where to come." Josh pulled out a chair for her to join them. She hesitated, and saw Josh look quickly away. She sat down and took a beer. Josh and Toby grinned at each other, lifted beers, clinked them against hers and made a toast to "Jo's Heavies." And suddenly, Jo no longer felt a stranger.

Ironic that it should happen in the company of the family's two interlopers, but then, that's exactly what she was, wasn't it? She was as external a part of the privileged, inner circle of the Fitzgerald family as they were. She suddenly felt that it didn't matter what had gone on between her and Josh before—all of that was water under the bridge. They were mates again.

"So, tell us Joanne—Joanna? Blimey," said Josh, "—just realized I don't know your name."

"Josephine. After Jo from *Little Women*."

Josh raised his eyebrows.

"Wow! Josephine. Nice name. Josie. Jose. Josefina."

"Jo."

"Right. So tell us Jo. How was the rest of your evening?"

She pulled a face. "Not sure he got the message, to be honest."

"Oh dear. Were you too subtle?"

"I told him I didn't want to go out with him."

Josh nodded slowly, never taking his eyes off her. "Nope," he said softly. "You weren't too subtle."

"And he took it really well and then kept saying, sort of, 'if it happens, it happens.' "

"Oh."

"I've got an idea!" cried Toby suddenly. "Why don't you two go out with each other?"

There was a crippling silence.

"Nice try, Mr. Matchmaker," said Josh. "Josephine from *Little Women* has an extremely good-looking boyfriend at home."

"Jo," she smiled.

"As good-looking as you?" Toby asked his brother.

"I don't know," answered Josh merrily, turning to Jo. "I've never asked her."

They looked at each other, Jo at a loss for words.

Just then her phone rang.

"Saved by the bell," murmured Josh into his beer.

Jo looked at the number on the screen.

"Oh dear," she sighed. "It's home. Mum wants to tell me that Dad hasn't eaten enough vegetables."

They watched her answer her phone.

"Hello?"

"Can I speak to Josephine Green?" came a male voice.

"Dad!" cried Jo. "It's me. What's up?"

"It's Mum."

"What's Mum?"

"She's had a stroke. Can you come home?"

Chapter 18

Jo was awake before six. She stared at Mickey and wondered why on earth she should be witnessing his arms in those positions. For one thing he looked like he was performing something unspeakable, and for another, she should be too fast asleep to notice. Then she realized she was still fully dressed. Then she remembered her father's call. And then she heard someone beside her on her bed. She stared at Josh, lying next to her, stirring. He opened his eyes, and they looked in befuddled shock at each other.

"Alright?" he croaked.

"Mm," she said, and jumped out of bed and into the bathroom. There she tried to rehearse the speech to Vanessa that Josh had helped her with last night, but it was hard to concentrate on the matter in hand.

Josh had been amazing. When she'd started crying, he'd soothed her, calmed her, put his arm round her. Toby had gone off to sleep, and Josh had poured her a stiff brandy and then sat with her, while she'd wept and blamed herself. She cringed in her shower at the memory. And then he'd sat on her bed as she talked, reassuring her until she'd fallen asleep.

When she came back into her room, Josh was lying awake and fully clothed on top of the bedclothes. He looked rough. It suited him.

"The shower's free," she whispered. "Do you want a coffee?"

"I'll do it," he said. "You tell Vanessa."

"Are you sure?"

"Yup. Good luck."

"Thanks, Josh."

Vanessa was already in the bathroom—she never used the en suite shower in the mornings, it ruined her hair—and Jo tapped on the door. Vanessa opened it a crack. She was brushing her teeth, about to spend her Sunday in the office, making last-minute preparations for tomorrow's pitch.

"Oh he-o," she said. "Any-hin wron?"

"My mother's had a stroke. I've got to go home."

Vanessa stopped brushing her teeth. Toothpaste began to dribble down her chin.

"Ho'd on," she said, and went to rinse out her mouth.

Jo leaned against the bathroom door.

"Right," said Vanessa. "Your mum's not well—"

Jo shook her head and started to cry. Vanessa put her arms round her.

"Come on," she murmured. "She'll be fine."

"I have to look after my dad," squeaked Jo.

"Of course you do."

"He's only got two arteries functioning in his heart."

"Oh dear."

Jo sniffed.

"I'll come back as soon as I can."

"Don't even think about that. We'll get a temporary nanny. It's not a problem," said Vanessa, already planning which phone calls she would have to make and which she could delegate to Dick.

"When are you planning on going?"

"Tomorrow—"

"Shit!"

Jo nodded. "My dad needs me," she squeaked.

"Of course he does," said Vanessa, hurrying to her bedroom to dress. She turned to Jo at the door. "Good luck." She shut the bedroom door behind her.

At the sound of the bedroom door slamming, Dick jumped awake.

"Wake up!" Vanessa told him. "Jo's leaving."

"What? What did you do this time?"

"I didn't do anything. Her mother's ill, so she's going home because her father's a man."

"Eh?"

"She has to help him live or something. *Wake up.*" Vanessa had one foot in her tights and was hopping around the room.

Dick rubbed his eyes. "How come Jo's mother's the one who's had the stroke, Jo's the one who's leaving, and yet it's her father who's the bad one?"

"For God's sake, Dick," snapped Vanessa, falling on to the bed. "I haven't got time to argue.

"How useful."

"Of all days for this to happen. I can't do a thing about it today and tomorrow's the VC pitch."

"Oh dear," said Dick, swinging his legs over the side of the bed. "God forbid a family crisis should get in the way of your career climb."

Vanessa hitched her tights up over her crotch and grabbed a blouse from the wardrobe.

"Sod off, Dick. If we get this, I'll get a bonus that will keep us in food for the next year. Can't you shut the shop up next week?" She zipped up her skirt. "Or will your customer mind?"

"How would that help?"

"You could look after the children?"

"No I couldn't!" shot Dick. "I wouldn't know where to start."

"Well you can't make a worse job of it than you've made of the shop," she said, brushing her hair in the mirror.

"Thank you. Your wifely support is most appreciated."

Vanessa turned to face him.

"For God's sake, Dick!" she cried. "Don't just stand there! Get dressed! You've got phone calls to make."

Downstairs, Josh brought Jo her coffee while she stared at her rucksack.

Josh surveyed her empty room. "How long are you going for?"

"As long as they need me. Maybe for good."

Josh sat down on her bed and watched.

"Can I do anything to help?" he asked. "Do you need a lift up there?"

Jo turned to face him. "No thanks."

"I don't mind," said Josh, holding her clock. "I could take tomorrow morning off work. I hate work."

"No, thanks. My dad's meeting me at the station and taking me straight to the hospital."

"How long's your mum going to be there?"

"Hopefully she's coming home at the weekend. It was only a mild stroke." Jo steadied her breath. "She'll have a carer in twice a day, but most of it will be down to my dad."

"And you."

Jo opened her rucksack and looked at it. "Yep."

"Here." Josh stood up and took the rucksack out of her hands. "You just sit down and tell me what to pack."

Jo landed heavily on the bed. "Everything," she said.

There was silence.

"Right," said Josh. "Everything."

★ ★ ★

"*Pants*, Zak!" screamed Vanessa early Monday morning.

"I don't want to wear them!"

"Well you can't go to school without them."

"*Good!*" Sometimes his parents were so stupid.

"Zak, sweetie," coaxed Vanessa. "Mummy's own Superman. Super-mummy has a very important meeting to get to. Do you want her to have a nervous breakdown?"

Zak shrugged.

"Thank you, darling. So nice to know you're on my side."

"Why can't you stay with us?"

"I will," said Vanessa. "From tomorrow. I'll be with you all day."

Dick had phoned all three nanny agencies they knew. Unsurprisingly, none of them had a spare nanny who needed an indefinite temporary post starting Monday morning. They'd just have to pray for Jo's mother to make a speedy and full recovery. Until then Vanessa would take time off work.

"But just for today," she explained again to Zak, "you're going to have lots of fun with Jo's friend Pippa and Tallulah's friend Georgiana."

"I want Jo. Georgiana's a prissy cow."

"I know," agreed Vanessa, too stressed (and deep down, too impressed) to argue. "But Pippa isn't, and if you wear your pants like a good boy, she'll show you her tattoo."

After lengthy, complex negotiations, Zak wore his navy blue pants (instead of the stupid bright blue pants) with the red skull and crossbones on (instead of the stupid red anchors), and Vanessa was able to leave his room before bedtime.

Ten minutes later Tallulah was crying.

"Look!" shouted Vanessa. "*This* one's pink!"

Tallulah howled so loudly that Vanessa feared she might perforate something. She rushed to the wardrobe and pulled out an even pinker top.

"Ooh, look," she encouraged. "This one's even *more* pink. Mmmm."

Tallulah froze. Vanessa froze. For an instant Vanessa didn't know which way this was going to go. And then the instant was over and Tallulah bayed to the child moon with grief and horror.

Cassandra wandered in carrying Tallulah's Barbie top.

"Are you looking for this?" she asked over the noise. "She left it in my room last night."

Tallulah rushed to her Barbie top like a mother to her infant, and then, with it safely in her hands, started the slow descent to posttraumatic shock.

"Thanks, Cassie," said Vanessa. "You clever girl."

"S'okay," Cassie said.

By ten to nine that morning, Jo was standing at Paddington Station, staring up at the train timetables, holding a large black coffee, and wearing a rucksack. In the end, Josh had only packed the essentials, and she was now very grateful. She kept having the oddest feeling that she'd left something behind at the Fitzgeralds'. Was it her Mickey Mouse clock? No, she decided firmly, as the timetable flicker-flacked the arrival of her train. She felt she had finally outgrown him. Staring at her feet, she yanked her rucksack up her back and headed for her platform. Perhaps it was time for a mature person's clock, a clock to show her fully rounded personality. Lisa Simpson, maybe?

She found herself a seat, stored her rucksack, and settled down. She fixed her personal stereo and adjusted the earphones, checking the tape that she'd left in it. She hadn't listened to Travis for ages—not since before she'd left home. She remembered playing this album on her birthday, the evening she'd met Shaun and the gang in the pub.

As the train glided out of the station and the familiar minor chords struck up in her ears, tears sprang up out of nowhere, and Jo lost control big-time.

As Jo's train sped smoothly north, Vanessa's team sped smoothly through their pitch. She watched Anthony and Tom sing the jingle, play the parts of Alice and the White Rabbit, and produce the most impressive story-board she'd ever seen. Tom made a surprisingly effective Alice.

They left on such a high that in the cab on the way back to the office, even Tom was positive.

"If we don't get it, I'll shag my own mother," he said, beaming.

It was a tense afternoon.

At five o'clock, Vanessa stood with her junior Tricia, Max, Tom, and Anthony by the fax machine, urging it to spring into action.

"Push baby, push," coaxed Max, but the fax refused to be coaxed.

Piqued, he went to get a Scotch. Then suddenly, a trill tone, a click, a whir, and as if by magic, paper started jerking toward them.

"Here it comes!" he bellowed, racing back to prime position. He tore it off and read it breathlessly.

"We've got it!" he yelled, turning puce. "We fucking got it!"

Everyone was hugging everyone, and champagne was already out. They'd done it! Vanessa didn't even mind when Max kept calling Tom and Anthony "fucking geniuses" and completely forgetting to congratulate her at all. She decided to do something about it. "Congratulations!" she told Tricia loudly. "I couldn't have done it without you." Tricia looked at her as if she'd just spoken in Swahili.

"Right," said Anthony suddenly, putting down his champagne. "Must take a leak."

And with a quick glance at Vanessa, he was gone.

Vanessa stood still for a while, surrounded by the revelers, determined to enjoy her moment. And then she made a decision.

"Ooh," she said putting down her champagne, next to Anthony's. "Me too. Must be all the excitement."

Surprisingly, no one wanted to share Jo's seat all journey—Monday morning must have been a good time to travel out of London—so she had no excuse to stop crying. The only time she stopped was when the train whooshed into a tunnel and she found herself staring out at an all-encompassing blackness, interrupted only by her sorry reflection. She closed her eyes and concentrated on the tunnel enveloping her, protecting her, as if she—inside the train—had given it meaning. For a moment all was well with the world. Then as suddenly as the train had entered the tunnel, it shot out of it again, into the white, cold daylight, and Jo felt her tears return.

Vanessa, back squashed against the Silly Nibble cupboard door, front squashed up against Anthony, took a deep breath, rested her head on his shoulder, and slowly sucked chocolate out of her molars. When he moved away, she started to pull her blouse back on.

"I'm sorry," she said.

"That's okay—"

"I shouldn't—I don't—"

"Shhh."

"Do you think they noticed?" she whispered, as her body slowly slipped back into focus.

"Dunno," said Anthony. "So how long are you going to be gone?" he asked, retying his tie.

"Fortnight at the most." She buttoned up her blouse. "The nanny's mother's ill."

"Bitch," he muttered, straightening his tie.

"You can joke," tutted Vanessa, tucking her blouse into her skirt. "It's not your life it impinges on."

"I wasn't joking," said Anthony, smoothing down his hair. "And yes it is."

Some believe that in every office, someone somewhere is in a stationery cupboard with someone else, sharing an illicit moment of not looking for stationery together. In fact, only a month earlier, Josh had been known to frequent a certain stationery cupboard with a certain person where together they had forgotten all about stationery. And now that certain person was approaching. As Sally reached his desk and perched on the edge of it, he tried to work up enough momentum to smile.

"What's wrong, lover boy? Someone died in your family?" she murmured.

He upped the effort and tried to laugh. "I'm just a bit down at the moment," he replied.

"Oh dear," she soothed. "Perhaps I can try and get you"—she leaned forward—"up again."

He stared at her, trying to remember her good points. "Nah, you're alright, thanks."

"I know I'm alright," she shot. "I'm fine. It's not me I'm worried about."

"Don't worry about me."

"Fine." Sally shrugged.

"I'm just a bit down."

"We've established that."

"Sorry."

"I don't really care for your sympathy, Josh."

"Sorry."

"Not half as sorry as I am for you."

Josh nodded. "Yep. That makes sense. I'm a complete mess."

"Yeah well, I'm a tidy girl—"

"I know—"

"No room for mess—"

"I know—"

"So seeing as you're an immature, messy scrap of humanity who can't bin something he doesn't need anymore, and I'm the adult in this 'shag-ationship,' it looks like I'll be the one who's binning you."

Josh tried to smile again.

"Consider yourself binned, Josh."

"Thank you. You're a truly good person."

"Don't patronize me, you sod."

"Sorry."

"I'd bought a basque as well," she muttered.

"Sorry."

She got off his desk. "It's alright," she said. "Just because you won't be seeing it, doesn't mean no one else will."

"I have every faith—"

"Don't *patronize* me."

"Sorry."

And with that, Sally walked away, head high, ignoring the rib ache from her basque.

Josh stared at his phone, wondering how long the journey from London to Niblet-upon-Avon was.

Jo arrived at the station. Two whole minutes earlier, she'd stopped crying. Then she spotted her father standing alone on the platform and started all over again. They shared an awkward embrace and headed off to the hospital in silence. The hospital was tiny. It was where Jo had been born, and as they approached it, Bill started recounting his feelings on walking there twenty-three years earlier. He touched on the previous miscarriages Hilda had suffered, the doctors' gloomy prognoses, and their joy when Jo was born. The nearer they got, the more Jo felt she was still carrying her rucksack.

"She's just down here," said her father, as they approached a ward to the right. Jo kept her eyes ahead and followed him as he veered toward the end bed.

They found Hilda wide-awake. Smaller than Jo remembered and with slightly more squashy hair, but apart from that, surprisingly similar to before. She even managed a glint of recognition and half a smile on seeing her daughter.

She was already making clear sounds and just beginning to move the left side of her body. The nurse explained that if the physiotherapy and speech therapy went to plan, she should be almost good as new within six months.

When Jo and Bill returned home later that evening, they were too tired to eat. Bill sat in the lounge, flicking through the channels, and Jo shut the lounge door and sat in silence in the hall by the phone. She looked down at her mother's spidery writing on the notepad. *Jo's phone numbers*, it said. There was her mobile number and the Fitzgeralds' number. *Best times to ring: Weekdays—between 9pm and 11pm and weekends—not in the morning!* Jo rested her head in her hand.

"Cuppa?" Her dad appeared in the hall.

"Mm, lovely," she said, and picked up the phone. She left a message on Shaun's voicemail. She tried Sheila and did the same. She told them she was home and would love to see them. She didn't phone Pippa.

Vanessa was still in the office midevening when her phone rang. It was Dick.

"So how did it go?" he asked.

"How did what go?" asked Vanessa warily, hiding a Silly Nibble chocolate bar in her top drawer.

"The pitch. Did you get it?"

"Oh yes!" said Vanessa. "We got it."

Dick nodded slowly. He should have guessed.

"Well done, Mzzz Superwoman," he said. "Even with your home life crashing around your ears, you still don't miss a single rung up that ladder."

"Did you actually phone for a reason, Dick?"

"Just wanted to say well done."

"That was 'well done,' was it?"

"Yes. Would you like me to say it again?"

"No I certainly wouldn't. Anything else?"

"Just to say that after such hard work, you really deserve a fortnight off with the children."

"Just remember the deal. If Jo's gone for more than two weeks, it's your turn."

"Fine," said Dick generously. "I could definitely do with a break."

"Is that all you called about?" she asked.

"Nope. Thought you might like to know that the children are going to bed now and send their clever mummy all their love."

"Thank you," said Vanessa. "Tell them Mummy's looking forward to using up two weeks of her precious holiday looking after them while Daddy sits in an empty shop scratching his balls."

"Oh, I have to go, darling," rushed Dick, "one of them needs the toilet."

"I hope it's Tallulah," replied Vanessa, "because the others have been managing on their own for a while now." And she slammed down the phone.

Dick held the phone away from his ear, then very slowly put it down. Then he started rocking backward and forward, head in hands.

Chapter 19

Jo was so busy in her first week at home that she didn't have too much time to brood on why Shaun hadn't returned the phone message she'd left him on her first day back. Looking after her mother was far harder than looking after any children because Jo was so emotionally drained. Hilda needed twenty-four-hour care and could only move fractionally. It was like looking after a baby, while coping with the grief of losing a parent.

However, her mind wasn't so one-tracked that she didn't notice something was up with Shaun. She started replaying recent conversations with him and realized they'd hardly spoken more than twice a week in the past month, and even then their conversations had been short and full of unspoken resentments. She kept thinking back to when he'd come to visit her in Highgate. On the surface, things had gone well between them—if anything, they'd been happier than they had been for a long time. And then she thought of how things had felt under the surface. And then she pushed all thoughts of Josh to the back of her mind. Until night-time, when in the safety of her bed, in the safety of the dark, she scrunched her eyes shut, faced the bedroom wall she'd faced all the way through childhood, and let her mind free-fall from a great height, whizzing past heaven and landing in hell, just thinking of him.

When she had a spare moment from worrying about her mother, musing over Shaun, and dreaming of Josh, she thought about Sheila. Sheila had also not phoned her back since her return. It dawned on Jo that she hadn't actually spoken to Sheila since the call when Sheila had asked about Pippa, when Jo had had to leave midconversation. It only occurred to her now, in the cold light of day, how insensitive that was. And that was weeks ago—or was it months? Sheila hadn't returned one of her voice messages since then.

When Shaun finally phoned, a week and a half after she'd got home, she hardly recognized his voice.

"Oh hello," she said warily. "How are you?"

"Fine thanks," said Shaun. "You?"

"Mm. Fine."

She was just about to ask him whether he'd got her message, when he asked how her mother was. She did a little hop, skip, and jump over concern and landed on anger.

"Fine."

"Oh good."

"She's back home."

"I'm pleased to hear it."

"Thank you."

They arranged to see each other that Friday night—in two days' time, nearly a whole two weeks after she'd come home. Neither seemed particularly excited about it.

Things were going just as badly at the Fitzgerald home. Vanessa stood motionless in the middle of her kitchen, silence percolating through every pore, her naked eyes fixed on the clock—11:15 A.M. Were the clock batteries running low? She considered going back to bed until Tallulah needed to be picked up. Ironically, taking this time off to be at home had felt, at first, like supremely beneficial timing—she hadn't had to face Anthony after their scramble in the Silly Nibble cupboard. But as the time had passed, she realized it was the worst thing she could have done. All it meant was that she hadn't been able to tell him immediately that she'd made a terrible mistake. She'd had to nurse her guilt for a whole fortnight, her only company being all the loved ones she'd betrayed. It bordered on torture.

She had thought about phoning Anthony at the office, but that would have implied that their dalliance—dalliance? Did it even count as that?—held some significance for her. And also someone at home might find out. Oh God, had it come to this? Added to the stress of that, the isolation of being at home was doing her head in. Every morning, she had her daily update phone call with Tricia and Max, but their efficient brusqueness against the background office noises cut like a knife. Every time they were about to say good-bye she had to stop herself asking them to stop and chat. Was she like this on the phone when she spoke to Dick, in his empty shop? Did she make him feel this excluded, this irrelevant? And then the phone call would be over and Tricia and Max would hang up abruptly, leaving her to a day of relentless, mind-numbing silence.

She felt like her soul was slowly shrinking. And in only a few days, she had become a different person. She hardly recognized herself. She'd become dangerously introspective and started talking to herself. Her beautiful home had transformed into a prison, and she felt swamped by a need to get out of it. Unfortunately, the more swamped she felt, the less she was able to extricate herself from it. But when she did manage it, she seemed to have turned into a madwoman. She'd start striking up inane conversations with shop staff, she'd try and make eye contact with passersby, she'd even chatted to the *Big Issue* seller she usually ignored, until his eyes glazed over. Her all-time low was one morning when she'd managed to rationalize to herself the possibility of inviting in the dustmen for coffee. She wasn't one for poetry but after nearly two weeks at home as a full-time mother, she felt like she was a flower rooted in the shade, wilting silently against a cold brick wall. The thought that she might never again find a nanny like Jo, who would stay with them for long enough to give the children stability, and that the only possible solution might be that she give up her day job, had started to haunt her in the dead of night.

It wasn't as if she was idle. Keeping house—to the standard she'd grown used to with Jo living there—was a thankless, invisible, and twenty-four-hour-long job. It made her office job look like sheer bliss. At least with an office job, everyone at the office might treat you as a form of underclass, but the outside world treated you with some respect. At home not even your own children respected you. In those seemingly endless hours between afternoon and evening when the children needed her attention most and when she had least reserves of energy or emotion, she'd think of Jo and want to weep.

As she stood in the silent kitchen, thinking such thoughts again and again, the phone made her jump. Was it Max? Anthony, maybe? She braced herself and picked up the phone. "Hello, Vanessa Fitzgerald," she announced.

"I should hope so," said Dick cheerfully. "Otherwise, I'll have to start paying you."

"Ha-ha."

"How's it all going?"

"The kids are at school, and I'm just about to make a coffee to give me enough energy to kill myself."

"Oh. Don't do that, darling."

"Give me one good reason."

"Who'd pick up the children?"

She slammed down the phone and cried until it was time to pick up Tallulah.

With only one more day to go before the weekend, Vanessa wore mascara to celebrate. Three layers of it. She spent twenty minutes doing her makeup. It probably made her weigh two pounds more, but it had been worth it. Tallulah had watched with awe and, once permission was granted, had played ecstatically with mummy's pinkest lipsticks, and they'd managed to while away almost an hour tidying her makeup drawer.

They hadn't bothered with Tumble Tots or ballet all fortnight—Vanessa decided they might as well make the most of just being together, and anyway, she wasn't exactly sure where they were held and didn't want to interrupt Jo on her time off. She also didn't want to risk getting Tallulah's hopes up and then not be able to find the place.

On their last Thursday together, by the time they were ready for their teatime walk, both were pleased with the way their afternoon had turned out. Tallulah was wearing Summer Sunshine nail polish and Vanessa had a tidy makeup drawer. Tallulah had learned how to make pizza from scratch, and Vanessa didn't have to prepare any tea. It didn't give her the same buzz that her job did, but it did make her feel she wasn't such a failure as a mother.

The next morning, her last Friday off from work, Vanessa woke with a start after dreaming of falling down a hole in the ground and never reaching the bottom. She got out of bed in one bound.

While Vanessa clattered round the kitchen, Josh lay awake listening. He'd been having problems sleeping again, just like old times. And every time he woke up in the morning, after a night of thinking it would never come, his first emotion was dread. He hated walking through Jo's room. Every time, the same thoughts, the same feelings. He'd try not to, but end up looking at her bed and remember lying on it watching her falling asleep the night she'd got her dad's call; then he'd think about her with Shaun and remember the noises he'd heard through the stud wall when Shaun had come to stay; then finally, he'd think about them being together now. And then after his shower, he'd walk back through her room again into his room to dress and have exactly the same memories, the same thoughts, the same feelings. And then he'd have to walk through her room again, out into the kitchen and have exactly the same memories, the same thoughts, the same feelings. Three little journeys to hell every morning before breakfast.

And every evening he'd have to listen to Vanessa and Dick arguing about giving up on Jo and getting a new nanny. Vanessa was adamant Jo was coming back, Dick was concerned that she wasn't and they'd never find a nanny as good as she, or one who would stay. One evening when Dick had suggested that maybe after all, the children just needed their mother, they'd had the biggest row he'd ever heard.

After work, Josh climbed up the steps from Highgate Station, slowly but surely, and made his way to his dad's shop. Although there was a light drizzle, the spring evening smelled of flowers trying to bud. There was an almost tangible optimism in the air, like God's own version of supermarket's baked bread and Muzak. Summer would be here before he knew it. And yet he was depressed. He watched the traffic as he paced through Highgate. *Weird*, he thought as he neared the shop. *I never noticed how popular white Clios were before.*

Jo wiped her mother's mouth gently with the napkin and put the spoon back in the bowl.

"There," she said. "Well done. Can you believe Dad made it out of his own brain?"

Her mother smiled a slow wonky smile that squeezed at Jo's heart.

"He never even knew there was such a thing as a parsnip before making it," Jo said briskly. "You almost had parsnip soup without the parsnip."

Hilda laughed as Jo put the bowl on her bedside table.

"Do you want to wait a bit before you move on to the cheese and crackers?"

Hilda nodded.

"Sheila still hasn't called back," said Jo quietly. Hilda looked at her. "I think I upset her when I was in London," she explained. "Didn't call enough. Made her feel used." She looked up at her mum. "I don't think I called anyone enough," she whispered. Very slowly, Hilda lifted her hand and placed it on Jo's. They exchanged thin smiles. Jo picked up the plate with the cheese and crackers.

"Right," she said. "Tell me when you've had enough."

They'd phoned! Three o'clock on the Friday before Vanessa was due back and they'd phoned! It had taken them two weeks to need her, but need her they did! Vanessa was buzzing. She had a deadline—Max wanted some facts and figures that only she could provide, and he wanted them fast. "Fucking fast," in fact. *Tra bloody la,* thought Vanessa. A few emergency phone calls and she was back in the driver's seat. Tallulah sat with Mummy at the kitchen table and pretended to be an advertising accounts manager while Vanessa delegated the most basic of jobs and got one of the most efficient PAs she'd ever had. Better still, it stopped Vanessa thinking too much about Anthony, her marriage, her responsibilities, and the mess she was making of her life.

"Thanks for coming straight from work," said Dick to Josh. "I really appreciate it."

"Anytime, Dad," said Josh. "You must know that."

"Yes but on a Friday," said Dick. "I know all you city types usually go out for a well-deserved drink—"

"Yeah and I hate it. I'd much rather be here."

Josh never ceased to be amazed that his father didn't realize that he'd probably swallow fire for him. That's the way parenting works. Children could smell parental love like dogs could smell fear. Love your child unconditionally and they could one day leap up and ferociously attack you. Act as if you don't really care, and they slavishly adore you.

"What's the latest, Dad?" he asked.

Dick sighed. "I'm giving up on Jackie."

Josh stared at his father, then started nodding slowly.

"I can't rely on her anymore," said Dick. "And I may not have the time. I need someone I can really rely on. Someone I can trust."

"Mm?"

Dick grinned at his son. "You're going to make me ask you, aren't you?"

Josh mirrored his father's grin. "Oh yes."

"Josh."

"Dad."

"I'm sacking my accountant. Please will you do my accounts?"

Josh sucked in air and shook his head, pretending to consider.

"Of course I'd pay you!" rushed Dick.

"Don't be ridiculous—"

"I'm not being ridiculous," said Dick. "I have, amazingly enough, still got my pride. God knows how, but—"

"Dad, it would be like a hobby for me—I mean, I'd love to actually keep the books for a place I care about instead of some massive, faceless company—"

"Well we certainly aren't massive."

"I don't want the money."

"Stop it, Josh—you're doing more than enough already."

"Hardly. And as we both know, if it wasn't for that bloody stupid n—"

"It wasn't Jo's fault—"

"I know!" broke in Josh, astonished. "I was going to say that stupid *night,* not that stupid *nanny.* If it wasn't for that stupid night and me being a prize moron, we'd be in a much better position—*you'd* be in a much better position. It's my fault, so the least I can do is help out."

"I'm very grateful. Please look at my books and let me know if it's worth carrying on. I can't live like this for much longer."

"You'll take my professional opinion?" asked Josh.

"Of course."

"But . . . you didn't when I told you not to fall for Jackie's sales pitch. Remember?"

Dick smiled. "You were still studying then. Give me a break."

"I just needed to check."

"I trust and respect your professional opinion."

"Wow," said Josh. "And what will you do if I suggest the worst?"

Dick took a deep breath. "Sell."

"And then what?"

"I'll jump off that bridge when I come to it," said Dick. "One thing at a time, eh?"

Josh nodded again. Dick came across and shook his new accountant by the hand.

Friday evening and Jo was more nervous about seeing Shaun than she had been when he visited her in London. Still at home, she brought down the dinner tray and placed it on the kitchen table. Her dad, wearing a pinny, put the dinner plates straight in the sink.

"Oh good," he said, looking at Hilda's leftovers. "She's eating much more isn't she?"

"Well it's so delicious," Jo said, looking up at the kitchen clock.

"It's Nigella."

"Ah."

"Will you give me a hand carrying the TV upstairs before you go, love?" asked her dad. "She wants to watch *Midsomer Murders.*"

"Course."

"I don't want to make you late for Shaun," he added.

"No worries. He took long enough to call me back."

Bill followed her into the lounge. "You're not playing games with him, are you? Men don't like that."

"Dad," breathed Jo, lifting the TV. "How old am I?"

"Old enough to know better. *Steady*."

"No, that's you. I'm old enough to make my own decisions. I've got it, stop pushing."

"Alright alright. Left a bit. I just don't like to see a good man treated badly."

Jo decided to concentrate on maneuevering the television round the tight corner of the stairs instead of maneuvering her father round the twisted corners of her mind. Half an hour later, she lounged upstairs on her mum's bed watching TV, while her dad chatted to Shaun downstairs.

"Don't . . . stay . . ." murmured Hilda.

"I suppose I'd better go," agreed Jo. "Before Dad bores the pants off him. Have a good night. Enjoy the TV."

As she got to the door, she turned round and looked at her mother. Hilda opened her eyes wide.

"Good . . . luck," she whispered.

Jo smiled and made her way downstairs.

She stood outside the lounge for a second before opening the door. She was terrified of Shaun being indifferent to her, cold or just strange.

She needn't have worried. He looked terrified.

"Alright?" he said.

"Alright."

There was a pause.

"Right, well," said Bill, leaving the lounge. "I'll leave you lovebirds to it."

They all went to the hall, Bill going upstairs as they opened the front door. "See you when we see you Jo," he called from the stairs.

Jo considered smiling at Shaun, but didn't.

"They're watching what my mother wants on TV tonight," she explained to the cold spring evening.

"Oh."

"Quite a night, as you can imagine."

Shaun did something in between a smile and a laugh.

By the time they reached the restaurant, Jo was beginning to fear that Shaun was planning to propose again. All the signs were there—he'd gone quiet and pale like the other times, and she was filled with a vague sense of foreboding.

They sat down at their restaurant table and faced each other.

"Jo," started Shaun.

"Don't, please—"

"Don't what?"

There was a pause.

"I don't know," said Jo. "Sorry. What were you going to say?"

"Don't *what*?" he repeated.

"I don't know—"

"Then don't *what*?"

The waiter appeared.

"Would you like some drinks?" he asked.

"Yes," they said.

The waiter took their orders, and they started again.

"Jo," said Shaun.

Jo took a deep breath.

"Yes," she answered with a bright smile.

"I'm not going to propose again."

She let out a heavy sigh of relief.

"After this one last time," he finished.

She stopped breathing altogether.

"I don't understand what's happening in your world," he said, gesturing vaguely near her head. "I don't know how you're feeling, I don't know why you went to London, I don't even know what you think of me anymore."

"I—"

"Let me finish, please, Jo."

"Sorry."

"All I know is that I can't go on like this any longer."

"God, I'm sorry—"

"Please, let me finish."

"Sorry."

"It's really very simple, Jo."

She blinked and waited.

"You either want to be with me or you don't."

She blinked again.

"You either want to marry me or you don't."

She nodded.

"You just have to tell me so I can get on with my life."

She blinked and nodded.

"So," he said. "You have to decide."

She stared at him.

"What's it to be, Jo?"

The waiter appeared. "Are you ready to order?"

"Yes," said Shaun.

"No," said Jo.

"I'll come back when you're both ready," said the waiter.

Jo looked at Shaun.

"I love you Shaun," she whispered.

She saw him take a deep breath.

"But I can't marry you."

She watched him let out a heavy sigh.

As they sat there, she realized Shaun was right. It had been very simple after all. Now all she had to do was work out who was going to help her make big decisions like that in future.

After the last meal Jo and Shaun were to have together, it occurred to Jo that she had never loved him more than she did then. When he asked for the bill, she loved him for his quiet ability to take control; when he helped her into her coat, she loved him for his little gentlemanly acts. When he drove her home, she loved him for his kindness. When he kissed her gently on her lips for the last time, she loved him for having shared an intimate world with her. Sitting in the passenger seat of his car, she began to ache with loneliness.

"Bye, Shaun," she said, sniffing.

"Bye, Jo. Always remember that I love you."

She got out of the car and walked to her parents' house.

She shut the front door and leaned against it. She could see a crack of light from upstairs, which meant that her parents were still awake. She knew they hadn't expected her to come home that night and yet at the same time, they had. She climbed the stairs. When she reached the top, she heard her father call out from their bedroom. She tapped on their door.

"Come in," he called.

Her parents were sitting up in bed together, a sight that made her feel envious and comforted at the same time.

"Your mother wants to know if you had a good evening," said her father. "I told her to mind her own business, but . . ."

Jo sighed and nodded, the tears speaking for themselves.

"I'll be fine," she said eventually. "Night."

"Your mother says to tell you we're here if you need us," her father said gruffly.

"Thanks, Dad."

Her mother made a gesture with her right hand. Jo waited.

"No . . . matter . . . what," whispered Hilda.

Jo smiled at them both and blew them both a kiss. She shut their bedroom door behind her and went to bed.

Chapter 20

Monday morning came bright and breezy. Hilda had come downstairs for the first time since her stroke. Jo had been home for two whole weeks and it felt like she'd never been away; the sun was out, and it looked like summer was coming early. Which, of course, meant it would rain the next day.

Jo had phoned Vanessa the night before to explain that she couldn't come back yet, but would as soon as her mother was able to walk upstairs unaided. She'd begged Vanessa to keep her job open for her and told her how much she missed them all, and had felt hugely relieved when Vanessa had sounded emphatic about wanting her to come back whenever she was ready. She'd even alluded to giving Jo a raise. But Jo had felt as if she was phoning another world. She wondered who else in the family was in the room while Vanessa spoke to her and felt a yearning to be there.

Without a downstairs toilet in their house, Hilda either had to stay upstairs twenty-four hours a day or start using a commode. She had gone for the latter option and Jo had offered to be her commode emptier—"just like in the olden days," she'd winked at her mum—when Bill had proved too squeamish. Jo was happy to do it as long as he kept up the cooking regime. She was convinced her mum would improve fast—she could sense her fingers itching to get back to feeding her father, especially after a night when he'd made himself steak and chips.

While Bill settled Hilda into his armchair, Jo put the kettle and her mobile on for the first time that day. While she was pouring hot water into the pot for her parents and the new cafetière she'd bought for herself, her mobile rang.

At first she didn't recognize Pippa's voice, but once she did, she was delighted to feel a surge of warmth toward her new friend. After a whole fortnight away from London, Jo was relying on her gut instinct to see if her life there had been genuinely good or had been her putting on a brave face. She had wanted to phone Pippa often, but had felt too guilty about phoning her before speaking to Sheila. She could have hugged Pippa.

"Hi, stranger!" cried Pippa.

"Hi!" Jo almost laughed the word out. "How are you?"

"I'm fine! I'm having sex! With a policeman!"

"Which one?"

"Nick, of course! I've been Nicked!'

"So you're going out with him now?"

"Um," said Pippa. "Actually I'm staying in with him, more than going out with him. If you get my drift."

"I'm *so* pleased for you, Pip."

"Well, it was all due to you."

"Don't be daft. I only introduced you. The rest was all your own work."

"I know. And I owe you big-time. We really miss you!" said Pippa. "When are you coming back?"

"Oh God, I miss you, too!" replied Jo. And then, inexplicably, her happiness tipped over straight into misery. Like a baby trying to hide the fact that she's ready for bed, Jo suddenly found herself crying. She decided it would be a fine time to tell Pippa about Shaun and her.

"What shall I tell Nick?" asked Pippa, after making all the right noises, then leaving a long enough pause.

"Why?" Jo sniffed.

"Because, honey, Gerry's still after you," explained Pippa. "And he's a cop who's used to getting what he wants."

"God," sniffed Jo. "How terrifying."

"I'm just letting you know the way the land lies in Boy World."

"Does it make any difference what I want?"

"Apparently you don't know what you want."

Jo sucked in some air. "That's outrageous!"

"They had a bet on you and Shaun finishing before summer, and Gerry getting in there before autumn."

"Oh God." Jo closed her eyes. "You've put me right off my breakfast."

"I told Nick you weren't interested," continued Pippa, "but he said you may have been playing hard to get and not telling me the truth."

"I *wasn't* interested," said Jo slowly and clearly, "I *wasn't* playing hard to get, and I *was* telling the truth."

"That's what I said. I told him girls don't think like boys."

"Thank God."

"He said everyone thinks like boys, girls just hide it better."

Jo made a face into the phone. "You have a very special man there, Phillipa."

"I know," said Pippa. "*And* he's good in bed."

"He'd better be."

"I'll tell him to tell Gerry you're not interested."

"Whatever."

"So," said Pippa, "how did you leave things with Josh?"

"Oh God," said Jo. "Have you got an hour?"

"That bad eh? You two looked pretty cosy at the cinema."

"I know. He went all nice on me again. And he was so wonderful when I got the call from my dad. He spent all Sunday helping me pack, helped me work out how I should tell Vanessa, he even stayed with me till I fell asleep the night I heard. I woke up the next morning, and he'd fallen asleep next to me."

"Blimey."

"But . . ."

"But?"

"I don't know."

"What's to know? You're single, he's single."

"That doesn't change what he said to me, about only wanting a shag because I was on tap. And he's a hypocrite because he hates infidelity but is helping his dad have an affair. And he's living at home rent-free in his midtwenties. And—"

"He looks like Hornblower—"

"—he . . ." Jo came to a halt. "I've forgotten what the fourth one was."

"How you feel about him?"

Jo groaned. "Don't confuse me."

"How do you think it'll be when you go back?"

"I've no idea. It feels more and more like it was all a dream, and I'm never going back. Like Dorothy—you know, I went looking for an answer, it was all Technicolor, but the answer wasn't really there, and now I'm back home again. Where everything's black-and-white."

"Oh my God. Profound."

"I think I've had too much time to brood."

"Listen," said Pippa, "as my mum always says, it'll all come out in the wash. You just have to believe it; otherwise, you'll go mad. How's your mum?"

After the call, Jo stood at the kitchen sink for a while. When the tea and coffee were both nicely stewed, she took them into the lounge on a tray. She felt a lot better after talking to Pippa. She realized that it was a new experience, talking openly and honestly to a friend who actively listened and who genuinely cared about making her feel better. Yes, Sheila had always been fun, and always been there, but Jo knew she could never have told her any of the things that she'd just told Pippa.

Too many new thoughts were shooting through her brain, and it felt like it was in danger of short-circuiting. She knew she was in a mood that needed a long walk by the river. She poured her parents' tea and her coffee and decided that her walk would be full of what she called Menu Moments; small but important decisions that always took her ages to make. She hadn't been to the river for a long time, it would probably do her a world of good.

Meanwhile, Vanessa felt like a bird released. Terrified that her wings wouldn't work and struck by her own frailty in the suddenly vast world. She put her head round Cassandra's door. Cassandra was silently dressing.

"How we doing?" asked Vanessa.

Cassandra smiled. "Fine."

"Give your old mum a hug before she goes in to her horrid office."

Cassandra squeezed her hard as they sat on her bed together.

"Why do you have to go to work?" she asked quietly.

Vanessa kissed her daughter's uneven parting. "Because it makes me feel good about myself." She redid Cassie's hair. "It makes me feel right. And it helps me be a nicer person."

There was silence.

"When will I feel like that, Mummy?" whispered Cassandra.

Vanessa clasped her child to her. "Ah, sweetheart. That can take a lifetime to work out."

Five minutes later, she rushed downstairs to give Josh some last-minute tips. He had surprised them all by announcing that he'd happily take time off to look after the children.

She couldn't work out whether she was pleased to see Dick so determined to work at his business and Josh so unusually generous, or whether she was furious that Dick had got away with it again. She decided to plump for the former for the sake of her marriage.

When she got downstairs, Josh was standing in the kitchen, frowning at the timetable on the fridge door. He looked at her like a hunted rabbit.

"Where's the pizza?" he asked.

"In the freezer."

"Where's the nursery?"

"Address is in the diary."

"Where's the diary?"

"Next to the telephone in the dining room."

"Do I have to make chips from scratch?"

"Only if you want to set the house on fire. Microwave ones are their favorites."

"Where are—"

"In the freezer."

"When do I give them their packed lunches?"

"Now."

"Superman one for Zak, Tweenie one for Tallulah, Buffy one for Cassandra."

"Correct. Well done." Vanessa smiled. "Thanks Josh, you're a star."

"It's a pleasure. Thanks for trusting me with them."

"If you swear in front of them, hit them, or let them die, I will hunt you down and kill you."

"Have a nice day yourself."

Vanessa took one look round the kitchen.

"Wish me luck," she said.

"Likewise."

As the front door slammed, Josh took a long, slow breath. He scoured the fridge door, his eyes resting for a moment on Zak's drawing of Jo as Catwoman before spotting Jo's phone number. His fingers itched to phone her, and his stomach squirmed at the idea. No. He could cope with this job. He was a man who had climbed the slippery slope of corporate accountancy, he could manage this rocky terrain. It was survival of the fittest, and he was going to win. This was not *Survivor, The Krystal Maze* and *The Krypton Factor*—this was Real Life, the toughest game of all. He rolled up his sleeves, flexed his proud muscles, took a deep, manly breath, and opened the dishwasher.

"Josh," came Tallulah's voice. "Will you wipe my bottom?"

The room went cold.

By the time Josh was driving toward Cassie's school, he was already running twenty minutes late and had sworn four times in front of the children. They were loving it. "What the . . . flippertygibbet is that driver doing, for . . . Fffreddy's sake?" he asked. It turned out he swore much more than he realized. "Doesn't he know there are children in this world who need to get to school?"

"Jo usually goes the other way," observed Tallulah.

"*What?*" cried Josh, looking in the rearview mirror. "Why didn't you tell me?"

"You didn't ask."

"Stop being a clever-dick!" he cried. "How do we get out of this traffic jam?"

"I could walk," offered Cassie.

"Would it be faster?"

"No," said Cassie. "Just more pleasant."

"Right," said Josh, swerving suddenly. "I'm parking. Tallulah, you're going on my back; Cassie, you're going on Tallulah's back."

Vanessa, coffee in one hand and briefcase in the other, hurried to work. The sun was almost breaking out from behind the grey clouds, and Vanessa fast-forwarded ahead by a month and imagined the vitamin D and ultraviolet rays skipping like lambs on to her skin. And then her office appeared.

Until that moment, Vanessa had always believed that her job turned the world round through simple economics, and her home life was a sort of fantasy subplot that she felt rather ashamed of believing in. It dawned on her she might have got that wrong. She clacked her way over the marble floor to the lift, keeping her eyes down while she waited for it to reach her. She walked to her office and closed the door behind her.

Before she moved forward an inch, she tensed. Someone had been at her desk. It was a complete mess. Her desk diary was open and her in-tray looked like an ashtray. How on earth was she supposed to start her day in a mess? Then she got a camera shot of how she'd left the kitchen for Josh. Followed by the sickening memory of Jo's weary resignation every morning at the sight of the kitchen. She must, she *would* give that girl a raise. If she ever came back.

No sooner had she sat down behind her desk and caught the framed laughing faces of her children than there was a knock on the door.

"Come!" she shouted.

Anthony opened it.

"Nearly." He winked. "But it has been two weeks."

Vanessa's body started humming a familiar tune.

"Oh God," she muttered.

"Tell me about it," breathed Anthony, shutting the door behind him.

"No I mean, Oh God, Anthony. I'm a married woman who's just spent two weeks with her children."

"I hear you, baby—"

"No, I mean—Anthony don't."

She pushed him away.

"What?"

Suddenly her office door flung itself wide open and Max stood beaming at its center. He stood there, arms wide, belly out, legs apart.

"Vanessa baby! Welcome back!"

Vanessa baby almost fell at her boss's feet. Instead, she turned politely to Anthony.

"Anthony?" she said. "Can we have a moment?"

"Of course." He smiled charmingly and left the room.

Pippa and Nick sat in a traffic jam up Highgate Hill, Sebastian James's car seat strapped into the back.

"If any of my mates from the station see a baby carrier in the back of my car," muttered Nick, "I'll never live it down."

"Don't be ridiculous," said Pippa. "You lived down that haircut."

Nick stared at her.

"What's wrong with this haircut?"

"I'm just making a point." Sebastian James belched. "And Sebastian James concurs," she added.

"I swear you feed him Swarfega," muttered Nick.

"I spoke to Jo this morning," replied Pippa.

"Oh yeah? She finished with lover boy yet?"

"She has, as a matter of fact."

"Blimey! He was right! Jammy bugger!" Then a thought occurred to him. "Shit. Your friend's lost me serious money—"

"No she hasn't, if you're talking about Gerry."

"Why?"

"Because she doesn't fancy him, that's why."

"Course she does."

"No she doesn't. I am telling you," repeated Pippa. "Jo just doesn't fancy him."

"Maybe she doesn't realize she does yet," conceded Nick, "but tell me this. How come she finishes with her boyfriend of six whole years just months after meeting him?"

"It's got nothing to do with Gerry. Other things have changed in her life recently."

"Believe me," said Nick. "Something's definitely happened to make her finish with him. It's too much of a coincidence. You mark my words."

Pippa looked at him as he drove and started to stroke the back of his head.

"Oh, you're so clever," she said. "I do love that in a man."

"Well of course," said Nick. "I'm in CID."

Precisely one hour later, Josh sprinted to the nursery, almost falling over his long legs with the effort.

Why had he been late all day? He didn't understand it, he'd done nothing, yet he'd been late for everything and the house looked so bad that if Zak came home just then he'd probably be distraught that he'd missed the burglars. Josh suddenly realized he hadn't eaten anything all day. It dawned on him that he'd never seen Jo have lunch, let alone take a lunch hour. Not only that but it felt like bedtime even though everything indicated to the contrary, such as his watch and the daylight. When he finally arrived at the nursery, with a stitch and low blood sugar, there was a big queue of women waiting. They all turned to stare at him. He tried to smile, but his stitch was so bad it came out as a grimace. The women turned away again. He wanted to ask them questions. How did they fit eating into their daily schedule? How did they get there on time? Every day? How did they keep their clothes so spotless? Would they—*could* they—teach him?

When Pippa ambled beside him, looking like a Timotei ad, he was overjoyed.

"Hello!" he cried. "Have you spoken to—have you seen—how are you?"

"Hi!" she beamed. "What the hell are you doing here?"

"Oh, just looking after the kids. Took some time off work. Otherwise, Vanessa might have to get another nanny in."

"Oh!" exclaimed Pippa. "I see."

"And I know how much the kids love Jo," he rushed.

Pippa nodded. "You look absolutely awful."

"Thanks!" he said. "I feel absolutely awful."

A four-year-old hurtled off his scooter and landed in the fence beside them.

"So have you heard from Jo?" asked Josh, stepping away from the fence.

A mother in front of them finally flipped. "*If you tell me one more time you're going swimming tomorrow,*" she told her six-year-old, "*I'm not letting you go.*" Her six-year-old turned round and told someone else.

"Yes," said Pippa, "I spoke to her this morning."

"Oh yes? How is she?"

"Her mum's downstairs and her talking's really improved, so they're just waiting for her to be able to walk upstairs and get to the toilet."

"And how . . . and how is Jo? She seemed a bit stressed when she left. I mean—"

"Well, she is a bit upset."

"Why?"

"Well, because of Shaun."

"Why? What's happened with Shaun?"

Pippa nudged him forward, and Josh suddenly found himself at the front of the row facing a Montessori teacher with an expression that told him talking would no longer be tolerated. He smiled warily at her.

"Name?"

"Josh."

"We don't have a Josh."

Pippa stepped nearer. "Tallulah," she helped. "And Georgiana."

"Oh I see!" grinned Josh. "Sorry. *I'm* Josh."

"I'll just check," said the teacher, unimpressed.

Josh turned to Pippa. "I'm definitely Josh," he said.

"I know, sweetie. She's gone to get Tallulah."

Tallulah was duly fetched. She came out with a small smile on her face.

"Hello, Josh."

"Hello, Tallulah."

Georgiana followed her and walked toward Pippa.

"Hello, sweet pea."

"Hello, Pippa, I painted a fish," said Georgiana, presenting Pippa with a picture of a something between a shark and an elephant.

"That's wonderful, darling," enthused Pippa. She grinned at Josh. "Well, I guess I'll see you—"

"Have you got time for coffee?"

She grinned. "Yeah! Why not?"

Josh turned to Tallulah. "Would you like that, Tallulah?"

Tallulah turned thoughtfully to Georgiana.

"Can I be the girl this time?"

"No," said Georgiana. "You have to be the boy because you're taller than me and you have darker hair than me."

Tallulah looked up at Josh.

"No thank you, Josh," she said quietly. "I'd rather go home, if you don't mind."

"Oh. Right." He turned to Georgiana. "Oh go on," he coaxed the little girl, "let Tallulah be the girl."

Georgiana ignored him. "Where's my baby brother?" she asked suddenly.

Pippa blinked.

"Oh dear. He's in Nick's car," she whispered. She looked at Josh.

"Josh, can we make that another time?"

"Yeah—yeah, of course."

Pippa grabbed Georgiana's hand and fled without a glance back. Josh watched her go.

After a moment, he felt a small hand slip into his and grip it firmly. He looked down and saw Tallulah. He knelt to her height.

"She says I'm like a boy," Tallulah explained in a very small voice, "because I haven't got hair like her."

"Well I don't think you're like a boy, gorgeous."

Tallulah gave him a slow grin and then, overcome by sudden shyness, dipped her head and looked up at him through her bangs.

"Oh yes," he said, squeezing her hand tight and kissing the top of her head. "You are all woman."

Nick and Gerry sat in their car, waiting for a call on the radio.

"So," said Gerry. "Jo's a free agent then, is she?"

Nick nodded through his hamburger.

"I think you owe me some money, my friend." Gerry smiled.

Nick finished his mouthful. "Apparently, she's not free for the reason you put the bet on."

"Oh yes? Go on, Nicholas. I am all ears."

"It turns out," said Nick, finishing his lunch, "that she just realized she wasn't in love with her boyfriend anymore."

Gerry let out a honk. "Yeah right," he said.

Nick turned to his friend. "You seem admirably confident, if I may say so."

"Well, my friend, it's my firm belief that she's just putting what politicians call a 'spin' on it."

"Gerrard," said Nick, "I love you like a brother, but I don't want to see you making a prick of yourself. Hard as it may be for us to fathom it, I don't think she fancies you."

"Convince me."

"She told her closest friend she doesn't. And girls tell their friends everything."

Gerry stared at Nick in dismay. "Call yourself a policeman?" he cried. "I'm disappointed in you, Nicholas."

"Why?"

Gerry resettled himself in his seat, facing Nick. "She's hardly going to tell her best friend she *does* fancy me, is she?"

"No," said Nick. "Because she doesn't."

Gerry sighed dramatically and shook his head. "No, because she knows her best friend would tell you, and you would tell me. And that would make her look keen. And the whole point of the chase is that the woman is not meant to be keen. Otherwise, there's no chase." Gerry tutted. "Honestly, Nicholas, you're meant to be in CID."

Nick shook his head.

"I believe Pippa on this one."

"Rule number one. Don't believe a woman who has intimate knowledge of Mr. Squiggly. Rule number two, look at the evidence, not at what's coming out of the suspect's mouth."

"Mr. *Squiggly*?"

"Evidence: She's finished with her boyfriend of six years right after meeting me."

Nick was silent.

"And she went on a date with me."

"Where you didn't so much as cop a feel. No pun intended."

"She was still someone's girlfriend then," explained Gerry. "She's a loyal lass; I like that in a girl."

Nick was silent.

"I'm telling you," said Gerry, "there's a chemistry there. She's the one who went all, 'Oh, I'm a stranger in a strange land,'" he mimicked. "'Look after me, you big burly policeman.'"

Nick smiled. "That was an uncanny impersonation, Gerrard. Sounded just like Julie Andrews."

"Nicholas. I am on her tail. And what a tail, if I may say so."

"You may."

"And, let's not forget, my good friend, that if it wasn't for her 'Ooh, and your friends can meet my friends blah blah blah' you wouldn't have even met Pippa. So aside from the fact that you owe me big-time, the least you could do is support me on this."

They sat in silence for a while.

Gerry was the first to notice the atrocious smell, but he didn't want to mention it. When it got unbearable, he turned to see where it was coming from.

"Jesus Christ," he whispered.

Nick followed his gaze.

"Not quite," he muttered. "Hello, Sebastian James."

Later that day, Pippa phoned Jo. "You'll never guess who I met at nursery today," she said.

"Josh?"

"Bloody hell! How did you do that?"

"I just said what came into my head first."

"That is frightening," said Pippa.

"What the hell was he doing there?"

"He's looking after the kids while you're away. And get this! He took time off work to do it. And, get this! He did it because otherwise Vanessa might have got another nanny in!"

"You're kidding?" gasped Jo.

"He asked me for a coffee, so I couldn't get any more than that, but I'll try and get some more tomorrow. I had to go suddenly because I realized I'd lost Sebastian James."

"He asked you for coffee? Maybe he fancies *you*. Oh my God, of *course*—"

"Shut up! Considering that he'd just asked me how you were, and I'd just told him that you were upset because of Shaun, I think it was more likely that he wanted to find out the real story about you."

"He asked about me?"

"Instantly. The minute he saw me."

Jo felt giddy with excitement.

"Unfortunately," continued Pippa, "so is Gerry. And it doesn't look like he is going to take no for an answer."

"Well he'll have to."

"Nick told me he once took a whole year to get a girl to go out with him."

Jo swore under her breath. "Just tell him I'm obsessed with Josh," she muttered.

"Oh yeah, right, tell a trained fighter exactly who his rival is when he knows where he lives. Do you want Josh beaten up again? I think once is enough for your conscience, don't you?"

"Bloody hell. Gerry sounds like a nightmare. That'll teach me to flirt."

"Aha!" cried Pippa. "So you admit, you *did* flirt with Gerry?"

"Well," said Jo, "Maybe I was trying to make Josh a little jealous. Nudge him into actually making a move. How was I to know Gerry was a freak?"

"Hmm."

"Why can't Josh be that determined to get me? And why can't Josh want more than a shag from me? And why can't Josh just be a nice bloke with no sides to him? And why can't I think of anything else?"

"Because that would be far too simple."

"Well, *you* got what *you* wanted."

"Are you calling my boyfriend simple?"

"No, I'm saying I'm jealous. You both liked each other, you both did something about it. The End."

"Ah," said Pippa. "But that's after years of complications. You've had it all too simple for the past six years. It's your turn for the fun and games now. Those are the rules."

Jo sighed.

"Anyway!" said Pippa. "I noticed your sharp nannying eye hasn't left you."

"Eh?"

"Do you want to know where I lost Sebastian James? And why I had to go to the local police station to pick him up? And what I had to tell my boss?"

Jo did want to know. She listened keenly and that night in bed, dreamed of Josh asking questions about her while picking up Tallulah from nursery.

Chapter 21

It was another few days before Sheila finally returned her call. They arranged to meet for lunch that day, in their usual café.

As they sat looking at the tablecloth, Jo realized she didn't know where to jump in on their conversational loop. The usual subjects of Shaun and her parents were too raw for her to broach. The only impartial subject she could think of talking about was Pippa. Before the silence got too agonizing, she told Sheila all about Pippa and how Pippa was probably the only reason she was staying in London and how much Sheila would adore her. When Sheila didn't respond, it hit Jo that Pippa was probably not the most tactful of subjects to have started on. Why couldn't she talk to her best friend anymore?

"How's work?" she asked Sheila finally.

Sheila looked up briefly from her food. "It's a job," said Sheila. "Certainly nothing to write home about."

Jo started eating. "How's James? I've missed him."

Sheila raised her eyebrows. "I haven't."

Jo frowned. "Where's he gone?"

"We finished a fortnight ago."

Jo gawped. "What? What happened?"

"We finished," repeated Sheila. "A fortnight ago."

"I thought you two were going to get married."

"Just shows you how wrong you can be."

"What happened, Shee?" Jo softened her tone.

"Turns out I was just waiting for something better to come along. And it came along."

"Who the hell came along?" Jo used her gossipy tone. "I have to know!"

"You 'have' to know, do you? All of a sudden, you 'have' to know?"

Jo sighed. "God, Shee, I'm so sorry if I made you feel—"

"You didn't make me feel anything," cut in Sheila.

"Then why are you being so . . . like this?"

Sheila stared at her food. "Sorry," she said eventually.

"It's not as though I've been having fun," said Jo.

"When are you going back?"

"As soon as I can leave my mum."

"Hmm."

"Anyway," said Jo, adopting her gossipy tone, "so who's the mystery man?"

Sheila gave a secret smile.

"Do I know him?" whispered Jo.

Sheila smiled again.

Jo gasped. "It's not John Saunders is it? Village idiot? Face like an albino rabbit?"

Sheila laughed. "Piss off!"

Jo laughed and waited for the moment to pass. "So how is James?" she asked.

"Oh absolutely fine," said Sheila. Jo looked astonished. "Turns out he was just waiting for me to dump him," explained Sheila.

"Men."

"Hmm."

"Hmm," said Jo. "I–I finished with Shaun, actually."

Sheila raised her eyebrows.

"You don't seem surprised," said Jo miserably.

"I'm not. To be honest."

"Oh," said Jo. "I was."

Sheila looked at her.

"Actually," said Jo, "he sort of helped me do it."

They finished their lunch. They looked out of the window. They looked round the café. They decided not to have another tea.

"So what do you mean, he helped you do it?" asked Sheila, as they paid the bill.

Jo confided to her best friend of ten years about the breakup of her relationship of six as they wandered out of the café.

After their lunch together, Jo and Sheila went their separate ways, and Jo took herself off to the river. She knew that her father would need her back within the hour, so she didn't have that long, but hopefully it would be long enough.

As she walked away from the High Street toward the bridge, she felt like she'd swallowed a black hole and it was sucking up her insides. She could barely stand up straight. She stepped gingerly onto the bridge where she and Shaun had had their first kiss all those years ago. She watched the water flow underneath and wondered how such a special memory could make her feel so sad. Then she thought about Sheila and the friendship that had been such a large part of her identity. And then she thought about her parents. Had she made her mother ill by leaving?

Staring at the river, her thoughts flowed too fast for her to keep up. Had she taken all the important things in her life for granted? Had she ruined all her memories? Or, even more terrifying, had she been getting it wrong all the time, building memories on such shaky ground that they couldn't withstand change? Had she been wrong to leave for London, or had it shown her that it had been time to move on? Had she left herself with nothing? Or shown herself that she'd started with nothing?

After what seemed like ages, she walked over the bridge and turned to the right, following the flow of the river. The sound of the gravel crunching underfoot almost made her weep with nostalgia. And then she reached the church graveyard. She forced herself to stop and look at it. Two ghosts appeared. Two fifteen-year-olds with everything to live for, sharing their first voluntary carcinogen behind the gravestone of a fifteen-year-old girl who'd died in a freak factory accident. Had she loved Sheila then? Would she have loved Sheila if she'd met her in London, almost ten years later? Would she even like her if she met her now? The thoughts were starting to make her feel morose.

She turned the corner and stopped to take in her favorite view. Against the bright blue horizon, trees swollen with buds waved gently at her in the breeze. Fields pregnant with potential rushed toward her, and she stared and then stared again, taking it all in like something the doctor had ordered. Slowly but surely, she began to feel hope and a flicker of fire in her belly. She hardly understood the emotions within her. How was that possible—to feel something you couldn't understand? And so she backtracked to the last time she remembered feeling like this and got such a jolt that she needed to sit down on the ground. After considerable soul-searching, Jo realized what had been wrong in her life. Dorothy discovered that the Wizard wasn't the one with her answer—it had been inside her all along.

A long way away, Josh Fitzgerald was having a rather different sort of epiphany. Tallulah was being picked up from nursery and taken to play with a friend, so he had taken the opportunity of being home midweek to see his mother for lunch in Fortnum's after she'd visited the Royal Academy to see their latest exhibition.

He'd got rather more than he'd bargained for. By dessert, he was sitting, slack-jawed in the restaurant, staring at his mother.

"Don't look at me like that, Joshua," said Jane. "The chef will poach you."

"I can't believe what you just told me," whispered Josh.

"What? That I don't blame Dick for leaving?"

"Yes. And the other thing."

"What? That I engineered his affair with that silly secretary?"

Josh hung his head in his hands. "I don't get it," he whispered. "Why are you telling me this now?"

Jane sat back in her chair.

"It's my therapy. Martin really is marvelous. He's made me look deep within myself, and I've seen that I controlled the whole thing. Your father couldn't control a TV remote. Why do you think he married Vanessa?"

"But why would you control the breakup of your own marriage?"

"Because I wanted out. And," Jane confided, "it turns out I had a classic passive-aggressive attitude to our marriage, so my only way of dealing with it was to force him into the role of abandoner because I wanted to be the angry one. It's actually very clever, when you think I didn't even realize I was doing it."

"So hold on," said Josh, "let me get this straight so that when I rewrite the past that you ghosted for me, I won't get it wrong this time."

"Oh, sweetheart, don't—"

"You're telling me that you have made Dad feel guilty for the past eleven years of his life because you weren't assertive enough to say you wanted to end the marriage?"

"Subconsciously darling," conceded Jane. "Men didn't like assertive women then."

"Oh, so it was all of men's fault, not just Dad's?"

"No, I just . . ."

Josh stared some more.

"How on earth did you 'make' him have the affair with his secretary?"

"Oh that was easy," said Jane. "I just kept telling him how beautiful she was, how sexy, drip, drip, drip, then stopped having sex with him."

"Aha!" Josh slammed the table with the palm of his hand. "That does *not* give him permission to have an affair. He *was* the guilty one there."

"And then I told him I thought we should have an open marriage, and I might sleep with the grocer. He had very big hands as I recall."

Josh did another fish impression.

"Josh, please don't look at me like that. It's so unattractive, I can't tell you."

"You mean you gave Dad permission to have an affair—practically told him to—and then castrated him for it?" he said. "How . . . how *dare* you?"

"I *know*," gasped Jane. "I feel *wretched*."

"He's been feeling guilty for the past eleven years; I've been feeling abandoned for almost half my life, Toby has wrapped a shell around him that's almost impossible to break through, and both of us have grown up feeling guilty about being men because of what happened to our poor mother!"

"Oh don't exaggerate, Joshi, you always did exaggerate."

"I'm not exaggerating!" burst Josh. "When I was fourteen years old—probably my most vulnerable—you convinced me that my father had abandoned me for his fucking secretary—chosen her over me—"

"He didn't leave *you*—"

"He *did* leave me!" cried Josh. "Of course he left me. You think he popped into my room every evening to see how my revision was going? You think he scooted by every morning to wish me good luck for my exams over breakfast? You think he was there for me when my body grew a mind of its own? He left me. My father left me. For some slut in his office."

Jane turned to the two women at the table next to them who had stopped talking and were now openly staring. She gave them a charming smile and stage-whispered, "He's just getting off antidepressants."

The women nodded sympathetically and turned back to their food.

"Mum!"

"What?" Jane was all innocence. "Everyone's on them nowadays."

Josh slumped over the table.

Jane stared at her son. "Martin would say it's time for you to own your own emotions, instead of blaming others."

"Fuck Martin."

"Ah well, I was coming to tha—"

"Mum. Please." Josh held his hand up to her, blocking his face. "One traumatic revelation at a time, thank you."

"For what it's worth," said Jane, "your father didn't want to leave you. I . . . well, I sort of forced him to."

"Oh God."

"He wanted us to live separate lives but in the same house, so that he wouldn't miss you both growing up."

Another fish impression. Jane let it go.

"But I'm afraid I couldn't allow it." She took some wine.

Josh hid his face with his hand. After a while, he started mumbling through it, and Jane had difficulty hearing everything.

"I've spent the past decade being wary of women," she heard. "I've seen every unattached woman as a threat to family life."

Jane frowned hard at her son. "Do you think that's why you have such a problem? With women?" she asked hesitantly.

"Pardon?" Josh looked up.

"Well, you always go for very easy women, darling, and then detest them for being exactly that."

"That's a bit harsh."

"What's the longest relationship you've ever had?"

"Two very long months."

"The one that ended because you thought she was having an affair?"

"Yes."

"So you cheated on her?"

"Yes."

"Twice?"

"Yes."

"I always wondered where your misogyny came from," said Jane. "Now I know." She took another gulp of wine. "Have you ever thought of therapy? Martin's marvelous. He's saved my life."

Josh bent his head down.

"I can't—I don't know—I . . ."

"I didn't know what I was doing," urged Jane.

Josh looked at his mother. "Up till now I thought you were the only one who was innocent in the whole mess that is my life," he said.

"Your life is *not* a mess." It was the first time he heard emotion in her voice.

"Mum," he tried to explain, "to me you were practically the Virgin Mother."

"Well, perhaps it's time you realized that's not possible."

He paused.

"I was speaking metaphorically."

"Yes, but, darling, I do think you have a tendency to *see women* metaphorically. Do you see? Rather than as flawed human beings, like men."

Josh blinked hard, "Maybe that's because my mother convinced me she was perfect, and my father was evil personified."

"Yes, well," said Jane with some difficulty. "When two people are involved, it's usually not as simple as that."

"You mean, you made mistakes too?"

Jane squirmed in her seat. "I am able to confess that . . . it was not entirely your father's fault that we divorced."

She looked down before pouring herself more wine.

"Excuse me," said Josh in a low voice, "while I just reposition my entire life map."

"I didn't do it on purpose, darling," insisted Jane. "I was desperately unhappy." She held his hand across the table. "Your father's and my marriage was doomed. We're both far happier without each other. The only good thing about our marriage was you and Toby. And you both still are. Why do you think we're still in touch at all? We've got the most amazing children in common."

"I need a drink," whispered Josh, wiping his face.

"Of course you do, my darling," said his mother, passing him her napkin. "I really am terribly sorry."

After two vodkas, Josh was able to see things more clearly.

"So," he said slowly, "Dad did not want to leave me and Tobe, you admit that he was not entirely to blame for your divorce, and I'm a misogynist."

"Yes," said Jane thoughtfully. "You know, perhaps you *should* try some antidepressants."

"Thank you, Mother," said Josh. "But not when I've only just come off them."

When Jo arrived home from her walk, she shut her parents' front door behind her and called out.

"I'm home!"

"We're in here!" came her father's voice from the lounge. "There's a pot just made."

Jo took off her shoes and left them by the front door.

Her parents were sitting side by side on the sofa, a sight she couldn't remember seeing since her father's new armchair had been bought ten years before.

"How was Sheila, pet?" asked Bill.

Jo sat down on his armchair and swiveled it round to face them.

"Not good," she said. "She's finished with James."

"What?" cried Bill. "And her with all that weight to lose? She'll never find another man. The girl's mad."

"She already has, apparently."

"Who?"

"She wouldn't tell."

"Blimey," breathed Hilda softly, and they laughed.

"And I finished with Shaun."

"What?" cried Bill.

"I finished with Shaun."

Bill knew this had to be handled sensitively. He took a deep breath before continuing.

"Are you stark raving mad?" he cried. "He had everything! Men like him don't grow on trees you know!"

"Well, you marry him then!" shouted Jo.

There was a stunned silence.

"Mum, Dad," she said quickly. "I've got something to tell you."

"Oh my God," said Bill. "You're pregnant."

"I am not!"

"Thank you, God," said Bill, genuflecting.

"Quiet," said Hilda.

There was quiet.

"I'm going to go to university," said Jo.

There was a pause.

"Over my dead body," whispered her father.

"Bill," said Hilda.

"*Well*," said Bill. "I'm speaking on your behalf, too, I know that." He turned to Jo.

"You're a sensible girl, Josephine—"

"Too sensible—"

"No such thing. It's going to London that's put stupid ideas in your head."

"No," said Jo firmly. "I've always wanted to go to university."

"Well," he said, "we all have silly dreams. I've always wanted to play for England."

"It's not a silly dream! How can it be so silly if so many people do it, Dad?"

"Because not everyone's as sensible as you!"

Jo fought hard to keep her thoughts on track.

"Dad," she said finally, "I love you, I respect you; but I'm not asking you, I'm telling you."

There was a silence.

She sat forward in her chair. "I'm twenty-three years old, and I'm not asking for permission," she said. "I'm just letting you know. And please don't make me feel that knowing my own mind is an act of betrayal. I won't need any money from you, I haven't had money from you for years—"

"Just a roof over your head."

"Well," said Jo. "I won't be asking for that because I'll try and study in London while I'm earning my own keep."

"Will you!" bellowed Bill, standing up. Hilda started moaning. "Look! You've upset your mother now."

"No, Dad," said Jo. "I think you getting angry is upsetting her much more than me."

"Don't you get smart with me, university girl!" He turned to Hilda. "Look at that, already answering me back, and she hasn't even gone there yet."

"Is that what it's about then, Dad?"

"What?"

"Scared I'll know more than you?"

"Don't you dare take that tone with me."

"I'm not taking any tone, I'm just trying to work out why you want to stop your only child doing what she wants to do with her life."

"Don't you see? It's *because* you're my only child that I want to stop you making a mistake."

"Why?" asked Jo. "Mistakes are part of life. Why can't I make any?"

Hilda chuckled.

"Don't you take her side," Bill told his wife.

"Leave Mum alone, you bully," said Jo. "She can think whatever she wants to think."

"She thinks what I think," said Bill.

"Oh yes?" asked Jo. "Shall we ask her?"

They both looked at her.

"Hill?"

"Mum?"

Hilda closed her eyes and breathed deeply.

"Bogdon-over-Bray," she murmured.

There was a long pause. Then Bill sighed heavily. "That's a cheap shot, Hill," he murmured.

"What was that?" asked Jo.

Bill sat down on the sofa again.

"Dad? Tell me."

"It's the bus stop where I met your mother. Jesus wept!" he laughed. "I'd forgotten all about that."

"And?" asked Jo.

Bill forced himself to speak. "I was only there because I'd got on the wrong bus and had to get off it and wait for the 24b to take me back the way I'd come."

"So?" asked Jo.

Bill sighed. "For someone smart enough to go to university, you're being rather slow on the uptake." He gave Hilda a long look before turning back to Jo. "I always used to tell your mother that if I hadn't made that mistake, I'd never have found the best thing in my life."

There was a long silence. Then Jo went over, hugged her mother, and left the room.

Eventually Hilda looked at her husband and found him staring at her. "Hmm?"

He looked uncomfortable. "I'm not a bully, am I, Hill?"

She laughed and lifted her right arm to stroke his cheek.

Diane, Vanessa's mother, was playing with her grandchildren in the garden. Jo had been back with her own family for nearly an entire month. And still they hadn't hired a new nanny. Diane didn't trust Josh with them—what on earth was a grown man doing spending his time with children, she wondered, as she heard him prepare the tea.

"Can we go in the playhouse, Grandma?" asked Tallulah.

"I don't think Grandma can fit inside, darling," said Diane. "I'll stay out here in case the door gets stuck. You know what it's like after it's rained. I tell you what! I'll watch you from here. Don't close the door tight." She sat in the tiny hammock and started flicking through a glossy magazine.

"I'll ask Cassie," said Tallulah. Cassandra was doing her homework at the garden table.

"Cassie?" asked Tallulah.

"Mm."

"Will you come and play with me in the playhouse?"

Cassie tore her eyes away from her math problems.

"What are we playing?"

"Mummies and daddies."

"Okay."

As they walked toward the playhouse, Zak zoomed across the lawn, carrying his cyberdog in his arms.

"My cyberdog's broken!" he cried.

"How come?" asked Cassandra.

"There were sparks coming out of his bottom, then he just stopped working!"

"Did he fart?"

"No he did not fart!" exploded Zak.

"We were just about to play in the playhouse," said Cassandra. "Do you want to play with us?"

Zak sniffed. "What are you going to play?"

"Mummies and daddies."

"No!"

"You can be the daddy," said Tallulah.

"Can I bring my cyberdog?"

They hadn't been in the house together for years. They'd forgotten how thrilling it was.

"I'm going to bed," Tallulah told Cassie. "You have to say good night to me."

"Why do I have to be the mummy?" asked Cassie.

"Because you're the oldest."

"I don't want to be."

"Zak!" ordered Tallulah. "You be the mummy."

"Okay."

"Who's the daddy then?" asked Cassie.

"You are."

"I don't want to."

"Why not?"

"Because daddies are boring."

"We could have two mummies," said Tallulah.

"That's gross," said Zak.

"No it's not," said Cassandra. "A girl in my class has two mummies."

"I bet she's gross."

"Zak, if you're not going to play properly," said Tallulah, "you'll have to leave."

"I know!" exploded Zak. "Lula and I are identical twins, separated at birth, Cassie's our baby sister, and Mummy and Daddy have gone on holiday without us," he started to whisper, "and Grandma's Hannibal the Cannibal prowling outside."

There was a pause.

"Are you alright in there?" called Diane.

When they all screamed with delicious terror, Diane tutted and returned to her magazine.

Dusk thickened into evening, the air echoed with the sound of setting car alarms, and Dick wandered home alone.

He passed streets full of houses just like his own: Victorian brick dividing him from mothers unable to hear the white noise in their heads over crying babies and demanding toddlers, in their self-imposed luxury prisons. When they needed a community, each one would switch on the radio and be traumatized by dramatic news stories of death and destruction. When they needed company, they'd turn on the television and be confronted with images of perfection and ads created to make them feel overweight, ugly, smelly, and sad. And when it all got too much, they'd pop Prozac and keep it to themselves.

Dick shut the front door behind him and trod over various toys in the hall. Putting his briefcase in the corner of the kitchen, he sifted through the post, sighing over every brown envelope. Without looking up, he made his way to the drinks cabinet, opened the door, and went straight for the whiskey.

"My, my," said Diane. "Whiskey before dinner?"

Dick swirled round. "Hello, Diane."

"Hello, Dick."

Dick smiled weakly.

"Drink?"

"Yes, Dick, I know what it is."

"I mean, do you want one?"

"No thank you. The children are in the playhouse. For some bizarre reason Josh decided that instead of insisting that they do what he says and eat their tea in the kitchen, he would teach them that if they insist enough, they will be rewarded for it and get their way."

"Pardon?"

"They had their tea in the playhouse and are now playing bedtime in it."

"Good."

"And Josh has gone to bed. He says he's exhausted. I'm hardly surprised. He had lunch with his mother today. That would be enough to exhaust anyone." She walked past Dick into the hall to get her things. "I really don't understand this generation."

"Thank you, Diane."

"I've missed bridge for this week."

"Sorry."

"Don't be sorry, Dick. It doesn't become a man."

"Sorry."

"Good-bye. Give Vanessa my love."

"I will."

Dick watched the front door close behind his mother-in-law. It was, he had discovered over the years, his favorite time to watch it. He stood there for a few moments, then found his way back to the drinks cabinet.

By the time Vanessa got home he was sitting watching television in the dark, an empty whiskey bottle on the coffee table.

"Oh hello," said Vanessa, startled that Dick was still up.

"No need to look so surprised," said Dick. "I do live here you know."

Vanessa sighed. "Dick, I was thinking," she started. "It might be nice to get the children a brand-new computer."

Dick stared at his wife in bemusement.

"Why?"

"I just think it would be nice. They've been very good about Jo leaving, and we've got the money—"

"We *haven't* got the money, and why should they be treated to an expensive present just because they aren't being brats?"

"We *have* got the money and they're not—"

"*We haven't!*" shouted Dick.

"*Well I have!*" shouted Vanessa back.

Dick took a moment.

"That's right," he croaked. "Rub it in my face."

"Rub what in your face?"

"The fact that you're a success and I'm a failure."

Vanessa started. "What are you talking about? We're a team."

Dick exploded. "A team? That's rich! You're always on about how the shop is crap. Well you're right. It's crap. I'm crap. I'm a crap provider. I'm a crap husband."

To her horror, he started crying. Vanessa came over to him.

"What are you talking about?" she whispered. "You're not crap."

"I am crap," he spat. "I failed at one marriage, and I'm failing again."

Vanessa felt her heart stop. "What makes you think you're failing?"

"Oh leave me alone," he moaned. "Just leave me alone."

Vanessa sat down next to him on the sofa. "You don't get it, do you?" she said. "I don't care about any of that."

"So why do you keep going on about it? Constant jokes about how the shop is crap."

"Because . . ."

"Because you've got no respect for me."

"No!" She almost shouted it. "Because I'm jealous. I'm so bloody jealous of you I could scream."

"*Jealous?*" Dick was incredulous. "What of?"

"Jealous that you always get the best bits."

"What are you talking about?"

Vanessa sank back into the sofa. Every word seemed to cost her effort and energy. "I don't always want to be Mummy. I can't be a full-time mother, Dick. I'm hopeless at it. It's bad for me to even try—it damages me. And yet, even though I work in London and you work locally, even though I have a mean boss in a cutthroat business and you're your own boss, I'm still the one who ends up having to deal with all the legwork of having kids as well as do my job. It feels as though my job will never be as . . . viable as yours. I've got to keep justifying it and defending my right to have it, as if I'm living on borrowed time. It's not fair."

Dick managed half a laugh. "If one of the children said that, we'd tell them life wasn't fair."

"Yes," conceded Vanessa quietly, "but unlike the children, I can leave home."

There was a long pause before she started again. "The more I think about it the more I feel motherhood is . . . a relative concept."

"What the hell does that mean?"

Vanessa sighed. "If we'd been living 150 years ago and were rich, I wouldn't have even been expected to breast-feed my babies, but I felt so guilty because I couldn't. If I'd been poor, I'd have popped them out in my tea break and got back to work." She started to talk fast. "If I'd lived in a biblical tribe, I'd have had all the women of the tribe supporting me, helping me, feeding me, and looking after me. Only *one* generation ago, I'd have probably had my family living down the street, would have known all my neighbors and would have spent the first fortnight of motherhood being looked after in hospital and sleeping off the trauma of giving birth. I don't have any family support apart from the occasional visit from my mum—your mum sees the kids once a year—I don't know my neighbors so I can't ask them for help, I was home from hospital making my family dinner the day after I'd given birth, and my workplace seems to think that my miraculous ability to have children is proof that I'm flawed, rather than proof that I'm helping the human race survive as a species. I mean, can you imagine any other animal in the animal kingdom treating their mothers like this?"

She stood up and was pacing the conservatory. "And yet I'm expected to feel *guilty* because I can afford *one* woman to help me. Well I *refuse* to feel guilty, Dick. Or evil. Or selfish. I admit it." She lifted her hand. "I need help being a mother. Everyone does. And if they say different, they're lying."

Dick gave a slight nod. Vanessa calmed herself down before continuing.

"I love my job. *Love* it. I *need* it. Just as there are some women who feel utterly complete being mothers, I feel utterly complete having a job. I don't mind the fact that you have the shop, what I mind is that you don't respect my job and how bloody good I am at it, and that you imply I've got something lacking in me as a woman because I prefer the company of adults to children. For all we know, I'll come into my own as a mother when the children are teenagers—or adults. Who knows? And what I mind is that you *resent* the fact that I bring home the bacon! I mind that I have to fight you to feel fulfilled. I mind that I thought you were going to be my biggest support but you've turned into my biggest block to happiness. I mind that I'm so angry with you that I can't remember how to love you." She was crying.

Dick was now rigid, as Vanessa took a deep breath before continuing.

"If you wanted to give up the shop and become a . . . a . . . carpenter, I'd happily support you. I'd support you in anything you wanted to do. I'm a born career woman. It doesn't mean I don't love my children, I'm not a freak of nature. I just love my job. Why can't I be allowed to be a woman with children who loves her job?"

Dick was pale. "Because you can do both," he wept. "And I can't do either."

"That's not true!" cried Vanessa. "I spent the last two weeks aching for Jo to come back. And so did the kids! I was hopeless. They were bored, I was bored—it was awful. I can't do it, Dick. I am just not cut out for it. Why should all women be able to do the same job just because they're female? Can you imagine expecting every man to be able to . . ." She thought frantically for a relevant job description . . . "I don't know . . . *garden*? Just because they're all men?"

Dick managed a smile. "I'm quite good at the garden," he mumbled.

A laugh hacked out through Vanessa's tears. "And you're a wonderful father. The kids adore you. You've got far more patience with them than I've ever got."

"But they don't need two fathers."

"I don't want to be a father, Dick, I just want to be me. And whatever the kids need, they need two happy parents."

"And a good nanny."

"And a good nanny."

Dick looked at his wife. "You can't remember how to love me?" he whispered.

She gave him a half smile. "I'm beginning to remember," she whispered back.

When the rhythmically raised voices of Dick and Vanessa lowered again, and Josh could hear his father crying, he felt a choking sensation rise in his throat. And for the first time, he felt pity for his father instead of for himself.

Outside in the playhouse, Zak, Tallulah, and Cassie huddled together under their blanket.

"Is Daddy going to leave us?" whispered Tallulah. "Like he left Josh and Toby?"

"No," whispered Cassie.

"How do you know?" sniffed Zak.

"Because we won't let it happen," said Cassie.

"How?" asked Tallulah and Zak.

They all tried to think of an answer.

"When did all the rows start?" asked Cassie eventually.

"When Jo went," sighed Tallulah.

"Exactly," said Cassandra. "So we're going to get her back."

"How?" whispered the others, in hushed awe.

"Easy," said Cassandra. "You see, it's all about knowing exactly who you're dealing with. Bringing out sides of people they didn't know they had themselves."

There was silence.

"We won't have to get Jo back ourselves," said Cassandra, "because Josh is going to bring her back for us."

Chapter 22

Stupidly early on the Monday morning of her fifth week at home, Jo was the first one up in the kitchen. She looked out at her mother's neat little garden, replaying the conversation she'd had with Vanessa the night before. Vanessa had sounded weary but resigned. Yes, they all wanted her back, but they had no choice but to give her only two more weeks before they started looking for a new permanent nanny. Jo had spotted her chance to say she desperately wanted to come back—but with a view to becoming their part-time nanny; she wanted to study and look after the children at the same time, she wanted to live in London and go to university, she missed the children, missed the chaos, missed the tension, but she needed more. Instead, she had felt the gap in the conversation where this was all meant to be said come and go without her even opening her mouth.

The birds were so loud she could hear them over the boiling kettle. She usually loved this fleeting moment between night and day—as if she'd caught God off guard taking a power nap. And she usually loved this moment best at exactly this time of year because it was so proud with potential, and she usually loved experiencing this moment in her parents' house before they'd woken up, because they were her comfort zone, yet sometimes the thought of them was less exhausting than the experience of them. Technically, this should have been up there in her favorite moments.

But not this morning. Something had changed—she had changed. Everything had changed. This morning the signs of summer made her itch with dissatisfaction at her life. And her parents' home had stopped being a comfort zone ever since the row with her father. He was still sulking, and she believed he might never get over it. And she hadn't been sleeping well because certain disturbing images of Josh Fitzgerald kept waking her up.

She heard her father pad downstairs. He was up early. She turned round and watched him come into the kitchen, pour himself a cup of tea instead of making a pot, then go upstairs for his bath without looking at her.

She filled the cafetière, took a coffee, and put them both on a little tray, opened the back door, and took her mug into the garden. She sat down on the B&Q bench by the gnomes and, with her mind somewhere between Niblet-upon-Avon and Highgate, watched the garden wake up.

Half an hour later in Highgate, Josh was feeling torn. When Vanessa had got the call from Jo saying she couldn't come back that week, he reluctantly said that he had to go back to the office. His job was meaningless drivel, but it paid the bills. And he could do with the break.

Josh now saw mothers in a somewhat different light. Instead of looking straight through them—as had been his wont—he found himself inclined to bow as they passed him in the street. And he certainly looked at nannies in a different light. As far as he was concerned, nannies and mothers had taken over the role of biblical midwives—silent, invisible lifesavers, giving their menfolk time to go round slaying each other and recounting ripping yarns about themselves. Up till now his arguments in favor of the superiority of his gender had always felt indisputable. Why was there no female Shakespeare, no female Einstein, no female Shackleton? he used to say in bars all over London to girls who would pout at him in mock anger. But now he knew the answer. They'd all been busy wiping babies' bottoms and doing finger-painting. *What a tragic waste*, he thought.

Of late, he had begun to notice a worrying habit of waking up, as if from a trance, in Jo's bedroom, and finding that he'd been sitting on her bed, or looking at her photos, or holding her stupid Mickey Mouse clock, or reading the spines of her books. He had seriously needed to get back to work.

When he told Vanessa and Dick that he had no choice, he had to go back to work, Vanessa had looked at Dick in a way Josh had never seen her look at him before.

There was a tenderness in it and yet an expectation of great things. Dick then said it was his turn to stay at home, and stay at home he would. In fact, he became positively evangelical.

"It's my turn to look after the children," he said firmly. "I'll only open the shop for a few hours a day when they're all at school. I'll be absolutely fine." There was a pause. "I'm a modern father, and this is a modern family." Another pause. "Now, how do you work the clothes dryer?"

When Josh wandered through the kitchen on his way out to the big wide world, Dick was staring at the timetable on the fridge door. He looked at his son with haunted eyes.

"Where's the spaghetti bolognese?" Dick asked.

"The mince is in the fridge."

"And what do I do with it?"

"Make spaghetti bolognese for the children to spread on their faces."

"Where's the recipe book?"

"Dad, it's mincemeat and tomato sauce. You'll be fine."

"Where the hell's Tumble Tots?"

"Address is in the diary."

"Where's the diary?"

"In the dining room by the telephone."

"Is Beavers what I think it is?"

"No. It's a club for little boys teaching them to obey mindless rules so that they can grow up to be unquestioning members of society. Zak loves it, don't forget his woggle."

"What the hell's a woggle?"

"He'll tell you. I have to go. Phone me if you need any help."

"Why? Will you come home and help me?"

"Nope. But I'll need a laugh."

By ten, Dick had tidied the kitchen, put the dishwasher on for the second time, changed all the bed linen, and put the third wash in. The house was buzzing with activity, and all thanks to him. He was the master of all he surveyed, the king of his castle, and all was well with the world. He stood at the ironing board, listening to a Radio 4 play and piling up his children's clothes. Why hadn't anyone told him that the act of ironing tiny clothes corresponded directly to the amount of love you have for their wearers? The knowledge that his children were eating what he had put in their lunch boxes filled him with satisfaction. The awareness that their last contact with home life before entering the big bad world had been Daddy made him yearn for them again. How come no one had told him these things? It was a conspiracy! Women had conned men for centuries that these jobs were unfulfilling, yet all this time their souls were being pumped with love.

By 11:30, the Radio 4 play was over, the ironing was done, the sheets were blowing in the sunshine (he'd decided against the dryer) and Dick knew that he never wanted to work outside his home again.

After finger-painting with Tallulah and getting her to tidy up faster than ever before by pretending it was a race; after picking up Zak from school and watching him shake hands with his teacher, which brought a lump to his throat; after picking up Cassandra and seeing her face light up at the rare sight of him; and after driving home while singing "Postman Pat" louder than all of his children put together, Dick's mind was made up.

This was what life was about, not worrying about money, not trying to sell records to people who really wanted DVDs, not sweating over figures that never added up and living in fear that any day you'd be found out as a failure. Life was about nurturing the next generation, giving them a sense of values that would give their world meaning, teaching them to have confidence in themselves and love for others. He may have been forced to fail Josh and Toby, but he wasn't going to fail his little ones. They were his future, and he had as much to learn from them as they had from him.

"Dad?" asked Zak.

"Yes, son," said Dick, smiling down at his youngest boy.

"What does bollocks mean?"

The Alice in Wonderland shoot would be in full swing. *And why on earth shouldn't I be popping along to it,* Vanessa asked herself once more, as the taxi carried her toward it. She was the account manager, she needed to see how the company's most important ad was going. And she needed to have a word with Anthony.

She paid the taxi, smoothed down her Nicole Farhi suit, straightened her back, and walked purposefully into the studio. The pungent aroma of fresh paint vied with the strong cappuccinos she knew they'd been drinking since dawn.

She stood safely at the back watching for a while. In front of her stood the Mad Hatter's Tea Party. Casting was perfect, and everyone was 360-degree beautiful, despite heavy makeup and costumes. The scene was one of three that were being set in Alice's Wonderland. The actress playing Alice was a TV presenter, which meant she had the body of a child with helium breasts. As soon as the camera light went on, she widened her eyes, curved her back, and bared her teeth and breasts in the obligatory pose once reserved for a top-shelf wonderland, but one that had now encroached fully on daily life, making everyone less satisfied with their own. As soon as the camera light went off, so did the light in her eyes, and she looked bored and a little hungover, as if the effort of breathing filled her with ennui.

Vanessa had long since got over the excitement of seeing a star perform the same three lines all day with decreasing finesse and patience, and this part of the process would be much more pleasant if everyone else involved in it, including the star, felt the same.

She tiptoed closer to the action. Anthony was standing near Tom, who was looking through the camera and moving his right hand to indicate to the Dormouse to move fractionally over.

The director was watching the action intently while authoritatively stroking his chin. Beside him, his PA, wearing more body piercing than clothes, watched her boss just as intently while authoritatively stroking his ego. Anthony turned round, saw Vanessa, and walked toward her, smiling. She immediately craved a Silly Nibble. They met in the middle of the studio.

"How's it going?" asked Vanessa coolly.

"God, you look amazing."

"Not here, Anthony. How's it going?"

"Who cares? There's a perfect cupboard in studio 3."

Tom turned round and grunted a greeting. Vanessa waved at him overeagerly and joined him at the camera.

"How's it going?" she asked with great earnestness.

"Typical nightmare," said Tom. "My vision is compromised in all senses of the word."

He moved over, allowing her to see.

She looked at the composition for a while, taking in every detail. "Is Alice's eye shadow purple?" she asked eventually.

"Why?" shot Tom. "Don't tell me they hate purple."

Vanessa kept her tone even but firm.

"I told you in the pre-preproduction meeting that they didn't want any purple because of the new Emiscar logo."

"I thought you said purple was their favorite color."

"That was in the *pre*-pre-preproduction meeting." Why didn't anyone concentrate around here?

"Well it's too late now," said Tom. "It's taken us all morning to get her to open her eyes. Asking her to close them again while someone changes the color of her eye shadow is far too risky. We'll change it in postproduction." Vanessa felt a presence at her side. She ignored it until it spoke.

"Would you like a mochachino?" asked the PA. "Some cinnamon toast? Bottled water?"

She stared at the girl for a second before realizing that she'd like all three.

"The color will be brightened up in production, won't it?" clarified Vanessa, back to the business in hand.

Tom smiled at her. "Thanks for your comments," he clipped. "All positive input greatly appreciated."

"Well, I'm just saying, it needs to be brighter than bright. The opposite of real life."

Tom stared at her as her postbreakfast-prelunch arrived. "Have I ever produced an ad that was too realistic?" he asked, loudly enough for Alice to look over and practice focusing. "I am aware I'm not Ken Loach, you know." He began a performance of a real-life artistic temperament at work. "I do know what I'm doing—selling promises, allowing the world to return to its thumb-sucking, halcyon days when happy endings really did come true. That's what all those awards in my office are for—"

"I was only saying—' interrupted Vanessa through a mouthful of cinnamon toast.

"*Yes, well,*" shouted Tom suddenly, "you can shove your 'only saying' where the sun doesn't shine."

The studio fell silent. Vanessa finished her toast and placed her coffee on the camera stand.

"For your information." she told him primly and loudly, "I have incredibly flexible joints and a private sun terrace, so that the cliché is totally redundant. But I take your point, Tom. Thank you."

Jesus, she had to get away from these tossers. She'd have to confront Anthony another time. She walked out to silence. As she reached the door, Anthony appeared at her side, as if from nowhere.

"About those flexible joints," he whispered.

"*Not now, Anthony,*" she said.

Anthony stared at her.

Her last thought as she left the studio was that Anthony looked in serious danger of bursting.

Josh's lunch hour was over. But he found it impossible to tear himself away from his father's books. The morning had flown by. He'd never thought he would enjoy bookkeeping, but doing it for somewhere he cared about had transformed it into a work of love.

At 3 P.M., when he looked up for the first time since lunch, he saw his office with different eyes.

He asked himself why he'd become an accountant and immediately knew the answer. He could remember, as if it was yesterday, asking his father what he should become when he was older.

"Don't do what I did, son," Dick had proclaimed with the solemn wisdom of regret. "Get yourself a profession. You can't go wrong with a profession."

And fifteen-year-old Josh had been impassioned by the idea of making his dad so proud of him that he'd come back home for good. He wondered now if Dick would even remember the conversation.

His thoughts pinballed round his brain as he stared blindly at the office ahead of him. Sitting in an office all day was shriveling his spirit. He needed to find something he believed in, something he could put his skills and his passion into. And he'd just found it.

Now all he had to do was tell his father.

Midafternoon, after returning from the shoot, Vanessa found a window to phone home. At the sound of Dick's voice she felt a rush of emotion.

"How are you?" she asked tentatively.

"Fine!" There was more warmth in his voice than she'd heard for a long time.

"And how are our children?" she asked.

"Fine!" said Dick again, with even more warmth. He had one eye on the clock, the other on the sandwich he was making. "Tallulah picked you some flowers on the way home from all the neighbors' front gardens. We ran the last fifty yards."

"Aah, sweetheart. Give her a big kiss from me."

"I will. I'm just about to pick up Zak."

"Don't forget his scooter. Walking's for girls."

"Oh right. Thanks. Then I'll make them lasagna. I'm making pancakes when Cassie gets home."

"Blimey. Good luck."

"Thanks."

"I'll be out in time to pick up Cassie from Mandy's," Vanessa told him.

"Okay. I'll be here with an open bottle of wine. Empty, but open."

"Excellent." Vanessa laughed. "Bye then."

"Bye, love."

Dick put the phone down, wrapped the sandwiches in foil to eat on the way to school, picked up Tallulah, the scooter, and car keys, and left the house.

Meanwhile, Vanessa sat looking at the phone. Something was different. What was it? Oh yes, she realized with a little start. They hadn't argued. And Dick was going to make lasagna.

The lasagna was disgusting. Even Dick couldn't eat it, and he was starving. So when Zak suggested whole wheat biscuits covered in golden syrup and chocolate buttons and Tallulah started getting so excited she hugged her daddy, Dick decided that food was for fun, and one meal really wasn't going to harm anyone.

By the time Josh came home, Dick, Zak, and Tallulah were so high on E-numbers they could have invaded a small unsuspecting island. Josh tidied them up, cleaned the kitchen, calmed them down and made them sit down to cheese on toast with Tabasco sauce followed by fruit salad à la Josh. Then he and Dick prepared the pancake mixture while the kids tidied up.

Stalemate reigned in Niblet-upon-Avon. Jo had started ignoring her father back, and every opportunity that could have been taken to make friends had become an opportunity to be the first one to ignore the other. Jo's new existence was punctuated every so often by emptying her mother's commode and taking headache pills.

She was in the kitchen taking her teatime pills, ignoring her father as he prepared Hilda's tea, when her mobile interrupted the silence. Her father ignored the noise. She ignored her father ignoring the noise. When she saw that it was Gerry, she stared at the phone, and it was only her father's grunt that made her answer it.

"Hello!" she greeted warily.

"Hi there," said Gerry. "Just wanted to see how you are."

"I'm absolutely fine, thanks," she said, surprised to feel warm and friendly at the sound of his voice instead of threatened and claustrophobic. "Thanks for asking." Her father grunted again.

"Don't be daft," said Gerry, "We've been missing you."

"Oh thank you!" She crossed her arms and faced her father, while speaking into the phone. "Tell you what, it's nice to know someone cares."

Bill looked at his watch, checked it against the kitchen clock and tapped it in Jo's face.

"I'd better go, Gerry," said Jo. "I'm needed."

"Okay," he said. "I'll call you again another time."

"Okay," said Jo. "Thanks." She put the phone down and told herself that this was not a man who couldn't take no for an answer. She had been frightening herself over nothing.

The pancakes were disgusting. Even Dick couldn't eat them and he was starving. But it didn't matter. The ice cream Vanessa had picked up while taking Cassie home was a grand success, and it only took an hour to clean the kitchen up afterward. No one was surprised that the kids disappeared for this. While the grown-ups tidied, the children had important issues to discuss.

"Right," said Cassandra, upstairs. "I call this meeting now open."

Zak and Tallulah looked up at her excitedly.

The meeting didn't take long at all. Cassandra chaired it with confidence and purpose. Zak and Tallulah loved their roles and admired her terribly. They had no time to lose. Operation Jo had to start immediately.

Downstairs, things weren't quite as exciting. While Vanessa showered, Josh and Dick spoke quietly in the kitchen.

"Well?" asked Dick eventually. "Are things as bad as I thought?"

"Do you want the bad news or the bad news?" asked Josh gently.

Dick sighed.

"The bad news," said Josh, "is that to my estimation, you're about six months from bankruptcy."

"Jesus." Dick took a swig of whiskey. "And the bad news?"

"And the bad news is that I'd like to buy it off you."

Dick stared at his son.

"Come again?"

Josh took a deep breath, "The thought of being an accountant for the rest of my life depresses me more than you can imagine. I spoke to my bank today, and they'd give me a loan. I want to take over the shop, Dad."

Dick shook his head. "Son, son, son."

"Listen to me! No one else will buy it. This is your only chance. As well as mine."

"Please don't make the same mistakes I did."

"I haven't. I've got a profession, I could keep the books far more effectively than you ever could."

"Owch!" grimaced Dick.

"All thanks to you. Thanks to your sound advice when I was a kid, I have a structure with which to support my dreams. I can learn how to run my own business because I've seen how businesses succeed and fail. I won't be doing it blind like you had to. And if it fails, at least I'll have tried, and I'll just go back to being an accountant. I'll never be unemployable, Dad. You made sure of that."

"I got something right then." Dick smiled.

"Yes. And now I'm going to do what you told me not to do and follow your example. I want to sell music."

"Music? Not records?"

Josh shrugged. "Some records, but CDs, too, and DVDs."

"So you're going to buy my shop and then sell out?"

"No, I'm going to make it work. And I won't sell out, because it won't be a pop music shop. It will be eclectic. Unique. Very Highgate. I also thought I might do a coffee bar, you know at the back there, where you've got the old jukebox."

"You've really thought this through."

"Dad," said Josh, "I haven't felt this excited for . . . I've never felt this excited before."

Dick shrugged. "Well," he said eventually, "who am I to stop you?"

"But do I have your . . . blessing?"

"Do you need it?"

"You know I do."

"You have my blessing whatever you do, Josh."

Josh smiled.

Just then, Tallulah padded into the kitchen in her pajamas.

"Hello, sweetie," said Dick. "How's my sunbeam?"

"Tired," said Tallulah.

"Do you want me to come up and tuck you in?"

Tallulah shook her head and pointed to Josh.

"I want Josh to."

Dick and Josh grinned at each other, and Josh tried not to feel smug.

As Josh took the stairs two at a time, feeling smug, Dick poured Vanessa a Baileys and took the stairs one at a time. Both men wavered for a moment before entering the rooms.

Dick wavered slightly more than Josh. As he closed the bedroom door behind him, he could hear Vanessa still in the shower. He undressed and put his clothes in the empty laundry basket. He noticed Vanessa's blouse on the bed. The shower stopped. He picked up the Baileys and wandered in.

"Thought you might like this," he said, as Vanessa wrapped a towel round her.

"Oh wow!" she smiled. "Perfect."

"Do you want that blouse cleaned?"

"Oh, it's dry-clean, I'll do it over the weekend."

"I'll do it tomorrow."

She looked at him.

"You sure?"

"Yep. I'm going into the village anyway to get in some shopping."

"Great."

"Coming to bed?"

"Yes. I'll just comb my hair out."

Vanessa gave her husband a smile, then watched him leave the room, slowly turned, and stared at herself in the mirror.

Josh pushed open Tallulah's door and was surprised to see the light off and Tallulah curled up in bed, with Cassie beside her.

"Hey," he whispered. "What's this? A powwow?"

"Lula's been having bad dreams," whispered Cassie. "Haven't you, Tal?"

Tallulah nodded.

"Come on then, move over," said Josh, sitting on the bed. "I can't have my two favorite girls having problems sleeping. What's up?"

Tallulah sucked her thumb, and Cassandra sighed.

"Come on," soothed Josh. "You can tell me."

Tallulah shook her head.

"Sweetheart!" said Josh, dismayed. "What can't you tell me?"

Tallulah sighed.

"Can you tell Mummy or Daddy?" tried Josh.

"No!" said Cassie quickly.

"Why?" he asked, starting to worry. "What's going on, Cass?"

Cassie turned to Tallulah.

"Can I tell him, Tally?"

Tallulah barely nodded.

"She's been having nightmares," whispered Cassie.

"What sort of nightmares?" whispered Josh.

Cassie opened her eyes wide in the dark. "Nasty ones," she said in hushed tones.

"How nasty?"

"They're about . . . they're about . . ."

"Go on . . ."

"They're all about . . ."

"Cassie, you have to tell me."

"They're about Jo."

Josh sat up straight. That he had not expected. And then to his horror, Tallulah curled up even tighter and started weeping. He put his arm round her and made soothing noises.

"Jo keeps dying in her dreams," explained Cass.

"You're kidding!" said Josh. "That's terrible."

"And Lula's trying to catch her—"

"Catch her? Is she falling?"

"Yes. She's always falling. Off a cliff."

Josh gasped.

"We're scared something terrible's happening to her." Tallulah's elbow jerked out and nudged her sister. "And we miss her," added Cassie, her head down.

"Yes," said Josh. "I know. We all do."

"Mummy and Daddy didn't row as much when Jo was here," whispered Tallulah through her thumb. "Now they row all the time." She started crying into her hands again.

They had a point, thought Josh. There was that hideous row the other night that was so loud it woke him up, then he'd heard Dick crying. And God only knew what it was doing to Dick's self-esteem shutting up the shop for most of the day and being at home with the children. He was putting a brave face on it, but it couldn't be good for him. But what to do?

"What can we do?" asked Cassie.

"I don't know, darling," said Josh. "Hope and pray to God that she comes home soon."

"Mummy said God is a man-made construct to stop people being ambitious," said Cassie.

"Oh."

"Shall I phone Jo?" she asked.

"I don't think that will be a good idea."

"Oh," said Cassie, and then started whispering again. "We thought we might go and get her."

Josh looked at his half sibling with wonder. "Did you?" he asked.

"Yes. But then Zak said he'd have to use the girls' toilets with us, so we couldn't."

The three of them sat on the bed for a while.

"G'night, Josh," came Tallulah's voice in the dark.

"Oh, good night pumpkin," said Josh, and gave her a kiss on her soft, dry cheek. He and Cassie left Tallulah's room, closing it softly behind them. In the hall, Cassie looked up at Josh.

"Thanks for helping," she said.

"I didn't do anything."

"No, well," said Cassie, disappointment in her voice, "thanks for trying anyway." With a heavy sigh, she went to her bedroom.

As Josh stood on the landing, he heard a noise from upstairs that sounded like someone snorting a vacuum cleaner. After a while, he realized it was Zak sobbing. He bounded upstairs and knocked on his door. The sobbing stopped.

"Zak?" whispered Josh. "Can I come in?"

After a while, there was a muted "Yes."

Josh pushed Zak's door slowly, catching the flying cyberdog as it flew toward him and jumping over the trip wire. He sat on Zak's bed.

"What's up, little man?"

Zak wiped his face.

"I had a nasty dream."

"Was Jo falling off a cliff?"

There was silence in the dark.

"No," whispered Zak.

"Go on."

Zak sat up in bed. "Mummy left us"—he sniffed—"because, because she had to go and be a nanny . . . for Jo . . . in the north somewhere. And then Daddy left us because he couldn't live without Mummy."

Josh hugged his brother. "Mate," he said, "no one's ever going to leave you."

Zak leaned into Josh and sniffed. "Jo left," he whispered.

"But she'll be back. I know she will."

They sat up until Josh was woken by the sound of a lawnmower in his ear. Zak was snoring.

After tucking Zak in, Josh went downstairs and walked slowly through Jo's empty room to his own. Sitting on his bed, he made up his mind. For the sake of the children, for the sake of the family, there was only one thing he could do. He was going to bring Jo back.

Chapter 23

Josh woke early the next morning and found the kids watching television in their pajamas. Soft sounds of adults abluting upstairs filled in the gaps left by the Teletubbies.

"Right! Kids," he began—

"Shh!" said Tallulah.

"This is boring," said Zak. "It's for babies."

"So you should enjoy it then," said Cassandra.

"Right, kids," repeated Josh. "I'm going to bring Jo back."

The children tore their eyes away from footage of a little girl finding a slug under a tree for the third time.

"I know," said Josh. "It was a bit of a surprise to me too, but, well. There it is."

And when they all leaped on him, he knew he'd made the right decision. He explained that they had to keep it a secret from the adults, and did they think they could manage that, and they said yes, and then they hugged him again, and that morning, he went to work with a spring in his step and a great big dollop of happiness in his heart.

On Saturday morning, the children, including Toby, woke early. Vanessa and Dick were delighted that they all wanted to help Josh wash Jo's car—even Toby—and when Josh offered to take it for a spin to keep the battery charged, they said he could use it until Jo came back.

After an hour, Toby and Josh were finishing off cleaning the car and Cassie, Zak, and Tallulah were inside finishing off chocolate biscuits and diluted orange juice.

"So how do you know she's going to come back?" Toby asked Josh while polishing the bonnet.

"I don't," said Josh, giving the roof a final rub. "But it's worth a try. The kids are a mess without her. And the other day I heard Dad and Vanessa having an awful row."

Toby seemed unmoved.

"Tobe, Dad was crying."

"Shit."

"Yeah. We need Jo back."

Toby nodded.

"How's Anastasia?" Josh winked.

"Wicked." Toby grinned.

"And how's the terrifying Todd Carter?"

"Very nice. Offered to do my math homework for me the other day."

"What did you say?"

"I said 'Piss off, I want to pass.'"

"Shit," whispered Josh. "Be careful, Tobe."

"I was joking. I said thanks, but no thanks."

"Good."

Toby opened the car door to clean the inside.

"Oh, lame!" He emited an abrupt laugh.

"What?"

"Look!"

Toby leaned across and took out Jo's dashboard cuddly toys.

"Put those back, Tobe."

Toby made a sound like a cow dying.

"Stop laughing," said Josh. "You really can be a prat sometimes. This is the woman who's got two CID policemen as mates, and you're taking the piss out of her cuddly toys."

Toby studied them in his hands. "Actually," he said. "They're quite cute."

"Put them back and help me finish."

Toby put them back. "So why aren't you telling Dad and Vanessa about going to get Jo?" he asked.

"'Cos they might not understand," said Josh.

"What's not to understand? You miss Jo, so you're—"

"The *kids* miss her," interrupted Josh. "Two nightmares in one night. And Tallulah keeps getting them. And Dad and Vanessa have been rowing really badly. I'm doing it for the family."

"Why?" asked Toby.

"'Cos I'm nice, that's why."

"What's this family ever done for you?"

Josh and Toby faced each other over the roof of the car.

"Tobe?"

"Mm?"

"Let's go for a quick ride. Might let you drive if we find an empty parking lot."

Toby jumped into the passenger seat.

Josh did let Toby drive. And he also told him about the conversation he'd had with their mum. And he explained that whether he liked it or not, Cassie, Tallulah, and Zak had nothing to do with Dad leaving Mum, and just as he'd had to grow up sharing his dad with them, they'd had to grow up knowing they had to share their dad with a boy who hated them. And they were going to be his brother and sisters all his life, and they would never forget how he treated them now.

Toby was quiet on the way home. When they stopped at a petrol station, Josh bought him some chocolates to cheer him up.

When they got home, Toby raced in.

"Oy! Lula!" he shouted at Tallulah, who was drawing at the kitchen table.

"*It's Tallulah!*" yelled Tallulah.

"What have I got in my hand, *Tallulah*?" Toby held up a closed fist. Tallulah flinched, got up from the table, and walked quickly into the garden.

"What did I tell you?" shouted Josh.

Toby opened his fist. Inside was a squashed chocolate.

"I was going to give it to her," he said in a strangled voice, before rushing upstairs.

Josh would have gone up after him, but he had to get to Niblet-upon-Avon.

Later that afternoon, the children had a meeting in Tallulah's room. Zak was only too pleased, as Toby had shut him out of their room all afternoon.

"I think we can say the plan went well," began Cassie. She looked at her watch. "Josh should be arriving at Jo's within half an hour."

They all giggled.

"And Zak," continued Cassie, "your timing was superb. I think Josh was moved by Tallulah's act, but it took yours to clinch the deal."

Zak frowned. "What act?" he asked.

Cassie looked at her little brother.

"Never mind," she said. "We did it. That's what's important."

★ ★ ★

When the doorbell rang at Jo's parents' front door, Jo was vacuuming the lounge while her father helped her mother walk upstairs.

"Get that, will you?" he shouted.

Jo made her way to the door and glanced absentmindedly at the hall mirror on her way. *Amazing what a bit of difference good country air can do for you*, she thought. Her skin was glowing.

She opened the door and found Sheila standing there with a self-consciously sad smile and an enormous bunch of red carnations.

"Shee!" cried Jo. "How nice! I didn't expect you, come in—"

"I can't stay for long," said Sheila quietly.

"Is something wrong?"

Sheila shook her head, then looked at the floor. Nonplussed, Jo stepped back and opened the door.

"You'd better come in," she said.

Very contritely, Sheila stepped over the Green family threshold, as if she hadn't spent every weekend there during her teens, and handed Jo the flowers.

"Wow. Thank you, Shee. They're gorgeous."

Sheila stood coyly in the hall, eyes still down.

"Come into the kitchen," said Jo.

"Thank you."

Jo led her friend to the kitchen table.

"Tea? Coffee?" she asked.

"I'm fine thanks," said Sheila.

"Didn't ask how you were," said Jo automatically. Sheila didn't laugh. She didn't even smile. Jo clicked the kettle off, left the flowers in the sink, and sat down at the kitchen table with Sheila.

"I've got some news," said Sheila eventually.

"What's happened?"

"I'm engaged."

Jo's eyes widened with surprised relief.

"That's wonderful!" she cried.

"It's going to be a June wedding," said Sheila.

"Wow! That was quick."

"Not really," said Sheila. "When you know he's the one, you know."

"Do you?" sighed Jo. "You lucky thing."

"Anyway," said Sheila. "We've known each other for ages. Only as friends for years but . . ." she took a deep breath . . . "we had a couple of flings, but nothing serious. We were both with other people at the time."

Jo nodded.

"But it became serious last month."

"Great."

"When you left."

"Oh."

"*Because* you left."

Jo frowned at Sheila. "Oh dear," she said. "Was I stopping you from something . . . ?" And then ran out of things to say.

Sheila finally lifted her eyes and Jo was looking at the personification of pity.

"Don't be upset, Jo," whispered Sheila.

"Why would I be upset? I'm delighted for you."

"We didn't mean to hurt you."

"You haven't! I don't know what the hell you're talking about."

Sheila sighed and tossed her hair back.

"Shaun . . . Casey . . . and I are getting married in June," she said very slowly and clearly. "Shaun. Your Shaun. Well. Actually, my Shaun. Shaunie. He asked me as soon as he'd finished with you."

Jo went cold.

"He didn't finish with me," she monotoned.

"Yes, he did, Jo," said Sheila, her voice softening and her head tilting on every word. "You just didn't notice."

"He proposed to me again, Shee," Jo said.

"Because he knew you'd say no." Sheila's apologetic tone was getting firmer. "I helped him make up his speech: '*I'm not going to propose again. Except this one last time, blah blah blah.*' Sound familiar?"

Jo lost feeling in her face.

"I was the one who decided which restaurant he should take you to," continued Sheila softly.

"But that was where we had our first date," whispered Jo.

Sheila nodded. "I know," she said. "I thought that might be more romantic."

Jo could hear blood pumping through her ears. "What do you mean you had a couple of flings?" she managed.

"Oh nothing serious," said Sheila. "You know, under the mistletoe, the odd party here and there—"

Jo held her hand over her mouth.

"Oh God, sorry, Jo. I didn't think you'd care this much. To be honest I thought you'd be relieved he was so happy. It would be awful if he was heartbroken, wouldn't it? Our Shaunie?"

Jo tried to nod. Her mind couldn't keep up with the altered reality being offered to her. It was so surreal.

"Shaunie wasn't convinced though," continued Sheila. "He said we shouldn't tell you for a while, but I said we had no choice. The invitations are going out next week. I didn't think it would be fair for you to be the last to know."

"He proposed four times, Shee," whispered Jo, wiping tears off her chin.

"I know," said Sheila, "I was furious."

Jo frowned a question.

"Well of course!" said Sheila. "There he was getting off with me at every opportunity while pretending to be serious with you. It was shocking behavior." She gave a little laugh. "I'm really very cross with him."

"I thought you said the odd party?"

"Well." Sheila shrugged. "There were a lot of parties. And a lot of mistletoe. It *was* six years."

"But why? Why not just finish with me?"

"Well I think he got rather attached to you really. I mean, you're very nice. And of course, it did his male ego no end of good. I remember telling him once that for all we knew you and James were two-timing us at the same time." She smiled. "We had a bit of a laugh at that."

"Two-timing? I thought you said it was just the odd fling?"

"Oh, whatever. The point is—"

"Does James know about this?"

"Oh yes," said Sheila easily. "He's always known. In fact, I was with Shaun before him. How do you think I met James? Actually, I thought you might have guessed from that; you know, thought it was too much of a coincidence. Anyway, James was more than happy with the arrangement. He wanted a girlfriend who was never going to push him into any commitment. In fact, he's going to be our best man." She sighed. "D'you know? I think I would like that cup of tea, now I think about it."

"But you hated Shaun!"

"Oh, that was his idea." Sheila yawned. She finished her yawn. "Oh, excuse me! Bit of a late night last night. Yes, we had to pretend we both hated each other so you wouldn't catch on."

"But he *really* hated you!"

"Well," Sheila stiffened. "Actually . . . I suppose I might as well tell you. I wasn't going to, but it might explain things a bit better: he'd already got off with me at Melanie Blacksmith's party and Philippa Fuller's party and Matt Wright's party that summer you were away in Norfolk with your folks—gosh, nearly seven years ago now. It was before he even met you."

"He met me at kindergarten."

"You know what I mean. Once he found out we were friends—"

"Best friends—"

"Yeah, he asked a lot about you. Said you were his first ever crush at school and it was every man's dream to actually . . . well, you know . . . I think the word he used was 'screw' the first girl you ever fancied. That was when I knew he was going to make a play for you. And, then because you're so . . . well, because you're so . . . " She stopped short. "Hmmm . . . how shall I put this?"

Sheila paused, trying to find the best way to put it.

"Tactlessly?" suggested Jo.

Sheila skipped a beat before continuing. "I suppose *straitlaced* is a nice way to put it, he had to date you—for a considerable while, as I recall—to screw you, and before he knew it, he was dating one of his most bullish employee's daughters, the whole neighborhood knew, blah blah blah. And so." She shrugged helplessly. "Right from the start, we had to pretend. It's such a relief to be honest after all this time, I can't tell you."

Jo tried to speak, but her body sank onto the kitchen table and spoke for her. Sheila got up and came and put her hand on Jo's shoulder, but Jo jerked away. Sheila stood for a moment.

"I understand," she soothed. "I really do."

"Paper towel," sniffed Jo into her sleeve.

Sheila rushed to the roll and tore some off for Jo. Jo blew her nose and, surprisingly, felt a little better.

"I'd better go," said Sheila.

Jo blew again. "You think?" she said.

"I'm sorry, Jo."

"Yeah, right."

Sheila turned to go. As she reached the kitchen door, Jo called her name. Sheila turned slowly round.

"Yes?"

They looked at each other for a while.

"When did you stop liking me?" Jo asked.

Sheila looked impatient. "This isn't about you," she said. "It's not even about you and me. It's about me and Shaunie. You just happened to be in the cross fire. No one meant to hurt you."

Jo looked at the paper towel in her hand.

"When did you stop liking me?" she repeated.

After a pause, Sheila just shrugged.

Jo nodded, exhausted.

"We're going to have Shaunie's nieces as bridesmaids," said Sheila quietly. "I know we always said we'd be each other's—"

"Just go."

Jo managed a wry laugh at Sheila's nerve, which, once the front door clicked shut, turned into a choked sob.

Meanwhile, Josh had stopped at the traffic lights on Niblet-upon-Avon High Street and was staring, baffled, at a map. Unfortunately, the map was upside down and the lights were green. He turned the map the right way up. Nope. No clearer. It had obviously been drawn by people who wanted Niblet-upon-Avon to stay unspoiled by tourists. He looked up from it and found himself gazing at green lights. With a jump, he glanced in his rearview mirror and saw a man in a hat at the wheel of the car behind. The man waved. Bemused, Josh drove on. It was like a different country. Then he pulled into a side road and took out his mobile phone.

Jo was hunched over the kitchen table, head buried in her arms. Every time she thought she was feeling better, a stab of fury, humiliation, and pain hit her again, and she heard a strangled sound that seemed to emanate from deep within her. When her mobile phone rang, she supported her head in her hands. When it occurred to her that it might be Shaun, she picked it up.

"Hello?" she said, her voice thick with tears.

"Bloody hell," said Pippa. "You sound awful."

"That's nothing." Jo started sobbing again. "You should see how I look."

"What the hell's happened?"

"Shaun was two-timing me!" wept Jo.

"*What?*"

"With Sheila."

"Oh my God," breathed Pippa through Jo's crying. "Do you want me to come and see you?"

Jo nodded into the phone. "No thanks," she sniffed. "I don't think I could take seeing anyone right now. I-I can't take it all in."

"Would you like Nick to come and beat Shaun to a pulp?"

"No." Jo managed a smile. "Maybe he could mess Sheila's face up a bit though."

"Yeah."

Jo wept some more. "They've made such a fool of me."

"No they haven't," said Pippa. "They've made fools of themselves."

"They're getting married!"

"Hah!" cried Pippa. "More fool her! Can you imagine marrying someone who was dating your best friend all the way through your courtship? With your knowledge? Can you imagine what sort of marriage that's going to be?"

Jo stopped crying for the first time since Sheila's revelation.

"Believe me," said Pippa. "You are best out of it. He was bad news."

"I thought he loved me," said Jo pathetically.

"I know, hon. There'll be others. Much better than him. There's already two in the wings."

Even though that didn't feel strictly true, what with one of the men in the wings being a freak stalker and the other a hypocritical scrounging bastard who was only interested in a shag, the thought did somehow made Jo feel better.

She wished she could get to see Pippa, but neither of them could afford the time off. So Jo made do with the phone call. When it was over, she washed her face at the kitchen sink and decided to go for a walk.

Josh put down his mobile. The local station had been very useful. He was practically on top of Jo's house. He started the engine, turned the car round, went through some red lights, and headed toward her.

By the time the doorbell went for the second time that day, Jo's skin wasn't glowing quite as much as it had been earlier. In fact, as any beautician worth her salt will tell you, if you want your skin to look good for a special occasion, it's advisable not to spend the entire hour beforehand weeping.

Her body jerked in shock at the sound of the bell. It must be Shaun.

She padded quickly to the door, roll of paper towels under her arm, the used one in her hand, slippers flip-flopping against the carpet.

She opened the door wide. She looked up at a tall dark stranger who made her heart squeeze. She stopped. Her eyes took in lots of information that her brain then vomited back out. She blinked and tried again.

There was a Jehovah's Witness at her door—one of those incredibly smooth, good-looking chaps who have a strange light in their eye called Jesus. No, silly. She was dreaming and this was God.

When God said, "Jesus F. Christ, you look like shit," she realized it wasn't God. And then she realized it was Josh.

Josh certainly hadn't intended to wrap Jo in a prolonged, full-bodied bear hug. He'd had a long enough journey to get his greeting planned just right, and nowhere in it was there a prolonged, full-bodied bear hug. In fact he didn't really know where it had come from. But he'd done it, and she was sobbing into his sweater, and he was stroking her hair, and he felt like he didn't want to do much else in the world, so it was probably all for the best. Maybe her mother had had another relapse. Poor lamb. *God, life can be cruel. Some people get all the short straws*, he thought, looking at her hall.

When he spotted a barrel-chested man standing on the stairs staring at him with all the warmth of a raging bull he almost jumped out of his skin. He released Jo and stood her at a safe distance.

"H-hello," he said to the man on the stairs.

The man's eyes narrowed. "Who the hell are you?" he whispered, "and what have you done to my daughter?"

"Dad, this is Josh," sniffed Jo.

"Josh?" queried the man with such confused disgust in his voice that Josh suddenly became aware of how odd his name was. *"What sort of a name is that? And who's 'Josh' when he's at home? And why are you crying?"*

Josh stood stiffly. "I didn't make her cry, I-I-found—"

"Was I talking to you?"

Josh shook his head.

Bill looked at Jo.

Jo started trying to speak. Then she realized she didn't know where to start. Then she realized she and her father weren't talking anyway. Then she realized Josh had come all the way from London to see her. Then she realized she must look like a blowfish. She ran blindly into the kitchen.

The kitchen door slammed shut and Jo's father turned slowly to face Josh. Josh's mouth formed itself into something approaching a smile while his stomach formed itself into something approaching an ulcer.

"I'm Joshua Fitzgerald," he said in a small voice, holding out his hand. "It's an honor to meet you."

The man grunted and continued to stare. Josh's throat contracted. He moved his hand down to his side.

"I like your hall," he croaked, his mouth dry.

The two men stood looking at each other in silence for what felt to Josh like the better part of a year. A bad year. Droughts, diseases, famine, that sort of thing. He had the strongest sensation that if Jo's father had had antlers, they'd be piercing his groin by now. He was about to say that he'd pop back later, now was obviously not a good time but it had been a delight to meet Jo's family and what a very lovely hall, when Jo appeared. She was clearly still upset about something, but she invited Josh into the lounge, instructed her father to be nice unless he wanted her to leave home that night, then walked stiffly upstairs where she would, she explained to them both "attempt to rectify my face."

Josh waited in the lounge and stared at everything, trying his best not to stare at the commode. He could hear muted voices at the top of the stairs, which he assumed must be Jo's parents because the higher one was speaking much more slowly than the lower. When the door opened, he stood up. Jo's father grunted at him again, and he smiled gratefully.

"Nice horses," he said, nodding to the ornaments. "And foxes. And cats. And the otters are sweet. And the commemorative plate. What a tragic waste, eh?"

"The wife likes them," said Bill. "Bugger to dust."

"Oh, I bet." Josh nodded, as though dusting had always been a major consideration in his life.

Then Hilda appeared next to her husband, holding on to the door. Josh stepped forward and shook her hand ever so gently.

"Mrs. Green," he said, "Joshua Fitzgerald. So pleased to meet you."

She smiled at him, and he saw the same eyes as Jo's, although Hilda's were a paler blue as though exhaustion had washed them out. He felt inclined to give her a bear hug, too, but reined himself in.

"She's just coming," said Hilda slowly.

"Thank you."

"Please," murmured Hilda. "Sit . . ." He sat obediently. "Down." He cringed inwardly.

The next instant, Jo appeared, and he bounced up again.

"Right," she announced, putting on a jacket and tying her hair into a ponytail at the same time. "We're going to the river."

"Now, young girl," started her father. "Mind you—"

"*Bogdon-over-Bray*," Jo told him in a tone that would brook no nonsense. Her father shut up.

Josh, baffled and not unafraid, nodded a farewell to Jo's parents and followed her out of the house.

"Bogdon-over-Bray, eh?" he attempted, as soon as they were at a safe distance.

"It's a long story."

"I bet." He nodded, as though long stories had always been a major consideration in his life.

He walked alongside her in silence until they reached the stunning vista of a bridge over a stream. He stopped.

"My God," he breathed. "It's beautiful."

"Mm."

Jo slowed down with him, and together, they walked onto the bridge. When he stopped in the middle of it and leaned to look over the stream, she did so too. "Thank you for coming, Josh," she said quietly.

He turned and smiled at her. Their shoulders were almost touching.

"My pleasure," he said.

"It's nice having you here."

"Thank you."

"On this bridge."

"Oh. On this bridge. Well, it's a nice bridge."

"New memories and all that," said Jo.

Josh took this in.

"I bet," he nodded eventually, beginning to bore himself.

"This is where I had my first kiss with Shaun," said Jo.

Josh moved away slightly.

"Not exactly here," she laughed, pointing to a spot a foot away. "There."

"Ah," said Josh, following her hand with his gaze.

Then to his surprise, she linked her arm into his and thanked him again for coming. He put his hands in his pockets, tried not to look too happy, and told her again that it was his pleasure.

They strolled off the bridge and past the church. Again, he stopped and took in the view.

"God," he whispered. "It's stunning."

"Mm."

He listened to the gurgle of the stream, clear against a silence so pure that it was broken by the whisper of a breeze.

"How could you have left?" he whispered.

And then he listened to the clear, pure sound of Jo sobbing.

They found a bench near the pub, and Josh put his arm round Jo as they sat down. After a few false starts, she updated him on how her life had changed since he'd last seen her. She told him about Shaun's proposing again. About her confronting the truth and their relationship finally coming to an end. About the pain she felt in ending such a big part of her past even though she knew it was the right thing to do. About her guilt for hurting him and disappointing her parents. About Sheila, her best friend, popping round half an hour ago for an overdue girlie chat. About discovering the sham that was her relationship with Shaun. About discovering the sham that was her friendship with Sheila. About her humiliation. Her anger. Her confusion and her pain.

Throughout the dizzying tale, Josh stared at the fields ahead, his grip on reality steadily loosening as his grip on Jo's shoulder tightened. He couldn't believe it. It just couldn't be true. Surely there was a mistake. But no. It wasn't. Jo was actually single.

He couldn't think of anything to say, so he just held on and rested his head on hers.

"I'm so sorry," he said.

And then he realized that he could say more. He told her that from a man's point of view, there was no way Shaun would have gone out with her for that long if he didn't want to. And he certainly wouldn't have risked proposing to someone he didn't want to marry.

Jo considered this. "You mean you've never gone out with someone just because you couldn't be bothered to chuck her?" she asked.

"Not for that long," he confessed. "And I certainly wouldn't have proposed to her. Four times. You're only hearing Sheila's side, remember."

Jo moved away a fraction to consider this.

"So, what does that mean? She's making it all up? She hates me that much?"

"No," he said pensively. "For all you know, she told you what she'd love it to have been, but not exactly what it was. I watched—*saw* Shaun with you, and that was not a man who was obsessed with someone else."

There was a silence.

"It sounds to me like Sheila's just probably in a lot of pain," concluded Josh.

"In pain?"

"Yeah. Well, by her own account, she's been waiting for Shaun for a long time. Even longer than he was waiting for you. And maybe she's had to resort to using the old rule book 'all's fair in love and war.' Which, let's face it, we've all used at some point or another."

"I haven't."

Josh smiled, and said gently, "Maybe you've never needed to."

Jo moved away another fraction to think.

"I suppose I thought Sheila loved me, not him."

"Yeah." Josh sighed. "That's got to hurt."

"It does. I don't know who's hurt me more."

"Yeah."

"And you know what really hurts?" Jo continued. "Really *really* hurts?"

"No."

"James's knowing. They've all been treating me like a child for the past six years."

"Not really." Josh shook his head. "They're the ones who have been acting like children for the past six years. You've been the only adult in the equation."

She looked at him. "When did you get so wise all of a sudden?" she said fondly.

Josh turned to her with eyes as warm as a winter fire.

"We really miss you, Jo," he whispered. "All of us. Turns out the Fitzgerald family needs you in order to function."

Three layers of foundation hid Jo's blush. "Oh," was all she could manage.

"The kids are having nightmares. It's horrid." He sighed. "And Scary Spouse is terrifying my dad into a state of almost permanent paralysis."

"Vanessa isn't scary," she said softly.

Josh snorted and moved his arm from Jo's shoulder onto the back of the bench.

"Believe me," he said, "that woman could terrify for England."

Jo recalled Josh's and Dick's whisperings and felt a sudden, visceral loyalty to all betrayed women.

"I hardly think that's fair," she said.

"Trust me," smiled Josh. "I know. I know all about Vanessa and Dick's marriage—"

"—You can say that again—" she muttered.

"—And Vanessa is one scary woman."

Jo tensed. "Well," she said. "Perhaps she needs to be."

Josh paused for a beat.

"Why?" he asked.

"Sometimes a man needs a bit of scaring," said Jo. "Especially when . . . he's the kind who plays away from home."

Josh stared at Jo. She put her head down.

"Sorry, but that's how I feel."

Sometimes," he said, "a woman pushes a man into playing away from home." He ignored Jo's gasp and continued, "And then she piles on the guilt after he's been forced to look elsewhere for love and ruins his life."

"That's an atrocious thing to say!" said Jo. She stood up and walked back toward the river. Josh followed.

"No it's not," he said. "A woman might resort to being manipulative, you know—subconsciously. And a man can't help it if he stumbles into the arms of someone else. Believe me, I know."

"How can you say such things? After your dad did that to your mum? How can you condone his affairs? How can you help him have them?"

"I don't condone—"

"You do! You just said—"

"He only had one—"

"Oh don't play that with me. I know all about you and Dick and your sordid little secret from Vanessa."

"What?"

"D'you know? You're all the same. You disgust me. Men disgust me."

"Is that why you keep so many hanging on at the same time?"

Jo gasped. "What?"

"You're a prick-tease."

She slapped him hard on the cheek, and tears sprang to both of their eyes. Josh bit his lip, his hand on his cheek.

"Anyway," he said, slightly muffled, "they want you back."

"Fuck off." She turned and walked back toward the bridge. Josh followed her.

"Oh come on," he said, when he'd caught her up on it. "It's great money, thanks to your little raise."

"Oh yeah," she spun round. "And you understand all about money."

"I do actually," said Josh, his hand still on his cheek. "I know what happens when there isn't enough. It can tear people apart just as much as affairs."

"Tell me," said Jo, hands on hips. "Is that why you scrounge so much?"

"What?"

"You heard."

"I don't scrounge. I don't need to."

"Oh no, that's right. You earn an absolute fortune, then live rent-free off your dad like a spoiled child, while the rest of us scrimp and save to earn a living."

"How do you know what I earn? And who told you—"

"Vanessa told me you were living rent-free ages ago. At your age! It's disgusting."

"Well!" Josh was now beginning to shout. "That just goes to show that Vanessa doesn't know everything."

"She certainly doesn't!" Jo shouted back. "You and Dick Dastardly make sure of that."

They stood facing each other, the river flowing fast beneath them.

"Right," he said. "I think I'd better go."

"I think you better had."

"Nice to know what you think of me."

"Yeah, strange that," she said. "Two-faced, hypocritical, scrounging bastards with a Peter Pan complex are usually my type."

Josh blanched. And then walked away.

Meanwhile back in Highgate, Scary Spouse was enjoying a rare moment alone. Dick Dastardly had gone to the shop for the day, the children were playing together in the playhouse (they seemed to be spending an awful lot of time together recently—even with Toby), and she was reading the Saturday papers to a background of radio ads. She didn't know where Josh was and frankly she didn't care because it was rather wonderful to be alone in her own house. Things had felt a lot better between her and Dick after their little chat. It had just felt so good saying those things out loud to him—her anger hadn't appeared once since then. And he seemed to be treating her differently, too. She had even started to see glimmers of the man she married.

The front door opened and shut. She looked up at the kitchen clock and sighed. Well, she'd had twenty minutes, what more did she expect?

She didn't look up from her paper when Josh wandered into the room. But she did look up when he went straight to the drinks cabinet. So she was somewhat surprised to discover that Josh was in fact Dick.

"Hello!" she said, surprised.

Dick didn't turn round as he took a swig of whiskey.

She stopped herself from her knee-jerk reaction of asking if he was celebrating selling a record.

"Hello," she repeated.

When Dick eventually turned round, he was so pale he was almost translucent, except at the edges where he'd gone a sort of green. Vanessa was on her feet fast.

"What's happened? Have you been robbed? Attacked?"

Dick shook his head as she led him to the kitchen table, sat him down, and poured him another drink. Then she knelt beside him and stroked his back as though he were being sick.

"I'm fine," he said weakly.

She sat on the chair next to him, never taking her eyes off him. She waited as he took another swig, then hung his head in his hands.

"I've just found something out," he groaned, almost inaudibly. "It involves you. And affects the children."

Vanessa stopped breathing. Blood pumped to her heart.

When Dick took another gulp of whiskey, she stood up to get herself one. He put out his glass. She took it and poured them both one.

"What?" she whispered urgently. "What have you found out? Dick?"

And then to her horror, he started sobbing into his whiskey. Great huge, racking sobs that shook his whole body. She sat in wretched pity, nursing her drink, feeling she had forfeited her right to soothe him. Eventually he stopped and, exhausted, looked up at her. She looked down quickly at her glass.

Dick stared at his wife miserably. How did he get here? How did he make such a mess of his marriage that when he needed his wife most, all she could do was sit in stony silence?

"Well?" she asked again.

Dick had no choice but to explain.

"I popped up to the flat today," he whispered. "They've gone. Vanished. No rent, no nothing. They've taken most of the furniture with them and left the flat in a mess. I'll never get new tenants in and can't afford to do it up again."

Vanessa frowned. "Is that all?"

Dick let out a short, bitter laugh. "Not really," he said. "The missing bit of information is that they've been paying for everything except Jo's salary for the past two years because the shop's been making such a steady loss."

Vanessa frowned some more. "How does that involve me?"

"Well I've been conning you for years, and I can't keep it up any longer."

Vanessa dropped her head in her hands and took long, deep breaths. After a while, she sat up.

"So how have you been paying for Jo?" she asked, confused.

He started crying again.

"Dick?"

Dick took another swig. "Well, while my wife's been paying the mortgage and keeping the children in clothes, my son's been paying the nanny."

"What?" she cried. She thought frantically of how on earth Zak could be paying for Jo. Maybe Dick was having a breakdown and was talking gibberish. She started to get scared. She wanted her old Dick back!

"Dick!" she cried. "For God's sake, try and explain!"

Dick took a deep breath. "When I realized I couldn't keep you in the manner to which you'd become accustomed, the only thing I could think of doing was to go to Josh for help. The bank wouldn't give me another loan, and I didn't know where else to turn. To save my pride, Josh pretended he wanted to live with us—to 'bond' a bit—though why he'd want to bond with his failure of a father I don't know." He took a big sniff before continuing. "Anyway, I pretended to believe him because it was the only way I could save face. So he's been paying me 'rent' so that it looked to you like I could easily afford Jo. By the way, giving her that raise when she called the police didn't help, 'cos Josh couldn't afford the difference." He shrugged. "Meant the shit hit the fan about two months earlier than it would have anyway."

Vanessa blinked. She could almost hear her brain churning from the effort of trying to take in the information. "*Josh?*" she repeated.

Dick nodded, wiping his eyes and nose with his shirtsleeve.

"What about his flatmates?" she whispered.

Dick let out a half laugh, half sob.

"They didn't go traveling, did they?" asked Vanessa slowly.

"Still all living in the flat in Crouch End," Dick spoke in a low monotone. "Josh is still paying rent there. That's why he doesn't go out. He hasn't got much money to play with."

Vanessa sank into her seat.

"So," said Dick, "now you know everything." Vanessa stared at him. He couldn't even raise his eyes as he spoke. "You're married to a man who needs help from his son from the first marriage he fucked up, to support the second marriage he's fucking up."

Vanessa looked away.

"Yes," she said finally. "I know everything. I know you couldn't talk to me when you needed me most, didn't believe that I loved you unconditionally, yet loved me enough to try everything to save our marriage."

Dick turned to her in surprise, and then it was his turn to be horrified at the sight of her crying into her whiskey.

Chapter 24

Josh was so livid he could barely drive out of Niblet. When he passed a picture-book pub, he stopped, parked the car, and stormed into it.

"We don't open till seven," said a stunned landlady.

"I'll give you £100," said Josh.

"What'll you have?" She smiled.

"Vodka. Double."

He sat at the bar and downed his double vodka in exactly the manner he assumed a two-faced, hypocritical scrounging bastard with a Peter Pan complex would.

Vanessa snuggled up to her husband under the duvet. He gave a contented groan.

"How come Josh wants the shop then?"

"He says he's sick of being an accountant," said Dick. "Wants to give the shop a go. Wants to buy the flat above it as well, either to rent out or to live in himself if he can afford it."

Vanessa sighed.

"It would save my life," said Dick. "I wouldn't be able to sell it for half as much to anyone else. But of course, he's pretending I'd be doing him the massive favor, as usual."

"Wow," she said. "I'm beginning to see him in a new light."

"Good."

"Now we just have to work on Toby."

Dick sighed. "Poor lad. By the time he was Tallulah's age, I'd already left."

There was a long pause. "God," breathed Vanessa. "I never thought of it that way."

"Thank God we're not going to repeat that pattern," whispered Dick.

"Of course not!" said Vanessa, kissing his cheek.

"I thought we were going that way," Dick whispered, hiding his face in her hair.

"I can't believe you thought I loved you for your money," she said.

"I didn't think that exactly," said Dick. "I just thought you'd love me less for having less of it."

She held his face in her hands and made him look at her.

"If you said you wanted to give up work tomorrow and be a house-husband, I'd be the happiest woman in the world."

Dick stared at her. "I want to give up work tomorrow and be a house-husband."

Vanessa stared back at him. They stared at each other in the dark.

"Really?" she croaked.

"You didn't mean it did you?" said Dick, turning away.

"I did."

He turned back to see the expression on her face.

"We'd have to do without Jo, of course," he said.

"Why?"

"Well, we'd only have your salary."

"I want to get a better salary, move jobs. I was going to tell you tonight."

"You want to leave your job?" he asked.

"Yep."

"Why?"

She shrugged and looked away. "More money. Better job. Want to be appreciated. Meet new people. Stop meeting the morons there."

"Because we need more money?"

"Not especially. I just think it would be nice, don't you? But anyway, I'd have had enough to pay for Jo now, if only you'd come to me."

Dick smiled. "Didn't I marry well?"

Vanessa smiled. "Not as well as me."

Dick tutted. "Typical. I can't even beat you at that."

She laughed and kissed her husband. They lay back, staring at the ceiling together.

"But will you want Jo there all the time?" she asked. "Won't she cramp your style with the children?"

Dick considered this for a moment. "I don't actually have a style to cramp."

"I mean, you'll want to be your own boss where they're concerned."

"But they'll miss her terribly," said Dick.

"Mm."

"So will I. She's a pro, and I've got a lot to learn."

"Yeah. She'd be training you, I suppose, like any job. And it's nice having her around too."

"Hmm," said Dick. "It would be great to keep her as a sort of part-time nanny."

"God. That would be ideal wouldn't it?"

"Too good to be true."

"Worth asking, I suppose," pondered Vanessa. "She could always do other nanny work to fill in the time."

"Who knows? She might not have to if we don't lower her salary too much. Then she could sort of be on call if I need her."

"Why don't we offer to just take off the raise we gave her?" suggested Vanessa. "So she'd be doing half the hours, still living in, for the same pay she moved all the way to London for."

"Can we afford that?" asked Dick.

"Of course! Maybe one less holiday, but who cares? You and I will be busy changing our careers. We can have two holidays next year when I'm earning more."

"You're sure?" asked Dick. "I'd be at home all day with home help and you'd be supporting us all, plus a part-time nanny? It's a massive responsibility, Ness."

"At last!" grinned Vanessa. "Recognition!"

Dick gave her an intense look. "I've always recognized how brilliant you are at your job, Ness." Vanessa searched his face. "I just felt so crap at being bad at mine," he explained, "I couldn't be proud of you. Pathetic. And I'm sorry."

"Apology accepted."

"And I certainly think of you as a real woman." He moved in closer to the warmth of her body.

"Good."

He sat up suddenly. "Let's phone Jo now!"

Vanessa sidled over. "In a bit," she whispered, stretching her leg over his.

"Oh if you insist." He sighed, lying back down again. "I suppose it can wait."

Still standing on the bridge, Jo was so angry with Josh she literally didn't know what to do with herself. She kicked some gravel, then raced over the bridge a couple of times and shouted at the river a bit. She considered running to tell Sheila everything, then remembered she couldn't, which made her even angrier. She shouted at the river some more, clenched and unclenched her fists, and shouted again. Then she bought a doughnut from the corner shop and ate it in two bites, which actually helped quite a bit. Then she went for a long stompy walk through the fields, getting her shoes all wet and not caring.

Then she walked home, past the church, where she swore—not too loudly in case the vicar was about—and back over the bridge again where she swore again, rather more loudly.

When her house came into view she felt even angrier. She stopped and looked at it properly. Really looked at it. And felt a few things shift into a new perspective. She stood there for a while, just looking and thinking before walking toward it.

She slammed the front door shut behind her before climbing the stairs.

She sat on her bed. She got up and sat at her dressing table. She looked in the mirror and almost started in shock. She looked like a madwoman. Which made her *really* angry. There was a knock at her door.

"What?"

Her father opened it, and Jo sat rigidly, waiting for him to tell her off.

"Your mother wants to know what's up," Bill said.

"Oh, you're talking to me now, are you?"

He grunted. "If you're going to be like that—" He started shutting her door.

"Like what?" asked Jo, spinning round to look at him. "Like *I'm* allowed to be the one with feelings for once? Instead of the one indulging everyone else's feelings? Like your feelings? Or Shaun's?"

"Eh?"

"You heard."

"I don't like your tone, young lady."

"Well get over it." She turned back to her mirror.

"How dare—"

"I haven't liked your tone for years, Dad," she told his reflection in her mirror, "but I've just had to live with it. So now you don't like mine. Okay. I'll do you a favor and move out."

Bill watched her as she furiously did her face.

"There's no need—"

"Oh I think there is," Jo said. She scrunched up her face and shut her eyes, as if concentrating. "I'm going to try and sort out a part-time job first thing Monday morning. In London. While signing up for a university course." She opened her eyes.

"What about your mother? You're walking out on your mother?"

"Mum's fine. She's already able to walk up stairs with you standing next to her. She's far more capable than you give her credit for. She's looked after you all these years, hasn't she? And I'm not walking out on her—or you—I'm just living my life."

"Sounds like being selfish to me."

"Well of course it would!" cried Jo, swiveling round to face him. "What's self-preservation for you is selfishness for me and Mum. I only have to watch you with the remote control to see that. It took Mum having a stroke before she was allowed to watch what she bloody wanted to on TV. Thirty years with a man who doesn't *permit* her to watch what she wants on TV. Can you even begin to imagine what that's like, Dad?"

The skin round Bill's eyes thinned. "A man has to be king of his own castle—" he muttered.

"And what must a woman be? In her own home? Chief servant? You think that's fair?"

"Your mother's not my servant."

"No, you're right," shot Jo. "That would mean paying her a wage."

Hilda appeared behind him. Jo looked at her parents and felt her anger drain out of her body.

"What happened?" asked Hilda. She still spoke quietly, but her speed was improving.

"Oh," sighed Jo. "I had a horrid row with Josh. And now I'm taking it out on Dad."

"Did he make you cry?" demanded Bill, his fury transferring outside the family with ease. "He looked the type. Too clean-cut. Too smooth. Never had to try hard in life to get what he wanted."

"No he didn't make me cry," Jo said. "That was Sheila. It turns out Shaun—the perfect Shaun you're so desperate for me to marry—has been two-timing me with my best friend all the way through our relationship. That's right, with Sheila. Since before our first date, almost seven years ago. Good thing I didn't listen to you and refused him every time he proposed, eh, Dad?"

Hilda gasped. "Josie!"

"Oh I'll be fine," said Jo wearily. "I needed to get rid of him for years, just didn't know how." She let out a bitter laugh. "Didn't want to hurt him. Didn't want to rock the boat. Hah! Typical!"

"How did you find out?" asked Hilda.

"Because I finished with him the other night. Or he finished with me. Not sure which, you'll have to ask Sheila. Anyway it doesn't matter."

Bill sat down heavily on her bed. "I can't believe it," he said.

"I know, Dad," said Jo. "Believe it or not, that's another reason I didn't finish it sooner. I knew how much you wanted him for a son-in-law. I was trying to want the same things for me as you did. A bit of a pattern, it appears."

Bill gave his daughter a baffled stare. "You dated him for me?"

"No," said Jo slowly. "At first I dated him for both of us. But after a while . . . I suppose I was in denial." She let out another sharp laugh. "Didn't want to disappoint the men in my life. And I didn't even notice how much that was disappointing me."

There was a pause.

"Well," said Bill quietly. "Well."

Hilda came slowly into the room and sat next to Bill on the bed.

"You both seem to have missed something rather important," she said breathily.

They looked at her.

"I came up the stairs on my own," she said.

The slam of the front door woke Vanessa and Dick out of their slumber. They heard Josh clatter into the kitchen and make more noise in there than when the children got their own breakfast.

"Bloody hell," said Dick. "What's wrong with him?"

"Shall we go and see?" asked Vanessa. "I owe him an apology anyway."

"Yeah," said Dick. "And we can tell him about Jo, too."

They jumped into their clothes and went downstairs, where they found Josh standing by the kettle.

"Josh!" greeted Vanessa. "How nice to see you!"

"I went to see Jo," he told the kettle. "And she's a fucking bitch."

Vanessa and Dick stopped in their tracks.

"Ri–ight," said Vanessa thoughtfully. "I just wanted to say—"

"You're better off without her." Josh turned to Vanessa, his face pale with anger. "I went all the fucking way to no-man's-land, where I had to be polite to her father—a man who makes the Godfather look like

Mahatma Fucking Gandhi—to tell her how much the kids miss her and how much you two need her to save your doomed marriage because Dad's so scared of you he's—"

"Son—" began Dick.

"Sorry." Josh took a breath. "Sorry. And guess what? Did she thank me for my pains? Did she buggery. She called me a 'two-faced hypocritical scrounging bastard with a Peter Pan complex.'" He stopped and laughed. "'A two-faced hypocritical scrounging bastard!'" he repeated.

"Why?" asked Vanessa and Dick at the same time.

"With a Peter Pan complex!" he finished.

"Why?" they repeated.

"How the hell should I know?" he asked.

"Oh dear," said Vanessa. "What did you say to her, Josh?"

"Oh it's my fault, is it?" burst Josh. "Of course! I should have known—it's always Josh's fault. Even when I'm the one trying to save the day—*especially* when I'm the one who's trying to save the day. Josh the Accident Waiting to Happen. Josh the Guilty until Proved Innocent—"

"I didn't mean that," interrupted Vanessa. "I just thought maybe you'd triggered something, and we might be able to work out why she said that."

"Well," he said, "I clearly said something a two-faced hypocritical scrounging bastard with a Peter Pan complex would have said."

He looked at their pained faces.

"She accused me of living here rent-free while earning a fortune, neither of which is remotely true—"

"Oh dear," said Vanessa.

"I wish they were!" continued Josh. "I wish I did earn a bloody fortune—it might help me deal with the fact that I hate my job and the fact that my dad lives in fear of his wife."

"About that, son—"

"*And* she said I helped Dad have affairs. Helped him! Said we had some sordid little secret from Vanessa."

"Well we did," said Dick. "When you think about it."

Josh stopped.

"What?" he clipped.

"Well, we were colluding to keep my money problems secret from Vanessa."

Josh stared at his father.

"Which meant lots of whispered conversations," continued Dick. "Lots of secret looks—"

"Dad!"

"Maybe Jo just overheard us or noticed something. She was a perceptive one, was Jo."

Josh stared at Vanessa.

"It's okay, Josh," said Vanessa. "I know all about it."

"Crikey," said Josh. "I was only away for one day. What else did I miss? You haven't had another baby or anything?" He turned to his dad suddenly. "How come you're home on a Saturday?"

Dick explained everything, and for the third time in as many weeks, Josh's world map was picked up, shaken vigorously, and replaced in a different location—a location offering improved views and amenities that he was sure to appreciate once he'd got over the travel sickness.

Afterward, Vanessa came over to him and put her arm on his.

"Josh," she said. "I owe you an enormous apology. You were right; I have always assumed you were at fault. I've been very unfair to you, and I'm sorry. I'm also deeply grateful that you actually sacrificed your own comfort to help your father's marriage with a woman you hated. Even though I'd have much preferred it if Dick had come to me, I am aware that what you did was unbelievably big and I think you're . . . well, amazing."

"I didn't hate you," said Josh quietly. "I just thought you hated me."

"Oh dear." She sighed. "You thought I hated you, and Dick thought I loved him for his money. And there you both were, plotting to keep me in the picture. You're misguided fools, but in a good way."

There was silence in the kitchen for a while.

"And that's another thing!" Josh suddenly exploded. "She said I disgusted her. *Disgusted* her."

Vanessa and Dick watched mutely as Josh picked up Jo's car keys, muttered something about going for a long drive over a short cliff, and left the house.

"What shall we do now?" asked Vanessa, after the echo from the slamming door had died down. "When do you think will be the best time to tell him we've decided to give Jo an offer she can't refuse?"

Dick thought long and hard.

"Cup of tea?" he suggested eventually.

"Shall we still phone Jo?"

"Don't know."

"I'd love one, thanks."

"Hmm," said Dick as he switched on the kettle.

They stood watching the kettle boil, which, it being the latest Alessi, didn't take long.

"I think we should call her just to find out what happened," said Dick.

"But do you think it's fair to get her back in the house when Josh feels like this? I don't want to alienate him any more than I already have. I want him to feel welcome here."

"Maybe we can try and clear it up," said Dick, taking milk out of the fridge. "Anyway, he'll be moving into the flat as soon as he can. And I need Jo. They need never see each other again."

"I wonder what happened between them?" Vanessa took out the only two mugs not in the dishwasher. "Should I tell Jo I got it wrong about Josh not paying rent?"

Dick grimaced. "Do you mind not? I don't really want our—my—personal financial situation dissected."

"Of course not," said Vanessa, getting out the tea. "Silly suggestion. And I'm sure it's irrelevant anyway—it'll hardly have been about that."

Dick spooned the tea into the teapot.

"It was awfully good of Josh to go all that way to get her back for us," murmured Vanessa, watching Dick pour water into the pot. "I really have underestimated him."

Dick smiled. "He's a good boy, my Josh."

Vanessa patted her husband's cheek. "Just like his dad." They kissed.

A retching noise came from the garden. They turned to see Toby framed by the French windows.

"Do you mind?" he said. "There are children present."

"I'll phone Jo," whispered Vanessa.

"I'll bring you your tea," said Dick, and watched her go.

Jo and her parents were sitting at the kitchen table. They'd celebrated Hilda's first solo stair walk with a nice cuppa and were all feeling much calmer and able to take in all the different pieces of Jo's news. She and her father hadn't actually apologized to each other, but he'd made the tea, and when he handed her her cup, she'd said thank you.

When the phone rang, they all stopped. Hilda wasn't expected to answer the phone anymore. Bill would have done it, but had just made the tea, yet Jo was emotionally fragile and had just pointed out that he had been selfish for the past thirty years. The phone continued to ring.

"I'll get it," said Jo eventually.

"Thanks," said Bill.

Hilda and Jo exchanged glances as Jo left the room.

Bill and Hilda strained to hear the conversation in the hall as they sipped their tea.

Jo was somewhat surprised to hear Vanessa's voice at the other end of the phone and felt a surge of sisterhood toward her. When Vanessa explained that Dick was selling his shop and was going to become a house-husband and that they wanted her to come back as their part-time nanny for a tiny reduction in salary, she could hardly believe her ears. On the one hand it was too good to be true—a message from heaven, the answer to all her prayers. On the other, she'd just told Josh to fuck off. Not only that, but she'd have to spend most of her working day with a cheating husband, which, especially after what she'd just discovered about her own cheating man, would not be easy. And could she live in such close proximity to Josh? The thought brought an angry flush to her face.

"I know about your argument with Josh," said Vanessa quickly.

"Oh," said Jo.

"And it might help if you know that he'll be moving out soon."

"Oh," repeated Jo.

"Yes," said Vanessa. "He's the one buying Dick's shop, and he'll be moving into the flat above it. So you've got nothing to worry about on that score."

"Oh."

"He's a good boy really," said Vanessa.

Jo was silent.

"Turns out I've been wrong about him in the past," continued Vanessa. "He's been much maligned."

"Hmm."

"So let's just forget everything I ever told you about him."

"Hmm."

"Let's all start with a clean slate."

Jo started playing for time.

"Wow," she said slowly. "I don't know what to say."

"You'll get loads more free time for practically the same money," urged Vanessa.

"You could get another job if you wanted, or take up some course or something."

Jo closed her eyes. "I always wanted to study," she said quietly.

"Excellent!" cried Vanessa. "Perfect!"

"Mm," said Jo.

"You must say yes," pleaded Vanessa. "The kids miss you so much. And so do we. Dick can't do it without you. It's a big step for him, he really wants to be the best father he can be. We've had a long chat, and we're going to make a fresh start."

Aha, thought Jo. It sounded like Dick had finished his affair and confessed all to Vanessa and this was their solution. It certainly sounded as though something had changed. "Okay." She grinned. "I'll do it. I'll come back."

She laughed at the sound of Vanessa cheering down the line.

"When?" asked Vanessa.

"When do you want me?"

"Tomorrow?"

Jo let out a quick guffaw. Then she decided that was a very good idea. And her mother could now walk up the stairs unaided.

"I'll see you tomorrow," she said. "As soon as I can get there."

When Josh returned home that evening from his drive, the kids bombarded him with hugs and kisses and tried to shout over each other. Dick and Vanessa watched, smiling hopefully, from the conservatory sofa.

"Wait!" shouted Josh, Tallulah in his arms, Zak holding on to one arm, and Cassie on the other. "One at a time!"

They all shouted again.

"Cassie!" shouted Josh. "What the hell's going on?"

Cassie jumped up and down.

"You did it! Jo's coming back! Tomorrow! You did it, Josh!"

Josh looked up at Vanessa and Dick.

"Is that true?" he asked.

"Yes but we can explain," said Dick. "Full-time at first, but then part-time. Just to help me get into the swing of things. We weren't going to do it, but you'll hardly know she's here."

"Great," said Josh, shaking the children off him like rain off a raincoat. "Just great."

"I told her I was wrong about you," rushed Vanessa.

"I couldn't give a damn what she thinks about me," said Josh quietly. Dick and Vanessa nodded.

"I just think she's a . . ." He looked at three happy young faces and let his sentence hang in the air.

"Babe?" grinned Toby.

"Oh shut up, Tobe!" flashed Josh. "Why must you always say what you know people don't want to hear? Do you *want* to be disliked, is that it?" Toby went silent.

"I think Jo's almost as pretty as Mummy," said Tallulah.

"Anyway," said Josh, "I'll be moving out as soon as the flat's been cleared. I would move back to Crouch End, but my room's been rented out."

"We knew you'd be all right about it," said Dick.

"We wouldn't have done it otherwise," added Vanessa.

"Oh don't worry on my account," said Josh. "I couldn't care less whom you hire."

"Right," said Vanessa.

Josh gave a curt nod. "I'll be in my room," he said, and left them to their evening.

Jo stood for a while in the hall before going back into the kitchen.

"That was Vanessa," she told her parents as she sat back down at the table.

"Oh yes?" said Bill.

"They want me to come back as a full-time nanny first, but then part-time on practically the same pay. Which means I'll be able to support myself at university."

Her parents were quiet.

"When?" asked Hilda eventually.

"I'm going back tomorrow," said Jo. "If that's alright."

Hilda and Bill looked at each other.

"What you asking us for?" said Bill.

Jo sighed dramatically.

"You're a big girl now," he continued, taking another digestive biscuit. "You know what you want."

Hilda smiled. "Better pack," she said quietly.

"Tell you what!" said Bill. "After you've packed and we've washed up the tea things, let's all go down to the Witch's Arms to celebrate."

They stared at him.

"*What?*" he cried. "Anyone would think I had two heads or some-thing."

They continued to stare at him.

"Alright," he said. "Let's *not* go, it's all the same to me."

Hilda got up to wash the tea things and Jo rushed upstairs to pack.

Chapter 25

The next morning, Jo stood in her bedroom, checking her packing for the fourth time. This time there would be no farewell party at the station. There was no possibility that Shaun or Sheila would come to see her off—which funnily enough, just felt more honest than last time, not more sad—and she'd told her parents she'd be able to get the bus to the station because there was so much less to carry. They didn't offer to give her a lift. All part of them allowing her to be a grown-up, she assumed. She stared thoughtfully at her rucksack as if it might be able to add something useful to the conversation in her head. Instead she found herself remembering the last time she was packing, with the help of Josh, and thinking how different her life was then.

"All packed?" came her mother's voice.

"Think so," she said quietly.

Jo turned as she heard her father appear behind her mother. They looked nice together like that, framed in her doorway. She looked at them.

"I love you both, you know."

Surprised, touched, but most of all embarrassed, her parents left her in peace. Jo smiled in some wonder. All these years, and the morning she leaves home she finally works out how to do it.

The journey to London was hugely frustrating. She hadn't remembered it taking this long. She sat in the train urging it to move faster, although she wasn't quite sure why. Every time she thought of the Fitzgeralds her stomach twisted. She tried to imagine how Josh had reacted when he'd discovered she was coming back. She tried to recall exactly what she'd said to him in the heat of the moment yesterday, but found it impossible to bring back the precise words. She started to consider the possibility that she might find it hard to be in his presence. When he was nice it was wonderful, but when he was the other Josh she found it painful just to be near him. Then she gave herself a stern telling-off. This was her dream come true, the job of a lifetime, and she wasn't going to let him spoil it for her. She would just have to cope with Josh Fitzgerald living in the room next door. It was only short-term, after all.

She had to wait four minutes for the High Barnet tube train, and she paced the platform impatiently. When the train arrived, she jumped on it and paced again. When she got out at Highgate Station, she found she was breaking into a grin as she walked along Southwood Lane, admiring the urban yet cosy houses. As she turned down the High Street her mind flipped briefly to Shaun and Sheila, and she waited for the pang. While waiting, she popped in at Costa Coffee and got herself an espresso. By the time she hit Ascot Drive she was practically running, and she rang the doorbell three times. At the familiar sound of stampeding buffalo, she started hopping from foot to foot.

The door opened wide, and there was Dick, surrounded by the children. Even the cats had come to see what all the fuss was about.

"Hello!" he shouted.

"*It's Jo!*" yelled Zak. "Mummy! Lula won't give me back my—*It's Jo!*"

Tallulah raced up to her and gave her legs a big hug, her face nestling into her thighs.

Cassandra stood in the hall, leaning against the banister, a smile lighting up her face.

"I'm growing my hair to be like yours," she said, stepping forward slightly.

"Gimme a hug, gorgeous," said Jo. Cassie obeyed. Tallulah giggled, and they all squeezed tighter.

Zak took hold of Jo's hand. "I've got a new dinosaur," he announced, overjoyed that there was someone new to tell. "It's got green eyes and roars and moves its head like the real thing. Dinosaurs are extinct, I like your top."

"How's your mummy?" asked Tallulah, letting go of Jo's legs.

"Much better, thank you, sweetheart," said Jo.

Vanessa came into the hall. Jo braced herself and looked up. No Josh.

"Stop hassling the poor girl," Vanessa instructed the children. "Jo, welcome back. Please come in. Let me take your coat. Your room is all ready for you. Come and have tea. There's a surprise."

"*We've got a cake!*" exploded Tallulah.

"Well, there goes the surprise." Vanessa laughed.

They all followed Jo into the kitchen. No Josh.

"Go and put your stuff away, freshen up if you want, Josh is out," called out Vanessa as she set the table.

Jo walked into her room feeling excited and disappointed at the same time. The room was smaller than she remembered. She glanced over to the door separating her room from Josh's. *So,* she thought. *He's out.* She didn't know if she was relieved or insulted. All she did know was that she'd spent the entire journey being psyched up to seeing him, and her body was full of nervous energy with nowhere to go but her nerve endings. Mr. Bojangles had nothing on her. Then she heard the front door bang shut, and her nervous energy found its direction with impressive alacrity. She nipped into the bathroom.

Once inside it, she looked at herself in the mirror, tutted, and walked out again. As she did so, Josh walked into her bedroom. She stopped still. He stopped still. The room stopped still.

"I—" she explained.

"Don't mind me," he said, walking through to his room. "I'll be out of your hair in a sec, just forgot something." When he came back she hadn't moved.

"Well, I came back," she said, as he reached her door. "In the end."

He stopped and raised his eyebrows. "Mm?"

"I just . . . I hope it won't be difficult. For us—for you. I mean—"

"Difficult?" he laughed. "Why on earth should it be difficult?"

"Well, we . . . you know. I said things—"

He shrugged.

"And so did you," she said.

Another shrug. "So? No big deal. I'd forgotten all about it."

"Oh! Great! So, me being here isn't a problem for you?"

He smiled pityingly at her. "Get over yourself." He shook his head.

Jo gave a tight smile. "I didn't think I was under myself."

Josh fixed her with an intense gaze. "Listen," he instructed. She listened. "They wanted you back, you came back. Great. It's got sod all to do with me. I couldn't care less what you do."

She watched him turn and go, her teeth gritting hard. "Tosser," she muttered halfheartedly—which made her feel a bit better—then joined the tea party.

Within an hour of arriving, Jo felt completely at home. Vanessa and Dick were bickering amid the sexual tension, the kids were rowing, the cats were unnerving her, and Josh was a dark, oppressive force invading her life. Home sweet home.

Monday midmorning, and Vanessa's hand hovered over the phone. After a moment, she changed her mind and phoned Tom.

He answered after only fifty rings.

"Tom? Vanessa."

"Vanessa! What a delightful surprise! I take it you've seen the rough edit?"

"I have, Tom."

"She has, Tom. Oh yes she has, in that tough yet womanly voice."

"Would you like to know what I think of it?"

"I would like nothing more, Vanessa. My life so far has been a prelude to this moment."

"It looks rougher than a badger's arse, Tom."

There was a long silence.

"Ah," said Tom eventually. "Don't tell me. In the post-post-pre-preproduction meeting they said specifically that they didn't want the badger's arse look, because of the award-winning Badger's Arse ad."

Vanessa raised her eyes to heaven. "Something like that, yes, Tom."

"Between you and me, Vanessa, that 'badger's arse' look is a complete fucker to create."

"Well, you managed it."

"Why, thank you. Credit where credit's due. Was there anything else?"

"Yes, Tom, I'd like to have a quick word with Anthony."

"I bet you would. I'll just put you through."

Vanessa waited, staring at her desk.

"You're a tough woman," came Anthony's soft voice, "but I like it."

"Yeah, sorry about that."

"Not a good rough edit, I take it?"

"Not if any of us want a decent bonus this year," she said.

"Shit. We'll get on it. Perhaps we should meet up."

"Mm."

"In a cupboard somewhere."

"I thought perhaps this evening. In Nachos."

"Oh! Great."

"Shall we say seven?"

"Seven it is."

Vanessa put the phone down and counted the hours to the end of her time as a scarlet woman. Only seven to go.

At three minutes past seven, Vanessa watched Anthony make his way toward her through the crowded bar.

"I know what you're going to say," he whispered in her ear as soon as he reached her side.

"Do you?" she asked.

"Yes. And it's not a Silly-Nibble in my pocket, I'm just pleased to see you."

Vanessa turned away.

"I'm just ordering," she said. "What would you like?"

"I'll have a Vanessa Fitzgerald please. On the rocks."

She had to physically move him away with her hand.

"Anthony." Something in her voice caught him short. He waited. "This is really difficult for me to say."

Anthony's features altered fractionally.

"Why? Is it in Greek?" he asked.

Vanessa gave him a look. After a pause, he started nodding and looked down. While he looked like he was resisting the urge to put his fingers in his ears, shut his eyes, and start whistling, Vanessa explained it as it was.

"It's all for the best," she concluded.

He nodded again.

"Come on," she said. "It was a one-off. It was hardly serious."

Another nod.

"We only did some heavy petting," she pressed the point. "Please don't make me feel like I'm finishing an affair."

Anthony looked round the bar. "We only did heavy petting because I'm a gentleman, and we'd only just started."

Vanessa shook her head. "No," she said. "I'm a happily married woman. I've got three children. I love my husband."

Anthony snorted. "You weren't thinking of them in the Silly Nibble cupboard, were you?"

"Actually I was," said Vanessa. "It was more about anger than lust."

"Cheers."

Vanessa sighed. "You're not making this very easy."

"Neither are you. Can you at least try to look ugly while you do this or . . . belch or something?"

"I can't belch to order."

"Typical."

"Look," lied Vanessa, "there are some things in life we'd like to do but can't. It's as simple as that."

"Why?"

"Because we have to be grown-up."

"Why?"

"Because that's what we are. Grown-ups."

"That's what got us into this mess in the first place. Believe me, if you were a child, we wouldn't be in this position."

Vanessa started collecting her coat and bag.

"I'm going to leave now," she said. "Can I . . . do anything? To make it all a bit easier?"

"Yeah, you could wear longer skirts."

She smiled.

"And keep your jacket on all the time," said Anthony. "And don't smile."

"I was thinking more of not appearing at meetings that aren't absolutely necessary."

"And get a run in your hose once in a while. Everyone else manages."

"I should leave."

Another nod.

Vanessa got up to go, and Anthony stared at the floor while she walked away. As she reached the tube station, he was still staring.

Jo began her first evening back in London sitting on her bed in her room, thinking seriously and maturely about unpacking. To her surprise, one of the cats appeared on her bed, stretched out and graciously allowed her to pet it. Then she lay on her back and fell asleep. She was woken by the sound of her mobile phone doing a samba. It was Pippa. She felt excited at the thought that Pippa was no longer her long-distance friend, and they arranged to meet the next day.

Then Jo told her her latest update.

"As soon as Dick sells the shop he'll be at home, and I'll be on practically the same salary part-time!"

"Go to the top of the class!" cried Pippa. "Part-time nanny on full-time pay! You should give talks."

"I didn't do anything," said Jo. "It's all because of Dick."

"Hmm. Guilty conscience?"

"Well, I think he may have finished the affair," confided Jo. "I don't think I'll be able to last working with him if he hasn't. I certainly won't be keeping any secrets for him like his son."

Then she explained about Josh coming to Niblet-upon-Avon and dissected the row they'd had.

"I don't believe it!" cried Pippa.

"I know. Bastard."

"He came all the way to see you!"

"He called me a prick-tease."

"He drove all the way to beg you to come back?"

"He called me a prick-tease."

"How many miles is that?"

"I think you're missing the point."

"Well one of us is."

"He called me a prick-tease."

"Hmm," said Pippa. "I wonder how he knows?"

"Pippa!"

"Listen, you're going to have to say something to Gerry," said Pippa.

"Oh God, why?"

"Because he's planned your children's first names. Did you know you were going to have four?"

Just then Jo heard Nick come into Pippa's room, and had to listen to Pippa telling him all about Jo being back. She heard Nick tell Pippa to say hi and invite Jo to join them later that night. She also overheard Nick say, "We can invite Gerry. Make it a foursome."

"Oh no!" cried Jo into the phone. She wasn't going down that road again. "No need to tell Gerry about me being back for a while, is there?"

Pippa's voice was slightly muffled.

"Too late for that. Nick's already on the phone."

"Oh God!" cried Jo. "Give me a moment to get my bearings."

"I don't think Gerry wants you to get your bearings. Much easier to sweep you off your feet if you're already wonky."

"You know," said Jo, "I think we may be overreacting a bit with Gerry. He phoned while I was at home, and he was so friendly it was really nice. And when I couldn't speak to him, he was absolutely fine about it. Better than Josh, who came in person and then blew me off. Did I tell you I slapped him?"

"Oh my God!" exclaimed Pippa. "How exciting!"

"Not really," said Jo. "It was horrid, I flipped. It's nothing like it looks in the films. It's ugly and embarrassing."

"How do you think you'll be when you see him?"

"I already have."

"How was it?"

"Absolutely horrid. He's back to the nasty version. All hard and cold."

"Oh dear. At least with Gerry you know where you are."

"Yep." Jo sighed. "With someone I don't fancy."

Jo explained that she had to phone her parents and tell them she was safely there and rung off. She lay back and closed her eyes, giving herself a moment before phoning her parents. When the samba started up again, she didn't need to guess who it was.

"Hello, Gerry," she said warmly, wondering if Josh could hear her.

"Hey! You knew it was me!" He laughed.

"Yup," she said.

"So!" he said, after a fraction's pause. "I hear you're back then."

"I am." She laughed. "It's a short but effective grapevine."

"And I hear you finished with Shaun."

"Actually it appears he finished with me."

"Great!"

"Thank you."

"I mean—"

"Look, Ger—"

"I wondered if you wanted to go out sometime."

"Thanks, but not now," she said.

"Oh. Okay. Give you some time to settle in."

"Well, I think I'll need a bit of time to adjust to more than that."

"Just in case you change your mind, we'll all be at the Flask from eight."

"Right," said Jo slowly, thinking that it would be nice to see Pippa and Nick, even if she wasn't so sure about Gerry. "Thanks."

"And I hope everything's alright," he said.

"Thanks. I'll be fine."

"Excellent. If you ever need to chat, just give me a call."

"Thanks," said Jo, considering that he might come in handy.

"Bye then," he said cheerfully.

And he rang off. She massaged her temples for a while and phoned her parents.

"I'm here," she told her father.

"Where?"

She smiled.

"In the bedroom."

"Ah," he said softly. "It's nice, smaller than I'd imagined, but nice."

She closed her eyes and smiled a bit wider, concentrating on her father's voice.

"How's Mum?"

"Fine. She's just watching *The Antiques Roadshow*."

A warm silence linked them over the line.

"I gave her a permission slip," he added.

Eventually, she rang off, sat up slowly and, after a moment of sitting cross-legged on the bed and humming, started unpacking.

Chapter 26

Things at the Fitzgeralds' abode were changing fast. Josh and Dick had exchanged contracts on the shop and the flat above it, and the family was to have a celebratory dinner that night. Cassie was going to be allowed to stay up for it. Even Jo was invited because Vanessa had said it was good news for her, too, because it meant Dick could spend more time at home so she could start looking for a course. There was a great feeling of excitement in the house that night.

"Why is it such good news, Jo?" asked Zak, as Jo popped up to check that he was getting himself ready for bed. Vanessa was on her way home, so she was getting the littler ones ready for bed while Dick finished dinner. He'd be up later.

"Well," she said, "it means you get to spend much more time with your dad, and it means Josh can resign from his job."

"Does it mean you won't be here anymore?"

"No, of course not," she said. "It means we'll both be at school at the same time. That's all." Just the thought of it made her excited.

"Why are you going to school when you're a grown-up?"

"Because I didn't do it when I was younger."

"Weren't you clever enough?"

Jo smiled. "No. I just didn't do it. And now I really want to."

"Oh." He eyed her suspiciously.

When she came downstairs, she found Josh leafing silently through her university prospectuses. At his sudden awareness of her, his head moved fractionally, but he kept his eyes fixed on what he was reading. She tidied like a little tornado around him.

"Going back to school then," he commented.

"Mm."

He looked up. "What course are you going to do?"

She stopped, surprised. "I'm not sure. I'd like to do anthropology, but I don't know if I've got enough qualifications."

Josh snorted. She stopped what she was doing.

"What does that mean?" she asked, her tone ice-cold.

His face was blank. "Qualifications are overrated," he said. "Totally meaningless."

"No they're not."

"Yes they are."

She started to stack the dishwasher. "That's like someone with money saying money isn't everything. Without qualifications you can't get good jobs."

Another snort. "Define 'good jobs.'"

She stopped stacking.

"Alright—accountancy."

He smiled. "You fell right into the trap there," he said. "Accountancy's overrated."

"But the salary's good isn't it?"

"No. Not particularly. Not for the hours you're expected to put in."

"Oh, and nannies don't put in long hours?" She looked up at the kitchen clock. "Which one of us is still working?"

He frowned. "Who's talking about nannies? I thought we were talking about accountants."

"I'm just making the point that with qualifications, I probably wouldn't be working this late in the evening, and I'd probably be earning more."

She waited for Josh's counterargument, and when none came, continued. "And don't tell me it's because nannies don't use their brains in this job, because I've just spent ten minutes playing a game of Question and Answers that will have huge implications for a bright, emotionally vulnerable eight-year-old."

Josh nodded.

"Anyone can add up sums," she concluded.

That sounded quite harsh, she thought, and it occurred to her that now might be an appropriate moment to apologize for slapping him. She looked at him. And remembered him calling her a prick-tease. And saying she was certainly on tap that night. And whispering with his dad about cheating on Vanessa. And she remembered Vanessa's prescient words of warning about the Joshua Fitzgerald charm. Then she remembered what Josh looked like in just his jeans. She could feel a headache coming on.

"I . . ." started Josh, "probably shouldn't have called you a prick-tease."

Jo was so shocked she didn't know what to say. Just then her mobile rang. She went to her bag and answered it without looking to see who was calling. She stared back at Josh as she answered. He was running his fingers through his hair while glancing at her prospectus.

"Hi, Gerry." She sighed weakly.

She missed the first half of Gerry's speech because she was too busy watching Josh. He looked up from her prospectus, stared baldly at her as if she was some sour milk he'd accidentally smelled and walked out toward the living room, saying composedly as he passed, "Excuse me."

She wandered mindlessly into her room, shutting the door behind her.

Gerry didn't want to turn into a pest, he said, but it just so happened that Nick, Pippa, and he were meeting up again tonight, and Pippa had wondered if she fancied joining them at the pub. Nothing fancy, just friends getting together. She said she couldn't, she was celebrating with the Fitzgeralds. When there was a knock at her bedroom door, she braced herself and, interrupting Gerry midflow, yelled for Josh to come in. He knocked again.

"Hold on, Gerry," she interrupted, and walked over to the door with the phone at her ear.

When she saw Shaun standing there, in front of Josh, she felt goose bumps up her neck.

"I have to go now," she told Gerry, looking through Shaun to Josh, who had obviously let him in.

Gerry kept talking in her ear. "Gerry, I have to go now," she repeated, and clicked off.

Josh turned and left the room.

She stared at Shaun. He was grave and pale. She wondered why he hadn't phoned to say he was coming. She wondered why he'd chosen to-night. She wondered where Sheila was. She wondered what had happened when Josh had answered the front door to him.

"Hi," said Shaun.

She nodded.

"Can we talk?"

"It's not a great time, Shaun. You should have phoned."

"Sorry."

"Not here," she said, shutting her bedroom door behind her. "We'll go to the park."

As they passed the living room, Jo popped her head round the door. Josh was staring at the television.

"Um," she started. "We're just off to Waterlow Park."

He kept his eyes on the television. "Don't have to check with me."

She clenched her teeth. "If Vanessa gets back before I do, please tell her I'll be back soon."

"Sure."

"Obviously, start dinner without me. Obviously."

"Obviously."

She paused.

"Right," she said.

No answer.

"See you soon," she told him.

Silence.

Then as she left the room she heard a sly, "Have a good time."

Her mind flitted through all the possible answers this deserved. "Oh don't worry," she said softly. "I will."

As she sped up the hill, Shaun following fast behind, she hoped Josh stewed in it. Meanwhile, Josh sat staring at the TV, stewing in it.

Shaun and Jo reached the park in ten minutes flat and sat down at the first bench they reached.

"So," she said. "You've got half an hour."

Shaun sighed.

"I know she told you everything."

"Yeah, that's right," said Jo. "She even reminded me of how long it took you to 'screw' me."

"It wasn't like that, Jo."

Jo shrugged. "Who cares?"

"I do."

Shaun leaned forward, clasped his hands together, and gave his side of the story in a fast monotone. He explained that he had never been serious about Sheila right from the start, and assumed Sheila hadn't been serious about him. When she mentioned that she was Jo's friend, he couldn't believe his luck. He'd had such a crush on her from nursery school—he was determined to meet her again. Yes, he may have told Sheila it was every boy's fantasy to sleep with his first crush, but that was before he'd met her again, and, anyway, it was true. Of course he couldn't remember saying it now, but if he had, he'd probably said it to put Sheila off him. How was he to know she was staying for good and was taking notes? Sometimes we say things about people before we really know them.

Anyway, when he did meet Jo again, she was everything he'd ever imagined she'd be. He'd wanted to go out with her, and of course, yes, he'd wanted to make love with her, he didn't see anything wrong with that; in fact, there'd have been something wrong with him if he hadn't. When Sheila found out that they'd started dating, she was furious and told him that she'd tell Jo everything, including what he'd said about her before he'd met her again. He was terrified he might lose her. And so began Sheila's power over him, which she went on to wield for the next six years. And the truth was he got used to it. In a way she was the antidote to the niceness of their relationship—and the occasional fling with her was always incredibly passionate, although it always filled him with remorse.

Yes, he had wanted to marry Jo. But when she went to London, he and Sheila suddenly had nothing to hide. And he found himself confiding in her. He discovered that the original lust he'd had for Sheila in the early days was still there, plus something else, an honesty about his darker side he'd never wanted to show Jo. Plus he and Shee knew what it was like to love someone too much, and they found themselves able to understand each other. Before he knew it, they were as good as dating. But they were in a stalemate situation. She wanted him to finish with Jo, yet part of him still wanted to marry Jo. So he persuaded Sheila that if he proposed again, Jo would most definitely refuse him again and he'd have the perfect escape clause. What he never told Sheila was that maybe this time Jo would say yes.

Jo listened with a sober detachment.

"So you're marrying Sheila when part of you wanted to marry me?" she checked.

"Well, if I'm completely honest"—he gave a big sigh—"I don't think I could have given Shee up even if I had married you."

Jo started laughing.

"Me and Shee—we're two of a kind," he said simply. "It makes much more sense marrying her instead of you." He looked up at her, squinting in the evening sun.

"Anyway," he added quietly, "I couldn't get you, could I?"

She shook her head. After a few moments, she looked at her watch.

"I have to get back," she said.

"Right."

They walked to the house in silence, Jo an anxious step ahead the whole way. They'd taken an hour. When they reached the front door, Shaun took both Jo's hands in his.

"What are you thinking, Jo?" he asked.

She walked him away from the living room window, braced herself, and went for it.

"Did I lead you on, Shaun?" she asked. "Was I a tease?"

He glanced away for a moment. "Nah. You didn't need to. I was doing it enough myself."

They looked sadly at each other and finally shared a resigned half smile.

"I hope you and Shee are happy," Jo said.

"Do you?"

"Yes. And I think you will be."

"I do, too, actually," he said quickly. "It's been like getting off some damaging drug—when you went to London it was cold turkey, and now I'm through the worst and living a normal life again."

Jo stared at him. "Thank you, Shaun," she said.

"I didn't mean you—"

"It doesn't matter—"

"It does—"

"No," she said firmly. "It really doesn't. I have to go back inside now."

She let him hug her, feeling unmoved by his embrace, then watched him get into his car and drive off.

After a moment, she turned to the house and went inside.

Vanessa was home, and Dick and Cassie were putting dinner on the table. She counted to three, then counted to ten and on fifteen walked into the living room. It was empty. She went back into the kitchen and paced a bit.

"Where's Josh?" she asked the room lightly. "I thought he was watching TV." Vanessa glanced over from picking at Dick's new improved lasagna recipe.

"Oh, he got a call from a friend," she said distractedly. "He went out to the pub."

"Shame," Dick said to Vanessa. "I really wanted to celebrate with him."

"You can celebrate with him on the weekend, darling," said Vanessa, carrying the lasagna to the table. "Tonight you're celebrating with the women in your life." Jo joined them at the table and tried to participate in the bonhomie. But from the plummet in her emotions about Josh's sudden disappearance, she knew conclusively that she was in serious trouble. It was hell when he was there, but even worse when he wasn't. She stared as Vanessa dished out the salad. Thank God Josh was moving out; otherwise, she wouldn't be able to cope with this emotional roller coaster for much longer. *This is my office*, she told herself firmly. *I cannot risk losing my job by being so emotionally vulnerable.* She managed a smile when Cassie made a face at how much green stuff had been put on her plate.

"Josh and I popped into the flat this evening," said Dick through his lasagna.

"Oh yes?" said Vanessa.

"He hadn't realized how bad it was, even though I'd told him. Says he might as well do some construction work on it—won't be able to move in for months."

"That's okay," said Vanessa. "It's great to have him round the house. And the kids love him." She turned to Jo. "You're both over your little quarrel, aren't you?"

Jo nodded.

Dick and Vanessa smiled, and Cassie cheered.

And Jo decided it was time to move out.

Chapter 27

Lunchtime a week later, Sebastian James sat bulkily on top of Pippa, almost visibly growing, while Pippa and Jo wolfed down a sandwich together. Jo had given Pippa her application form for her university course. When Pippa finished reading it, Jo calmly informed her that she had to move out of the Fitzgeralds'.

Pippa put down her pannini.

"Where will you live?"

"Well," said Jo. "I was wondering . . ."

"Move in with me!" cried Pippa. "I've got a spare room the size of a *massive* cupboard!"

Jo smiled with relief. "Your family won't mind?"

Pippa laughed. "You've been there! It's the attic flat! It has nothing to do with their home—separate front door and everything."

"How much is the rent?"

"Nothing! I don't pay, and you being there won't add anything to my rent. It'll just be nice to have you there. I mean it *is* small, but I'm at Nick's on weekends, so you'd have the place completely to yourself."

Jo nodded, and Pippa returned to her pannini before Sebastian James had a chance to smear it on his face.

After a while Pippa looked up at her. "Not hungry?" she asked.

Jo shook her head.

"What's up?"

Jo looked away.

"It's Shaun isn't it?" whispered Pippa.

"I hate Josh," breathed Jo.

"Oh."

"I can't bear it." Jo wiped her tears. "I feel like I played it all so wrong."

"Stop blaming yourself, honey," said Pippa, holding Jo's hand over the table and squashing Sebastian James's face into her chest. "It takes two to tango."

"He was so wonderful in the beginning. I mean *wonderful*. I was seriously considering chucking Shaun."

"I know."

"And then he went so cold." She blew her nose. "And said all those horrible things. And then at the cinema it looked like we were friends again, and I even managed to get out what I wanted to say to him, and everything was brilliant. Then he came to see me and . . ." She shook her head. "I just don't understand. It all went sour again. I just don't understand."

"You know what the trouble is, don't you?"

"No. What?" Jo concentrated hard.

"Well, what usually happens in something like this is that the reason you can't make up is because you can't say the one thing that will sort it all out."

"What's that?"

"That you fancied him rotten but were not going to chuck your boyfriend because he was your safety net. It doesn't mean you're a prick-tease, it just means you're mad about him."

Jo clenched Pippa's hand tight and nodded.

At precisely the same time, Josh Fitzgerald was discovering the efficacy of the office grapevine. Half an hour earlier he'd resigned. Now at the watercooler he was being congratulated by a bloke he'd only had a nodding acquaintance with in the lift.

He went on to spend the rest of the afternoon answering questions about his future plans, questions posed by everyone from the sandwich boy to his biggest rivals. Most of the office were as delighted for him as they were for themselves. He wasn't going to a better job in one of the top five firms, he was choosing to drop out of the race, and they were all man enough to congratulate him on taking a risk they'd never be stupid enough to take themselves.

Josh saw behind their smiles and was glad because it reminded him why he was leaving. And he was grateful to have so many people choking up his day because it took his mind off other things.

That night he went out for a drink with some mates to celebrate. By the time he got home, amply drunk, Vanessa and Dick were alone in the kitchen.

"Have a good evening?" asked Vanessa.

"I got rat-arsed," said Josh. "So it was good enough for me."

"Don't wake Jo up when you go to bed," said Dick. "She's only just turned off the light."

Josh nodded slowly, turning slightly to her door.

"Fancy joining us for a nightcap?" asked Vanessa.

"Why not?" he said. "Give her time to fall asleep so I don't wake her."

"Ah, that's good of you," said Vanessa.

Josh shrugged.

"She got the interview for her course," said Dick, pouring him some wine.

"Did she?" asked Josh, taking his glass and downing most of its contents. "Great." He nodded firmly.

"And she's moving out," said Vanessa.

Josh nodded again and downed the rest of its contents. He held out his glass for more.

"How come she's moving out?" he asked.

"She's going to move in with Pippa," said Vanessa.

"When?"

"Next week. Said she just needed a change. Shame."

"Maybe we've been taking advantage of her in the evenings," said Dick.

"Oh hardly," countered Vanessa. "Anyway, while she's here she might as well take part in the family."

"Exactly," said Dick. "Now she won't be here, she'll have her evenings to herself. Probably be able to start dating again. She can hardly do that when she's stuck here helping us."

They continued their discussion, hardly noticing Josh.

"Right," he said suddenly. "Night all."

"Night," whispered Dick and Vanessa, as he opened Jo's bedroom door.

He closed the door behind him and tiptoed through the pitch-black into his room, the sound of Jo's breathing telling him she was out cold. Once inside his room he fell flat on his futon, where he considered the pros and cons of walking past her sleeping form to brush his teeth.

"I think it's a shame," Vanessa told Dick, leaving her glass in the sink. "I thought we'd all just started to get used to each other."

Dick turned off the lights as they left the kitchen.

"Well, she won't be needed as much once I've finished sorting out the shop for Josh." He yawned.

"Yes, but that won't be for a couple of months yet," said Vanessa, following him up the stairs. "He'll still need you there in the day."

"I know. But in the evenings I'll be home. I don't blame her at all." He turned off the landing light and followed Vanessa into their room.

"I'm rather hurt actually," admitted Vanessa.

Dick put his arm round his wife. "Don't be," he said.

"Okay."

They kissed, then drew apart, fingertips touching as they wandered into the bathroom.

"Any news from the headhunters today?" asked Dick.

Vanessa shook her head. "I think it may prove more difficult than I thought. Companies are so much smaller than when I was last looking."

They stopped at their his-and-her sinks and looked at each other in the mirror.

"Are you unhappy there?" asked Dick.

"No," allowed Vanessa. "But I would rather be somewhere else."

"You don't regret taking on this responsibility? I can always—"

"No," she interrupted. "It's my turn to be doing it because I have to. You've done that for long enough."

Dick watched her as she tried to put her thoughts into words.

"I think I understand more how you were feeling about your work," she said. "I don't have a choice anymore. My job isn't a right, it's a responsibility. It was before—we needed both our incomes—but to me it didn't feel like I *had* to go in every day, it felt like I *wanted* to go in every day, because . . ." She smiled and shook her head at herself. "Because I had a husband. I had an economic safety net. I hadn't realized how much of a difference that made to me, psychologically. It meant I had the luxury of seeing my career as something to fulfill me, not as something to feed my family."

Dick nodded. "If you want me to get a part-time job—"

"No," insisted Vanessa. "You need to be with the kids, and they need you, and I want you to be happy. It's just . . . it's just different now."

"What if you can't find another job?"

Vanessa shrugged. "I'll stay where I am. Once I've exhausted all the options I'll have a word with Max, ask for a raise, see what happens."

"There's no rush financially, is there?"

She shook her head. "No. No."

"And your home life should improve. You won't be squeezing the supermarket shop in your lunch hour anymore. Or sorting out the kids in the morning. You can focus on your job, quality time with us, and relaxation."

They smiled at each other.

"We'll get there," said Dick.

"I know," said his wife.

It was a long night. By the time Josh had finally fallen into a fitful sleep, Jo was wide-awake, considering the pros and cons of moving in with Pippa. By the time she finally fell asleep again, Josh was wide-awake, considering the pros and cons of tiptoeing near Jo's sleeping form, getting himself another drink, and tiptoeing back past her sleeping form. By the time he finally fell asleep again, Jo was wide-awake, considering the pros and cons of knocking on Josh's door and apologizing for slapping him. By the time she finally fell asleep, Josh was wide-awake again, considering the pros and cons of tiptoeing past Jo's sleeping form, having a quick cold shower, and tiptoeing back past her sleeping form. By the time he finally fell asleep again, Jo was wide-awake, considering the pros and cons of knocking on Josh's door, opening it wide enough for her to be able to see him properly, and telling him that she didn't appreciate him always thinking the worst of her. It was hard enough moving out from home—not that he'd know, of course, still living at home—and she didn't need him making it even harder by being so cold with her. By the time she finally fell asleep again, Josh was wide-awake again, considering the pros and cons of tiptoeing past Jo's sleeping form and just taking it from there. By the time he fell asleep again, Jo was awake again, considering the pros and cons of knocking on Josh's door and just taking it from there.

Only moments before Mickey's white-gloved short hand reached the six, they were both out cold.

Later that day, while making the children tea, Jo's mobile rang. She read Gerry's name on it, and made a noise between a scream and a groan. *Right,* she thought, stirring their pasta sauce. I need to clear this up. She closed her eyes and pictured Josh's reaction to the last time he called.

"Gerry!" she cried more angrily than she'd intended. "Again!"

"Hi," said Gerry slowly. "Shall I call back later?"

"No! I think we have to talk."

"Actually I'm not sure I've got time."

"But you phoned me."

"Yep, but something's just come up."

"Gerry," she began.

"Another time perhaps—"

"I will say this only once," she continued. "I like you. You are really nice. But I do not like you in that way. I was lonely and depressed and trying to prove to—"

"I'll call back at a better time—"

"I do not, repeat *not*, want to go out with you."

"I think the line's going a bit—"

"*I don't fancy you, Gerry.*"

There was silence from the other end. She closed her eyes.

"Of course you don't," soothed Gerry.

"Thank you."

"Not now. It's a bad time."

"*No!*"

"I can wait."

"*Gerry!*"

"Woman's prerogative and all that."

"*What?*"

"We all know women change their minds a lot," he said good-naturedly. "That's how come they're so clean!"

"Gerry—" she said over his laughter.

"Listen, my mum refused my dad ten times before she said yes."

"*Gerry!* You're not listening."

"Mind you, she knew her mind over the divorce."

"Gerry, listen to me carefully. The womb does not take up brain space. They are in completely different places."

"Eh?"

"I know my own mind."

There was a pause. "Right."

"And I really like you, but I don't fancy you now, and I never will."

Another pause, during which Jo was cringing at the cruelty of her words. "Right."

"I'm sorry if I gave you the wrong impression."

"You did actually, yeah."

"Well, I'm really sorry about that. Maybe I like flirting as much as any red-blooded adult. I was very, very grateful to you for being so nice to me, but—"

"Ah shit!" he cried. "Not 'nice.' Don't call me 'nice.'"

"But you were."

There was a silence.

"Not ruggedly handsome and captivating?"

"No." She smiled. "Not to me. Maybe to someone else. But to me you were nice, Gerry."

"Bugger."

"I'm sorry."

There was a pause.

"You don't just want to still see each other as friends?" tried Gerry.

"No thanks."

"No strings?"

"No thanks."

"With Nick and Pippa?"

"No thanks."

Another pause. Jo knew she'd have to get off the phone quick, before she relented out of pure pity.

"I have to go now," she said, stirring the sauce.

"Can't blame a bloke for trying."

"No. And you certainly tried."

"Well"—he sighed—"if you really want something, you have to fight for it."

Jo paused from her stirring and pressed her eyes and mouth shut to stop herself from relenting.

"I'll say good-bye then," said Gerry.

"Bye."

She hung up, threw the phone in the air, and caught it just before it landed in the pasta sauce.

By the time Josh came home, Vanessa and Dick had tidied up from dinner.

"Mary Poppins in?" Josh asked, before going to his room.

"Nope," said Vanessa. "She's gone out with the girls. She's going to have to do all her packing on Saturday at this rate."

"When's she going exactly?" asked Dick, looking up from the paper.

"Day after tomorrow," said Vanessa.

They all mulled that for a moment.

"It won't be the same without her," said Dick.

"No," agreed Vanessa, as Josh left the room.

Chapter 28

On Friday afternoon, Cassie made a moving-out card with Zak and Tallulah, and they presented it to Jo at teatime. When she cried they felt awful.

When Jo put Cassie to bed that night, Cassie apologized for making her cry.

"Don't be a silly poppet," soothed Jo. "I'm crying because I'm so upset at leaving you all."

"Then why are you going?" asked Cassie.

"It's a long story."

"Is it 'cos of Josh?"

Jo stared at Cassie.

"What makes you say that?"

Cassie shrugged.

"'Cos I used to hate him, too. He's just another boy. But he's nice really."

Jo smiled. "He's very nice."

"So why are you moving out?"

Jo sighed. "It's a long story."

"You said that already."

Jo leaned across Cassie's bed and stroked her hair out of her eyes.

"You're a very clever little girl, aren't you?"

"If he likes you, and you like him, why are you moving out?"

"That's just it," said Jo, surprised at how good it felt to talk about it. "I don't think he does like me. I think I did something to hurt him. And it's horrid to spend time with someone who doesn't like you."

Cassie studied her, then Jo leaned forward and kissed Cassie gently on the cheek.

"Good night, sweetheart. I'm going to miss you very much."

Cassie hugged her, then snuggled down and closed her eyes.

Later that evening, Jo lay on her bed staring at the ceiling. She couldn't bring herself to pack. Nor could she bring herself to go out clubbing. She just didn't have the heart for it. But she couldn't stay in either, waiting for Josh to come home and ignore her. It looked like he was out for the evening. Her last evening in the house. He couldn't have made his position more clear.

Ten minutes before she was due to be picked up by Pippa, she got herself ready. Pippa came into her room and cast a look around.

"I'm picking you up tomorrow, right?"

"Yep."

"So when were you thinking of packing?"

"Tomorrow?" suggested Jo.

"Do you need a hand?"

"Oh yes, please," said Jo. "I can't bear the thought of doing it on my own. Not while he's in there." She nodded toward Josh's room.

"Is he there now?" whispered Pippa.

"Course not," said Jo morosely. "That might convey the impression that he liked me enough to stay in on my last night here. He's out for the evening."

"And so are you, girlie," announced Pippa. "And you're going to have fun whether you want to or not."

Jo grimaced.

"And then first thing tomorrow morning, I'll be round with coffee," said Pippa. "Double espressos all round."

"Why?"

"Because we're gonna need it after tonight."

"I'm not getting drunk," said Jo. "I'm going to be good."

"Yeah right."

"I am," said Jo, picking up her handbag and shutting her bedroom door behind them. "I need my wits about me tomorrow, and, anyway, I haven't got the energy."

Chapter 29

Next morning, Jo's brain was Pot Noodle. The first thing she was conscious of was the pain in her head caused by the sound of Pippa standing over her bed tutting.

"Shhhhh," she moaned. "I've got a headache."

Pippa thrust a take-out coffee under her nose.

"It's noon," shouted Pippa. "We have to get started."

"Witch," whispered Jo through cracked lips.

Pippa opened the curtain onto next door's building site and opened the window.

"Ah!" she said. "Breathe in all that fresh concrete. Last night's rain has highlighted its piquant aroma. That reminds me, do you remember falling in the puddle and thinking you were drowning?"

Jo turned her head away and tried not to cry. She heard Pippa turn on the shower, come back into the room, and pull her duvet off her.

"Don't!" she shrieked, pulling the duvet back. "He might come in. He doesn't knock anymore."

"Josh is watching TV in the living room," said Pippa. "He was the one who let me in."

Jo glanced up.

"How did he look?"

"Um," considered Pippa. "Tall, dark, and handsome?"

"I mean how did he seem?"

"Quiet."

"Quiet sad or quiet happy?"

"For Christ's sake, Jo, just tell him how you feel."

Jo sat up and counted, using her fingers.

"I feel one: furious, two: misrepresented, three: misunderstood, four: hard-done-by, and"—Jo stared hard at her fifth finger—"and a bit sick."

"Get in that shower," ordered Pippa.

Jo stumbled into the bathroom.

Josh, meanwhile, sat watching the living room television while sorting out his latest bank statement. Vanessa and Dick were driving to Brighton for a day trip alone, and he'd happily said he'd baby-sit. He was using the opportunity to sort through his accounts, a job he did religiously, every single time he remembered. For an accountant, his own personal accounts were in rather a state.

After an hour, he realized he'd left some receipts in his room. He knew that Pippa had arrived and had heard the shower going and the kettle boiling, so he was fairly sure Jo was up. He wandered through her room, nodding briefly to Pippa as he did so and glancing at Jo's rucksack and the boxes which had crept into his room.

"Sorry," Jo said stiffly. "We'll move everything if it's a problem. It was just easier."

"No problem," he told Pippa, before striding out.

Jo looked over at Pippa.

"See?" she said.

Josh shut the living room door behind him and continued with his accounts. The predictability of sums always calmed his mind. Just when he realized he was hungry, Toby poked his head round the living room door. He coughed slightly, and Josh turned to him.

"Alright, mate?"

"Yeah."

Toby came and sat down.

Josh turned off the TV and his calculator. "What's on your mind?"

"What do you get a girlfriend for an anniversary?" Toby tried to look cool.

Josh frowned. "How long have you been seeing her?"

"Two months."

"Blimey, mate, in teenage time you're married."

A look of panic flew across Toby's face.

"Joke. What do you want the present to say?"

Toby shrugged.

"What are her hobbies?"

Toby shrugged.

"What does she like to buy?"

Toby shrugged.

"What were you thinking of buying her?"

Toby shrugged.

Josh nodded slowly. "I see you've thought this all through."

"Clothes?" ventured Toby.

"Too risky."

"Makeup?"

"Too insulting."

"Condoms?"

"*What?*"

"Joke."

They thought for a while, before saying at the same time, "Flowers."

"Universal language, mate," explained Josh.

"Yeah." Toby grinned knowingly.

"For 'I give up.' "

Toby snorted into a laugh that danced recklessly around the octaves, and Josh decided it was the perfect time to say something that had been on his mind for so long now it had made an imprint.

"Tobe. Are you happy at school?"

Another snort.

"Do you remember me when I was at school?" he continued.

"Yeah, you had to wear a poxy uniform that made you look like an 'idgit.' "

"Do you know why I had a uniform like that?"

" 'Cos of the school you went to. Stupid."

"Yeah, and do you know why my school is different from yours?"

"Yeah, course. Mum and Dad had to pay money for yours."

"That's right."

Toby waited.

"Do you mind about that?" asked Josh. "That Mum and Dad sent me to a private school that pushed me hard to achieve good grades? And they sent you to the local comprehensive?"

He watched Toby mull the question for a bit.

"Did you enjoy school?" Toby asked him eventually.

"No."

"Do you like your job?"

"No. Hate it."

Toby shrugged. "Nah. I don't mind that you got the raw deal. Besides, I wouldn't have met Anastasia if I'd gone to a lame private school in that budgit uniform."

Josh felt his shoulders lighten.

"Josh," mumbled Toby.

"Mm?"

Toby took a deep breath and proceeded to speak in staccato phrases. "I'm sorry . . . I said . . . you thought Jo was a babe. I wasn't . . . trying to piss you off."

"It's alright."

"I didn't know you didn't want me to say it."

"It's alright."

Toby frowned. "I just thought . . . it was funny.".

"Mate. It's alright. But sometimes you have to think how other people feel before opening your mouth. It's called empathy. Kicks in after adolescence and—" he stopped midsentence.

"You alright?" asked Toby.

"Mmhm," said Josh quietly, motionless.

"Right," said Toby. "I'll be off then."

Josh looked up, as if from a trance.

"Answer me one thing," Josh said.

"Mm."

"Are you too old for a hug?"

"Yeah, piss off," retorted Toby. "I mean—sorry—"

"Stop apologizing. It's weird."

"Right." After a moment, Toby sauntered out of the room, whistling. Josh flicked on the television and stared at it.

When the door opened again, he spoke without looking round.

"It's too late for a hug now," he said. "Should have had it when it was offered."

"Thank God for that," said Pippa.

Josh swung round. "Oh shit," he said. "I thought you were Toby."

"No worries," said Pippa as she came and sat near him. They watched television for a while in silence, Josh seemingly engrossed. Eventually Pippa spoke.

"You like bowls, do you?" she asked.

Josh stared at the screen. "How's the packing going?"

"Fine."

"Good."

"Actually," said Pippa slowly. "It's not going as well as it might."

Josh nodded, eyes still on the screen.

"Between you and me," said Pippa slowly, "I think Jo's very upset to be leaving."

Josh gave a little shrug and spoke into his chest. "Then she doesn't need to leave, does she?"

"I think she's just upset generally, actually."

"Really?" he turned round. "Worrying about which bloke to dangle on the longest piece of string today?"

"No," said Pippa. "Just worrying about one bloke."

Josh turned back to the bowls. "Poor bastard," he muttered.

"Actually," muttered Pippa, "this one's a bit of a dick-head."

Josh crossed his arm. "Funnily enough that doesn't narrow it down enough for me. Could be either of them."

"Who do you mean?"

With a heavy sigh, Josh turned the television to mute. "Well, she obviously can't decide between the charms of PC Plod and the double-crossing excuses from Ex-Man."

Pippa let out a sharp laugh. "She's been trying to get rid of PC Plod since she met him. He just wouldn't take the hint."

"That's not what it looked like from where I was sitting."

"Well maybe your seats were restricted view," she shot back, watching the television.

Josh was silent.

"Anyway last night she finally got it through his thick skull. She spent most of the night celebrating. Wow!" she cried at the TV. "That was a good one. It does grow on you, doesn't it. Bowls?"

"What about Shaun then?" Josh asked in a low voice.

"Oh when he came to see her she wished him and Sheila joy," she said, eyes still on the telly. "Seems to be completely over him. Says she'd been over him for years—it's probably why she came to London. She just didn't know it. Was too scared of hurting him. But that's our Jo! Too nice for her own good!"

Josh didn't move.

"Right," said Pippa. "I'd better get back to it. Poor Jo needs cheering up. She was saying earlier how unbearable it is to be misunderstood and always thought the worst of. Don't know what she was talking about, but I just know it keeps making her cry. See you!"

And she left the room.

★　★　★

Meanwhile Toby, feeling full of optimism, wanted to share it with his half siblings. He took the stairs three at a time and knocked on Tallulah's door, where they were having a meeting. They all shouted at him to go away. He opened the door.

"It's alright!" he said, wandering in and lying on the floor. "It's only me. Big brother."

He became aware of an uncomfortable silence.

"What?" he said. "What's happened?"

"Toby," said Cassie, cautiously but with a firmness he'd never heard before, "we don't want you in here with us."

Toby looked up at her. "It's alright, Catastrophe," he said calmly. "I don't want you in here with me either."

Nobody laughed. Not even Zak.

"No. We mean it," said Cassie. "This is private."

Toby looked at Tallulah.

"Come on Lu—"

"It's Tallulah!"

"Alright, keep your knickers on."

"My knickers are on! Stop being horrid and just go away."

Toby stared at her. He stared at Zak.

"Bro," he said. "C'mon. Me and you against the girls."

Zak looked down. "I don't want to be against the girls," said Zak.

Toby swallowed hard.

"Sorry, Toby," said Cassie. "We're all rather busy at the moment."

"Right," said Toby nonchalantly. He stood up slowly and walked to the door. "Your loss," he told them all, and closed the door behind him.

He stood in the dark hall for a few minutes, then suddenly ran down the stairs. He raced past the lounge and straight out into the garden. He didn't notice Jo, who was sitting on the patio, staring blankly at the trees.

She turned as she heard him. "What's wrong?" she gasped.

Toby wiped his face angrily. She got up and walked toward him, and, to her astonishment, he ran toward her and hugged her fiercely. She couldn't imagine what could possibly have happened. He drew away quickly and resumed the angry face wiping.

"Don't tell anyone I'm crying," he ordered her gruffly.

"Course not," she said. "Especially if you say please."

"Don't tell Josh," he squeaked. "Please."

"Come on," she whispered. "Let's walk down to the end. Tell me all about it."

By the time they got to the bottom of the garden, Toby was sniffing violently and thrusting his hands in his jeans pockets as far as they could go. The image reminded Jo of his big brother.

"What's up?" asked Jo.

Toby wiped his eyes again. "They hate me," he squeaked, plonking himself on the lawn.

"Who hates you?"

"The others. Lula, Cassie, Zak."

"Of course they don't."

"They do!" he shouted. 'They're having a 'meeting' in Tallulah's room, and they won't let me in."

"Toby, all brothers and sisters fight."

Toby shook his head.

"Sweetheart," said Jo, "what brought all this on? I didn't think you really cared about them."

After he'd stopped crying again, Toby told Jo that he was trying to be nicer to them.

"Why?" asked Jo, as gently as possible.

With immense difficulty, Toby told her that he didn't hate them any-more. He just didn't. After a bit more gentle coaxing, he told her that he knew it wasn't their fault that his dad had left. He told her what Josh had told him about their mum and dad's divorce. He explained how his mum confessed to intentionally forcing Dick out of their relationship, by nudging him into an affair, then accusing him of betrayal. Jo fell silent.

"I always blamed them for Dad leaving," said Toby. "That's why I treated them like shit—sorry—like dirt. But Josh told me it wasn't their fault, and they never asked to be lumbered with me either." He started crying again. "So I've tried to be nice, but they hate me."

Jo put her arm round him. "Sweetheart, why aren't you telling all this to Josh?"

" 'Cos he told me this would happen if I wasn't nicer to them, and I didn't listen." He started crying again. "I don't want to tell him. Please don't tell him."

"Oh don't worry," she said. "He's not talking to me."

"Oh yeah. That's all my fault, too."

"Don't be silly."

"It is. I said he thought you were a babe."

"Pardon?"

Toby shook his head. "Everyone hates me."

"Give it time," she murmured. "Once they realize that you want to be their friend, they'll idolize you as their big brother."

"But I've *tried*."

"What have you tried?"

"Being nice."

"Have you tried apologizing?"

There was a pause.

"I can't," he squeaked.

"Why not? You'd be surprised how effective it can be."

Toby stared at the grass.

"Can you imagine how much fun you'll all have together if they like you?" asked Jo.

Toby managed half a smile.

"Come on," said Jo, getting up. "There are some choc-ices in the freezer. You can give them all one and then tell them how you feel." Toby stayed sitting on the grass. "Just be honest," she said. "It'll make you feel so much better."

He grimaced.

"Come on," she urged.

He shook his head. "I'm scared," he whispered.

"Of course you are," said Jo, kneeling beside him. "Otherwise, the apology would be meaningless."

After a moment's thought, Toby slowly got up, and they walked thoughtfully back into the house.

When Jo returned to her room, she landed heavily on her bed. Pippa looked up from sorting a box that had found its way into Josh's room.

"Feeling a bit better?" she asked. She saw Jo's expression. "Oh dear, what's up? You look like you've seen a ghost."

Jo recounted her conversation with Toby, while Pippa sat next to the box, leaning back against Josh's bed.

After Jo had finished, she seemed to run out of energy. "That explains what Josh said to me," she said in a monotone, "about how sometimes a woman can push a man into adultery."

"Yeah, but that's still no reason to blame all women for men's affairs," remarked Pippa, glancing round Josh's room. "He's messy isn't he?"

Jo frowned. "I don't think he did blame all women. I think he referred to just one man and one woman. He was talking about Dick and Jane, and he knew it was true. And that was when I told him that he disgusted me."

"You were disgusted because he's helping his dad have an extramarital affair," said Pippa, her eyes fixed on some pieces of pink paper by her feet.

"I know, but—"

"But nothing," said Pippa, idly picking up the pieces of paper. "That's how you felt, and you had a right to those feelings. He's got double standards. The man's a woman hater—it doesn't matter why."

"But it explains why he got so annoyed with me so quickly. I must have really hurt him."

Pippa went silent. After a moment, Jo looked across at her. Pippa was staring, ashen-faced, at two pieces of pink paper.

"What are you looking at?" asked Jo.

"Jo-oh," said Pippa slowly.

"Yes?"

"Did you say Josh was living here rent-free?"

"Yup. Another reason to hate him. Thank you, I was beginning to forget."

"And how much is your monthly salary?"

"Why?"

"Just tell me. To the penny."

"It's a really weird amount because of my raise," she explained before giving her exact monthly salary.

Pippa put her hand over her mouth. "Oh dear," she whispered.

"What?" Jo came over and looked at the pieces of paper. Pippa let her take them out of her hand.

They were receipts, in Dick's handwriting. They were called "Josh's rent—May" and next to the amount was the word "Paid." And the amount was exactly—down to the last penny—the same amount as Jo's salary.

As they stared at it, their eyes alighted on an imprint, underneath, that slowly, like children's invisible ink, grew more and more legible. And the more legible it grew, the more cold Jo felt. In Dick's scrawl were the words, "for Jo—June."

"Why did you think he wasn't paying rent?" asked Pippa eventually.

Jo sat down next to her, leaning heavily against Josh's bed. "Vanessa told me."

They stared at the receipts.

"And do you think," asked Pippa, ever so softly, "that it's remotely possible that Dick and Josh"—the words hung in the air—"kept it a *secret* from Vanessa? The fact that Josh was . . ." Again, the words hung in the air.

Jo forced herself to finish the sentence. ". . . Paying my salary?"

They continued to stare at the receipts.

"What did we actually hear them saying in the kitchen that time?" asked Pippa.

Jo furrowed her brow. "I don't remember."

"Did they actually talk about an affair?"

"Well, there was a woman mentioned."

"A lover? Did they say lover? Because she could have been anyone, right? She could have been someone from the shop. A buyer? Or someone to do with money? A rent collector or accountant or something?"

"I s'pose," murmured Jo.

"Didn't Josh at one point tell his dad he should have gone to him first before turning to her?"

"Oh my God," whispered Jo. "Maybe they were talking about an accountant. A female accountant."

"Has been known."

"But why be so cloak-and-dagger about an accountant?"

Pippa shrugged. "Maybe Dick keeps his accounts a secret from Vanessa."

"He did keep saying she'd leave him if she knew the truth."

"Yeah, well that fits. He probably thought she'd leave if she found out how bad it was."

"Oh come on, surely not. She's not that bad."

Pippa shook her head. "That's not the point. The point is Dick thought she might be."

"Maybe that's why Josh called her Scary Spouse," Jo said quietly.

Pippa laughed. "That's brilliant!"

Jo gave her a look.

"Sorry," said Pippa. "He may be a bastard, but that's funny."

Jo sighed. "Oh no."

"I think it's safe to say there was no affair," concluded Pippa, holding up the receipts.

"And that Josh and Dick's real secret was that Josh is in fact a generous, trustworthy type, taking responsibility for his father's actions by paying your salary."

They took a moment to reassess the situation so far.

"And as such," concluded Pippa, "you have fucked up big-time."

Jo groaned.

"Do you have anything to say in your defense?" asked Pippa.

"He hid the secret very well," whispered Jo.

"Yes," agreed Pippa. "We can add clever to his list of attributes then."

Jo sank her head back against Josh's bed.

"This is all good, hon," soothed Pippa. "It means he's a hell of a lot nicer than you thought. You're not obsessed with a nasty bloke, you're obsessed with a really decent *catch*."

"Nngh," agreed Jo.

"I have only one question."

"Hm?"

"What are you still doing in here?"

Jo tilted her head. "I'm waiting for the ground to swallow me up."

"Just apologize to him."

"Where should I start?"

"How about with absolutely everything you've ever said to him?" suggested Pippa. "That might make a good start."

"I *can't*." Jo hid her head in her hands.

"Course you can."

"I can't."

After a moment's silence, Pippa spoke again.

"Course you can."

"I *can't*."

At which point Pippa gave up.

Chapter 30

Toby carried four choc-ices upstairs and waited outside Tallulah's bedroom door until a strategy occurred to him. Unfortunately, the choc-ices were considerably faster at melting down his hands than the strategy was at occurring. When they started dripping, he had no choice but to knock on the door.

Cassie, Tallulah, and Zak yelled at him to leave them alone. He stared at the door handle, stared at his creamy knuckles and knocked again. There was more yelling. He poked his head round the door. The yelling started up again. He showed them the choc-ices. There was an aborted yelp of joy from Zak, followed by a thoughtful silence.

Toby used the moment to squeeze in a broken explanation for his past behavior and an apology that would have melted the heart of anyone.

They stared at his red eyes, and they stared at the choc-ices. When Tallulah crossed the room, took the choc-ices, and reached up to kiss him on the cheek, they all knew he was forgiven.

And a good thing too. Toby's contribution to the meeting proved vital.

While the children concluded their business for the day in a most satisfactory manner, Jo and Pippa were going round in circles.

"Okay. I've got to say sorry," repeated Jo.

"Yup."

"But I can't."

"Why not?"

"Because he hates me."

"Because you haven't said sorry."

"Okay. I've got to say sorry."

"Yup."

"But I can't."

Pippa looked at her watch. "I have a flight to catch in two months."

"Right!" announced Jo. "I'm going to say sorry." And she got up and walked out.

As she strode purposefully through the kitchen toward the living room, she saw Toby in the hall opening the living room door, followed swiftly by Tallulah. In one fluid movement, she turned on her heel and strode back into the kitchen, where she busied herself frowning and humming.

When Cassie and Zak bounced in, she gave them an absentminded smile.

"Thank you, Jo!" yelled Cassie. "Toby just gave us all choc-ices!"

They came over and hugged her.

"We've got something to show you," said Cassie. "But we can't show you here, Toby might see. It's a secret."

"Where shall we go?" asked Zak.

"I don't know," pondered Cassie. "Toby mustn't hear us. Where is he?"

"In the living room with Josh," said Jo.

"Where can we go where he won't hear us?"

"I don't know," said Zak, looking out into the garden.

"Shall we go into the garden?" suggested Jo, following Zak's idle gaze.

"Yes!" they both cried.

They went into the garden, and Zak got so excited he started running in place.

"I know!" he cried. "Let's go into the playhouse! Then no one will see us!"

Cassie frowned. "Jo won't fit."

"But I want to do it in the playhouse!" insisted Zak.

"Of course I can fit," Jo told Cassie. "Let's go into the playhouse. I think it's a great idea."

"Oh, alright." Cassie sighed.

They bent down and single-filed it through the door. Once inside, they sat in a cosy little circle.

"Well, go on then," Cassie told Zak. "Give it to her."

"I haven't got it," said Zak.

"I gave it to you!"

"No you didn't!"

"I did! I put it on your bedside table!"

"Well, then, you didn't give it to me, did you, Clever Clogs!"

"Guys!" shouted Jo. "Why don't you just go and get it?"

There was a pause.

"You go," Cassie told Zak.

"No!" said Zak. "You go!"

"No!"

"Guys!" shouted Jo again. "Why don't I go and get it?"

"*No!*" they yelled.

"Okay then, why don't you both go and get it?"

"But you might go away," said Cassie.

"I promise you I won't leave this spot until you come back."

"Cross your heart?"

"Cross my heart." Jo obliged, and from their expressions of total trust, felt as if she'd just signed a contract in her own blood.

They disappeared out of the tiny door, and she heard them giggling together before they even got inside. It always amazed her how children could forgive each other so easily. Why did adults lose that ability?

She leaned back against the wall and breathed in the woody smell, which was even more pungent than usual after the night's rain. She found it surprisingly soothing. Through the tiny window she could just make out one of the cats sitting in a tree, watching the proceedings. Perhaps she should just never come out. She closed her eyes and waited for the children to come back. They must have been quite a while because the next thing she knew she was jumping awake at the sound of the little door being slammed shut with some ferocity.

She turned and looked. And gasped. Josh had squeezed his tall frame into the house backward—she had to shuffle back before he trod on her—and Toby had just slammed the door shut behind him. "*Okay!*" yelled Toby from outside. "Now you can turn round and open your eyes." Then she heard the children disappear into the house in hysterics as Josh, with some difficulty, turned round to face her.

To say Josh was surprised to see Jo was an understatement. He was so shocked that he forgot he was in a playhouse and jumped up to leave, thwacking his head on the roof before he'd even sat up properly. He crouched down again, his head in his hands. Then at the same moment they both lunged for the door and pushed with all their might. Nothing. It was not going to budge. Jo knew. She'd spent hours in here in her time—usually with Tallulah—just waiting for the wood slowly to shrink back to its usual size. She considered asking Josh if he wanted to play imaginary tea party, which had been known to keep Tallulah contented for so long Jo had got repetitive motion injury from so much imaginary tea pouring. But as he was holding his head in pain, she decided it probably wasn't a good idea.

"I always thought this place could do with a chimney," she whispered eventually. "Nice period touch."

Josh grimaced. "Yeah, I'm fine thanks," he said, stretching his legs as far as they could go—one out in front of him, the other bent to the side, both taking up precious space around her.

"Hey," said Jo, trying to shift herself out of his way. "This time it was not my fault you got hurt."

"Yes it was." He tried to stretch his bent leg.

"How was it my fault? Do you mind? That's my bottom."

"You shocked me. Can I—' He indicated for his leg to go behind her.

"I was just sitting here minding my own business, thank you very much," she argued, inching forward.

"Yeah," he muttered, fitting his leg behind her, "waiting to give me the fright of my life."

"I had no idea you were coming in here," she said, lunging forward. "If I had, I'd have tunneled out."

"So what are you doing in here then?"

"Waiting for Cassie and Zak."

"Well you're in for a long wait."

"Why?"

"Because they're inside watching TV."

"What? They can't be. They told me to wait in here. They made me cross my heart." Josh leaned back against the wall, his head in the eaves, all the fight suddenly out of him.

"Little bastards," he snarled. "We've been set up."

"Josh," said Jo. "Will you please get your thigh off my bottom?"

"No," shot Josh indignantly. "You get your bottom off my thigh."

She lean forward and ended up practically eating his nose. She sat back again. "What do you mean 'set up'?"

"Toby—my Judas of a kid brother—persuaded me, with some difficulty, to come in here backward with my eyes closed because he had a surprise for me."

Jo stared back at Josh. "Little bastards," she agreed. "I thought they were my friends."

Josh nodded back at her. "Well, they clearly hate us both."

"So," he said. "As soon as you've managed to prise your bottom off my thigh, I vote we go back inside and kick their little heads in."

He turned toward the door, entangling most of Jo in his legs.

"Careful!" she yelped.

"Oh, come to help?" he asked. "How good of you."

"You'll never open it. It sticks in the rain. Last night was a downpour, I nearly drowned."

"Damn," muttered Josh, banging hopelessly at the door. "Those pesky kids."

Despite herself, Jo started to giggle.

"I don't know what's so funny," said Josh. "I'm claustrophobic."

"Oh dear."

He turned to face her. He was so close that her natural instinct was to jerk her head back. It walloped the wall behind her. "A condition not improved," he whispered, "by someone's entire body weight making my knees go numb."

Jo whipped herself away from him so fast he ended up lying half on top of her.

"That's better," he said pleasantly. "Where were we?"

"Ow," she moaned.

With some effort, Josh twisted his body away from hers, leaving them both just enough space to half lie next to each other, heads against the door. Then he sat up as far as he could, leaned his weight onto his right hipbone, and started to push the door hard with his upper body.

Jo had little choice but to watch, being unable to turn her head away without knocking noses with him. He was trying so hard to open the door that the veins in his neck were starting to bulge. After a while, he paused.

"Anytime you fancy," he breathed hard, "you're more than welcome to join in. No pressure."

Jo tried to speak. Josh looked at her and couldn't believe his eyes.

"Why are *you* crying?" he asked. "I'm the one who's claustrophobic. I should be in hysterics."

Jo sniffed.

"I'd get you a tissue from my jeans pocket," he said, "but in this space it might make you pregnant."

She laughed, then started crying some more. He gave up trying to open the door.

"Hey," he said, his tone softening slightly. "Come on. It can't be that bad being stuck in here with me."

She shook her head. "How can you be so hateful and so nice at the same time?"

"Just gifted, I guess."

"I'm sorry."

"It's alright. Cry all you like. Better out than in. Bit like us in here really."

She started to cry again.

"Come on," he soothed. "What's up? Is it Shaun?"

Her crying came to a slow, ugly halt.

"You want to get out so much," she whimpered.

"Well of course I do," he said. "I need oxygen."

She laughed, then stopped herself.

"So what's up?" he asked.

"I just told you. You want to get out so much."

He looked astonished. "That's why you're crying? Because I want to get out?"

She nodded, her eyes firmly shut.

"Don't you want to get out?" he asked gently.

She turned away, her eyes firmly shut. "I'm sorry," she blurted out.

"It's alright," he said. "I'm getting used to seeing you crying. It's quite sweet actually."

"I mean I'm sorry about . . . you know." She ground to a halt.

"Not really," he answered. "Perhaps you could narrow it down a bit."

"I found out," she whispered, turning suddenly toward him and giving him an intense look.

"Found out what?" he whispered back, squeezing his hips away from her.

"That you've been paying my salary."

He gasped. "Bloody hell."

Jo clutched his arm. "Why didn't you tell me?"

"I-I haven't—I've just been paying my rent."

"Which is exactly the same amount as my salary."

He stared from her eyes to her lips and back to her eyes. He blinked hard.

"I-I was helping my dad," he managed.

"And I was so horrid to you," moaned Jo, clutching him a bit more.

"No you weren't—" he said, trying to keep every part of his body very still.

"I was! But you went so cold on me. Not like you were in the beginning. In the beginning you were lovely. And I'd been so scared of meeting you for the first time after all those horrid phone calls—"

"What phone calls?"

"Every time I spoke to you on the phone, you took the piss out of me. And then you got your office to listen in. I thought you'd be horrible."

"Ah. Yes. Those."

"But you weren't horrid at all. You weren't what I expected at all."

"No, you weren't either."

There was a pause.

"I thought you'd be mean and fat," sniffed Jo.

"I thought you'd be stuffy and ugly."

"Did you?" asked Jo breathily.

Josh forced himself to look away.

"About those calls," he said. "When I agreed to come here, I really wanted to help my dad. I thought I was over all my jealousy of the kids. But every time I spoke to you on the phone you were so . . . disapproving, so—"

"I was terrified."

"Terrified?"

"Yes! The first time I had the whole family watching me, and I was convinced it was some nanny test. The next time Diane was scrutinizing my every word to see that I was a good enough nanny for her precious grandchildren."

"Ah," said Josh. "I see. She is a bit special."

"And you got your office to listen to me like I was some big joke."

"I'm sorry. You're right, that was horrid. But I do have an explanation."

Jo waited.

"I guess it's a long story."

"Well," she said. "It looks like we've got a long time." She didn't risk pushing the door again, and neither did Josh.

Instead, he began. "When I was at school and college, my mum had no help bringing me and Tobe up," he said, the words as new to him as to her. "She had to have a part-time job filing, so I had to pick up Tobe from a friend's on my way home, let us both in, make us both tea, keep him occupied till she got home. No biggie—there are worse things at sea, and I'm not complaining. I'm not emotionally scarred or anything. Well, I didn't think I was. But every time I spoke to you on the phone—and you sounded *so* different from how you were . . . in the flesh"—he looked down at her legs and Jo's flesh went hot—"I was reminded that for Dad's new improved children, things were very different."

"Oh, I see," whispered Jo.

"I don't feel that way now," Josh rushed on.

"No?"

"No."

"How?"

"Well, I feel completely different now."

"Really?"

"Yes. Quite the opposite in fact."

"Really?"

"God yes," said Josh. "I love the kids now."

"Oh. I see."

"It was all mixed up with my misunderstanding about Dad leaving."

"Oh. Right."

"It's only now that I can see I was bearing a big, unhealthy grudge. And of course it was easy to direct it straight at you."

"Oh."

"But it wasn't just that."

"No?"

"No. When I met you, I tried my best to hate you," he looked up at her. "Kept waiting for the hatred to kick in." He shrugged. "But it never did. And then before I knew it, I started to like you."

Josh looked down suddenly, and Jo took the opportunity to breathe out.

"And I've found out things about my mum and dad that have altered"—he thought for a moment—"everything for me."

Jo whispered, "Toby told me."

Josh paused and looked at her questioningly.

"I hope you don't mind. Earlier today," she explained, "he was distressed about something, and it came up."

"Is he okay now?"

"Fine." Jo nodded. "I think we sorted it."

"Who's a clever nanny then?" Josh smiled, moving his head back slightly.

"Oh yeah," quipped Jo. She looked away, her hair falling on his arm. "I'm a real Mary Poppins."

Josh looked away from his arm. "My turn to apologize. Horrid nickname."

"Understandable."

"Actually," he confessed, head down, "she was my first crush. I had a poster and everything."

Jo stopped breathing. When Josh squirmed a bit, she started to gabble.

"I'm so sorry I accused you of helping Dick have an affair."

"Oh yeah, where the hell did that one come from?"

"Pippa and I overheard a conversation you had with Dick about him meeting a woman," rushed Jo, leaning into him in her eagerness to defend herself, "and you were trying to persuade him to tell Vanessa about her, and he was saying that would end his marriage."

Josh blinked slowly, trying to focus on what she was saying.

"Don't worry," said Jo, leaning in some more. "We worked out it wasn't a lover. It must have been someone to do with Dick's business—a client or a buyer or his accountant."

"Oh! That complete bitch. His accountant. She just stopped returning his calls. He was so stressed, it was terrible. And the longer it got left, the worse it got. That woman was literally ruining him. I told him years ago not to go to her and begged him to let me do his books, but"—he gave a deep sigh—"I suppose I was still a trainee then. I guess it takes a while for parents to take you seriously."

Jo nodded. "Dick certainly relies on you."

"D'you think?"

"He adores you."

Josh beamed and shrugged.

Jo smiled.

"Bloody hell," cried Josh suddenly. "So you and Pippa put two and two together and made twenty-two."

They stared at each other. Jo was just about to apologize again when Josh spoke.

"You must have thought I was a right shit," he whispered. "Helping my dad have an affair."

"Well," Jo, clasping the nearest thing to her, which happened to be Josh's thigh. "That's why I said those things to you when you came to . . . see me."

Josh nodded. "Ungh."

There was silence.

"You don't . . . disgust me," she whispered. "At all. In fact."

"Thank you," said Josh. "You don't disgust me either. At all."

"And I'm so sorry I called you a scrounger."

"A two-faced, scrounging, hypocritical bastard with a Peter Pan complex I think it was. I can hardly remember."

"I thought you were living here rent-free—which was none of my business, I know," she interrupted herself. "But I found that quite immature and the truth was"—she steadied herself against the wall and mumbled—"it had begun to matter."

There was silence for a moment. Josh cleared his throat.

"I'm sorry I called you a prick-tease," he said quietly. "It did just seem—"

"I was."

"Pardon?"

"Flirting. I was. With you."

"Oh."

"I wasn't teasing, I was flirting," insisted Jo. "It wasn't something I thought about—I kept telling myself we were just friends—"

"Me too—"

"And I know I should have told you about Shaun, but I didn't want to—"

"No—"

"Because I was scared that if I did—" She slowed down, her eyes on the floor. She was unable to finish the sentence.

The silence was deafening. She'd have loved to have seen Josh's expression, but that would have meant looking at his face.

"And then you went all horrid," she went on whispering.

"I know," he whispered back. "I'm sorry."

"Why did you do that?"

The pause was unbearable.

"Wasn't it obvious?" he whispered.

Jo couldn't answer. She heard Josh give a big sigh.

"So you and Shaun, eh?" he started.

"Who?" Jo gave him a little smile.

"You seemed very cut up about it that day."

"Well, yes of course," she said. "You came at a bad time. It had only just happened. I was in shock. It was like . . . Sheila had just rewritten my past. If that doesn't sound mad."

"Nope. I know just what you mean."

"I just had some rethinking to do."

"Right."

"Bend myself to the new facts."

Josh got an image of Jo bending and quickly concentrated hard on the grains of wood in the playhouse wall.

"And I've done it now," said Jo. "Bent myself to the new facts."

"Wow," said Josh, staring hard at the wood. "That was quick."

"Not really," she admitted. "I should have finished with Shaun years ago."

She looked up, realized how close Josh was, went wobbly and looked down again.

"I hope he and Shee will be very happy together," she said. "And I think they will be. Anyway, I don't really care anymore. I've got other things on my mind."

There was a long pause.

"So," said Josh lightly, leaning down on his elbow, shifting along the floor space, and looking up at her. "I've been reliably informed that you told Gerry to get lost."

"Yes," she said, shifting herself down into a mirror image next to him. "Finally. Suppose I took my time."

"Well, sometimes these things are hard to do," he said softly.

He let his top leg drop toward her.

"Sometimes it's very hard to say what you feel," murmured Jo.

She let her top leg mirror his.

"God yes."

"Especially when you feel"—she didn't move her thigh when it accidentally brushed his—"so much."

"Much," he echoed.

"Maybe I just wanted to make you jealous," she whispered.

The playhouse shrank.

"I was jealous anyway."

"Were you?"

"Yes. Very."

"Who of?"

"Everyone. Even the kids. Bastards."

"The kids? You mean the ones who got us in the playhouse together?"

Josh laughed. "Looks like they're quite adult when they put their minds to it."

"Yeah," whispered Jo. "It's just us who need to grow up."

"I'm feeling particularly grown-up at the moment," he said. They were now lying facing each other, nose to nose, grin to grin.

"Ooer." She giggled.

Josh groaned playfully. "You are so gorgeous," he whispered.

She closed her eyes, and could feel his breath on her cheek and neck.

"That time you fell out of the sink," he murmured. She giggled. "Up till then I'd convinced myself that I just liked you, but oh God."

"I thought you were going to kiss me," she breathed into his neck.

"Kiss you?" He turned his head to hers. "I wanted to eat you."

She gasped, every nerve ending in her body on full alert.

"And then you told me you had a boyfriend." Josh moaned. "God, it was so awful."

"I know," she breathed. "I was just feeling so guilty and confused and . . . and horny."

Josh nudged himself nearer, so their hips were gently touching.

"And," whispered Jo, "I didn't want to spend our first kiss feeling guilty."

Josh's lips gently found hers.

"And then you needed help getting to bed," he whispered into her ear, "and I had to listen to you cry without being able to soothe you like I wanted to. And I had to help you get into your nightshirt." He groaned.

"Did you see anything?" asked Jo suddenly.

"Nope. Even in your inebriated state, you still managed to ask me to turn around."

"Really?" she murmured, her hand stroking the back of his jeans. "Not much of a prick-tease really then, am I?"

"Not then no."

He started stroking her hair all the way down her back. Her spine tingled.

"So how did you feel about Shaun that night?" asked Josh.

"The truth?"

"The truth."

"I could hardly remember his name when I was with you." He nudged his thigh ever so gently in between hers.

"That night he came to stay," whispered Josh. "It was hell."

"I know."

"I was in the next room for Christ's sake."

"I know. I was . . ."

"Yes?"

". . . thinking of you."

Josh lengthened his neck nearer to Jo.

"You don't need to just think of me anymore."

"Ooh! Mr. Fitzgerald!" mocked Jo. "What *do* you mean?"

"Do you think," he managed, hitching himself up, so he was lying above her, one hand lightly touching the back of her thigh, "we should kiss and make up?" His lips brushed hers.

"I don't know," she murmured, her arms finding their way up to his neck. "I can't think of anything at the moment."

"Oh."

"What do you think?" She closed her eyes and saw rainbows under her eyelids as Josh explained to her, as best he could, that he thought yes.

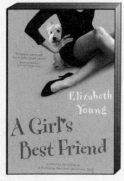

AVON TRADE...

because every great bag deserves a great book!

THE CHOCOLATE SHIP
by Marissa Monteilh
0-06-001148-3 • $13.95 US • $21.95 Can

THE ACCIDENTAL VIRGIN
by Valerie Frankel
0-06-093841-2 • $13.95 US • $21.95 Can

BARE NECESSITY
by Carole Matthews
0-06-053214-9 • $13.95 US

THE SECOND COMING OF LUCY HATCH
by Marsha Moyer
0-06-008166-X • $13.95 US • $21.95 Can

DOES SHE OR DOESN'T SHE?
by Alisa Kwitney
0-06-051237-7 • $13.95 US • $21.95 Can

LOVE AND A BAD HAIR DAY
by Annie Flannigan
0-380-81936-8 • $13.95 US • $21.95 Can

GET SOME LOVE
by Nina Foxx
0-06-052648-3 • $13.95 US • $21.95 Can

A GIRL'S BEST FRIEND
by Elizabeth Young
0-06-056277-3 • $13.95 US

RULES FOR A PRETTY WOMAN
by Suzette Francis
0-06-053542-3 • $13.95 US • $21.95 Can

THE NANNY
by Melissa Nathan
0-06-056011-8 • $13.95 US